To my family

Praise for *Hotel of Secrets*

"Glittering and golden, Diana Biller's *Hotel of Secrets* serves up decadence, intrigue, and a deeply emotional love story. Biller excels at immersive and atmospheric storytelling, and compelling voices with heart and just the right touch of humor. At once tender and exciting, *Hotel of Secrets* demonstrates why Diana Biller continues to be one of historical romance's very best."—Ruby Barrett, author of *Hot Copy*

"Gorgeously written and deeply romantic, *Hotel of Secrets* has a dream pairing: a buttoned-up virgin hero and a delightful, capable heroine falling for each other amid political intrigue and family drama. . . . While I couldn't wait for Eli and Maria's slow burn to ignite, I didn't want it to end. It's another wonderful romance from Diana Biller."—Emma Barry, author of *Earth Bound* and *Chick Magnet*

"Wit and charm illuminate this marvelous novel. *Hotel of Secrets* is dazzling. It will carry you through its pages as if in a glorious, heart-stirring dance, making you laugh, and spin, and come away feeling exhilarated. A delightful must-read for lovers of historical romance."—India Holton, bestselling author of *The Wisteria Society of Lady Scoundrels*

"Diana Biller's lavishly imagined *Hotel of Secrets* sparkles with champagne bubbles and winter moonlight. This unforgettable, intoxicatingly romantic tale of tangled family history and political intrigue will leave readers spellbound and breathless and ready to begin again. Written with originality, wit, and style, every page is pure magic."—Joanna Lowell, author of *The Runaway Duchess* and *The Duke Undone*

"A beautifully researched and emotionally complex experience, *Hotel of Secrets* is an opulent slice of Viennese tradition as rich as a torte and as layered as a complicated line of Strauss. With intrigue and danger that nips on the heels of its luscious waltz, Biller's lush and atmospheric escape is dolloped with romance and the deep, complicated, and sigh-worthy characters that always shoot her to the top of my auto-buy list."—Rachel McMillan, author of *The Mozart Code*

Also by Diana Biller

The Widow of Rose House

The Brightest Star in Paris

HOTEL
of
SECRETS

A NOVEL

DIANA BILLER

ST. MARTIN'S GRIFFIN
NEW YORK

First published in the United States by St. Martin's Griffin, an imprint of St. Martin's Publishing Group

HOTEL OF SECRETS. Copyright © 2023 by Diana Biller. All rights reserved. Printed in the United States of America. For information, address St. Martin's Publishing Group, 120 Broadway, New York, NY 10271.

www.stmartins.com

Designed by Meryl Sussman Levavi

Library of Congress Cataloging-in-Publication Data

Names: Biller, Diana, author.
Title: Hotel of secrets: a novel / Diana Biller.
Description: First edition. | New York: St. Martin's Griffin, 2023.
Identifiers: LCCN 2022051652 | ISBN 9781250809452 (trade paperback) | ISBN 9781250809469 (ebook)
Classification: LCC PS3602.I4368 H68 2023 | DDC 813/.6—dc23
LC record available at https://lccn.loc.gov/2022051652

Our books may be purchased in bulk for promotional, educational, or business use. Please contact your local bookseller or the Macmillan Corporate and Premium Sales Department at 1-800-221-7945, extension 5442, or by email at MacmillanSpecialMarkets@macmillan.com.

First Edition: 2023

1 3 5 7 9 10 8 6 4 2

This story deals with complex themes.
For a list of content warnings,
please visit the author's website.

HOTEL
of
SECRETS

Chapter One

He gave me a hotel. What the hell am I supposed to do with a hotel?

—Journal entry of Theresa Wallner,
Vienna, 7 June 1805

Vienna
New Year's Eve, 1877

There were twenty-eight minutes left in 1877, and as if the year had not seen trouble enough, Maria Wallner's father led Maria Wallner's mother onto the dance floor, clasped her amorously to his chest, and, with the first languid, delicate notes of Strauss's "Vienna Blood" waltz providing a suitably romantic background, began to dance.

Maria Wallner, current manager of the Hotel Wallner, hostess of the party her parents had just taken center stage at, and newly returned emergency plumber of the fourth-floor bathroom, stood in the doorway of the hotel's Small Ballroom and allowed herself precisely ten seconds of shock.

They made a stunning picture—or at least, Elisabeth Wallner, Maria's mother, did. At some point in her youth, Elisabeth had been told she resembled Empress Sisi, the Emperor's beautiful bride, and she had never forgotten. Everything from her hairstyle to her fitness regimen (strict gymnastics, every morning) was modeled from Sisi, and now, with her dark hair streaming down her back, studded with crystal hairpins, and her midnight-blue velvet gown frothing with silver lace, she looked every bit an empress.

Maria's father, Baron Heinrich von Eder, looked very much like the portly middle-aged aristocrat he was.

The couples around them were barely waltzing, fixated on the delicious scandal unfolding. The audience at the edges of the dance floor whispered and laughed, their eyes darting greedily between the couple and the stone-faced blond woman standing like a dignified statue in the corner of the ballroom.

Because none of this would have been particularly scandalous if her parents had been married. Or indeed, if they had not just broken the single rule governing the thirty-year détente between the Wallner and von Eder households: namely, that Baron Heinrich von Eder would refrain from noticing Elisabeth Wallner until Baroness Adelaide von Eder, his wife and the mother of his four legitimate children, had retired for the evening.

Her ten seconds over, Maria took a breath, brightened her smile, and began her own waltz, weaving through the crowd to check on the buffet. Smiling and laughing, pretending that nothing out of the ordinary was happening. (To be fair, in a way it wasn't—Maria had been a captive audience to this particular romantic drama her entire life. It was only the circumstances that were unusual.) She waved a server over to replace a group's empty champagne glasses; noticed a torn hem and discreetly alerted its wearer; and had almost made it to the buffet table when—

"Maria! When are you going to find *the man,* like your mother?"

There it was.

"If you know where he is, Mr. Schiller, please send him my address." She laughed, her response easy and light.

(As it ought to be. She'd been saying the same damn thing for decade and a half.)

The group of men around Mr. Schiller hooted in pleasure, and then mercifully turned back to the drama on the dance floor.

It didn't matter, she reminded herself, not entirely sure what *it* was, but if it wasn't about the Hotel Wallner's Triumphant Return to Society (yes, it was capitalized, yes, Maria did have a list with that title), then it didn't matter.

The caviar was low. She pulled one of the footmen aside and sent him running to the kitchen, catching a glimpse of her parents just in time to see Heinrich tenderly brush a curl from her mother's face. The crowd gave a pleased murmur. The story would be all over Vienna by supper the next day.

And that, Maria reminded herself, was what did matter. This was one of the scandals of the season, and the guests of the Hotel Wallner's New Year's Eve Ball had been the ones to witness it. Tomorrow, once they'd recovered from their traditional New Year's Day hangovers, they would go to supper with friends and say, "*Oh,* you should have been at the Hotel Wallner last night." Just like the old days, when the Hotel Wallner had been one of the epicenters of Imperial Vienna, its nights filled with scandal and intrigue and importance.

And this moment *did* look like something plucked from Maria's childhood memories. The newly cleaned and repaired chandelier dazzled. The freshly sanded and polished floors looked almost liquid, as if Elisabeth and Heinrich were dancing on a vast champagne sea, beneath a starry sky. (Maria was particularly proud of the starry skies. She'd repainted every single gold star herself, balancing on a rickety scaffold beneath the fifteen-foot ceilings until her back felt like it would break.) Perhaps she was deluding herself—it would take more than a single party to bring the Hotel Wallner back from irrelevance and disrepair—but she thought something like the old magical, golden wonderment shimmered in the air.

She'd do anything to give the hotel that magic back. Suffering some embarrassment and discomfort over her parents' behavior was nothing.

"I tried to stop him," said a soft, cultured voice over her shoulder, and Maria's smile warmed as she turned to her half brother, Macario von Eder.

Mac was the picture of a dashing young aristocrat tonight, Maria thought, as she brushed a speck of lint from his immaculately tailored evening suit. There was little resemblance between the siblings—both took after their mothers, Maria with dark eyes and darker hair, and Mac golden-haired and blue-eyed—but a great deal of fondness.

Maria shrugged. "They're impossible to stop."

He grimaced, his eyebrows drawn together in distress. "My mother's about to murder someone. Or have an apoplexy."

Maria waved to the hotel's resident clairvoyants, Madame Le Blanc and Frau Heilig, as they walked past, and glanced across the room at Mac's mother. To the ordinary observer she was entirely unbothered, but Maria had been looking at this woman for the better part of thirty years (despite never actually speaking to her), and she winced in sympathy.

"Can you convince her to leave?"

"Tried," Mac said. "But Count von Kaufstein is here, and she's afraid—" Mac broke off, sighing and rubbing his forehead. The crowd around them had noticed them talking, and were openly staring.

"Put your hand down," Maria said, with a bright smile. "We're being watched."

He laughed as though she'd said something funny, immediately smoothing his expression.

"Count von Kaufstein won't care about any of this," Maria said. "I've known him since I was in the cradle."

"The Count von Kaufstein you know and the Count von Kaufstein my mother knows are very different people," Mac said, through his own charming smile.

Maria opened her mouth to argue, but just then a server spilled a tray of champagne at the other side of the room.

"I have to—"

"Go, go," her brother gestured. "And Maria? It's a beautiful ball."

She squeezed his hand and hurried across the room, checking her watch as she went. Twenty-three minutes to midnight. The waltz was coming to an end.

She could see old Count von Kaufstein about ten meters away. It had been sweet of him to come. He was always sweet to them, the Wallners. It was widely believed that he and Maria's grandmother Josephine were half siblings, both by-blows of the Emperor two emperors deceased. Maria knew it was true of her grandmother; it was probably true of him as well.

Unlike Maria's great-grandmother, Count von Kaufstein's mother had been a highborn aristocrat, one who (also unlike Maria's great-grandmother) had never fallen out with the Imperial Court. The Count could have simply enjoyed a life of familial wealth and Imperial favor, but had chosen a career instead—steadily climbing the court ranks until he became the Imperial and Royal Chamberlain, the person responsible for the current Emperor's household finances.

Viennese high society had been surprised when the Count had announced his son's engagement to Annalise von Eder, Adelaide's oldest girl and Maria's half sister—the von Eders were wealthy and high-ranking, but there was that air of scandal attached to Heinrich, and the Count *was* very important. Consensus seemed to be that it was a love match; a claim Mac had vigorously denied in the Hotel Wallner kitchens two nights earlier, his mouth half full of cake.

"He's twenty years older than her, and she's never even

spoken to him," Mac had said, an expression of utter bafflement on his face. "She's not *that* pretty."

Reaching the scene of the dropped tray, Maria pushed the von Kaufstein–von Eder engagement from her mind. She was as unequipped to follow aristocratic marriage machinations as Mac would be to turn over a guest room.

Fortunately, the tray had carried only two glasses, and the server had dropped it at least a meter and a half away from the nearest guest. She helped him pile the glass on the tray, carefully keeping her gown away from the spilled champagne. Someday soon, she would have a full staff, who could render this sort of mishap invisible. Until then, she had footmen doubling as servers and three maids, all busy elsewhere. So for tonight, Maria was hostess, maid, manager, and occasional plumber all in one. She didn't mind.

When a Wallner woman loved something, she'd do anything for it.

The waltz ended. Her parents clung together briefly, several seconds longer than was appropriate. The party guests stared, thrilled.

"The stars aligned for you tonight," Madame Le Blanc said, coming up beside her. She was a tall Frenchwoman with a long white braid who had lived at the hotel for twenty years. Her specialty was astrology. "As I predicted."

"As *I* predicted," said Frau Heilig, a short, blond Czech woman whose mystical tool of choice was the tarot card deck.

Maria smiled. She had, out of politeness, consulted with both the hotel's occultists, and they had agreed that New Year's Eve was the correct date for the Hotel Wallner's Triumphant Return to Society.

"Your advice was invaluable." She didn't share her mother's obsession with the occult, but these women had lived at the Hotel Wallner almost as long as she had. They were family. "Both of you. It's marvelous, isn't it? Just like it used to be."

The women, sometimes allies, sometimes enemies, shared a glance.

"This room looks lovely," Frau Heilig said diplomatically.

Maria laughed, thinking of the Large Ballroom, with its ruined floor, and of the thirty-two currently unusable guest rooms. "Soon it will *all* look like this," she said. "We're almost back."

"Hmph," Madame Le Blanc said, looking over at Maria's parents, now standing too close together, drinking champagne, still sensationally unaware of their audience. "Well, *they* never left."

"No," Maria said, following her gaze. "They never did."

Another glance at her watch told her it was fourteen minutes before midnight. She had one more surprise in store for the guests, and it was almost time to reveal it. She said goodbye to the occultists, and with one last look at her parents—apparently returning to the dance floor, the beginning of Strauss's "Tales from the Vienna Woods" accompanying them—hurried from the ballroom.

The Small and Large Ballrooms were on the second floor of the Hotel Wallner, separated by a small lobby, with three floors of guest rooms above, and the family apartments above that. The kitchen and restaurant were on the ground floor, along with the lobby and Maria's office. A grand (and newly refurbished) staircase led from the lobby to the second floor. Maria took the tight servants' stair down instead.

She walked briskly to the kitchen, where every footman and handyman and waiter she'd been able to recruit stood in rented uniforms, holding cut-glass bowls, each bowl so large it needed two men to carry it. Hannah Adler, the hotel's chef and Maria's best friend, hurried along the line pouring water into the bowls.

"The metalworkers are out back," she said, and Maria swung through the back door into the small alley beyond, where six metalworkers waited, each carrying a small camp stove.

Every New Year's, the Viennese dropped bits of molten lead into cold water, and from the shapes formed divined their destiny for the year ahead. Usually, this was done with a bit of lead melted in a spoon over a candle, but the Hotel Wallner had once done things on a grand scale.

It was about to do so again.

Maria talked to the metalworkers, checked the uniforms of her army of bowl-carriers, and gave the signal to head to the second floor.

At five minutes to midnight, she returned to the ballroom and gave a nod to the orchestra leader. This would be the last waltz of 1877.

She took a breath, glancing down at the large sapphire ring on her hand. A reminder of her great-grandmother, the woman who had built it all. And then, with precisely one minute left in the old year, the last wild, sweeping notes of "Tales from the Vienna Woods" faded away, and Maria stepped onto the orchestra's platform.

"Good evening," she said, smiling at the beautiful people before her. Yes, the hotel shone, but so did they, the magic of the hotel reflected in their eyes. Her parents, side by side, smiled up at her, as caught in the fantasy as those around them. "The Hotel Wallner invites you to join us in bidding farewell to an old year and welcoming a new one." She turned to the orchestra leader. "Herr Weber, will you assist us?"

He bowed smoothly, and picked up his baton. With half a minute to go, the drummers began to count down the seconds with crisp beats, the audience counting along.

"Five—four—three—two—one—Happy New Year!"

The ballroom erupted in cheers and toasts, and 1878 began.

A fresh year. A fresh start.

When the cheers began to die down, she stepped forward. "And now, the hotel has prepared a little surprise." She smiled as the line of waiters began to enter. The cheers gave way to gasps, and then, as they noticed the metalworkers set up at their stoves around the ballroom, scattered applause. "Ladies and gentlemen, your destinies await. May they be brilliant ones."

The bowl-bearers had taken their places around the metalworkers, several bowls surrounding each stove. Three floating waiters at every station assisted the guests with their lead pouring, and conveniently kept an eye out for any long skirts traveling too close to the stoves. Maria had selected the safest model of camp stove, but fire of any kind was a risk.

She descended from the stage and picked up her waltz again. She spun from group to group, laughing, admiring destinies, pretending to see crowns and flowers, and once even the profile of someone's first love. The glow of the crowd built in her chest, until she felt as though she too was shining. They were happy—the hotel had made them happy. Later, they would wake up in the real world, with headaches to nurse and bills to pay and petty quarrels to fight, but right now they were in the magical fairyland of the Hotel Wallner, and they felt as though they never needed to leave.

May they never leave again.

She needed to check the desserts—Hannah had set them up during Maria's speech but she should double-check them—

"Trying to escape your destiny, Maria?" Madame Le Blanc asked from behind her, Frau Heilig at her side. For women who spent all their time arguing, they certainly spent a lot of time together.

"No," Maria said. "But—"

"Hmph," Madame Le Blanc said, taking her arm in a firm grip and leading her toward a lead-casting station. Maria didn't bother arguing. It would be faster to simply cast the lead, and the guests would like it.

A group of patrons gathered around her as the metal-worker helped her melt a small lump of lead.

"Maria, maybe this is the year you'll meet him," one said.

She laughed, wanting to roll her eyes. For a time in her twenties, Vienna had been very interested in *the man*. Who she would choose to have her daughter with, as her mother and grandmother and great-grandmother had done before her. Never mind that *the man* had rarely been good news: Maria's great-grandfather had very probably tried to have her grandmother and great-grandmother assassinated (this would forever be uncertain, as one didn't accuse an emperor of murder), and her father, while not threatening homicide, did produce an astonishing number of headaches. The best one by far was her grandfather, an unnamed aristocrat her grandmother Josephine had enjoyed a brief fling with before meeting her longtime love, Emilie Brodmaier.

"I'll wish for him," she said, winking, and then cast her real wish: *May the hotel flourish. May it grow and be prosperous.* And then, because the needling about *the man* actually did irritate her and she was feeling petty, she added: *And may we eclipse that damn Hotel Hoffmann.*

She poured the lead into the water, and watched as it formed a swirling, tangled circle. A waiter fished it out, placing it on one of the cloth-covered trays she had arranged for the occasion. She bent over it. "Hmm. Could it be a . . . a volcano?"

Covering the Hotel Hoffmann in lava.

Madame Le Blanc joined her. "Don't be ridiculous," she said, staring at the coin-sized lump. Her eyes flicked to Maria's, and then, disconcertingly, twinkled.

"*Mon Dieu,*" she said, loud enough for everyone in a ten-foot radius to hear. "He's tall. Clara, come look."

Oh no.

Frau Heilig joined them before Maria could stop her, bending her blond head over the lead, and then clasping her hand dramatically to her bosom. "Maria! It's finally happened!"

"No it hasn't," Maria hissed, through her smile. "They're joking," she said to the rapt crowd.

"*I do not joke about the will of the heavens,*" Madame Le Blanc declared in an offended tone.

Maria glared at her.

"He's handsome. Ooh yes," Frau Heilig said, giggling. "Dark-haired, definitely dark-haired. You agree, Matilde?"

With another glance down, Madame Le Blanc nodded graciously. "Yes. You have read it well."

Oh wonderful. They were *collaborating.*

"Madame Le Blanc!" a man called. "Is it him? Is it *the man?*"

"It certainly could be," Madame Le Blanc replied. "Nothing is decided. Merely an opportunity."

"A very handsome opportunity," Frau Heilig said.

There was a flutter in the crowd as—oh *no*—Maria's mother Elisabeth joined them.

"*Maria,*" she said, in a dramatic tone. Elisabeth spoke exclusively in dramatic tones. "Is it true? Is *he* finally coming?"

"No—"

"Oh!" Elisabeth clasped her hands together and looked heavenward, immediately becoming the star of the moment. "It's all I've prayed for! That you would find the happiness I have found with Heinrich! Your father!"

The crowd gasped.

Scandal of the season, Maria reminded herself. *Good for the hotel.*

It was a well-known secret that Maria was Baron Heinrich von Eder's daughter, but it had never been confirmed publicly.

Until now.

She looked over to catch Mac's stricken gaze, as his mother looked on expressionlessly.

It was going to be a difficult night in the von Eder household.

And this was why there would never be *the man,* no matter how many men in general Maria took to her bed. She had seen exactly what happened when there was one.

She would stick with the hotel. Here, if she worked hard, she could create . . . beauty. A magical, healing refuge. In the memories of the Viennese upper class, the hotel was a gossamer, ever-changing fairyland, but to her, it was solid. The home that always held her. The net that caught her when she was falling.

That was the spell of the Hotel Wallner. A spell she now needed to help it cast.

So she pinned a bright, beautiful smile to her face, the twin of her mother's. "How fortunate," she said, laughing. "I'll be looking for him. Day and . . . night." Another laugh, echoed in the crowd. "Oh! Countess von Fier, have you dropped your lead yet?"

Deftly, she turned the crowd away, toward other bowls and other scandals. Her mother, thankfully, had drifted away by the time she returned. Probably back to Heinrich.

They were being so flagrant tonight. Why? After thirty-odd years?

Taking a breath, she looked around the Small Ballroom. The tension drained out of her. No. Nothing could take this from her.

"You wiggled out of that one," Madame Le Blanc said.

Maria narrowed her eyes at the woman. "And *you* are a traitor." She glared at Frau Heilig too. "*Both* of you."

They snickered, unrepentant. "I only report what I see," Madame Le Blanc said, with wide eyes.

"Not funny," Maria said.

"*Very* funny," Madame Le Blanc replied.

"Ooh, Matilde, Hannah's put out her almond cakes," Frau Heilig said, eyeing the dessert table with interest.

"She has?" Madame Le Blanc turned abruptly. "We'd better hurry. They'll go quickly." The women turned to leave.

Thank God for Hannah's almond cakes.

"Oh, Maria," Madame Le Blanc said, over her shoulder as she left. "If I were you, I wouldn't sleep with any dark-haired men."

The women burst into cascades of laughter and sailed off to the dessert table, leaving Maria glaring behind them.

Chapter Two

*We're completely booked. Beethoven is premiering two
new symphonies tomorrow, and every intellectual aspi-
rant in the empire has traveled to see it. I desperately
wish I could go too, but someone must make sure they
all have food to eat when they return.*

—Journal entry of Theresa Wallner, 21 December 1808

The guests danced until streaks of silver began to lighten
the sky. And when the last one had either left the hotel
or stumbled upstairs to a guest room, Maria stood amid the
wreckage of the party and took it in.

It was the beginning.

No, there hadn't even been half as many guests as had
once crowded into the Small Ballroom, but then, it had been
five years since the room had seen any guests at all. This was
merely the start of the Hotel Wallner's Triumphant Return.

She walked to the supply closet hidden between the Large
and Small Ballrooms, and took out an apron and a broom.
The few remaining footmen and maids were upstairs, attending the guests staying over for the night. She'd get the cleaning started by herself.

Alone under the ballroom's starry sky, she tied the apron
over her ball gown and began to collect the dishes scattered
around the room. She hummed a few bars of the "Vienna

Blood" waltz as she worked, dancing in three-quarter time from table to table.

The Hotel Wallner had stood at 2 Annagasse for almost seventy-five years. It had been given to her great-grandmother Theresa, along with an Imperial decree allowing her and her descendants to operate it, before that particular love affair had . . . deteriorated. Theresa had eventually handed over the managership of the hotel to her daughter, Josephine—Maria's grandmother—who had operated the hotel during its heyday. Her reign had lasted forty years, until eight years ago, when she announced that she was exhausted and planned to retire to "devote her time to other pursuits." *Other pursuits* probably translated to *Emilie Brodmaier,* but Josephine was a mysterious woman. She could have taken up dinosaur hunting for all Maria knew.

She had, as tradition dictated, handed the hotel over to *her* daughter, Elisabeth.

That was where the problems began.

Elisabeth didn't really want to run the hotel. She wanted to enjoy its money and fame and premises. She already had her ongoing drama with Heinrich to tend to, and there wasn't much attention left over. Josephine and Maria had hoped she might . . . grow into the role.

She didn't.

Perhaps the hotel could have survived eight years of neglectful leadership. But in 1873, the Vienna Stock Exchange collapsed, triggering a continent-wide financial disaster. And then, two years later, there was an uprising in Bosnia (a territory of the Ottomans) that somehow, seemingly overnight, pushed Europe to the brink of war, with the empire caught between the Ottomans and the Russians.

Needless to say, this didn't help the economy.

Those were very lean years, and Elisabeth didn't know how to adapt. The hotel became shabbier and shabbier, the guests dwindled, and the Large Ballroom developed a catastrophic leak that destroyed its floors and two walls. Elisabeth fired much of the staff to keep the family profits up, but this only increased the rate of decay, and in eight devastating years, the Hotel Wallner went from the place to be seen to a pleasant, faded memory.

It was a relief when, two months earlier, Elisabeth had walked into the guest room Maria was cleaning, dropped the account books on the unmade bed, and declared her intention to retire. Immediately. Or rather in fifteen minutes, when Heinrich was collecting her for a romantic weekend at his hunting lodge.

In the ballroom, Maria piled as many dishes as she could onto a tray, and took them to the kitchen, where Hannah had collapsed in a chair, her feet propped up on an overturned crate. Light brown hair fell messily from her bun.

"Well?" she asked through half-closed eyes.

"A beginning," Maria responded, piling the dishes next to the sink and beginning to wash them. It was the word of the night. A good word.

Hannah nodded in satisfaction and closed her eyes the rest of the way. "What did they think of the cream puffs?"

"They loved the cream puffs."

"And the chocolate things?"

"They adored the chocolate things."

"And the almond cakes?"

"They—listen, I'm running out of synonyms. Everything you made was a sensation."

Hannah smiled slightly, yawned, and nodded again.

"Hannah?"

"Hmm?"

"Go to bed," Maria said.

"No," Hannah said, opening her eyes and hauling herself to her feet. "I'll dry."

Maria rolled her eyes and handed her a plate.

"I heard your parents made a scene," Hannah said.

Maria shrugged. "The guests loved it," she said. "They'll be talking about it for days."

Hannah raised an eyebrow but let it drop. "And I heard that Countess von Dasse snuck off to a linen closet on the third floor. With the new French spy."

"I heard that as well," Maria said, grinning.

"*And* I heard you have to swear off dark-haired men—"

Maria put the plate she was washing down and sighed. "They got to you." She looked over at her friend. Hannah's mouth was twitching.

"Well, it's just that I heard *the man*—"

"Were you hearing or cooking, woman?"

"I'm incredibly talented," Hannah said. "I can do both."

"You were tired a moment ago," Maria said. "Go back to that. That was better."

"Strangely I feel completely reinvigorated. But who do you think it could be? Who do we know that is dark-haired and handsome? Or no, it must be someone new—" Hannah stopped talking with an *mmph* when Maria shoved a cream puff in her mouth.

"I'm going to get the rest of the dishes," she said sternly. "And when I come back, you'd better be sleeping in one of the open rooms, because *someone* has to cook breakfast for the guests in about six hours."

"Fine, fine," Hannah said, through the cream puff. "How many stayed over?"

"Fifteen," Maria said. "Including Countess von Dasse and the new French spy. And we had ten rooms already booked."

Hannah dropped her dish towel. "That's . . ."

"The highest capacity in five years."

"We're back," Hannah said. "We're back!"

Maria smiled. She didn't correct her friend, but in her

head she added the word *almost*. They would be back, really back, when *every* room was booked. When both ballrooms were packed with people. When the restaurant could serve more than breakfast—

"Oh, Maria," Hannah said, as Maria took the empty tray and headed toward the stairs.

"Hmm?"

"At least there's the French spy. He's blond, so—"

Maria grabbed a dish towel, hurled it at her friend, and ran up the stairs.

An hour later she stood alone in the Small Ballroom, sweeping the floor. A now-half-empty bottle of champagne kept her company on one of the tables she hadn't broken down yet. She swept the last of the dust into a pile and took a swig, smiling as it shimmered down her throat. She was pleasantly tipsy, though whether it was from the champagne or the triumph that had been fizzing in her veins the last several hours she didn't know.

Maria took another swig, leaned her chin on the top of the broom, looked up at her starry sky, and for a moment, let herself dream of fine new upholstery and grand, unstained wallpaper.

Then she went and found the dustpan.

Soon. Soon every part of the hotel would shine again.

When the floors were swept and clean, she put everything away, took her now-three-quarters-empty bottle, and made her way down to her office. There was one last thing to do before the night was over.

The manager's office was small, just off the kitchen, and crowded with seventy-five years of account books and registration records. She lit the lamp and reached beneath the large wooden desk, turning the knob that released the desk's secret compartment and retrieving that month's innkeeper's diary. The Wallner women had kept these for almost as long as the hotel had stood, but because the diaries frequently included information that could be embarrassing to high-placed people in Viennese society they were always carefully hidden. The monthly diary was kept in the secret drawer, and at the end of the month it joined its fellows in a secure location.

Tonight was the beginning, Maria wrote, taking a swallow of champagne.

> *The Small Ballroom was beautiful, and so were the guests. Mother and Heinrich made a scene, and Adelaide saw. The guests enjoyed it.*
>
> *Hannah says she heard Countess von Dasse was seen leaving a linen closet with that new French spy. Claude something. If people are going to be using the linen closets for assignations, I need to refurbish them. What would be nice, but discreet? I can't exactly shove a velvet ottoman in a broom closet. Still, at the very least I should make sure there's a clear wall. And easy access. And fresh paint.*

She stopped to take another drink, only to find the bottle empty. Deciding that wouldn't do at all, she made her way to the kitchen and opened another bottle as she considered the mechanics of coupling in linen closets. Some kind of hand-hold on the back wall, at a conveniently placed height . . .

She sat down at her desk and continued to write.

> *Install a very secure shelf? No, that might present a head injury risk. I'll keep thinking. The desserts were very good. Hannah's almond cakes were particularly popular . . .*

She wrote for a while longer, her pen loosened by the champagne, recording who had attended, what they had worn, and what they had said to whom. By the time she closed the journal, she was surprised to see it was past nine in the morning. She needed to sleep, if only for a few hours.

But first—

The champagne was turning her sentimental, she thought as she stood, laughing to herself, but there was one more thing she wanted to do before she slept.

She wanted to toast the grande dame herself.

Taking the bottle with her, she wound her way out of the hotel, waving at Abraham, her head footman, standing alert at the front desk, and swung out the wide double doors into a crisp winter morning.

The sky was cold and blue overhead, and people dressed for work mingled with those in ball gowns and evening suits still enjoying the evening prior. The street was still closed for the night, as both the Hotel Wallner and the Hotel Hoffmann, across the road and two doors down, had hosted New Year's Eve balls, so it was quieter than usual, no shouting drivers and clattering horse hooves.

Somewhere up the street a violinist scratched out a waltz, and Maria hummed along. She pulled her velvet evening coat around her shoulders and wove her way across the narrow Innere Stadt street the hotel faced, to the square across from it.

In the summer the wide tree in the middle cast lovely, leafy shade over the four wrought-iron benches; now it was bare, the benches frosted. Still, a man sat on one, his wide shoulders hunched against the cold.

This was where she wanted to end her triumphant night: across the street from the pink and white façade of the hotel, admiring its five magnificent stories. Maria spared a glare for the Hotel Hoffmann, tipping her nose in the air at its pretentious marble columns.

"No magic," she said, scornfully, then dismissed it entirely, turning back to *her* hotel. "Not like you, darling."

She stepped out onto the cobblestone street and raised her bottle. "To you," she said, tipping it against her lips.

She heard the warning too late. By the time she heard the horses' wild cries and the shouts of the driver, she could only freeze, watching the carriage bear down upon her.

Time hung slowly. She noticed everything. The whites of the horses' eyes. The panicked expression of the young nobleman who'd lost control. The scream of a nearby woman.

And then *something* grabbed her arm and pulled, and she ran into something hard, and time moved once more.

Gasping, she stepped back, her head spinning from shock and champagne. Her stomach was suddenly extremely unsettled, and for a moment that took all her attention.

A man was talking to her. Touching her. The hard thing had been him, and even now he was steadying her with his hands. She looked at his hands. She looked at his chest. Finally, she looked up at his face.

He had stopped talking and was looking down at her with an expression halfway between concern and irritation.

He had dark, chestnut hair, styled sternly, and deep-set brown eyes. His skin was pale, his jaw sharp and clean, almost harsh. A severe face. Except for his mouth.

She blinked.

His mouth . . . was absolutely luscious. Wide and sensual and, at the moment, caught in a rigid frown.

That mouth, she thought, *is pure sin.*

It had been—she tried to calculate quickly but for some reason the numbers were rather fuzzy—at least a week since she'd had a man in her bed, which wasn't really that long, but planning the ball had been *very* stressful, and that mouth looked very stress relieving, and really the arms around her were pleasantly strong, and she had the vague feeling he might have just saved her life, which she had never experienced before and was discovering was every bit the aphrodisiac tawdry novels would have you believe, and she *did* need to test out her linen closet concept; after all, what kind of hotel manager would she be if she offered her guests an experience she hadn't *thoroughly* vetted first—

And then, with no warning at all, everything rushed back in. The sound of the street, the smell of the frost, the faint strains of the violinist, and, most important, *the color of his hair.*

Her stomach flipped again.

He's handsome, in a way. Ooh yes. Dark-haired, definitely dark-haired.

"No," she said. "They were joking."

"Are you all right?" He spoke in careful, American-accented German. A foreigner then. An incredibly gorgeous, dark-haired foreigner.

"No," she said, pushing his hands away. He retracted them immediately.

"You're not all right?"

The Hotel Wallner was back. Well, almost back. And the two occultists had simply been teasing her—they had wicked senses of humor—

Yes, but have you ever known them to lie about what they saw?

Maria gulped. "I'm fine," she said, cautiously, putting a hand on her stomach. It occurred to her that she had, perhaps, drunk too much champagne.

"You shouldn't have been in the street," he said, disapprovingly. Well. The words were disapproving. The mouth was . . . mmm. Stern.

Stop it, she told herself. *Stop it right now.*

"The street is closed to carriage traffic," she said faintly, as her mind spun through everything Madame Le Blanc and Frau Heilig had said. "That carriage shouldn't have been there."

The thing to do was to leave. On the off chance—on the off chance that Fate was an absolute bitch.

"I'm fine," she repeated. "No need for dark-haired men whatsoever. Thank you."

She tried to step away, but apparently her legs were still weak, and she stumbled. He caught her before she landed on the ground.

Strong. He was very strong.

She sighed in annoyance. "Yes, I see," she said, either to Fate or Madame Le Blanc, she wasn't sure. "He's very strong and tall and good-looking and *that mouth* is indeed quite something, but he's not *the man*."

"I . . . have no idea who you're talking to," he said, the impatience in his voice clear. "I think you're drunk."

"Yes, hold on to that. Good. Irritation is good. Just dump me on the ground and leave me. That's the wisest course of action. Above all, though, we cannot sleep together."

He dropped his hands. She staggered, but remained upright.

His expression of horror was . . . rather delicious actually. *No, not delicious. Absolutely not.*

"That will not present any difficulty," he said, and then he bowed crisply, and, bless him, walked away.

Maria staggered to a bench and sank down onto it. He'd *saved her life.* For one grisly moment she replayed the carriage racing toward her, the utter blankness of her mind, the feeling of it hurtling by as the man (not *the man,* though, very important difference) had held her in his arms—

She shook her head. Her heart was pounding. She felt as though she'd had not one near miss, but two.

She leaned over and vomited in the bushes.

Chapter Three

The papers report a revolt in one of the Ottoman ter-
ritories to the south, a region called Herzegovina. The
Catholics in the area (whom His Imperial Majesty ap-
parently considers himself the Protector of) have risen
up against the Ottoman governors, citing brutal over-
taxation . . . what the rebels want, though, the papers
can't agree on—one claims they fight for independence,
the other says they wish to join Austria-Hungary . . .
the former seems more believable. . . .

—Journal entry of Maria Wallner, 10 July 1875,
discussing the Herzegovina Uprising of 1875–77

Eli Whittaker, agent of the Secret Service Division of the
United States Department of the Treasury, had been in Vienna for precisely eight hours and forty-three minutes, and
already he desperately wanted to leave.

He had arrived at the train station (two days late, owing to
bad winds on the Atlantic crossing) with exactly one hour left
in 1877, and the entirety of Vienna out celebrating that fact.
It had taken him twenty minutes to find a driver, and then an
hour for his driver to weave through the clogged streets.

His first impression of the city had been formed from
strange, otherworldly flashes of light seen through the carriage
window: a man, in full evening dress, passed out drunk in the

entryway of a closed shop, a streetlamp painting his skin and the pale stone of the building behind him the same strange gold; a performer on a unicycle, dressed in garish yellows and greens, juggling oranges as he rode in circles around a barrel fire; an enormous group of partygoers in strange masks, carrying paper lanterns on sticks as they sang and waltzed; candlelight and gaslight streaming like the sun from buildings towering overhead, their strange, grand details appearing only in flickers, here and then gone.

He'd arrived at his hotel, wanting only to collapse into his bed, and had spent three exquisitely painful hours staring at the ceiling as the orchestra one floor below him played waltz after waltz after waltz, spinning, spinning, spinning, until he was dizzy simply from listening. When he thought he might actually scream, he had put his clothes back on and left his room, accidentally colliding with a couple leaving a linen closet on the way. He had stumbled outside, and seen the square across from the hotel. Outside was still loud, and surreal, and if he had been a man given to fantasy (he wasn't) he might not be entirely sure he was still in the mortal realm, but at least here there wasn't a bed to torment him with his inability to sleep.

And then—and then—

The woman.

What did she think we were going to do, he thought in outrage, *have relations in the middle of a public square?* All he'd done was save her life—after she half-wandered, half-danced into the middle of the street like a damned drunken fool— and then she'd commented on his appearance, and said that thing about his mouth, and *looked* at him in that way, like he was something delicious she might like to take a bite of—and then—and then!

Above all, though, we cannot sleep together.

There had been a day last September when Eli had been

kidnapped at gunpoint and held for seven very cold hours in an empty warehouse while three goons attempted to extract information from him. He had ended the experience with two broken ribs, a missing back tooth, two nasty black eyes, mild frostbite, and a dislocated thumb.

He wished he were back in the warehouse.

Eli recalled the incident fondly, stalking down a still-crowded street to the tune of a beggar's violin (another waltz—it was fortunate the goons hadn't thought to hire a musician). Vienna in the daylight was different, but no less overpowering. Where the night had been black and gold, the day was white and gold: the pale stone of the buildings; the gilt of their lettering; the snow-white coats of the powerful cab horses; the gold of the statues that lurked around every corner Eli turned. Women in evening gowns still twirled with men in fine black suits, seemingly unaware of the laborers in plain, sturdy clothing walking past them on their way to work. Across the street, three women danced in an empty fountain, apparently reenacting a scene from *Macbeth*. And on the opposite corner, a man covered in parrots announced the day's news.

The warehouse had been free of parrots. He hadn't considered this advantage before, but now it struck him powerfully. It hadn't been quiet, exactly, at least not until he'd overpowered his kidnappers, but there had not been any waltzes of any sort. Indeed, once the goons were unconscious, the empty building had boasted a certain peaceful quality. And then he'd gotten to arrest them, and once they were conscious again, they'd told him all about their employer, and two months later, after a meticulous investigation, he'd gotten an arrest warrant for a sitting United States senator, who was scheduled to go on trial in just a few weeks.

If torture in a freezing warehouse was a step up from the partygoer-riddled streets of Vienna, then the grim peace of a courtroom where a corrupt U.S. senator would come face-to-face with justice was, comparatively, a Utopia.

But no, rather than watching justice be served, he was here. Surrounded by more people than he'd ever seen in his life—likely more people than lived in the entire city of Washington, D.C.—every one of them loud, and drunk, and dressed in fabrics that probably cost the equivalent of his monthly rent at the boardinghouse.

Three weeks after receiving this assignment, he was no closer to understanding it.

The Secret Service Division of the United States Department of the Treasury, to which Eli had devoted his entire adult life—save for his years in the Union Army—was officially dedicated to the investigation of counterfeit currency, a problem that had plagued the nation for decades. At its peak, around the time of the Civil War, almost a third of the bills in circulation had been fake. The division had been created to ensure the stability of the nation's money.

Sometimes, counterfeiters were small-time gangs or wayward artists. And sometimes they were large, organized, criminal syndicates.

Eli's job was hunting down the latter.

For the last year, he'd been engaged in a meticulous, intricate, grueling investigation into a multistate web of criminals known popularly as the Bantry Gang. He'd endured the skepticism of his colleagues, the occasional derision of the press, the kidnapping, and three assassination attempts.

And at the end of it, he and his team had detained two congressional representatives, a federal judge, a Maryland State Chief Justice, and a United States senator for accepting bribes from the gang.

See, the thing about large, shadowy gangs of criminals was that they were rarely interested in *remaining* in the shadows.

Counterfeit money got turned into real money, which then got turned into judges and congressmen and senators, who somehow believed that their positions ought to protect them from shabby things like prosecution.

Eli didn't believe in God, or Heaven. He'd had all that starved and beaten out of him long ago. There was only one thing he believed in now: justice. It was his cornerstone, the rubric against which he judged his own actions and those of others.

So why was he in Vienna, thousands of miles from the courtroom in which that justice would be served, caught between a man vomiting on his right and a man carrying what appeared to be a snail in a golden cage on his left?

Probably someone, somewhere, knew. That person was not Eli Whittaker.

The case was straightforward enough: Someone was stealing American codes and selling them. An unsigned letter discussing the codes had been intercepted after being posted from a hotel in Vienna, leading the U.S. government to believe the codes were being stolen from the American Legation there. Someone needed to go to Vienna, investigate the hotel and the Legation, find out who was stealing the codes, and stop them.

What was less straightforward was why that person needed to be Eli.

He remembered the day he'd received the assignment much as he imagined one might remember a mugging. Everything had been fine. Good, even. It was the day after he'd arrested Senator Markham. His team had been in a good mood, teasing and laughing with each other. Agent Moreno had even plucked up enough courage to accuse Eli, who famously never smiled or laughed (even the senior bureaucrats called him Ol' Stoneface when they thought no one could overhear), of a certain lightness of expression.

And then, disaster had struck, in the form of a meek secretary, peeking his head in and requesting Eli's presence in Undersecretary Wallace's office.

From there, the memory assumed a surreal cast.

It was unusual to see Wallace at Treasury. He was more of a politician than a bureaucrat, a skilled one at that—despite being deeply ensconced in Washington's crony politics, he had somehow managed to escape every round of President Hayes's civil service reforms. Other than his dubious morals, his most noticeable feature was a large black mustache.

The man had ushered him in with a sort of accomplished familiarity. "Saw your father yesterday," he had begun. "Stepfather, rather."

They were playing a game, Eli had realized. But he didn't know what game. Three weeks later, he still didn't.

"He worries about you, you know," Wallace had continued.

That was probably true, and it bothered Eli. The Ambassador was a kind man, who loved Eli's mother very much. Eli was grateful to him. An uncomfortable emotion.

Eli had simply waited. The point, whatever it was, would be forthcoming. Eventually.

"You've been working hard," Wallace said. "He worries you're getting . . . run-down."

"I'm not." Eli doubted his stepfather had said anything of the kind, especially not to someone like Wallace, but that was the kind of sentence that needed to be immediately refuted when you worked in government.

Wallace had smiled. Kindly? In a manner Eli imagined was supposed to emulate kindness. "You're a hard worker," he said. "But Elijah, you've had two assassination attempts *this year.*"

It was three, but the undersecretary didn't need to know that. And it wasn't as though it was the first time someone had tried to kill him. For a brief, panicked moment he had wondered if his mother had heard about the attempts. Was that what was going on here? Had someone told his mother, and she had told the Ambassador, and the Ambassador had complained to Wallace?

If someone had made his mother worry . . .

"Elijah?"

"Yes?"

"Err, nothing. Never mind." The man had stared awhile longer at Eli's face, but quickly recovered his slick demeanor.

"The point is, you need a rest."

Eli had shaken his head. "I don't." What he needed was to get on with his day, file a significant amount of paperwork, and then find out who the hell had worried his mother.

Wallace was beginning to look annoyed. Eli was familiar with the expression. It usually emerged when someone expected him to be more than minimally polite. He'd thought the man would argue, but Wallace had abruptly changed direction.

"The truth is," he had said, leaning forward confidentially, "I need you to be tired."

"Excuse me?"

"I need you to be tired."

Politicians were slippery, the extremely ambitious ones particularly so. Eli had come to understand this in the fourteen years he'd lived in Washington, so he proceeded warily.

"Why?"

"Because the government needs you somewhere else."

Needs you . . .

"Where?"

"Vienna."

Eli had not responded, waiting to hear what the United States government needed him to do in Vienna, Virginia, and why he needed to be tired for it. The town was only a few miles outside of Washington, he could be there that evening if he needed to be. After the paperwork, and the investigation of the mother-worrier. And he would need to pack. Still, before midnight.

"Austria."

"I beg your pardon?"

"Vienna, Austria."

Eli had wondered if the man was drunk. He didn't look drunk. But how did you forget what department you were the undersecretary of? This was Treasury, not State.

"There's a problem at the Legation in Vienna," Wallace had continued.

"One involving the counterfeiting of American money?"

Wallace had chuckled indulgently. "One involving American *security*," he said. "Rather more important. We believe someone is selling our codes.

"Our *secret* codes," Wallace had continued, after a moment of dense silence. "That we use to encode our diplomatic messages. Someone needs to go there, find out who is doing it, and stop them."

That part made sense. Certainly, someone should. Someone from the State Department. Whose job it was.

"You speak German fluently," Wallace had continued.

True. He had lived near a German-American community as a child, and had learned it then.

"And, I believe, some Hungarian."

Also true. The man who lived next to him in the boardinghouse was a Hungarian scholar. Eli had learned some of the language. It had seemed minimally polite.

"And you're good with numbers, which means you're good with codes."

"I have no reason to believe my mathematical talent will translate to cryptography," Eli remembered protesting. "I've never studied it."

Wallace had literally waved this off, his hand arcing casually through the air. "It will. And anyway, mostly what we need is a good investigator. And you're our best."

This was true . . . at *Treasury*. He had to imagine there were equally talented people the State Department could turn to.

"And anyway, it's not a request," Wallace had continued. "Your government needs you. I've never known you to shirk a duty."

But he had duties *here*. "When do you need me to go?"

"Today."

"*What?*"

"You have a briefing at State in an hour. Officially, you'll be going to Vienna to give the Legation currency trainings. Your ship leaves tonight."

"But my case—"

"I'm aware of your work on the Bantry Gang case," Wallace had said, chuckling. "Caused a bit of a fuss yesterday, didn't you? Anyway, I hope you're not implying you and *you alone* can finish it up. If you've trained your team properly, they can do it."

"I . . ." A year. He'd worked for a year. His team *could* do the rest. Probably. "But . . ."

But Wallace was already standing, handing Eli a thick folder. The matter was settled.

And now Eli was here, four and a half thousand miles away from his team, his case, and justice; and yes, that was indeed a snail in a golden cage, and oh, he really, really, *really* wanted to leave.

The only way out is through.

Solve the case. Turn the culprit over to the appropriate authorities. Avoid being harassed by drunken women. Go home.

But first, he needed to sleep. At least for a few hours. He looked at his pocket watch. Half past nine in the morning.

Surely the ball was over by now. There had to be a limit to how long people could dance before physically collapsing. If he went back now, he could get at least an hour of sleep before the Legation opened.

Clicking his watch shut, he turned on his heel and went back the way he had come. As he approached the square across from the Hotel Wallner, where the incriminating letter had been intercepted and where he was staying, he slowed, scanning for a woman in midnight-blue silk, with short, wavy black hair. It had been a ridiculous gown, with hundreds of crystals sewn on the skirt, forming the constellations of the night sky. The crystals were what had caught his eye first, sparkling in the bright winter sun.

He didn't see her, but he still approached carefully. No, she was gone. He nodded, relieved to avoid yet another complication.

He squinted up at the Hotel Wallner.

Well. He'd survived a kidnapping, a price on his head, and three assassination attempts in 1877. Surely 1878 couldn't bring anything worse.

Chapter Four

*I saw him today. He's aged so much—this unending war
with Napoleon. We slept together; I think more because
it was expected than because either of us wanted to. I
wonder how many more times he will ask for me. He's
never met Josephine—I don't suppose he ever will.*

—Journal entry of Theresa Wallner, 14 August 1809,
referring to her relationship with Emperor Francis II

That evening, after a few hours' sleep and plenty of Hannah's coffee, Maria sat paying bills in her office while Hannah prepared the dough for the next day's bread.

She'd woken with a foggy memory of making an absolute fool of herself in front of a very good-looking man and then vomiting in some bushes. At least, she hoped those had been separate events, and that the handsome man and the vomit had not been present at the same time. Oh, and she'd almost been killed by a carriage. Perhaps she should drink less in the new year.

She went back to her bills.

Hannah sang as she kneaded. She had a pretty voice: soft and gentle, just like her. The hotel didn't serve dinner currently, so the kitchen was otherwise quiet. Most of the guests had either checked in or out (though Countess von Dasse's room still sported its Do Not Disturb sign), so the lobby on the other side of the swinging door was quiet as well.

There was a knock on the kitchen's back door, and Garit the postboy rushed in with the day's mail. "Sorry I'm late," he said, thrusting the stack at Hannah. There were dark circles under his eyes. Maria walked out, taking the mail from Hannah while her friend gave the boy a cup of coffee.

"Thanks," he said, gulping it quickly. "Some night."

Maria suppressed a smile as she flipped through the mail. Most of Vienna was nursing a hangover today.

Garit handed the cup back, bowed to them both, and dashed back out the door.

"He's still got half the neighborhood to do," Hannah said, washing the cup.

"Mmm." Two more bills, a letter to her mother with no return address (probably Heinrich), and something from the Hotelkeepers' Guild. "They can't want more money already," Maria said, tearing the letter open.

She read it. She read it again. And then she read it a third time.

Dear Fraulein Wallner, the letter began.

I'm writing to you with some urgency. Last night, shortly after their New Year's Eve ball, the Hotel Hoffmann suffered a catastrophic leak. The damage is significant. As you know, they were the planned location for our annual Hotelkeepers' Ball, which is three weeks hence, on January 26, and for which the tickets have already been sold. Most of our hotels have events too close to that date to serve as a replacement venue, but I heard of your success last night, and I remembered the Hotel Wallner. Is it possible for you to host the ball? Let me know as soon as possible.

Sincerely,
Ryker Koch, Guild Master

"Hannah," she croaked. Inaudibly. She cleared her throat and tried again. "Hannah!"

"Hmm?"

"The guild—the ball—" She thrust the letter at her friend. "Read."

Hannah took the letter. Maria collapsed against the kitchen table.

The Hotelkeepers' Ball.

Vienna's winter balls were famous across Europe. Technically, ball season began in November, but really it began January sixth, the first day of Fasching—Carnival. These were not the piddly balls of other European capitals, with their small orchestras and watered-down punch. These were *real* balls, grand, soaring, wild, each-one-must-outdo-the-last events, where a prince and a scullery maid might dance together.

And the Hotelkeepers' Ball was one of the best.

Hannah's mouth was open. She finished reading and looked up blankly. They stared at each other.

"My New Year's wish," Maria said. "Was to eclipse the Hotel Hoffmann."

Hannah nodded. "A leak. Terrible for them."

"Tragic."

They stared at each other for a moment longer before Maria shook herself.

"I have to answer," she said. "I have to answer immediately!"

She ran to her desk, Hannah behind her. Hand shaking, she pulled out a crisp sheet of Hotel Wallner stationery and began writing.

"—*be delighted*—" she muttered, her hand dashing across the page.

"I have to invent a new dessert," Hannah said. "Where's my notebook?!"

"We need someone to deliver this," Maria said, standing as she blotted the letter.

"I'll get one of the footmen," Hannah said, putting a hand to her cheek and leaving behind a streak of flour. "I'll—" She stopped on her way to the door. "Oh."

"What?"

"Maria."

"What?"

"The ballroom."

The words pierced like arrows into a hot air balloon. Maria hissed and sank back into her chair. "The ballroom."

She chewed her bottom lip. The Large Ballroom had been unserviceable for several years, since it had suffered its own catastrophic leak. The Hotelkeepers' Ball would likely have more than five hundred people in attendance. The Small Ballroom could fit a hundred and seventy-five. In a pinch.

Maria shook her head and stuffed the letter into an envelope. "I'll figure it out."

"But—"

She sealed the envelope and addressed it. "This is what we've been working for. This is our moment to remind all of Vienna who we are. Who we have been and who we will be. I won't lose this opportunity. Not even if I have to sand every square centimeter of those floors myself."

Hannah hesitated, then nodded. "All right," she said. "I'll get a footman."

"I'll tell my grandmother," Maria said, handing Hannah the letter. "We'll need her advice." She looked at the clock. It was just past six in the evening. "Hotel meeting," she decided. "In an hour. Bring your notebook."

The Wallner family apartments were on the top floor, beneath the sloped roof of the hotel. Over the decades they had been built out, so now there were three suites, and a large unused attic area beyond. Maria lived in what had once been her great-grandmother Theresa's apartment, with her grandmother Josephine next door, and her mother at the end of the row.

She had taken the stairs at a run, so she was panting when she knocked on her grandmother's door.

"Come in," Josephine called, and Maria pushed the door open.

Her grandmother was dressed to go out, sitting before her vanity and winding her silver hair into the sharp, stern bun she had worn for as long as Maria could remember. She was a small woman in her seventies, with a perfectly straight back and dark eyes resembling Maria's own. She lifted an eyebrow. "You're in a hurry," she said.

"I have news," Maria said. She sat next to her grandmother, breathing in the familiar, comforting smell of powder and tobacco.

"Tell me then."

"The guild wants us to host the Hotelkeepers' Ball," Maria said, the words coming out so fast they jumbled together. She paused and added, "In three weeks."

Josephine said nothing, pinning her bun into place. Only when she was finished did she turn.

"The message?"

Maria handed it to her. Unlike Maria and Hannah, her grandmother needed only one read-through to possess herself of its contents.

"Hmm," she said, handing it back. "And what are you going to do?"

"I'm going to host it."

Josephine nodded. "All right. Do you want my help?"

"Yes. Please."

A slight gleam came into her grandmother's eyes. "Then I'll help you," she said. "Do you have a plan?"

"I want to have a hotel meeting at seven. Can you come? I see you're going out."

"Yes," Josephine said. "I was on my way to Emilie's. She'll understand if I'm late."

"Thank you," Maria said, standing. "Thank you, Grand-mother."

"The Hotelkeepers' Ball," Josephine said, an uncharacter-istically nostalgic tone in her voice. "We've hosted it three times before, you know. But the best one was in 1829."

She didn't appear interested in elaborating, standing and crossing to her desk. Maria hid a smile. She didn't know what had happened at the Hotelkeepers' Ball of 1829, but she would bet the hotel's entire operating budget that it had something to do with Emilie Brodmaier. There was really only one person in her grandmother's life who could produce that tone.

When a Wallner woman loved, *really* loved, it was forever.

An image flashed into her mind of strong arms and a grim, sensual mouth.

Maria frowned and brought herself firmly back to the present, said goodbye to her grandmother, and hurried out.

An hour later, she sat at the kitchen table with Hannah and Josephine, her notebook open before her.

"As I see it, we have two main problems," she began. "First, the Large Ballroom is not fit to be opened. The floors are buckled, the plaster is damaged, and the chandelier is broken. Second, we only have three weeks to fix all this."

"And plan an entire ball," Hannah contributed.

"And plan an entire ball," Maria said, nodding. "The floor and plasterwork are what's worrying me the most. I'm con-cerned we don't have enough time to get them finished. Even assuming I can find the money to pay for them."

Josephine pursed her lips. "I can get you the workmen," she said. "A few people still owe me favors. But the money—you'll have to go to the banks."

"I know," Maria said. They had expended every spare gulden already on the Small Ballroom and Lobby renovations. A loan was the only thing left to do.

A shadow flickered across Josephine's face, quickly vanishing. She'd never publicly criticized her daughter during Elisabeth's disastrous managership, but once, late at night, Maria had walked in on a quiet, devastating argument. It certainly couldn't have been pleasant, watching forty years of hard work vanish in less than a decade.

It would all be set right soon, Maria reminded herself. Hosting the Hotelkeepers' Ball was a sure ticket to fashionability. If they pulled it off, there would be no difficulty in filling their rooms. Their return would be assured.

"All right," she said. "The guild will transfer the portion of the ticket sales set aside for the event costs to our accounts tomorrow."

"It's not a lot," Josephine said. "The hotels usually have to cover extra. It's more than worth it for the benefits, but it's another cost."

Maria nodded. "It will have to be enough," she said. She wasn't worried about that. She'd made do for far less important opportunities than this one—the last eight years had been one long lesson in making do.

"Have you decided on a theme?" Hannah asked. "I'm going to make a dessert to match it—"

"Good evening, everyone!" Elisabeth trilled as she pushed through the lobby door into the kitchen. She was dressed for the evening, in a luscious emerald gown Heinrich had assuredly paid for. Her long dark hair curled prettily around her shoulders.

"Hannah," she said, smiling, "would you be a darling and make me some coffee?"

Hannah nodded and pushed away from the table.

"Actually—" Maria began.

"You all look terribly serious," Elisabeth said, laughing. "I hope nothing's the matter?"

"No," Maria said, resigning herself to the conversation. Her mother had to know about the ball anyway. "We're discussing the Hotelkeepers' Ball. The guild has asked us to host it."

"The Hotelkeepers' Ball! How marvelous! Oh, how exciting! Of course I was going already, but if it's going to be *here* I think I'll have to make a special effort, don't you? I'll send a message to Claudette immediately and tell her we'll be making adjustments to the dress. What's the theme? Oh, let's do something marvelous like Versailles, or the Romans!"

"Fairyland," Maria said, quietly. "The theme is Fairyland."

"*Perfect,*" Elisabeth said, beaming. "It's like you chose it just for me. I'll be a marvelous Titania, don't you think? And Heinrich can be Oberon—oh, perfect, perfect, perfect."

"Yes," Maria said. "Perfect."

Josephine said nothing. Hannah handed Elisabeth the coffee.

"Thank you, darling," Elisabeth said. "Last night was beautiful, but I do have the most terrible headache. I know your lovely coffee will chase it right away. Oh, a letter!"

She picked up the envelope addressed to her as she sipped the coffee, opened it, and began reading. Hannah sat back down at the table.

"Fairyland," she said, opening her notebook. "It's a lovely idea. It makes me think of spun sugar and an enormous amount of candied flowers, spilling out from everywhere. . . ." She trailed off as she began to sketch.

The alley door shut abruptly. Elisabeth had left.

It was silly to feel slighted, Maria told herself. Her mother had never once, in the whole time Maria had known her, cared one single bit about the hotel. If that hadn't changed during the eight years she'd been manager, it was hardly going to change now.

Josephine sighed and stood. "I'll message the workmen. It's a good theme. Cheap, too. You can do a lot with greenery—"

She was interrupted by an ear-piercing bang.

"Was that—"

"The lobby," Maria said, running to the door.

Chapter Five

Seventy-four souls drowned yesterday. A terrible tidal
wave overwhelmed them when the Danube broke
through an ice damn and flooded. . . .
            —Journal entry of Theresa Wallner, 1 March 1830

The bullet missed Eli's head by six inches, burying itself in the wallpaper next to the front doors he had just walked through.

Eli blinked.

"Sorry," the man waving the gun said, before aiming it at a fat upholstered chair a few feet away. "Thought he was going toward the door."

Eli assessed the situation. It was fairly clear. A husband had found his wife in bed with another man. The husband was drunk; the wife was on the stairs, half-dressed and crying; and judging from the bare foot Eli saw peeping out, the other man was hiding behind the chair.

"Come out, you coward," the husband shouted, his arm waving precariously.

"No," the man behind the chair replied, in a French accent.

This answer seemed to confound the husband. "You have to," he said, after a pause.

"No, I don't."

The door next to the front desk opened.

"Don't come out," Eli shouted, but a woman peeked her head around—

No. Not *a* woman.

The woman.

She took in the scene. She took in the bullet hole. She stared at the bullet hole. And then, rather than sensibly putting two and two together and *retreating,* she pushed into the room.

She was going to get shot.

Eli set his briefcase down and began edging his way around the room.

"Count von Dasse," the woman said slowly, ice edging her words, "are you responsible for the bullet hole in my wallpaper? My *new* wallpaper, that I got at thirty percent off because it was the very end of the roll, and therefore is *irreplaceable*?"

"But Maria, I found them *in bed* together—"

Maria. So that was the foolish woman's name. She had changed out of her ball gown. Now she was wearing a day dress in deep, saturated violet. A perfect dress to walk into the middle of a gunfight.

Maybe she was still drunk.

"So?"

"They were *copulating*!"

"I see. Were they doing it on my wallpaper?"

The Count scrunched his brow, confused.

"Well?"

"No," said the man behind the chair. "We were upstairs. On the desk. Though, may I say, it is lovely wallpaper. I would be happy to copulate against it."

"You!" The Count spun around and fired directly at the chair.

The Countess on the stairs screamed.

A half-naked blond man dashed out from behind the chair. The Count fired again.

"Stop shooting at me!" the blond man cried, darting behind a pillar near the front desk.

"Stop fucking my wife!"

"I *already have,*" the man said, reasonably. "I can hardly fuck her while you're shooting at me!"

Eli closed the distance between himself and the woman—Maria. He would push her back through the door—

Bang.

This time the bullet tore a chunk out of the marble pillar. Stone shards flew everywhere, and the woman behind him made a sort of growling sound. He whirled around.

"Are you hurt?" he asked.

"No," she said, baring her teeth. "But he's about to be."

And she stormed into the middle of the room, just as the Frenchman dove behind the front desk. The Count flourished the gun, his arm waving wildly, and Eli flung himself at Maria as a shot rang out, tackling her to the floor. A quick, hot pain tore across his arm as they fell.

He looked up in the sudden silence. The bullet had landed in the wall behind them. Exactly where her head had been.

Releasing a breath, he looked down and realized he was lying on top of her. Completely on top of her. His-torso-suddenly-knew-every-soft-curve-of-her-body on top of her.

He scrambled off her, walked to the Count, and took the damn gun away.

"Give that back!"

"No," he said, crossly.

He returned to Maria and knelt beside her. "Are you all right?"

"You," she breathed. Her eyes were wide, and he was about to tell her to rest, that she was probably in shock, when she pushed herself off the ground.

"I'm going to murder him," she announced, perfectly calmly. Apparently in no shock whatsoever. "Give me the gun."

"No."

"You're right," she said. "I need him to pay for repairs."

She marched across the room to the Count, who had collapsed drunkenly in the chair he'd shot through. Judging by the man's abrupt pallor when she started talking, she didn't have anything pleasant to say.

Eli unloaded the gun and tucked it in his pants pocket. He registered a slight pain in his upper arm when he moved, and remembered he'd been shot. He sighed.

"I think I must offer my gratitude," said a French-accented voice. Eli turned. The blond man was mostly naked, but he was wearing his pair of white drawers with the same ease as if he were in full court dress.

"You should put clothes on," Eli said. "There are ladies present."

The man shrugged. "Well, she's already seen it," he said, gesturing toward the Countess, who had joined Maria in yelling at her husband. "And I don't think that one shocks easily. My name is Claude Girard." He made a gracious bow.

Mad. They were all mad.

"Eli Whittaker."

"Yes, the American," Claude said. "I heard you were coming."

Eli frowned. "You heard—"

"You aren't *quite* what I expected," Claude continued, smiling charmingly, for all the world as if he hadn't almost been murdered. Multiple times. "I do hope I'll see more of you."

He bowed again, and then, blowing a kiss at the Countess—right in front of her husband—he sauntered up the stairs.

Suddenly Eli's head hurt. He needed to . . . leave. Yes. He would go to his room, and shut the door, and then he would be *inside,* and they would be *outside.*

As he turned, she called after him. He knew it was her without looking. Somehow he'd already memorized her voice.

"Sir!"

"Yes?"

"Thank you," she said. "For saving my life. Again, I think? I'm afraid I don't remember very much of last night—"

He nodded, curtly, and started walking up the stairs. He wasn't surprised she didn't remember anything.

"Err—"

All he wanted to do was go to his room. "Yes?"

"Are you—are you staying here?"

He looked up the stairs, and back at her. "Yes."

"Oh," she said, pursing her mouth. "Of course you are. Why wouldn't you be. Just . . . of course."

She was arguing with an invisible person again. "If that's all," he said, bowing, and headed up the stairs.

He stopped after two steps as a grave, obvious realization came over him. He'd been so concerned about her possibly being shot that he hadn't even stopped to question what she was doing in the hotel, or why she had emerged through the door he'd already mapped as leading to the kitchen. Slowly, he turned.

"Excuse me," he said, interrupting her whispered monologue.

"Yes?"

"Do you work here?"

"Oh," she said. "Yes. I'm Maria Wallner. The manager."

He nodded. It all made perfect sense. She was mad, and so was her hotel.

"Eli Whittaker," he said, curtly, and then he bowed again, and left.

His room had been cleaned while he was at the Legation. He had made his own bed, but it had been stripped and remade;

the curtains pulled back and the washbowl from the morning removed. At least whoever was in charge of housekeeping at the hotel was sensible.

He rang for the maid, and asked for a fresh bowl of water. After she delivered it, he eased out of his coat and examined the damage.

The bullet had grazed his arm, tearing the sleeves of his coat and shirt. As he unbuttoned his shirt, he frowned at the bloodstain on the white cotton. That would be difficult to get out.

He took his medical kit from the armoire and sat on the bed to dress the small wound.

Maria Wallner needed to be more careful. Twice in a single day she'd put her life in peril. She was surrounded by chaos— she *was* chaos—and chaos . . . chaos could so easily turn to danger.

As the manager of the hotel from which the incriminating letter had been sent, she was now also a suspect.

After washing himself, he rinsed the blood from his shirt as best he could and then left it to soak. The coat was better— the sturdy black wool hadn't absorbed the stain. He cleaned it carefully and set about mending the tear. It was only about an inch and a half long, with fairly neat edges, burnt from the heat of the bullet. When he was finished sewing, he held it up to the light and nodded. Likely no one would even notice it was there.

As he was hanging it up, another knock sounded at the door. He found the same maid on the other side, this time carrying a small silver tray with a glass of amber liquid on it.

"With the hotel's compliments, sir," she said, handing it to him and curtsying.

"I don't—"

But she was already down the corridor, so he simply frowned and shut the door.

He smelled the glass. Whiskey, he thought. He didn't drink alcohol. Carrying the glass with him, he sat down at the desk positioned before the large window and looked out over the city.

After an hour of sleep and his morning calisthenics, he'd gone to the American Legation, only to find it closed. Thinking perhaps the staff had simply left for a very late lunch, he waited. And waited. By four in the afternoon, it was obvious no one would be appearing. His mood even grimmer than usual, he had made some notes and then left. He'd stopped at a small restaurant on the way back, where he had been served a schnitzel approximately the size of his briefcase, and then had waded back through the already-thickening crowds.

Now, night had fallen. Vienna blazed below him, golden light pouring from windows and street lanterns and passing carriages. Faintly, through the glass, he heard a violin playing. A waltz, of course.

His boarding room in Washington had a pleasant view, a tree that leafed full and lush in summertime, and a brick sidewalk below. This was entirely different. Looking out on this land of light and music was like looking into another world.

In Eli's experience, other worlds tended to have teeth. And quicksand.

He stared at the alcohol in the glass. *She* had sent it, probably as a thank-you. Perhaps as an apology, hotel manager to guest.

He left it where it sat and went to change for bed.

Chapter Six

Herr Fritz and Frau Pichler are back, in room 306. If they break anything this time I <u>will</u> send a bill to his house, wife or no wife. . . . The crisis in the Balkans continues to worsen. Now that Bosnia has joined, the refugees are numerous—some papers say upward of 100,000. The larger European situation continues to be precarious. . . .

—Journal entry of Maria Wallner, 13 September 1876, discussing the Great Eastern Crisis

2 January 1878

The next morning found Eli freshly shaven and freshly determined.

He stopped for breakfast in the Hotel Wallner's restaurant, the room lushly upholstered in faded reds and pinks, the paint on the walls a butter yellow that had once, perhaps, been cream. It was as impeccably clean as the rest of the hotel, though, and the food was simple, filling, and excellent. The kitchen was as competent as the housekeeping staff, he mused, glancing over the morning paper. He felt a brief pang of sympathy. It must be difficult, working under a madwoman.

Frowning, he banished Maria Wallner's face from his memories, and settled into an article summarizing the latest developments in the war between the Russian and Ottoman empires. The Russians had made still further gains, marching ever closer to Constantinople. Most observers agreed the victor was already decided—the only question left was whether Russia would attempt to breach the Ottoman capital. All of Europe was apparently looking to Austria-Hungary, to see whether it would intervene on either side, but the empire's foreign minister was stubbornly silent, leaving the Brits, of all people, to intervene on the Ottomans' behalf.

Eli recalled his meeting at the State Department on the day he had left. He'd been ushered into a small room with a harried-looking young man, who had given him a brief—absurdly brief—overview of the Austro-Hungarian Empire. It had consisted entirely of information Eli already possessed: namely, that the empire was one of Europe's Great Powers; that it had been ruled by the House of Hapsburg since the thirteenth century; and that it consisted of a massive chunk of territory, bordered by the failing Ottoman Empire to the east and ever-growing Russia to the north. Fifteen minutes later, the young man had shoved some books and files at him and hurried to his next appointment.

Fortunately, the books and files were more helpful. On the Atlantic voyage, Eli had dedicated his time to study. After learning that over a dozen languages were spoken in the empire—German and Hungarian were the most common, but Polish, Romanian, Ruthenian, Serbo-Croatian, and Slovak were all used in various parts—he had found a Polish crew member and paid him for some basic tutoring.

He'd also learned that almost every major religion was represented (an outcome brought about by the Hapsburg strategy of collecting land through strategic marriage), but the State Department–provided materials were predictably biased toward Christianity. This was an annoying hurdle given that the shipboard library didn't exactly stretch to studies of comparative religion; one he wasn't able to remedy until they reached Trieste.

Perhaps the most interesting part of the files he'd been given was a geopolitical analysis written two years prior by a visiting scholar, concerning the shifting state of Europe. Historically the Austro-Hungarian Empire had regarded the Ottomans as its biggest enemy; now, faced with the fading power of the empire's old foe, the more recent threat of Russia, and the ever-increasing nationalist tensions within the empire, Emperor Franz Joseph's current policy was more one of conservation.

Keep the empire the same. Keep the Ottomans and the Russians the same. Keep Europe the same, for fear that if one single thing was allowed to fall apart, the empire—and thus the continent—would simply explode.

Reading that morning's news, Eli wondered if conservation was turning to paralysis, or if a deeper game was being played.

But while all that was useful context, it wasn't why he was here. Looking at his watch, he drained his coffee (excellent, and served at precisely the correct temperature), counted out a generous tip, and stood. Perhaps the staff of the Legation would deign to appear at their workplace today.

The Legation was a short walk from the Hotel Wallner, housed in a smart building of white stone. Eli walked confidently up the front steps, pulled on the door, and . . . discovered it was still locked.

He lifted his eyebrows and then stepped back and surveyed the building from the street. The windows were as dark and empty as they had been the day before.

His watch informed him it was almost ten in the morning. Tightening his scarf, he sat down on the cold front steps and prepared to wait.

"Hard to steal secret codes if no one ever shows up to work," he muttered, tucking his nose more deeply in the navy wool. He wasn't sure which he disapproved of more, the laziness or the treason.

The sun was almost perfectly overhead when footsteps finally approached the steps. Eli looked up, finding a pale, red-haired young man with bloodshot eyes staring back at him.

"May I help you?" the man said, in careful, schoolboy German that easily marked him as a product of a New England preparatory school. Phillips Academy to Yale, probably.

"I'm Eli Whittaker," Eli replied in English, standing. "From Treasury."

"Oh! The currency expert. Right. I'm William Collins, Director Farrow's secretary. Didn't expect to see you here today."

"My crossing was delayed. I sent a message at Trieste."

"I got it," Collins said, shrugging. "But it's the day after New Year's. I'm only in to clear the mail."

"It's a Wednesday."

Collins laughed. "Things are a bit different here than back home. Come on, then, let's stop standing in the cold."

He walked past Eli and unlocked the heavy front door. Eli followed him. It was marginally warmer inside the building than outside.

"We're on the second floor," Collins said, leading him up the wooden stairs. "I'll show you to your desk, though I'll tell you now, no one's going to be in for the rest of the week."

"Why?"

Collins shrugged. "It's ball season. Most of our work gets done at parties, anyway. Oh, I suppose it's different at Treasury. Mostly book work, isn't it?"

Eli made a noise that could be read as agreement, already feeling hampered by his undercover status. He'd been undercover before, but only twice, and each time for less than half an hour. In general he didn't like undercover work: it was inefficient, and prone to legal challenge. And lying wasn't his strong suit.

Another thing Undersecretary Wallace should have considered.

"Glad you're here though," Collins said, in a somewhat patronizing tone. "I'm the first to admit I can't make heads or tails of this currency stuff. We need a proper training, that's certain."

"My desk?"

"Here." Collins pointed toward an empty desk against the outer wall, and then squinted against the bright light pouring in through the windows. "Christ," he said, looking momentarily nauseated. "Forgive me, Whittaker, but I'm just going to take the mail and go. Here, take the keys." He tossed Eli a key ring. "Lock up when you leave."

Eli frowned down at the keys in his hand. "But—"

Collins waved a hand at him. "See you Monday," he said, and then he disappeared down the stairs, leaving Eli alone in the Legation.

All right. So security in general could be better.

Still, he wasn't about to question his good fortune. This gave him an unexpected opportunity to search the building.

He tucked the keys in his pocket, dropped his briefcase on the desk, and got to work.

Chapter Seven

Ritter von Wolf was in 401 last night with not one but two actresses: Sarah Willis, on tour from England, and Ilse Bauer, who had much success in last season's revival of Goethe's Egmont. *I was prepared to be indignant on behalf of his wife, but then she arrived as well, and if the noises I overheard while unclogging the fourth-floor toilet were any indication, the foursome passed a very pleasant evening.*

—Journal entry of Maria Wallner, 7 October 1872

The day after her most recent brush with death—two in twenty-four hours really was a bit much—Maria sat in a beautiful marble bank and listened to the man across from her explain why there was absolutely no possibility of the Hotel Wallner receiving a loan.

It was the fifth time she'd heard the speech that day. It seemed the empire had not recovered as entirely from the financial crisis of 1873 as Maria had previously believed, and then there was still the situation with Bosnia, and furthermore, there was significant banking legislation currently being considered by the government, laws that could result in a major reorganization of the financial sector. And of course, the hotel wasn't what it had been, was it? Oh, yes, they *had* heard of the New Year's Eve party—a friend had gone and said how wonderful it had been to return to the memories of their youth. But, Maria must understand, bankers couldn't use memories as collateral, no matter how beautiful, and no matter how much they, personally, wanted to.

"Now, if you came back to me in the fall," this particular banker, Herr Kis, said. He seemed a nice enough man, with silver hair and a neat mustache. "I might be able to give you a different answer."

"Unfortunately, there is some urgency," Maria said. "As I mentioned, we've been given the opportunity to host the Hotelkeepers' Ball—"

"Ah, yes," Kis said, smiling fondly, giving the impression of a particularly useless uncle. Or rather what Maria imagined a particularly useless uncle might look like, having none of her own to draw from. "I went to a Hotelkeepers' Ball at the Hotel Wallner, back in . . . oh, '28? '29? I was just a young pup. Your grandmother punched a man—laid him right out. Ah, those were the days."

"She did *what*?"

"Mmm," Kis nodded, pleased. "No one ever found out why. Well, you know your grandmother. No one was brave enough to ask."

Maria was torn between pursuing this point and returning to the more pressing one. As it usually did, money won out. "My grandmother will be assisting me with *this* ball," she said. Perhaps the man's apparent fondness of Josephine could be turned to advantage. "If we're successful, it would catapult us back into society."

"And I trust that will happen," he said, stacking the papers she'd given him and handing them back with finality. "You know, for a year after the crash we didn't lend at all. Even now we're lending perhaps a tenth of what we did before '73. And the property simply isn't in good enough repair to justify investment. It's a shame your mother—" He stopped talking, shrugged. "But in the fall—"

"Yes," Maria said, trying to smile, or at least look polite. "If we still need a loan, I'll try you again in the fall."

A few minutes later she stood at a streetcar stop on the wide sidewalk of the Ringstraße, the enormous new circular boulevard built where the old city walls had once stood. Elegant white stone buildings lined the wide street, far newer and cleaner and more elaborate than the Hotel Wallner. It was hard not to feel that the city had simply . . . moved on without them.

She looked down at her great-grandmother's ring, glinting a little in the fading winter light.

If the city has moved on, Maria thought, *we will simply haul it back.*

The sun was already setting, the twilight cold and gray. She looked at her watch—four o'clock. She was working the evening shift at the front desk at seven. Plenty of time to go back and decide what banks she was going to visit tomorrow.

Back at the hotel, she pushed through the alley door that led to the kitchen. And stopped abruptly, trying to make sense of the scene before her.

Every surface was covered with flowers. Sparkling white lilies lay side by side next to the sink. The stove was obscured by deep purple hydrangeas. The kitchen table had become a rose garden. Hannah stood at a counter, lower lip bitten in concentration, working on what might be snapdragons. Josephine was at the table reading the newspaper, her stern black dress at odds with the sugary spring around her. Emilie Brodmaier sat next to her, nibbling on a violet with one hand and working on her latest musical composition with the other.

"Hello," Maria said, faintly.

"You're back," Hannah said, looking up. Her hair was askew and dusted with sugar. "Try a tulip."

She shoved a yellow bloom in Maria's mouth. Maria chewed, then frowned. "It's a cookie?"

"It's a cookie!" Hannah said, picking up a bag of icing and gesturing with it. "The roses are spun sugar, and the violets are marzipan. These snapdragons are a sort of rock candy—"

"She's been like this for hours," Josephine said, turning the page.

"—and the hydrangeas, well let's not talk about the hydrangeas, and whatever you do *don't* eat them—"

"The violets are very good, Hannah," Emilie said, reaching for another. She was a soft-spoken woman around Josephine's age, dressed elegantly in light green silk that set off her cloud of white hair. She was something of a Viennese celebrity: born to one of the city's premier Jewish families, she had been a child piano prodigy, performing all over Europe before she was twelve. When she was twenty, she married Jakob Brodmaier, heir to a newspaper empire and her childhood friend, and largely retired. She rarely went anywhere but her own home and the Hotel Wallner, but every second Thursday she held a musical salon that was the most coveted invitation in Vienna.

"Try the snapdragons," Hannah said, shoving a plate across the island. Emilie nodded, carefully examined the flowers, chose one, and went back to work.

"I'm thinking a kind of edible bower," Hannah said, turning back to Maria. "I know it's expensive. . . ."

Hannah bit her lip, and Maria rapidly calculated the price of sugar. The empire and the beet-sugar manufacturers had been engaged in taxation cat and mouse for decades: the price went down when the manufacturers figured out how to evade the latest legislation, and up when the empire caught up. Currently, the empire was winning.

But . . . Maria looked at the flowers. They were magic. The kind of magic that would be talked about all season.

"We'll need to cut costs somewhere else," Maria said, and Hannah's face cleared.

"Here," she said. "Let me show you my sketches—where did I put my notebook—"

"Here you all are." Maria's half brother Mac walked in from the lobby. Maria frowned at him.

"Mac, how many times do I have to tell you the kitchen is for employees?"

"Frau Brodmaier isn't an employee," Mac said, sitting next to Emilie and eyeing the plate in front of her. "Can I have a violet?"

Maria narrowed her eyes at him. "Give him one of the hydrangeas," she said.

"I don't know why that sounds so dire," he said. "Take pity on me, Maria. My mother has Annalise reducing for the wedding. I'm half starved."

Hannah set a plate with a large sandwich in front of him. He looked at her as if she were the Empress herself and immediately began to eat.

"You can't help yourself, can you?" Maria said.

Hannah shrugged and went back to her snapdragons, a delicate brush of red now mingling with the flour on her cheekbones.

"Anyway, I came to check on you," Mac said, through a mouthful of sandwich. "Someone said you'd been shot."

Maria picked up a rose, still thinking about the price of sugar. "I wasn't shot," she said. "But that idiot von Dasse ruined my new wallpaper, the one I got on discount, *and* shot a chunk out of one of our pillars. Hannah, what do you think about doing a fairy feast? We could use good, simple food, but display it fantastically. Goulash in a fountain. Potato cakes, molded to look like golden eggs. You know, in all those stories there's a feast, and if you eat it—"

"You have to stay there forever," Hannah said, nodding.

"Oh, yes. Glamour, with a hint of risk. It's different. And cheap. We'll need larger than normal tables—really now, *where* did I put my notebook?"

She put a hand to her forehead, leaving behind a bright pink smear, and began lifting pots and pans and baking sheets in search of it. The others, even Emilie, stopped what they were doing to join the search.

Abruptly, Maria was struck by how dear they all were. How much she would give to never lose this, this family, this kitchen, this world.

Then she rolled her eyes at herself and joined the search.

"Here," Mac said, pulling the notebook from beneath some roses and handing it over. "But let's go back to the shooting. You're sure you're all right?"

"I heard she was rescued by a dashing American," Emilie said, selecting another violet. "Oh, hello, Mac."

"She wouldn't have needed to be rescued if she hadn't run out into the middle of a gunfight," Josephine said, turning over another page.

"Hello, Frau Brodmaier," Mac said. "Will someone please tell me what happened?"

"Count von Dasse found his wife in bed with another man," Hannah said. "Here, try a delphinium. He tried to shoot him, but instead he shot our new wallpaper. Maria went out to yell at him and almost got shot, but the American staying upstairs tackled her to the ground and saved her."

"It would have missed me," Maria said.

Josephine turned another page. "It wouldn't have," she said.

The certainty in her grandmother's voice shivered through Maria's spine before she pushed it away. She couldn't dwell on that.

She sat down, firmly directing her attention to the snapdragon forming beneath Hannah's talented fingers. The light through the window was strong and clear. Someone had recently hung a glass ball by the window, one with long, tangled tendrils on the inside.

"Who hung the witch ball?" Maria asked, to change the subject.

"Oh, your mother asked me to," Hannah said.

Josephine rolled her eyes, not looking up from the page. It wasn't necessarily that Josephine and Maria didn't believe in the supernatural, but Elisabeth took it a bit . . . far.

"What's a witch ball?" Mac asked, standing to take a closer look.

"It's to ward off bad luck and curses and so forth," Hannah said, a little shy now that Mac was next to her. "Um, you see these glass lengths, sticking up in the middle? It makes the bad luck get tangled."

"Incredible," he marveled, staring at it with wide eyes.

The door from the lobby banged open. "Is Maria—oh, thank God, you're back," Abraham, her head footman said. "Helga couldn't come in this morning. Her granddaughter is sick."

Maria frowned. "Then who—"

"Anita's managed the top two floors, but the guest rooms on the third haven't been cleaned yet," Abe said.

"It's past four!" Maria said, already grabbing an apron from the supply cupboard.

"It's 301, 302, and 306," Abe said. "306 isn't expected back until the evening."

Maria nodded. 301 and 302 were Madame Le Blanc and Frau Heilig. They both had weekly readings with her mother scheduled this afternoon, which meant they wouldn't be back to their rooms for at least another hour. Elisabeth refused to plan her weekly social calendar without consulting the resident supernatural experts. "I'll do them now," she said. "It was nice to see you, Emilie. Hannah, don't let Mac stay here and bother you all evening. He's rich. He can eat at a restaurant."

"But Hannah's food tastes better," Mac protested.

She didn't bother to respond, already hurrying up the servants' stair. Her guests were *not* going to return to find their rooms in the same disheveled state they'd left them in.

Maria had been cleaning rooms since . . . well, since she could remember, so the routine was as familiar to her as washing her own face. She took fresh linens from the third-floor closet, thinking absently of her plans to fit the linen closets out for assignations. As she was contemplating the various acts such a space would need to accommodate, her mind began to drift, sketching out a pleasant fantasy of a closet, and a man on his knees before her, his strong, large hands holding up her skirts. . . .

A man whose mouth bore an embarrassing resemblance to Elijah Whittaker's.

Maria closed the linen closet and got to work.

The occultists' rooms were the closest to the staircase, near the bathroom Josephine had installed twenty years before, when there had been plenty of money for improvements. The Hotel Wallner boasted a bathroom per floor, a luxurious amenity.

Madame Le Blanc and Frau Heilig had lived in their rooms since Maria was a child, and the units had long ago become more like apartments than hotel rooms. Because the women rented by the month, they did most of their own cleaning, but the hotel changed the linens once a week, and today was the day. Maria quickly stripped the beds and remade them, checked to make sure the women had all the supplies they needed, and hurried to the room down the corridor.

This one was still very neat—the occupant had made the bed, which always made her smile. People who made the bed in a hotel did so because the habit calmed them, rather than because they wanted it to be tidy. They knew it would be re-made later. She did so, then moved to the desk to clear it.

And froze when she saw the glass of untouched whiskey on the desk.

She hadn't asked what room he was staying in. She hadn't wanted to know.

Slowly, she looked around. Yes, it was his room. She recognized the shoes sitting neatly by the armoire. She'd seen them the day before, when he'd tackled her to the floor and then knelt next to her.

For a single heartbeat, she wanted to flee.

He's a guest, she reminded herself. Yes, a guest with a shockingly beautiful mouth who had saved her life twice, but that didn't make him less deserving of having a clean room. Rather the opposite!

She got back to work, and if she moved a bit quicker, to be sure she would be gone before he returned, well that was only good service. She pulled the curtains back, shaking them to keep them free of dust, and then cleared the glass from the desk and the shaving bowl from the dresser. She wiped the desk down, and was about to empty the small garbage bin next to it when a flash of dark red caught her eye.

She frowned into the bin. There was a handkerchief buried beneath some crumpled paper, stained with what looked like blood. A fair amount of blood.

It was then, of course, that the door opened.

Chapter Eight

Bad news from the Stock Exchange. My poor Heinrich looking very, very stressed. Mood in the hotel very dark as well . . .

—Journal entry of Elisabeth Wallner, 9 May 1873, referring to the crash of the Vienna Stock Exchange and the beginning of the Panic of 1873

"What are you doing here?"

It was her, *the woman,* Maria Wallner, standing between the desk and his bed, with her back to him. Going through his trash.

Searching it.

"I asked you what you were doing," he said, slowly.

"Were you . . . were you shot?"

"What?"

She tilted the bin toward him, revealing the handkerchief he'd used to clean his wound that morning. He'd thought he'd wrapped it properly, but it must have come open in the trash.

"When you saved me," she continued. "Yesterday. Were you shot?"

She looked up at him, those dark eyes wide again. He closed the distance between them and ignored her deflection. "Why are you searching my room?"

He was close to her now, close enough to see the two small freckles next to her nose.

It had been a trying day at the Legation. He'd found the latest codes written down (written down!) in three different locations. Anyone could have accessed them.

He was frustrated. With himself. With the staff of the Legation. And, walking back through *yet another* night of streets crowded with partygoers, with the entire city of Vienna. And then he'd come back to his room, looking forward to his evening calisthenics and a session of Polish study, only to find *her* rummaging through his garbage.

It occurred to him that despite the lack of success at the Legation, a lead had just presented itself.

She blinked up at him, her thick spiky lashes dark against her skin. For a moment they stayed like that, eyes locked, and then, abruptly, she grabbed his upper arm.

He hadn't expected it. He winced.

"You were," she said, dropping the bin, and suddenly *she* was the one closing in on *him,* pushing his coat halfway down his arm and peering at his shirtsleeve as though she could see through it.

"Stop that!"

She glared up at him accusingly. "You were shot? You were *shot*? And you just . . . walked up the stairs?!"

"It was only a— Ow! Don't do that!"

"Then *don't* say it was only a flesh wound," she retorted sharply, releasing the pressure on his arm.

"Fine," he said, trying to back away from her and somehow getting tangled between his coat and her arms. "I was slightly shot."

"Slightly!"

She was really so close to him, and she was touching him, and this was *definitely* not how an interrogation was supposed to go.

"And that hardly explains what you're doing in my room—"

"Who does that! Who gets shot and just walks away! We should have had a doctor, you should have gone to the hospital!"

"I can hardly see a doctor every time someone shoots me—"

"*Yes you can,*" Maria shrieked. "*That would be a very normal thing to do.*"

"Stop changing the subject," he said. Firmly. He was not going to allow her chaos to infect him. "What were you looking for, Fraulein Wallner?"

She blinked at him. "I was cleaning your room." Still holding the garbage bin, she gestured at the bed, then at the curtains. He looked around. The room had indeed been cleaned.

He lifted an eyebrow. "I'm expected to believe you do the hotel's cleaning?"

A slight—very slight, you would have to be watching closely to see it—bit of color rose in her cheeks. Ah-*hah.*

But then she emptied the garbage bin into a canvas sack, set it back in its place by the desk, and put her hands on her hips.

"Of course I do," she said. "When we're shorthanded. I have since I was old enough to carry a bucket of supplies. You can hardly run a hotel if you don't know how to turn a room over."

"Uh-huh. Dressed like that."

She was wearing an elegant dark-blue day dress with embroidered flowers across one shoulder. It was not exactly the sort of dress he tended to see maids in.

"Dressed in whatever I'm wearing," Maria said, evenly. "Chores in a hotel don't tend to wait on wardrobe changes. Now, if you're done with the interrogation—" She made to move past him, toward the open door.

He stepped in her way. "I'm not."

She huffed. "Has anyone ever told you you're a very suspicious man?"

"Yes," he said, looking down at her. Trying to see past her exasperated façade to the actual motives beneath. She was already a suspect, and now he had found her searching his room. . . .

She was, once more, very close. Abruptly, distractingly, he remembered the feeling of her body beneath his own.

Her breathing changed, becoming sharper and shallower.

And then voices came from the stairs, and she stepped back.

"—the stars disagree, Clara. When will you learn to look beyond—"

Maria exhaled sharply. "Oh Lord. Look, if you don't want a scene, you'll let me leave, or at least shut the door—"

"Maria, darling! Is that you in there?"

Maria stepped back, resignation in her eyes. "You brought this upon yourself," she said, cryptically.

"What—"

Eli turned just as two women, a short one and a tall one, both in their middle years, poked their heads in.

"Ohh," the short one breathed. "Oh dear, oh we're terribly sorry, yes we'd better go, *so* sorry to interrupt."

"Yes, what *were* we interrupting?" the tall one said, and somehow instead of leaving they were coming into his room. Eli frowned sternly at this invasion of his space. They ignored him.

"Hello, dear, you're certainly handsome, aren't you? Wouldn't you say so, Matilde? With such *dark, dark* hair?"

"Yes," the tall one, apparently Matilde, replied, eyeing his hair with a disturbing amount of mirth. "Quite dark. It is real, isn't it?"

This was apparently directed at him.

"My hair?"

"No, the salamander on your shoulder," she replied, voice dripping with condescension. "Yes, your hair. Is it dyed?"

For a moment Eli wondered if his German was less fluent than he had thought it was. Then he simply decided everyone in the Hotel Wallner was mad.

And everyone knew there was no point in engaging in conversations with madwomen. He bowed to the two women. "If you'll excuse us, we were—"

"Such good manners," the short one said. "Such dark hair."

"Stop," Maria said, from her position—across the room? In his chair? "It's not funny anymore. Actually, it was never funny."

"Wrong," Matilde said, firmly. "It was hilarious."

The short one nodded vigorously. "You should have seen your face, Maria—yes, like that! You looked just like that."

"This is my murder expression," Maria said.

The two women ignored her. Well, if they could ignore Maria, then presumably he could ignore them. He turned to Maria.

"Isn't it rather late in the day for cleaning?"

"Are you really not going to stop?"

"I will when I get answers."

"I've given you answers!"

"Allow me to amend," he said. "Truthful answers."

She had the nerve to sigh in exasperation and pinch the bridge of her nose, as though he was giving her a headache. The two middle-aged women watched them intently.

His frown deepened. He didn't really enjoy audiences at his interrogations.

"You know, the mouth only goes so far," she said.

"I—" He took a deep breath; sighed it out in annoyance. "I never understand anything you say. I thought it was because you were drunk, but you're not drunk anymore. Are you trying to throw me off? It won't work."

She narrowed her eyes, and then, abruptly and discerningly, smiled. "Elijah Whittaker, I want you to meet Frau Heilig and Madame Le Blanc, two long-term residents of the Hotel Wallner. Ladies, Mr. Whittaker is here on business from America, and he was *just* telling me about his interest in the occult."

"No I wasn't—"

"*Particularly,* Frau Heilig, about his interest in the mysteries of the tarot. I told him I was sure you—"

"Oh! My dear, I'd be delighted. Come here, young man, yes, sit right here, fortunately I have a deck on me at all times—" Frau Heilig took Eli firmly by the arm and began steering him toward the small table against the wall.

"But really," Madame Le Blanc said, her voice cutting sharply over Frau Heilig's softer one, "the stars are a much more *serious* subject—"

Maria stood, smiling, as he attempted to disentangle himself from hands and jewelry and at least two different scarves.

"I don't—stop—"

But she merely smiled sweetly at him as she passed. "*Do* enjoy your stay," she said, and then she was gone, closing the door behind her.

It took him several precious seconds to free himself and follow her, the confused voices of the occultists calling after him. He caught up to her near the stairs.

"I wasn't done talking to you," he said.

She turned quickly, sharp smile still on her face. "But I was quite done talking to you, Mr. Whittaker. You're very attractive, and I'm very grateful for your . . . *assistance* yesterday, but your manners are extraordinarily boorish. I will, of course, extend you every courtesy you deserve as a guest of this hotel, but other than that I do not anticipate we will have occasion to speak again—"

She was interrupted by a soft voice. "Oh, there you are,"

a woman with soft white hair and dreamy brown eyes said, drifting up the stairs and stopping in front of them. She smiled vaguely at Eli. "Hello."

He clenched his jaw. "Hello," he said. Was it impossible to go ten minutes without interruption in this hotel?

"Oh! You're the American who rescued Maria," she said. "I'm glad you saved her. I'm fond of her. Maria, do introduce us."

Maria sighed, but obeyed. "This is Frau Emilie Brodmaier. Emilie, this is Mr. Elijah Whittaker."

"Hello, Mr. Whittaker. Do you like music?"

"Do I— I beg your pardon?"

"Frau Brodmaier is a very celebrated pianist and composer," Maria explained. The white-haired woman continued to smile at him.

"Er, I . . . haven't had occasion to listen to it very much," Eli replied.

"Then you should come as well." She handed him a thick, creamy envelope—an invitation, apparently. "You might find you enjoy it. Maria and her family always come."

"I'm sure Mr. Whittaker is very busy—"

"I'd be happy to," Eli said, abruptly. Maria Wallner thought she could throw him off, did she? Well, he hadn't earned three assassination attempts in a single year because he lacked persistence. "Thank you," he added.

Maria compressed her lips. He'd annoyed her. Suddenly he felt almost cheerful.

"You're welcome," Frau Brodmaier said. "Your grandmother and Hannah and I are off to the woods, Maria. Hannah was wondering about trees made of candy. Or was it cake? I wasn't listening. But I thought perhaps the Spirit of the Forest might speak to me."

And on this incomprehensible utterance, she drifted back the way she'd come.

"I really—*why* would you accept—"

He looked at her blandly. "To listen to music," he said, and deciding he'd passed the window in which he would get any further information from her, he retired strategically to his room.

Chapter Nine

I am twelve today, and this is my first journal entry. Mother and I had a fancy luncheon, the two of us, and then she and Marthe and Hilda and I ate a cake Hilda made. It was very good.
　　　　　　　　　　　—Journal entry of Josephine Wallner,
　　　　　　　　　　　　　　　　　　14 December 1817

January 5

Jakob and Emilie Brodmaier lived in an estate on the outskirts of Vienna. Eli's cab drove slowly up a long drive bordered with golden paper lanterns, finally stopping in front of a large, elegant mansion. He stepped out amid a throng of other newly arrived guests, the women in lavish, jewel-colored ball gowns, their companions in conservative black.

In his haste to pursue Maria Wallner, he had forgotten exactly how much he disliked parties. They were large and loud, and the conversation was strained, silly, and usually filled with falsehoods. But the faster he found the culprit behind the code theft, the faster he could get home. Perhaps even in time for Senator Markham's trial.

Abruptly, it occurred to him that at *this* party, he would be the one telling falsehoods. Really, why did this investigation need to be undercover? He would probably be *done* by now if he could simply ask a straightforward question.

But his orders were clear, so he cut off further internal strife and joined the line of people walking into the mansion. He handed his invitation to a butler dressed better than he was, and was directed up a wide marble staircase.

The Brodmaiers' ballroom was, like the rest of the house he'd seen so far, large and elegant. Windows on one side looked out toward the lights of Vienna, and on the other toward a dark sweep of lawn. The room was already filled with people, though the music had not yet started.

The crowd parted, and he saw her.

She wore a gown of deep purple silk, its full skirts overlaid with pink and gold netting. Her dark hair was caught away from her face with a gold comb. She was laughing.

She looked like the night sky.

Eli frowned. Listened to that thought once more. Frowned deeper.

Maria Wallner was a suspect. One who had been caught searching his room. He was not there to—to admire her choice of evening gown.

He set his jaw and walked toward her.

"Oh, Mr. Whittaker," Emilie Brodmaier said, with another of her vague smiles. She was standing with Maria and two other women, one a beautiful woman in her middle years, the other a small, older woman with a stern expression and steely silver hair. "You're here."

He bowed again. "Thank you for inviting me."

"You're the American," the older, silver-haired woman said. There was nothing vague in her expression. Watchfulness. Assessment. Next to her, Maria was glaring at him.

He bowed. "Eli Whittaker."

"Hmm," the woman replied. "I'm Josephine Wallner. This is my daughter Elisabeth, Maria's mother. I suppose I owe you a debt of gratitude."

"This is the man who saved you?" Elisabeth Wallner said,

her hand fluttering to her bosom. He bowed a third time. Another thing he hated about parties—all the bowing.

"Oh, *thank you,*" Maria's mother continued, taking his arm. "She didn't tell me you were so handsome. Or that you had such lovely dark—"

"I'm sure Mr. Whittaker is very busy," Maria interrupted. "We mustn't keep him."

"No," Eli said.

"I beg your pardon?"

"I'm not busy."

She blinked at him. He stared back. Her eyes drifted to his mouth.

"Then you should sit with us," Elisabeth said, pulling him toward their table as more guests approached Josephine and Emilie. "Here's an empty seat."

She pulled a chair out and half pushed him into it, smiling brilliantly at him, and shooing Maria into the chair next to him. "Now," she said, sitting on his other side. "You must tell me about yourself. Where are you from?"

Perhaps he hadn't thought this through very well. "Washington," he said. That much at least matched his official cover. "The District of Columbia."

"Oh, marvelous," Elisabeth said. "So far away."

There didn't really seem to be anything to say to that. Unfortunately, Elisabeth seemed to be waiting for a response.

"Yes," he said.

She smiled as though he'd said something brilliant, and then trilled—trilled!—with laughter. She leaned forward, putting her hand on his arm. "And you're such a strapping fellow—"

"Elisabeth? Who's this?" A man in his late middle years appeared over Elisabeth's shoulder, staring at the hand resting on Eli's biceps. He was stout, with a gray mustache and thinning hair.

Maria's mother looked up, her smile growing even brighter.

"My love," she said. "Come meet Mr. Whittaker. The man who saved *our daughter*. Mr. Whittaker, this is Baron von Eder."

Next to him, Maria had stiffened. Eli made an addition to the increasingly complicated Wallner family tree. With complications came motives.

A flicker of discomfort crossed Baron von Eder's face, before disappearing behind a genial smile.

"Ah, I heard," he said. "Nice to meet you, young man."

Eli nodded, flicking a glance at Maria. She appeared absorbed by the floral centerpiece.

"You look dashing tonight, Heinrich," Elisabeth said, running a hand down von Eder's jacket. "Aren't you going to ask me to dance?"

"Later, my love," von Eder murmured, sidling back slightly. "Have to do the rounds first, you know."

Elisabeth pouted. She was very good at it—Eli would describe the expression not so much as practiced as *honed.*

"Ah, not that face, my pretty," von Eder said, chucking Elisabeth's chin. Eli barely stopped his lips from curling. "You know I'm weak to it."

"But I wore my prettiest gown for you," Elisabeth said, widening her eyes.

"Later, my beauty—"

"But Heinrich—"

"He can't dance with you until his wife goes home," Maria said abruptly. "You know that. It's been that way for thirty years. I don't know why it wasn't that way on New Year's Eve, but it's obviously that way again, so stop asking him."

"Maria!" Elisabeth's mouth was open. "How dare you—what's wrong with you?"

Von Eder reddened and looked around hastily. After apparently deciding no one had overheard, he simply . . . faded into the crowd. It was a remarkable move; had Eli not been watching him intently he might have missed it entirely.

This man was not merely a coward. He was an incredibly *accomplished* coward.

Maria stared down at the table, her cheeks pink. "I'm sorry," she said finally.

Her mother huffed. "For your information," she said, "*the way of things* may very well be changing."

Maria said nothing. She picked up a knife. Looked at it. Put it down.

"Adelaide may have finally overplayed her hand," Elisabeth said. "She thought I could be easily intimidated, but I am *not,* and I think Heinrich is finally seeing her for who she is—"

"I'm sorry," Maria said, abruptly. "I shouldn't have said anything. Let's not talk about this here."

Elisabeth sighed, and then stretched her hand across the table in front of Eli, resting it on her daughter's.

"It's been hard on you, hasn't it," she said. "Not having your father present—not having him there for you."

Maria closed her eyes. "Not particularly."

"You put on a brave front, but you must long to have a proper relationship with him."

"It's not a front," Maria said, the waves of agony almost visible around her.

"Ah, my poor darling," Elisabeth said. "Don't you worry, I'm going to take—"

"Would you like to dance?"

Shocked silence fell on the table.

It took Eli a full second to realize he had been the one to ask the question. A question he wasn't sure he'd ever asked before. In any language.

Maria and Elisabeth stared at him.

He willed his expression to remain impassive. After all, he reasoned, the whole point of coming to the party had been to stay close to her. This was logical. A very sensible way to stay close.

The silence continued.

Perhaps, though, his timing had been off.

Silence.

Yes, he should take it back. And probably apologize. The music wasn't even playing yet. He opened his mouth—

"Yes," Maria said, standing. "Thank you."

Oh.

He blinked. She stared at him. He stood.

"Maria—"

"Later, Mother," Maria said, smiling brightly and taking his arm. "After all, a handsome dark-haired man has asked me to dance."

"Oh," Elisabeth said, nodding and waving a hand, just as the orchestra leader announced the next dance. "Of course. Go, go."

Silently, Eli led her to the dance floor. He looked at the couples around him and mimicked their position, placing one hand gingerly on her back and the other on her waist. The music started, and he began to dance.

He'd never waltzed before, so for the first minute he focused on the steps. He'd seen them several times, and it wasn't hard to understand the basic mechanics. Once he was confident in them, he returned his attention to the woman in his arms.

"Thank you," she said, not meeting his eyes. "And I'm sorry. It was not my intention to . . . display our family quarrels in front of you."

He nodded briefly. There was nothing to say to that. He was there to learn more about her, and he had done just that, until—

Until you couldn't watch her suffer any longer.

Until I had learned all I could in that setting, he replied firmly.

She was stiff in his arms, her cheeks pink.

"Nothing to apologize for," he said. "It didn't bother me."

She huffed out a laugh. "You must have been shocked," she said. "I understand America is quite strict. And we're a little scandalous even for Vienna."

"Strict families have their own scandals," he said, without thinking. He stopped speaking abruptly, but she didn't seem to notice anything odd.

"That's gracious of you," she said.

Relief flooded him.

They fell silent. She had relaxed a little. The steps were rather like doing algebraic equations; they soothed him. She felt nice in his arms. Almost comforting—

She's a suspect. You're not here to be comforted *by her.*

Then what was he there to do? Interrogate her in the middle of a ballroom?

Yes! That's exactly what you're here to do!

He looked down. Her cheeks held only a hint of their former blush, but her eyes were downcast and she was nibbling her bottom lip.

Interrogations were the part of Eli's job he was best at. He almost always knew the *right* question to ask. It wasn't like in detective stories, where the suspect immediately confessed— but there was often truth to be found even in the lies, if the question was right. Sometimes it was in the flick of an eye or a laugh that went on too long. Sometimes the key question wasn't even one he asked the guilty party—sometimes it produced an important detail in a witness statement, or persuaded him of a suspect's innocence.

But from the first evening he'd set foot in Vienna, it was as if this sense had abruptly abandoned him. He felt . . . bumbling. Why? Perhaps it was being undercover—

"Although," she continued, "you wouldn't have been there to hear it if you hadn't been following me. Why are you following me, Mr. Whittaker?"

Apparently other people were not having the same difficulty.

"I thought I made myself clear," she continued.

"That I have boorish manners."

"Yes."

"And that you like my mouth," he added, for some unknown, idiotic reason.

"The latter doesn't excuse the former."

"Why were you in my room last night?"

Maria groaned. "Not this again. You're unbelievable. Why are you so concerned about it?" Suddenly, her expression turned cold. "Oh. You think I was there in hopes of tumbling you."

Eli choked.

"We're not that sort of hotel, Mr. Whittaker."

"*No,*" he said. "*No.* I want that to be completely, perfectly clear."

She stared at him. "Then what? Are you a spy or something?"

It was good he'd already choked. Was this how his suspects felt?

"Because if that's the case, you don't need to worry," she said. "We've hosted several, over the years, and *always* with discretion. In fact, during the Treaty of Vienna, right after the hotel opened, we had *seventeen.*"

"I'm not a spy."

"Well then, I'm afraid I have no idea what cause you have to be upset," she said.

"I'm a very private person. And it's hard for me to believe you're so short-staffed you couldn't find a single maid to clean my room. Even if that was the case, you could have simply left the room uncleaned."

"No, I couldn't."

He lifted his eyebrow. Her tone was both shocked and certain, as if he'd just proposed she murder someone.

"I know the hotel might look a bit shabby," she said, her cheeks reddening once more. "But that doesn't mean our standards aren't at the highest possible level. *Of course* your room had to be cleaned. *And* your garbage emptied, even if your bizarrely suspicious mind can't seem to fathom it. And on that subject—"

The music stopped, and the dance ended. She continued talking.

"—hotel garbage cans are not really the place to hide confidential items. *Someone* has to empty them, after all."

"I know that," he said, annoyed. At who, he couldn't precisely say.

They were arguing in the middle of the dance floor. He pressed his lips together and steered them to the side of the room, ignoring the curious glances directed toward them.

This wasn't getting him anywhere. It was time to change tactics. His fellow agents had occasionally suggested a softer interrogation manner. *You catch more flies with honey,* one had said. A revolting metaphor.

Still, he wasn't getting anywhere with his usual techniques.

"Err," he said. Cleared his throat. "Are you all right? After the gunfight? You must have been shocked."

She frowned at him, suspicious. "I wasn't the one who was shot."

"Barely—" He watched her eyes narrow and stopped. Tried again. "And I was rude. When you expressed concern."

Her eyes were practically slits. He wasn't very good at this.

"Yes," she said. "Well. Thank you for the dance, and the rescue. I'm going to leave now. Certainly you. Hopefully also the ball. Good night."

"Wai—"

But she was already gone.

Well. That was the worst interrogation you've ever conducted.

He took some careful breaths and walked to the refreshments table to get some water, keeping half an eye on her as she went to gather her things.

Get it together, Whittaker. She's obviously trying to shake you off her trail.

Damn it. It was working too.

She said goodbye to her mother, and was making her way from the room when she was stopped by a footman, who bowed and handed her a note.

Interesting. Eli moved closer.

Maria read the note, then glanced up in what looked like excitement. She put the paper in her pocket and began to walk, this time with more urgency.

Interesting and *suspicious.*

Obviously, he followed her.

Chapter Ten

My Dearest Diary, I've met <u>the man</u>. I knew it was him as soon as I saw him. His name is Heinrich von Eder, and he's a Baron. . . .

—Journal entry of Elisabeth Wallner, 3 February 1845

The idiot is back again. Elisabeth won't stop running around with him. . . .

—Journal entry of Josephine Wallner, 17 February 1845

That *man*. Maria fumed as she hurried across the wide Brodmaier lawn. His effrontery! His absolute *gall*! The nerve of him—

No. Now was not the time. She made herself push him out of her mind and focus on the note in her pocket.

Fraulein Wallner, it had read. *I spoke to my superiors this morning about your request. I know I initially denied your loan, but yesterday I couldn't put the Hotel Wallner from my mind. My superiors do, however, have a few questions, and when I saw you here, I wondered if we could simply sort them out now. I'll be in the first greenhouse until ten.*

Sincerely,
Rudolph Kis

It was almost ten now. Maria had spent the day as she had the ones before it, going from bank to bank and hearing no after no. And now, just as she had crossed off the very last bank on her list, this note had arrived. Like magic.

The music of the party faded as she walked, the night closing soft and velvet around her. The Brodmaier greenhouses were quite famous. Jakob Brodmaier was never happier than when he was surrounded by plants. Over the last thirty years he had installed four enormous glass greenhouses, filled with everything from Russian wildflowers to American cacti to sixteen different varieties of edelweiss.

Maria let herself into the first one. It was warm and dark inside, the moonlight drifting through the arched glass ceiling the only illumination. This was the orchid house, the fragile, strange plants lining four long benches. She walked down one of the aisles.

"Hello?" she called. "Herr Kis?"

Silence. She squinted at her watch. There were still five minutes until ten. Perhaps he was running late. No matter— for this, she could wait as long as necessary.

She wandered along the aisle, humming the theme from Emilie's latest waltz, peering at the orchid blossoms in the moonlight and returning to her argument with Elijah Whittaker. Well, more an interrogation. How *dare* he interrogate her? About *her* business?

You should be grateful for his obnoxiousness, her inner scold said. *Two minutes more in his arms and you'd have been looking for a linen closet.*

She bit her lip. It was a *little* true. Dancing with him had been . . . an experience. His arms were more than strong, they were capable. Apparently, his whole body was. The first few seconds of the dance she had been sure he'd never waltzed before in his life, but within the minute he had mastered it.

Oh, she doubted he'd ever be a truly gifted dancer, not with that stern personality, but he had achieved competence in sixty seconds.

Capable. Competent. She wouldn't have thought, before meeting him, that she'd find those words so appealing. Maria had enjoyed a great number of men, but they tended to be charming, lighthearted. They smiled a lot, and they left easily when the time came.

She didn't think she'd ever seen Elijah Whittaker smile.

And that made her think about his mouth again, which had looked *truly* luscious from her vantage in his arms, and that was simply not productive. No. She was *not* going to think about him anymore—

And then she didn't, because something cracked into her head.

Maria landed hard on the floor, her skull ringing with pain. "What?" She looked up, disoriented, to find a dark figure looming over her.

"What?" she said again, and then the figure lunged at her, and she stopped asking stupid questions and scrambled back.

The person grabbed her ankle, and she finally gathered her wits enough to scream. They pulled her toward them, and she kicked out hard with her foot, making contact with their knee. They grunted in pain, but didn't let go.

She screamed again. The figure lunged forward once more, pulling her toward them and covering her mouth with their hand.

Maria bit them.

They swore, but didn't let go, so she bit harder, sinking her teeth into their leather-gloved palm until they hit her, hard, with the other.

Her head banged hard against the floor of the greenhouse,

cold slate she knew was blue-gray in the daylight. Her skull rang with the impact.

Someone was trying to kill her. The realization infuriated her.

She kicked out once more, screaming until they slapped her again, but she didn't feel the pain through her panic and anger. Hands closed around her throat, closing off her air, and she was struggling, but she couldn't get free, the attacker's weight was on her and they were too heavy—

And then, suddenly, the weight was gone.

Disoriented, her vision blurry in the dark, she sat up, coughing, and saw two people struggling against one of the workbenches. Her throat was hoarse and painful. She was surrounded by broken orchid pots.

How dare they, she thought. *Jakob* loves *these orchids.*

She made herself stand. Her legs gave out when she was halfway up, and she fell against the bench next to her. Her vision slowly cleared.

She wasn't surprised when she saw Elijah Whittaker. Of course it was him—really, she'd already assumed. The two of them were grappling, Elijah pushing her attacker against the bench. In the moonlight, she saw that the person—she thought it was a man—was wearing a black mask.

Elijah punched the attacker, a hard crack against the jaw. He went down, dragging Elijah with him. She thought Elijah was trying to restrain him, so she grabbed a coil of cord from the bench, but as she turned there was a flood of light, and the greenhouse door swung open.

"What is going on—Maria! Are you all right?"

It was Jakob Brodmaier and a few other men from the party. Eli glanced up, and her assailant took advantage of the distraction, shoving him away and rushing the men standing in the door, pushing past them.

For a moment Elijah started to follow; then he looked at Maria and stopped. "Go after him," he snapped at the men.

"Right. Come on," Jakob said, and the group took off into the night.

Maria dropped the cord. Elijah Whittaker came toward her, stabilizing her with his arms. She hadn't known she was swaying.

"The orchids," she said. She tried to move, but either her legs or Elijah's arms refused to oblige.

"Where are you hurt?" he asked, his voice urgent. One hand braced her back, and the other touched her face, her arms, the back of her head.

"We have to save the orchids." Her voice was trembling. Her whole damn body was trembling, which was extremely annoying, because she needed it to do things. She mustered her strength and pushed away from him, kneeling clumsily and pulling a fallen tray toward her. She didn't know anything about orchids.

"Someone else can clean up the damn plants," Elijah said, kneeling across from her. "You need to tell me—"

"How dare he," she said. "How *dare* he. These are Jakob's pride and joy. He wins awards for them! And I don't—I don't know how to save them—they're exotic, they're not like normal plants—"

"Maria, someone just tried to kill you."

"And he failed. But he's going to kill—he's going to kill Jakob's beautiful flowers—"

To her disgust, her throat closed up, and a tear trickled down her nose.

Elijah closed his eyes briefly, the moonlight illuminating his impatience. When he opened them, his voice was brisk. "They'll be fine," he said, beginning to efficiently separate the plants from the broken pots. "Orchids are hardier than people realize. We'll cover the roots for now so they don't take further shock. Help me scrape up that bark." He stood, looking for something, the broken pieces of pot now in a neat pile.

Sniffling, she obeyed. His instructions were clear and steadying. She gathered the bark mixture the plants had been in, and by the time she had a mound of it, Elijah was back, carrying a very large pot.

"We'll put them in here," he said, and then proceeded to do so, arranging the complicated bundles of root and stem and flower with calm competence. His motions were quick, but his hands were gentle.

There was nothing in that to make her cry. So why were the tears flowing again?

"There," he said, arranging the last one. "Look. They're going to be fine."

She nodded.

"Can you stand up?"

She nodded again, but when she told her legs to do so, they simply . . . didn't.

Elijah sighed. "All right," he said. "Come on."

He reached down to lift her up, but she shook her head. "Just . . . just help me stand," she said.

It looked as though he would argue, but he simply pressed his lips together and steadied her as she rose.

"How does your jaw feel?"

"Sore. I don't think it's broken."

"And the rest of you?"

"Bruised," she said, taking stock of her arms and legs and torso. "Also not broken."

"Good," he said. Slowly, they left the greenhouse and began to cross the wide expanse of lawn. Music and light still spilled from the ballroom windows, a strange reminder that hardly any time had passed. Twenty minutes, perhaps.

Twenty minutes she might not have seen the other side of.

"Did you recognize your attacker?"

"No." She let out a shaky breath. "He was masked."

Elijah nodded. "Did you notice anything—"

"How did you know about the orchids?"

A pause. "Pardon?"

"Do they . . . do they grow in America?"

He frowned. Frowned, but after a moment, answered her. "Some species do. My mother and I . . . there are two women we're close to." His words came slowly, as if he was choosing them carefully. But then, Elijah Whittaker seemed to choose all his words carefully. "In Boston. One of them keeps orchids. She taught me a little about them. Do you know why someone just tried to kill you?"

"No." She said it softly, as if that might keep the attack from sticking, from hardening into reality.

Her jaw hurt. Her back hurt. And the tears hadn't stopped, flowing down her cheeks, constant but strangely distant. She wiped them away, but it was pointless. They kept coming.

"Tears are a natural bodily reaction to extreme stress," Elijah said.

"Oh," she said.

They reached the servants' entrance, and pushed through it into the bustling kitchen. They stumbled in, meeting stunned silence, before they were swiftly whisked into the butler's office, out of the way. Eli asked for ice, and within moments a maid handed him some in a neatly wrapped cloth, and left them alone.

He steered her into a chair and knelt. "Maria. This might sting," he said, before carefully placing the ice on her jaw. Vaguely she wondered when he had started using her first name. His voice was like his hands, gentle but efficient. "Can you think—"

"Maria!" The door to the butler's office slammed open, and Josephine and Emilie ran in. "Maria!"

Her grandmother came to a stop, her hands desperately running over Maria's head and body. "Jakob sent a messenger—you're all right? You're all right?"

Maria caught her grandmother's hands. She'd never seen Josephine so distressed. It snapped her back to herself. "I'm fine, Grandmother. I'm fine. You don't need to worry."

Josephine took a deep breath and stepped back. "Thank you, God," she said. "Thank you."

And then, in one clean motion, she took a gun from her skirts and held it to Elijah Whittaker's head.

Chapter Eleven

Spies, spies, spies everywhere. I might as well install windows between the rooms for all the good the locks are doing.

—Journal entry of Theresa Wallner,
1 December 1814, during the Congress of Vienna

"Grandmother!"

Eli looked up at the small, steel-haired woman holding the gun to his head. She held it confidently—it wasn't the first time she'd pointed a firearm at someone. He was certain he could disarm her, but not entirely sure he could do so without harming her. So, he waited.

"Talk," she said.

"Grandmother! He had nothing to do with it—he saved me—"

"He's a spy."

The sentence, short, definitive, and shocking, stunned Maria into silence.

It should have been terrible. Eli's heart should have dropped, he should have started sweating, he should have done anything, everything, to persuade Josephine she was wrong.

But all he could think was *Good.*

His muscles relaxed.

Josephine's lips curved in a grim smile. She lifted her eyebrows. "You're not going to deny it?"

He probably should. *Definitely* should.

He couldn't even open his mouth to form the denial. It had been a stupid order. Now maybe he could get something done.

"To be fair, Josie, Jakob says he's more *undercover*," Emilie said, in the slightly distracted tone he was beginning to understand was simply her permanent state. "Here about the American code theft."

If Jakob Brodmaier, who ran a newspaper syndicate, knew . . . it was safe to say his assignment was no longer a secret. This was objectively bad. But it was like looking at a catastrophe in pictures. It didn't touch him. He felt light.

Until he met Maria's eyes, and saw the confusion and hurt and embarrassment in them.

"Spy or undercover or secret, I don't care," Josephine said. "What I care about is that you've been present three times when my granddaughter's life has been put in danger. So, talk."

"He didn't—" Maria let out a breath. "Spy or not. He didn't have anything to do with what happened. Any of those times. He didn't push me into traffic, or make Count von Dasse a terrible shot. And he didn't attack me tonight. He saved me." Her voice was tired, a hint of a question threaded through it.

"I didn't harm your granddaughter."

"Oh, so you can speak."

He glanced at Maria's grandmother. They looked alike, he realized. It was easy to see the resemblance between Maria and her mother, but that was only surface deep. These women had the same determined fierceness.

"She's a suspect," Eli said.

Silence. Three faces stared back at him in shock. He made himself meet Maria's eyes, something that shouldn't be guilt thickening in his stomach.

"Maria?" Josephine dropped her arm abruptly. "*Maria* is a suspect?"

"Yes," he said. "You are too, I suppose. And your daughter."

"Elisabeth wouldn't even know where the American Legation is," Josephine said, blinking.

"That's true," Maria said, her voice dazed. "A suspect? I'm a suspect?"

Finally, he could ask the questions he needed to. "Earlier, you asked why I was following you," he said. "That's why. You were searching my room. And the only link I have to the theft is a letter sent from your hotel."

"I was *cleaning* your room," she said, her voice suddenly sharp. She thrust a piece of paper at him. "Here. If you must know all my business . . . I was cleaning your room because we only have three maids. Because the hotel is broke. I've spent the last two days desperately trying to convince someone to give me a loan, and no one will, and then whoever attacked me lured me outside with this—"

She broke off, pressing her lips together and turning away.

He read the message. Recalled the slightly faded feeling of the hallways. Maria's upset over the ruined wallpaper. The sudden hope in her face when she'd received the note in his hands.

She'd been cleaning his room.

"Let me see that," Josephine said, snatching the missive away and reading it quickly.

There was a commotion in the hall, and a tall, elegantly dressed man pushed into the room. "*Again,* Maria? You've almost died *again*? And who the hell is this?"

"It's all right, Mac," Maria said, visibly pulling herself together. "I'm fine."

The man continued to bristle at him, and Maria sighed.

"Macario von Eder, this is Elijah Whittaker. He's . . ." She stared at Eli blankly, obviously at a loss. "The American."

Eli connected the man's last name with that of Maria's father and drew his own conclusions.

The door opened again, and Jakob Brodmaier entered. He was a small man, probably in his seventies, fit and wiry.

"We lost him," he said. Eli grimaced. He hadn't really expected a group of elderly men to catch the attacker, but his stomach sank anyway.

Jakob was still talking, wiping sweat off his brow. Emilie handed him a handkerchief. "He ran into the woods. We were able to track him for a while, but—" He broke off and shook his head. "It was too dark, and he was too fast. Do you want me to summon the police?"

Maria immediately shook her head. "No."

"Why not?" Mac exclaimed. "You almost died!"

"They won't be able to do anything," she said. "And the story might get out, and then people would be talking about that instead of the hotel."

"So your plan is to . . . move on? Pretend it didn't happen?"

"What else am I supposed to do? Reporting it won't do any good. They'll ask me some questions I don't know the answers to, file a report, leak it to the press, and never look at it again."

"What questions?" Eli asked.

"What?"

Her innocence didn't change the fact that it was all one hell of a coincidence. The letter had been sent from her hotel, and tonight she'd been attacked. Every instinct Eli possessed said she had *something* to do with the case. "What questions don't you know the answers to?"

She frowned. "I don't— Why do you care? I appreciate

you saving me—again—but I'm not the person you're look-ing for. I understand why you were following me. Now we can go back to staying away from each other."

It was an undeniable dismissal. She looked at her grand-mother. "I want to go home," she said.

Josephine nodded, the fake missive still in her hand. "Then we'll go home."

Mac came to Maria's side, putting his arm around her shoulders. Her grandmother took the other side, and the Brod-maiers crowded around her, so that she was escorted from the room in an embrace of friends and family. So many protectors.

Where were they, then, when she was wandering in front of a carriage? When she had a gun pointed at her head?

Where were they when she screamed? When she was fight-ing to breathe?

Not your assignment, he told himself. *The job is to find the code thief. Not protect Maria Wallner.*

Enough. He needed to investigate the crime scene.

Stepping into the kitchen, he was startled to find it still bustling, strains of yet another waltz drifting in. Apparently not even a murder attempt could stop a party in Vienna.

He slipped through the kitchen door and out onto the frosted lawn. The music was louder here, winding through glass doors that opened onto a series of balconies. Partygoers stood there despite the cold, laughing and shouting, and in the shadows, embracing.

Eli stood, staring up at them. He wondered how Jakob Brodmaier had heard Maria's scream. He couldn't have been in the ballroom at the time. No one could hear anything in that clamor.

Walking across the lawn, Eli surveyed his surroundings, mapping the sequence of events. He had followed Maria from the ballroom, but he'd been at least a minute behind her. She'd been barely visible ahead of him, especially in her dark gown. Still, he was confident there had been no one between them, so the attacker either had been in the greenhouse already or had approached from the other side.

He reached the first greenhouse but didn't immediately go inside. There were four of them in total, all large, elaborate glass buildings. They were lined up, about twenty feet between each one. The in-between space seemed to be both test garden and tidy equipment storage, with bags of—he sniffed—manure piled neatly next to a tidy toolshed.

There was a small space between the bags and the shed, perhaps eighteen inches wide. The ground was too hard for footprints, but Eli didn't need them. He wasn't a gambling man, but he would wager a hundred dollars that that was where Maria's assailant had waited. It commanded a view of the lawn and the greenhouse, but was concealed from both. And it allowed the attacker to arrive second and block the door.

He entered the greenhouse. No one had been in yet to clean—he would ask that the scene be preserved before he left. He would need to see it in daylight.

Walking carefully along the adjacent aisle so as not to disturb evidence (though he'd destroyed plenty, he imagined, in his attempt to act as orchid knight), Eli played the attack out in his mind. She'd fought, that was obvious. The assailant had snuck up behind her—cowardly—and struck her. She'd fallen, then recovered enough to push him back. That was probably when Eli had heard her scream.

The memory curled uncomfortably in his stomach. He frowned and pushed it away.

She hadn't bought enough time to get away. The attacker had hit her again—he could see where she'd landed, among the spilled earth on the tile floor.

Then he had held her down and choked her.

Eli's brain went gray and red again, the same way it had

when he'd run in and seen it happening. He made himself take a careful, deliberate breath.

He'd been angry during investigations before. It was impossible not to be. But that was righteous anger, the kind that fueled him, made him cold and hard and calculating. This anger . . . this was hot, and clouding. It lived in his body, not his brain. It made him want to hit something. It was emotional.

And it was emotion that had led to the mistake that would haunt him. He'd had the attacker in his grip. And when the man had broken away, when Jakob and the others had come in, he should have given chase. He could have caught him.

Instead, he'd looked at Maria, and he'd wanted to be sure she was all right.

He'd been making stupid mistakes ever since he'd arrived in Vienna, but this one was the stupidest. He'd stayed to make sure she was all right, and because of that, her attacker had escaped.

That was what excess emotion did. It led you to mistakes. To carelessness. To harm. He had made an emotional decision, and because of that, the attacker was free to try again. Because of Eli.

Well. It wasn't the first sin he'd had to live with. And Maria—*no one* would be aided by him dwelling on it. He set his shoulders and walked briskly from the greenhouse. He had a footman to interview.

Chapter Twelve

Grandmother and Hannah and I went to the Brahms premiere tonight—"Variations on a Theme by Joseph Haydn." It was a reserved crowd. This season is already so much more spartan than last year's. Mother hasn't said anything, but I peeked at the book and reservations are down, down, down. . . .

—Journal entry of Maria Wallner, 2 November 1873

January 6

On the first day of Fasching, the morning after the attack, Maria sat in her small office with her jaw swollen and painful and wrote everything down. Perhaps her hand shook a little as she did so, and perhaps there were one or two small moments where she stared at the wall for an undetermined amount of time, but down it all went, every detail.

That, after all, was the Wallner way. Wallners loved obsessively, had a single daughter when it was time, and wrote everything, *everything,* down.

She heard a banging from the direction of the kitchen and frowned. The room should be empty, Hannah having already completed the morning baking. She put the pen down and went to investigate.

The noise was coming from the back door. Maria froze in the empty room, the memory of the dark greenhouse flooding through her. She grimaced, her hands balling themselves into fists. Damn it, she didn't have time for this. And it wasn't as though would-be attackers were likely to announce themselves by banging on the back door.

Still, she held her breath as she yanked it open.

Only to abruptly release it when she saw her mother, bent over, dirt on her face, a trowel in one hand, and a shoe (a shoe?) in the other.

They stared at each other.

"Mother?"

Elisabeth laughed charmingly and straightened. "Maria, you gave me a fright. My poor girl, those bruises are terrible! You must put ice on them, my love, and then crushed strawberries. I'll tell Heinrich to send some right over—of course he was *terribly* concerned."

"Mmm," Maria said. "What are you doing?"

"Well, you know, I was speaking to one of my supernatural contacts," she said, lowering her voice to a whisper on *supernatural contacts.* "And we haven't been paying *nearly* enough attention to the hotel's spiritual protection."

"I see."

"We're practically defenseless! So I'm burying this shoe."

Maria looked at the small patch of earth by the door. There was a good-sized hole—Elisabeth must have been working at it for some time, given how hard the earth was—and several bulbs in a discarded pile off to the side.

She would miss those irises in the spring.

"And the shoe will . . ."

"Well, *everyone knows* burying a shoe is one of the best wards there is," Elisabeth said. "And this is one of your father's! So I'm sure it will be *even more* protective, since it will be protecting you and me! His *family.*"

Yes, it looked like it had belonged to Heinrich. It sported

an ornate buckle that managed to look both expensive and tasteless at the same time.

"Maria?" Abe leaned through the door between the kitchen and the lobby. "Count von Kaufstein is asking for you."

Thank God. "I need to go," she said to her mother. "Err, good luck."

Elisabeth sent her a cheery wave and bent back to her task.

"Do you know what he wants?" Maria asked Abe. "It's not Tuesday."

In addition to their unacknowledged familial attachment, the Count was one of their most regular clients. He had met his longtime mistress, Mrs. Fischer, here some decades before, and had faithfully visited every Tuesday afternoon, between three and eight, since. Mrs. Fischer had once been an actress, but now was simply a charming middle-class woman married to a merchant.

Maria had always found their long attachment rather sweet.

"He's not here to see Mrs. Fischer," Abe said. "He says he's here with a business proposition."

She frowned, and followed Abe out to the lobby.

Count von Kaufstein was a tall man in his early seventies. He was thin, and his back a bit curved. He had a white mustache, a wife that had been dead some years now, and a single son, the one who was now engaged to the half sister Maria had never met.

Vienna was a very small world.

Briefly, Maria tried to calculate what relation von Kaufstein was to Franz Joseph, the current emperor. If he and Josephine were both by-blows of the emperor two emperors ago, and this emperor was the . . . nephew of that emperor's father . . .

She gave up. It didn't matter, though she wondered how

it felt, being so close to Imperial power and knowing that, but for a different mother, he could have sat on the throne instead.

It didn't seem to bother him. Count von Kaufstein lived a simple life. He referred to himself as a servant of the empire and the Hapsburgs, and appeared to be perfectly satisfied with his lot.

"Count von Kaufstein," Maria said, curtsying neatly.

"Oh, no need for that, Maria, we're old friends," the Count said, smiling gently. "I think I've been coming to this hotel longer than you've been alive."

"And we appreciate your patronage."

He laughed, his eyes twinkling.

"Abe said you wished to speak to me?"

"Yes, my dear. Do you have a moment?"

"Of course," Maria said. "May I offer you some refreshment first?"

"Oh, perhaps some tea," the Count said, and Maria nodded and popped into the kitchen to relay the order to Hannah. When she returned, the Count was sitting at a table by the window. She joined him.

"I heard about this," he said, gesturing to her face.

Maria grimaced. She'd forgotten about the bruise. "Yes," she said. "Not pleasant."

He regarded her with sharp eyes. "Did you speak to the police?"

"No," she said. "They couldn't do anything."

"Mmm," he said. "You're likely right. I'll have my people look into it."

"Oh, you don't have to—"

He held up a hand. "Don't," he said. "As I said, I've known you since you were born."

Hannah brought the tea out herself, placing it carefully on the table and smiling at the Count.

"Hello, Hannah," he said. "Looking prettier every day."

"Thank you," Hannah said. "Enjoy your tea." She walked back to the kitchen.

"Well, this is a business matter so I will be blunt, my dear," he said, and Maria gave a confused nod. "To be frank, your visits to the banks have not gone unnoticed."

"Oh," Maria said, heat abruptly surging to her cheeks.

"No need to be embarrassed," he said, waving his hand again. "Everyone knew the Hotel Wallner was in a bad state. If anything the news was a positive turn for you—we all heard about the Hotelkeepers' Ball, as well."

"Yes," Maria said, trying to keep her voice even. "We're very excited to be able to host it."

"But you need money."

"Er—" She needed a polite way to tell this nice old man that the financial state of her hotel was none of his business.

"Oh, don't snap at me," he said, laughing. "I deal with money professionally, remember? That's all it is, just money. Coins and little bits of paper and metals of different color. And you *don't* need very much, not really. I'm here to give it to you."

"What?"

"The loan you want. I'll give it to you."

"That's not—"

"Now don't be stubborn," he said.

"I—it's very kind of you—"

"Not particularly," he said. "It's an investment. I believe in you, and your capabilities. And . . . well, this *is* where I met Mrs. Fischer."

"Yes," Maria said, faintly. After everything, someone was just going to . . . hand her the loan she needed?

"But no," she heard herself say.

"*No?* My dear girl, are you sure?"

"It's extremely kind of you," she said. "But this is a family matter. And we'll take care of it accordingly."

"So you'll take it from a bank but not an old friend?"

She smiled at him, ruefully. "Perhaps especially not from an old friend."

"But then what?"

"I—I know what I need to do," she said, and as she looked down at her hands, folded neatly on the small marble table, she realized that she did.

Over lunch, Maria sat across from her mother and grandmother in the hotel kitchen and told them she was going to sell her great-grandmother's ring.

"No!" Elisabeth said. She was wearing her own inheritance from Theresa, a large emerald set in gold filagree. "How could you even think it! It's a family heirloom! Someday it will go to your daughter, and then her daughter— No. Absolutely not."

"The hotel needs the money," Maria said, flatly. She always felt flat, next to her mother. "I've been to every bank in town, and they won't lend to us."

"I'll ask your father."

"No," Maria said. "This is a family matter."

"Maria! He's your *father*—"

"I'm not asking for permission," Maria said, calmly speaking over her mother. She looked at Josephine, who had taken the news silently. "Though I suppose I'd like your blessing, Grandmother."

Josephine took a sip of coffee. "She left it to you, Maria. It's your decision."

That would have to do. Maria nodded and stood.

She didn't remember Theresa Wallner. She knew her through the memories of her mother and grandmother, from the journals she'd written in, and from the portrait in the hotel lobby of a dark-haired, dark-eyed woman holding a rose.

"Maria, don't you dare," Elisabeth said, rising from her

chair. "I'll never forgive you. You want to sell it for what, some pine floors? It's so mundane!"

What Elisabeth had never realized was that it was the mundane that allowed the fantastic. There were no balls without floors to dance on.

"You're talking about selling our family legacy—"

"The hotel is our family legacy," Josephine said, finality in her tone. She took one last sip of her coffee, clinked it down, and stood. "My mother didn't give a damn about the jewelry, Maria," she said, and then she left the room.

"Mother!" Elisabeth said, following her, apparently preferring that argument to the one with her daughter. Maria wondered if Josephine had drawn her off on purpose.

The sky was blue and bright when she stepped out of the hotel, the air cold and still. She pulled her coat tighter and walked to the nearby horse-tram stop. Already the city felt slightly fizzy around her—excited for Fasching, for the decadence that would begin that evening.

Fifty-five minutes later she stepped out of a jewelers' shop with her pocket satisfyingly full. The sapphire had glinted cheerfully in the jeweler's desk lamp when she had slipped it off her finger: one final wink before it was examined, appraised, bargained over, and finally sold, for slightly more than Maria had been prepared to accept. Enough for the floors, the plasterwork, and the paint, and perhaps even for someone to repair the grand chandelier, so long as she polished the crystal drops herself.

There wouldn't be any surplus with which to augment the ball's budget; that would have to come solely from the portion of the ticket sales the guild allotted them. Maria had seen the number this morning, and it wasn't promising. Eight years ago she wouldn't have believed the hotel could host a hundred people for that amount, let alone five times that number.

But where money was short, creativity and hard work must

suffice. No money for this season's gowns? Buy outmoded ones at the secondhand markets and have them remade. No money for a professional artist to repaint the Small Ballroom ceilings? Take up ceiling painting as a relaxing evening hobby.

No, Maria wasn't worried about the ball. She and Hannah had creativity and willingness to work in spades. The ball *would* be a triumph.

She would make Theresa proud.

She was already making a mental list as she swung back through the front doors of the hotel. There was no time to waste.

Abe was behind the front desk. "You look cheerful," he said. "And determined. It's a little scary."

Maria reached over the desk for one of the hotel note cards and drafted a note to Josephine's floors contact. She needed to get the crew working as quickly as possible. "It's a good day," she said, addressing an envelope and stuffing the note inside. "Can you have this delivered?"

He nodded and took the note, already hailing a footman. She smiled and hurried up the grand staircase.

Only to stop abruptly, three steps below Elijah Whittaker.

"Oh," she said. "Hello."

He nodded.

She hadn't seen him since the night before. Since he'd saved her life for a third time. Since he'd revealed that the reason he'd been hanging around her was that she was a *suspect*. For a crime she barely even understood.

Since he'd knelt before her and held ice to her jaw, his hands as gentle as if he were touching a butterfly.

Apparently they weren't going to talk about any of that, though, because after a tense moment, he simply nodded again and walked past her.

She let out a breath and continued up. This was good. She'd told him to stay away, and it looked like he was going to.

"It's not my business," he said. She turned, unnervingly quickly.

"It's not my business," he repeated. He hadn't turned, only tilted his head to the side as he paused on the stair. "But . . . you didn't go out alone, right? No. Even you wouldn't do that the morning after an attack by an unknown assailant. Right?"

"I—" *Didn't even think about it* was the end to that sentence. Which in hindsight was . . . extraordinarily foolish.

The truth was, she had no idea *what* to think. The attack seemed like a terrible dream—she could hardly believe it had happened. She didn't know where to put it in her mind. It was, sixteen hours later, as utterly inexplicable as it had been while it was happening.

And because she didn't know what to do about it, there hadn't seemed any point in thinking about it. In remembering the man on top of her, the terror of—

"I have a hotel to run," she said, slowly. "I can't do that if I can't leave the hotel. I'm not insensible to the risks, but . . . I also can't ask someone to go with me every time I need to run an errand."

"Why not?"

"What?"

He finally turned, his mouth set in a grim line. "You're always surrounded by people. You have a mother, a brother, a grandmother, a grandmother's lover, a grandmother's lover's husband, not to mention employees—"

"None of those people are in charge of the hotel—"

"So my question is, of all those people, why can't *one* of them go with you on whatever errands you need?"

"I—" She stopped. Frowned. The answer was simple: because she wouldn't ask them. "They have their own business," she said. "Their own lives. I can't just ask them to stop whatever they're doing to play nursemaid."

"I see," he said, and hesitated, before walking up toward her, taking her arm in his, and pulling her up the stairs.

"What are you doing?"

"Playing nursemaid," he said, curtly. "Is there someplace private we can go?"

And it was *completely* inappropriate, given the very serious context, but Maria immediately thought of linen closets.

"I—"

They were on the second floor. He opened the door to the Large Ballroom and nodded. "This will do," he said, pulling her through and shutting the door behind him. He looked at the buckled floorboards and then led her into a smooth patch in the middle.

"Do for *what*?"

"If you're going to insist on going out alone, then you should at least know how to defend yourself. Do you know how to fight?"

His mouth—*Stop looking at the mouth, Maria*—was distracting her. It took her a moment to understand his words.

"This is . . . kind of you," she said, slowly. "But—"

"I understand if you don't wish to be around me, after last night. But—I would consider it a courtesy. If you let me help you." He cleared his throat. "As an apology."

Oh no. If Elijah Whittaker was devastating when stern, he was downright lethal when he was sincere.

But he was right. She was keeping her head in the sand when she should be facing the problem head-on.

"My grandmother taught me how to shoot. But if you mean fisticuffs, no."

He nodded. "For someone with no training, you fought well, in the greenhouse. I could see it in the wreckage."

The compliment warmed her, lightening the stab of dark memory.

"But you're very small, and once he was on you, his weight

gave him an enormous advantage." He spoke dispassionately, as if he were giving a lecture. "So your first goal is to scream and get away before that happens. You did the first part last night, and it saved your life. If that doesn't work, your second goal is to get him off you. And your third goal is to incapacitate him."

"Incapacitate him?"

"By whatever means necessary."

The set of his mouth told her everything she needed to know about *that*.

"How did he attack you?"

"He hit the back of my head with a flowerpot," she said. "At least I assume it was a flowerpot. It was hard. I fell down."

His expression turned from grim to terrifying. Which she *absolutely* should not find attractive. He stepped toward her.

"You did not mention another head injury," he bit out, and then he was touching her again, his hand gently feeling the back of her head until he found the knot. He swore in English.

"I forgot about it," she said.

Elijah speared her with *a look*. She imagined it served him very well in the intimidating-criminals-and-subordinates department. It had a rather different effect on her.

He must have seen some hint of that in her face, because he abruptly dropped his hand and stepped back. He cleared his throat.

"You should have said something," he said, not making eye contact. "It ought to have been iced. And you should have seen a doctor."

"I can hardly see a doctor every time someone hits me on the head with a flowerpot," she said, tossing his words back to him in an attempt at lightness.

He stared at her. Clenched his jaw. Very emphatically did not laugh.

"What happened then?"

"He tried to hold me down," she said. The memory tried to close around her. She pushed it away. "I kicked him—I think his knee. It hurt him, but he didn't let go. He put his hand over my mouth. I bit him."

He nodded approvingly. Absurdly, she had to resist the urge to preen.

"He hit me. And then—" She bit her lip and looked at the floor.

The floor, at least, was safe to think about. What about her and Elijah, together on the floor? A pretty image, one she probably shouldn't be courting, but if it was between that and the greenhouse . . .

"All right," he said. His voice was still impersonal, but when she looked up she saw lingering darkness in his eyes. "Let's start with vulnerable points. The knee was a good idea, but it's not easy, and you can hurt yourself if you kick wrong. The eyes and the groin are simpler. Those work standing or grappling on the floor. For the eyes, anything sharp you have at hand is obviously best, but your finger will work. I'll show you."

He demonstrated, once at normal speed, and then several times slowed down. "Now you try."

She struck out with her fingers at an imaginary target.

"Good," he said. "That's good. If that works, you try to get away. Immediately. The goal is always, *always,* scream and run away."

Maria nodded. She had no temptation toward heroism. But, looking at Elijah, at the way his body loosened when he was demonstrating fighting technique, she doubted he followed his own advice.

"Let's move on to the groin," he said. Her mind made the predictable connection, but she managed to keep her expression clear. "So if someone grabs you from the front, a knee to the groin is often very effective."

He demonstrated the mechanics of the move, and then

stood in front of her and set his hands on her shoulders. "All right. Try it slowly."

Cautiously, she raised her knee. It was more difficult than she had imagined.

"Try again."

She did. It was a bit easier. "Your life must be rather dangerous," she said.

"Your skirts are a problem," he said, and her mind provided several excellent ways he could help her with them. "Let's try this in the air."

He stepped away from her. She tried the knee strike again, and realized her skirts *were* a problem. They were heavy, and the petticoat underneath was boned, which made them move unpredictably.

"That was me prying, by the way," she said, continuing to practice.

"Yes," he said, dryly. "I'm familiar with the method. That's looking better. You can try it a bit faster."

"Are you not allowed to talk about it? Your life? Is that part of the whole being-a-spy thing?"

A tic in the right side of his jaw. "I'm not a spy," he said. "I *was* undercover. Clearly not well."

"Don't feel badly about it. It wasn't anything you did. Apparently everybody knew before you even got here. Well. Not me, obviously." She tried to turn it into a joke, but the words fell awkwardly between them. His mouth twitched, as if he was suppressing a flinch.

When he spoke, though, his voice was even. "The leaks are that bad?"

She shrugged. "Perhaps we're just used to it. There are a lot of spies in Vienna."

"I see."

"So if you're not a spy," she said, "what do you do in America?"

"I work at the Treasury," he said.

All right, not exactly what she had expected. "With . . . money?"

"I'm in charge of tracking down people whose illegal activities with currency fund larger, even more illegal activities," he said.

"Ah. Suddenly the dangerous life makes sense."

"It's not that dangerous," he said. "Keep working on the knee strike later. It's much better now. You've figured out the balance of your skirts. Next let's try a palm to the nose."

He demonstrated, a quick upward punch of the arm with an open hand. She realized he was modifying all the moves to suit her height—whoever his imaginary attacker was, they would have to be a giant for their nose to be that high, but if she mimicked him, her palm would land very near Elijah's nose. He was a surprisingly good teacher.

"Higher. You want the thickest part of your hand to do the work. Here—" He took her hand. "Feel how much stronger this is. Hit someone with this part, and it hurts. Hit someone higher, near your fingers, and you break your hand."

His fingers were on hers. She stared down at where their skin touched. His hand looked like the rest of him, large and stern and competent.

He'd stopped talking. She looked up at him, just as he, too, looked up from their hands, and suddenly, she stopped breathing.

There was no mistaking the look in his eyes. She'd seen desire directed at herself many times before. But she'd never before seen desire this . . . raw.

And then someone cleared their throat, and the moment shattered. Elijah stepped away swiftly, as though she were a hot coal.

"I beg your pardon," a crisp, educated voice said. Blinking, Maria looked toward the door, where a neatly dressed, middle-aged man stood. "I was looking for the restaurant."

"Down the stairs," she said, dazed. "To the right."

"Thank you," the man said. He bowed and disappeared through the door.

Maria smoothed her dress. "I—" She needed to leave. "Need to work," she settled on. "Thank you for the lesson."

And before he could say anything, she fled.

Chapter Thirteen

The Hotelkeepers' Ball was a success last night. Not as good as '29, of course. But still, so far, the event of the season. The champagne rain was a sensation. . . .

—Journal entry of Josephine Wallner, 1841

Eli stood in the empty ballroom, the memory of her hand lingering on his skin.

He barely knew the woman, but he knew the way her body felt against his, the line of her jaw under his fingers, the warmth of her hand—

And had they been interrupted even two seconds later . . .

No. He wouldn't finish that sentence.

A waltz floated through the ballroom windows from the street below, thin and wispy. Always, perpetually, off-balance.

He had wanted to kiss her. Had almost *felt* the kiss taking shape between them.

Eli walked to the side of the ruined ballroom, pressing a hand against the cool plaster wall.

He was attracted to her.

It was, in hindsight, embarrassingly obvious. He'd probably had a crush on her from the moment she'd looked up at him after the carriage incident, with those wide, wondrous dark eyes.

This was . . . this was trouble.

It wasn't that he hadn't been attracted to people before

her. He had a very efficient system in place to handle it—he ignored it.

Attraction was danger. Attraction was . . . vulnerability.

But he *couldn't* ignore Maria Wallner. Not with this nagging feeling that she was somehow connected to the very case he'd been sent to Vienna to solve.

He walked to the window. The ballroom was in shambles, but the windows were sparkling. He wondered if Maria had cleaned these too.

He'd spent most of the day interviewing the staff at the Brodmaier estate, unfortunately with very little result. The footman who'd accepted the note was only able to confirm that the person who'd handed it to him had been a man, perhaps in his thirties or forties. Jakob Brodmaier had given him the invitation list, and Eli would dutifully sort through it, but he would be very surprised to discover that the assailant had possessed a legitimate invitation. The attack had been planned. He wouldn't want his name on any lists.

So he couldn't ignore her. Not until he knew whether she was connected to the code thefts or not.

Not until she's safe.

He didn't bother arguing with himself. He knew when something had transformed itself into a duty.

That was the plan, then: Solve the case. Keep Maria safe. Go home.

Home, where things were stable, and comprehensible. Where there were no trees made of candy, and no waltzes, and no beautiful, wide-eyed hotelkeepers. Where moonlit attacks were directed against him, and not against random women. Where he was in no danger of . . . of losing himself.

She'd handed him a nice clue today. *Everybody knew before you even got here,* she'd said, so casually. *Everybody knew.* Which meant someone in the American Legation knew, and had leaked it.

Tomorrow was Monday, and he very much hoped the staff would show up to work. He had some questions to ask.

The corner of his mouth twitched.

This part, at least, was going to be . . .

Fun, his brain whispered.

Satisfying, he responded. Working toward justice was always satisfying.

Monday morning dawned with a bright blue sky. Eli didn't bother hurrying. He did his exercises and enjoyed the morning paper in the hotel's excellent restaurant. It struck him that no matter how tired the furnishings, there was something that felt *good* about the Hotel Wallner. Maria was really very talented. What did it matter if the wallpaper was a bit faded, so long as the tables were immaculate and the food delicious?

After about five minutes lost to thinking about Maria's many positive traits, he cleared his throat aggressively and went back to his newspaper.

It also struck him that despite the emotional turmoil of the day before, this was the first morning since he'd arrived that he felt . . . calm. Like himself.

After breakfast, he returned to his room and spent an hour reading one of his books on comparative religion. Only when the clock in his room read half past ten did he collect his briefcase, don his coat, and leave for the Legation.

The Legation door was unlocked when Eli arrived at eleven. He hung his coat, introduced himself to the clerk at the front desk, and made his way to the second floor. He deposited his briefcase on his desk and walked over to where Secretary Collins sat, at a large desk in front of the Legation director's office, frowning down at a Hansen Writing Ball typewriter.

"Ah, Whittaker," Collins said. His eyes were still bloodshot. "Looking distressingly alert at early hours again, I see. Look at this awful thing."

Eli looked at the machine. It *was* an odd-looking thing,

but he'd purchased his own several years earlier. It made writing much more efficient—not to mention legible, given that his own penmanship was crude at best.

"Washington sent it," Collins said. "They can't mean *me* to use it, can they? We'll have to hire a girl." His expression turned lazily lecherous. "Well, at least it won't *all* be bad, eh?"

Eli stared at him, and Collins rolled his eyes and returned to the machine.

"Is Director Farrow available?" Eli asked.

"I should think so," Collins said, yawning as he stood. "I'll tell him you're here."

He knocked on the door and disappeared briefly inside. When he emerged, he left the door open and jerked his head toward it before sitting back down.

Eli entered the office. It was neat and stylish, like the rest of the building. Wood paneling covered the walls, and bookcases stretched floor-to-ceiling behind the desk, filled with expensive-looking reference books and legal tomes.

"Oh, Mr. Whittaker," Farrow said, standing and reaching across his desk to shake Eli's hand. He was a tall, lean, handsome man, with graying brown hair and a neat mustache. "Yes, we've been expecting you. Collins said you arrived last week and got right to work. As expected from you Treasury fellows! Sit, sit."

Eli sat in the indicated chair.

"Well, how was your journey?"

"Satisfactory," Eli replied, content to let Farrow set the scene. "Some slight weather."

"Ah well, didn't make you too squeamish, I hope."

"No, sir. Thank you."

"Collins was sick as a dog on our journey over. Thought he might toss himself overboard, just to end his suffering. Was tempted to do the deed myself, a couple of times."

This was a line calling for polite laughter. Eli was long

accustomed to the awkwardness that came in the unexpected silence.

Farrow lifted his eyebrows, and then filled the silence with his own laughter. "Yes, you Treasury boys are straight arrows, aren't you? Well, you're very welcome here. This currency issue is a tangle, no question about it. Most of the fellows here can't even summarize the issues well enough to send memos back home about it. I'm not sure even I can! How long do you think you'll need for the trainings?"

"I'm not here to do currency trainings," Eli said, in his mildest voice.

In the long pause that followed, Eli learned several things.

One, Farrow certainly knew why Eli was really in Vienna.

Two, he was deeply, *deeply* surprised to hear it acknowledged.

Three, he was a reasonably accomplished liar. One and Two were mere flickers of emotion on his face before his expression was schooled into perfect confusion.

"Aren't you—are you here to handle them for us, then?"

"No." Eli paused, reflecting on the *truly* dreadful memos concerning the currency crisis he had read last week. "Though I'd be willing to do some training while I'm here," he added.

"Then why—? I'm afraid I don't understand."

"I was sent here to investigate the theft of American secret codes from this Legation," Eli said. "It was intended to be an undercover operation, but I have discovered it was compromised before my arrival."

Farrow let out a long breath, his eyebrows apparently permanently raised. "The codes."

Eli nodded.

"I see. Of course, I'm aware of the supposed code theft," Farrow said, slowly. "Though, to be perfectly honest, I'm not persuaded there was a theft at all. The boys back home aren't as . . . secretive . . . as they perhaps believe. Two years ago they published the damn things in *The New-York Times*."

That was quite true. And before Maria's attack, Eli had been prepared to consider the possibility that there had not actually been a theft. But then she *had* been attacked. Coincidences happened, but they weren't usually quite so dramatic.

"I'm certain I'll be able to discover the truth in my investigation," Eli said, mildly. He pulled out his notebook. It felt good in his hand. "Now, if you don't mind, I'm going to ask you a few questions."

"Questions!"

"It's procedure, sir."

"I have to say, I'm not sure I approve of this," Farrow said.

Eli blinked, all mild surprise. "Surely you must want to get to the bottom of this, sir."

"As I said, I'm not particularly worried about these so-called thefts," Farrow said, and then sighed. "I suppose if you must, you must. It's all very irregular, though, and I *will* be telegramming both State *and* Treasury to confirm what you said."

"As you should, sir. Now, just so I can understand the context . . ."

In a few minutes he had the answers he'd expected: Farrow had seen nothing, done nothing, and suspected nothing. This was perfectly normal: supervisors, as a class, were not pleased when their workplaces were investigated, and tended to stonewall initially. After all, investigations turned up all kinds of crimes and scandals, not only the ones they were targeting.

"One last question, sir. You know your staff best. If someone here *did* sell the codes, who would it be?"

This was one of Eli's favorite questions, because no matter the answer, he learned something.

Farrow blew out another breath. "It would have to be the local staff," he said. "One of the maids, maybe."

Eli nodded. "Thank you," he said, standing. "If you could ask your staff to make time for me."

He was almost at the door when Farrow spoke again. "Whittaker."

"Yes?"

Farrow hesitated. "I'm not sure I should share this," he said. "I wasn't told all the details behind your assignment. But . . . I did get the sense you weren't sent here because you were in *good* standing at Treasury."

"I don't follow," Eli said.

"Perhaps you should think of this assignment as a time to reflect. You seem like a good lad, but you're rigid. You need to learn to bend, if you're going to make it in government."

It wasn't the first time he'd heard such an opinion expressed (often in rather more vulgar terms). But usually he understood what he was supposedly being too rigid about.

"I'll take you up on those trainings, though," Farrow said. "We *do* actually need them. Set it up with Collins later, will you?"

The director nodded, and the meeting was over. Eli returned to his desk, looking out his window onto the wide, pale boulevard beyond. His calm had evaporated with the morning frost.

He was missing something. It was like there was an invisible obstacle in his path, and ever since he'd arrived, he'd been tripping over it. He'd been looking for it in the codes case, but what if it wasn't about the codes at all?

Chapter Fourteen

Darling Diary, today I presented Heinrich with his first
child, his daughter, Maria. . . .
　　　　　　—Journal entry of Elisabeth Wallner, 23 May 1847

He wasn't able to reclaim the calm of the morning, but Eli
was used to working with unsettled questions looming
over him. After some deliberation, he sent a message to his
second-in-command, Robert Kasinsky, asking about the status of the Bantry Gang cases. If he *was* in disfavor at Treasury
(more than usual, that was), then it was probably because
of something he'd done, or not done, on that investigation.
Of course, this being the United States government, there
was also the possibility that he had worn the wrong shoes
to a meeting. In the decade he'd worked for Treasury, he'd
learned that things in government bureaucracy didn't necessarily need to make sense.

He briefly considered sending a second telegram, to his
stepfather, Ambassador Thomas, but decided against it.

Eli had been sixteen when his mother had met and married his stepfather. For two years, before he had left for the
Union Army, he'd lived in the man's house (mansion, really),
and watched him. No investigation he had led since had been
as thorough as the one a young Eli Whittaker had conducted
on George Arthur Thomas, former ambassador to the United

Kingdom, former secretary of state, and current giant of politics. The man who could have been president, but had married Eli's mother instead.

At the end of Eli's investigation, he had reached two crucial conclusions. First, Ambassador Thomas was basically a moral man. He had flaws, and in his youth had been mightily attracted to power, but his middle years had brought . . . a kind of thoughtfulness and clarity that Eli, even at sixteen, suspected was rare. Second, the man would shoot himself in the head before he ever laid a hand on Eli's mother.

The latter was really the only finding that mattered. After everything—after everything, his mother deserved that.

Sometimes Eli wished he had a softer disposition. Ambassador Thomas was a good man, and he loved Eli's mother. And just for that, just for keeping his mother loved and happy and safe, Eli owed the man an unpayable debt. He wished that when the Ambassador was warm, he could be warm in return. That he could express his gratitude.

The best he seemed capable of, though, was careful, formal politeness, and never adding to that debt. Asking the Ambassador to look into his standing at Treasury would do so.

Telegram sent to Kasinsky, he filed Director Farrow's words into the part of his brain reserved for unsettled questions and got to work.

The rest of the day was spent in interviews, and in arguing with Secretary Collins about which records his clearance entitled him to, and then, once he had won that argument, sorting the mountain of files that appeared at his desk, Collins apparently resorting to the time-honored technique of "bury your opponent in paperwork."

Fortunately, Eli enjoyed paperwork.

He stayed at his desk long after the Legation staff had departed (which was shortly after teatime). He was vaguely aware of the fading light, but it wasn't until a violinist began a waltz directly beneath his window that he realized night had fallen. He pushed his chair back and stretched, his back popping in annoyance.

The clock informed him it was just past six. Still early, then. Eli stood and walked to the small kitchenette along the side wall, squinting in the room that was now only illuminated by his small desk lamp. He made himself a pot of tea and settled back at his desk.

At half past ten, after uncovering two extramarital affairs and realizing that the currency trainings needed to be scheduled *immediately,* he closed the file he was working on, yawned, and collected his coat.

Outside, the city had descended once more into black-and-gold madness. He sidestepped a group of jugglers (no one wanted one juggler, let alone a group of them), escaped a tense situation with a mime, and narrowly avoided being waltzed with by a group of rampaging youths. Eli thought he had been getting used to the insanity of nighttime Vienna, but tonight it all seemed to be even more chaotic than usual. He paused when he reached Annagasse, the small street on which the hotel was located, quickly straightening his tie and smoothing his hair.

He braced himself as he walked into the lobby of the Hotel Wallner, but it was Abraham behind the front desk. Deciding the deflated feeling in his chest was relief, Eli nodded to him and walked up the wide staircase to his room, intending to get some exercise in and then sleep.

Instead, he found Josephine Wallner sitting at his desk. Apparently his exercise would have to wait.

He stopped in the doorway. "Good evening."

"Close the door," she said.

He obliged. She gestured to the unoccupied armchair, and he sat.

For some reason, the corner of his mouth twitched again.

"So," she said. "Elijah Whittaker, undercover American agent."

"Not undercover anymore."

"It's hard to keep a secret in Vienna," Josephine said, and then smiled, a small, grim little thing. "Even for the Viennese. Though I think perhaps you never had a chance at keeping yours."

"So it seems," Eli said, mildly.

"You don't seem particularly put out."

Eli shrugged. "I don't really like secrets. They tend to be a lot of work without a lot of reward, in my experience."

"Mmm," Josephine said, another faint smile crossing her face. "There we disagree. I quite like secrets. It is only when they threaten those I love that I cannot allow them."

Her meaning was clear enough. "I pose no threat to Maria."

"*You* may not," Josephine said, but didn't elaborate. "Well, let's talk."

Eli nodded, relaxing into the chair. This was obviously supposed to be a threatening conversation, but something about Josephine felt easy. Like he didn't need to put quite so much work into translating his thoughts to words when he spoke, because at some level, they thought the same way. "The attack," he said.

"Yes. So? What do you know?"

"Not much," he said. "I went to the Brodmaier estate to-day."

"And did you find anything?"

"Not really. A very vague description of the attacker. What about you?"

She lifted an eyebrow, but after a pause, nodded again, very slightly. "The same," she said. "And not a whisper in town. No one knows anything."

"Someone was following her."

"Yes."

The note that had lured her out had built upon the contents of an actual meeting. Someone hadn't just been following her, they'd been following her *closely.*

"Is there anyone you suspect?"

"Perhaps the Hotel Hoffmann," Josephine mused. "They can't be pleased about losing the Hotelkeepers' Ball to us, though this seems extreme for them."

Killing someone over a ball did seem extreme, but then, Eli was learning to not underestimate the importance of balls in Vienna.

"Another possibility is one of her former lovers," Josephine said. "I don't know all of them, but you can trust I will by the end of the night."

Eli nodded. "It's rather too much coincidence," he said. "That she was attacked while I was investigating her."

"I agree," Josephine said, dryly. "Though I'm hard-pressed to see the connection between my granddaughter and the secret codes of a backwater nation halfway across the world."

Eli ignored the slight. It was hard to argue that the United States was anything *but* a backwater when compared with the over-the-top magnificence of Vienna.

On the other hand, his neighborhood in Washington was blessedly free of roving gangs of jugglers.

"The letter that led us here was sent from your hotel," he said, instead.

"So you said." She shrugged. "We're a hotel. It's rather our nature to let anyone through the doors."

"So there's no one you suspect?"

"About your silly codes?" That faint smile returned, this time with an air of indulgence. "It's not a matter of suspicion. I simply can't see why anyone here would care. The most likely scenario is that someone from your Legation used our postbox."

That was the likeliest scenario, except— "Except Maria was attacked while I was investigating her."

"Except Maria was attacked while you were investigating her," Josephine agreed. "Still. Coincidences happen. Even if neither of us like them."

"Mmm." They looked at each other, both lost in thought.

"If someone here *was* involved with the code theft," Eli said, finally, "who would it be?"

Josephine snorted. "That wouldn't have worked on me when I was twenty," she said.

The corner of his mouth twitched again. Perhaps he was developing a facial spasm.

"Well, I'm due at Emilie's in thirty minutes," she said, and pinned him with a look, all trace of amusement gone. "I'm going to do everything I can to protect my granddaughter. I'd like your promise you'll do the same, on your side."

"I promise." It was, after all, part of the plan.

Josephine must have heard the intention in his voice, because she nodded and stood.

"Oh, Frau Wallner—"

"Yes?"

"Will . . . will the orchids survive?"

A faint smile ghosted across her lips. "Yes," she said. "Jakob says so, at least. Good n—"

A knock sounded on his door.

"If that's my granddaughter, this is about to become awkward," Josephine said, and a wave of heat flushed Eli's cheeks.

He ignored it and answered the door.

"Good evening, Whittaker," Macario von Eder said. Maria's brother was dressed for the evening, his blond hair slicked back neatly. His scowling expression, Eli imagined, was supposed to be intimidating.

This time, both corners of Eli's mouth twitched. There was a strange pressure in his chest.

He bowed.

"I thought we'd have a little chat—" Mac said, brushing past Eli into the room and freezing.

"Mac," Josephine said.

"Oh," Mac said, unsure.

"I'll leave you to your talk," Josephine said. She stopped as she passed Mac, placing a hand on his arm. "You're a good boy, Macario. Ask Hannah to feed you before you leave."

Color rushed into Mac's face. He bowed. "Thank you."

The two men watched Josephine leave.

"Well. I guess she's already threatened you," Mac said.

Eli nodded. She had, if implicitly.

Mac stuffed his hands in his pockets and looked sheepish. "That's taken care of, then. Do you want to get a drink?"

Eli blinked. "No."

"Oh," Mac said. "All right. Have a good night, then— Oh, hello, is that someone at the balcony?"

Eli turned. Frowned at the shape outside. Opened the balcony door. "It's three floors up," he protested, to the man on the balcony.

"I've been with the Countess, in the room above you," Claude Girard said, swanning into Eli's hotel room like it was a grand ballroom. "Thought I'd come down and say hello. Search your room if you weren't here. Hello, I'm Claude Girard," he said to Mac.

"Mac von Eder. Aren't you the new French spy?"

"One and the same," Claude said. "Didn't I see you at the Hotel Sacher the other night?"

"Oh! At the Christmas ball," Mac said. "Yes, I—"

"I don't mind you two furthering your acquaintance," Eli said, with what he thought was extreme restraint, "Only you doing so in my room." He tried to usher them toward the door.

"He's awfully grumpy, isn't he?" Claude said, evading him

and sitting on his bed. "But don't you think we should call for some alcohol?"

"I have some," Mac said, pulling a bottle of golden liquid from his pocket.

"What a well-prepared fellow you are," Claude said, admiringly. "Elijah, do you have glasses?"

"Eli," Eli said, reflexively. "And no—"

"Found them!" Mac said, producing three glasses from a cupboard.

"Look," Eli said, repressing an urge to rub his forehead. "As I said, I have no objection to you furthering your acquaintance—though, to be clear, Mr. Girard, I *do* have an objection to you searching my room—but perhaps you could do so elsewhere. Anywhere else."

"So grumpy," Claude said, stretching his feet out so they rested on Eli's desk chair. Mac flopped in the nearby armchair like an overgrown puppy. "I heard you caused a fuss at the American Legation today."

Eli stopped trying to pull Mac back up. "From whom?"

"The parrot man down the street," Claude said. "And he heard it from a man at the Café Landtmann. I don't know who that man heard it from." He examined his fingernails.

Mac sat up abruptly. "I'm hungry," he announced. "Let's go to the kitchens!"

"No," Eli said.

"A wonderful idea," Claude said. "Come on, Whittaker. If you come maybe I'll let slip something interesting."

"Oh, *spy* business," Mac said. "Do you think I'd be a good spy?"

"Oh my darling, no," Claude said. "But you're a *marvelous* aristocrat."

"You just met him," Eli said. "How do you know?"

"He's decorative, elegant, and seemingly useless," Claude said. "Everything an aristocrat ought to be."

Mac sighed. "I *am* very good at it," he said. "So is my father." He shook his head and stood. "Kitchens!"

"Kitchens!" Claude echoed, standing. The two tripped into the hall, and after a moment of thought, Eli followed. Claude Girard knew something. If the price for finding out what was following a puppy and a spy to the Hotel Wallner kitchens, then it was a low price indeed.

At the landing Eli turned toward the main stair, but Mac shook his head. "This way," he said, heading toward an unassuming door near the back wall. He opened it to reveal a narrow stairway.

"Servants' stair," he said.

Three turns of the stair took them to a door, which Mac pushed confidently open.

"Abe, I want you to try this— Oh. Mac." The woman at the stove was pretty, with warm brown eyes and light brown hair.

"Ah-hah," Claude whispered. "Now we know why he wanted to come to the kitchens."

The corner of Eli's mouth did the twitching thing again.

"Evening, Hannah," Mac said, smiling in what Eli imagined was supposed to be an ingratiating manner, and instead looked . . . nervous. "Oh, have you met? This is Claude Girard and Elijah Whittaker."

"The French spy," Hannah said. "And the American."

"None other," Claude said, sweeping a fluid bow. Eli bowed as well, though somewhat less gracefully.

"Well," she said, putting her hands on her hips and surveying what seemed to be her domain. "I suppose you've come to beg for food, Mac, which *you know* Maria doesn't like you to do. But, well, I *do* need someone to try the lilies." She nodded at the large table, covered in various . . . flowers?

Mac and Claude sat immediately.

"The pink ones," Hannah said, and went back to piping a wild-rose design on wax paper.

"What is that?" Eli asked, peering at the paper.

"I'm testing a design for a cake," she said. "For the ball. Maria's doing a Fairyland theme. Here, hold this." She handed him a bag of green frosting.

Eli watched as she competently sketched out a bloom with pink frosting. "The Hotelkeepers' Ball?" he asked, remembering Josephine's comment.

"Mmm. Green." He gave her the green-frosting bag and took the pink. A few gestures of her wrist created a twining vine.

"You're adding thorns."

"It's not Fairyland without thorns," Hannah said, focusing on her work. "It's our salvation, you see. The ball."

Eli lifted an eyebrow. "Salvation?"

"It's going to return us to fashion," she explained. "Fill our rooms again. Let me serve more than breakfast and tea in the restaurant. At least, it will if it's wonderful." She shrugged. Smiled. "But it *will* be wonderful."

She stepped back, looked at the design. "Not quite," she said, pulling a fresh paper down and moving the current one to the side. "Pink," she said, and they exchanged frosting bags.

"So, how are you finding Vienna?"

Fast. Confusing. Deceptive. "It's very different from home," he said, deciding to exercise diplomacy. "Grander."

"You must miss your family. Green."

"Mmm," he said, noncommittally. "They're fine without me."

It was Hannah's turn to raise an eyebrow, but she let it lie, focusing on an intricately braided rose vine.

"Pretty," Eli said, unthinkingly.

"Yes," she said. "You know, Maria's my best friend. Pink."

Eli did the bag switch and waited.

"It occurs to me that you don't know the legend."

"I beg your pardon?"

"About *the man,*" she said, and yes, those words were absolutely in italics. "Local legend says that for every Wallner woman there is one man in her lifetime. She'll meet him, love him, and have a child with him. A daughter."

"What a stupid legend," Eli said. "For one thing, at least one of the Wallner women seems to be in love with . . ." Eli paused. He didn't know how widely known the relationship between Josephine and Emilie was.

"*The woman,*" Hannah finished. "Well, I didn't say the legend was true. Though I suppose it could still be, technically. After all, it only specifies *one man,* nothing about other genders. And that's not the point. The point is that for a long time, when we were in our twenties, Vienna talked about him. Maria's *man.*"

"Hannah, can we try the camellias?" Mac asked.

"*No,*" she said, dropping her frosting bag and rushing across the kitchen.

Eli's stomach was sour. An entire city gossiping about one young woman's love life . . . it was disgusting.

He walked to the table, where Mac was attempting to flirt with Hannah, and sat next to Claude. "Tell me the rest, please," he said, plainly.

Claude plucked a petal from a rose and ate it. "All right," he said. His laconic expression dropped away, and Eli caught a glimpse of something serious beneath. "You have more than one leak in that building, and at least one person who is profiting from them. And before you ask," he said, cutting Eli off, "I don't have any names."

Eli nodded. "Thank you." He stood, bowed to Claude, and then to Hannah and Mac, and went back up the stairs to his room.

Chapter Fifteen

He's engaged.

—Journal entry of Elisabeth Wallner, 1 June 1847,
presumably referring to Baron Heinrich von Eder.
Page is notably scored with pen strokes.

January 8

Maria closed the journal and put it in its cabinet. She'd written about the ring, a little regret and a lot of determination in her chest as she did, and now she needed to relieve Abe for his lunch. After that, she needed to go to the furniture-rental warehouses.

Abe smiled as she approached, sketching out the events of the morning before leaving for the kitchen. The lobby was empty, their handful of guests still sleeping, most having returned from their Fasching balls after dawn. Eighteen rooms were currently occupied, with three more reservations scheduled to check in. It was a good number—down from the record high of New Year's, but five rooms higher than the same day the year prior.

And perhaps, in a few weeks, when everyone had heard about the success of the Hotelkeepers' Ball . . .

She glanced around the lobby, making sure everything was just so. The marble floor gleamed; the pillar Count von Dasse had shot a chunk out of had been repaired so you could barely see the damage. A plate of Hannah's almond cakes stood on a table near the desk, their enticing warm-honey scent threading through the air. A crystal pitcher of water sat next to them, accompanied by a samovar of tea. And Theresa Wallner presided over everything, smiling out in three-quarter profile from a gilt-framed portrait above the marble fireplace, her expression laughing. Her dark curls were piled casually on her head, and in one hand she held a rose. A bright blue shawl, embroidered with flowers, was wrapped around a white evening gown. The effect was one of almost arrogant joie de vivre, a woman in absolute command of her life, her surroundings, her heart, and her happiness.

"I sold your ring," Maria said, after checking that she was alone. "Grandmother said you wouldn't care, and I wish . . . I'm sorry I had to." There had been a comfort in the weight of it on her hand, a reminder that she came from strength, love, and determination. "The workers started on the floors this morning, and after Abe gets back I'm going to the furniture warehouses. Fasching has already started, so the selection will be bad, but—" Maria shrugged, trusting that Theresa understood. It would be fine. She would make it so.

She'd had these conversations with her great-grandmother since she was a child, late at night, waiting for her grandmother to finish whatever task she was engaged in. Listening to the hum of the hotel at night, soft but alert.

A carriage pulled up before the hotel doors, and Maria watched Franz, one of the footmen, spring up from his station in front of the hotel. The first of their new guests, arriving for the day.

She opened the reservation books—ignoring the small talisman written on thin parchment paper her mother had likely dropped within—and, when a woman descended first from the carriage, decided this must be the Novotný couple, traveling to Vienna for Fasching from their estate outside

Prague. When they came through the door, she was ready with a smile.

Forty-five minutes later, Abe returned, and Maria donned her coat, checking her reflection in the mirror by the door. She had her hand on the doorknob when Elijah Whittaker's words came back to her.

Of all those people, he had asked, *why can't one of them go with you on whatever errands you need?*

It *was* broad daylight. But . . . maybe she'd see if there was anyone in the kitchen who could go with her.

She walked across the lobby and poked her head into the kitchen. It was empty save for Hannah, who was bent in concentration over something on the counter. Quietly, Maria closed the door. She would just make sure she was back before dark.

The afternoon was cold and clear, a sharp wind tossing her curls and biting at her nose. She bent her head against it, watching the pavement a couple meters in front of her as she thought about rental furniture.

A pair of familiar shoes stopped in front of her. She glanced up.

For a moment, they simply looked at each other. He was wearing a navy scarf around his neck. The color set off the severity of his features, the harsh cut of his jaw, the deep seriousness of his gaze.

He sighed. Deeply. The kind of sigh that spoke of severe spiritual anguish. He even closed his eyes while doing it.

Maria bit her lip. No man should look that good while experiencing severe spiritual anguish.

"All right," he said, after he was done sighing. "Let's go."

"Sorry?"

"Wherever it is you were going. Let's go."

"I'm going to the furniture-rental warehouses," she said, confused and still a little distracted.

"Fine."

"Sorry?" she said. Again.

He was apparently tired of this particular conversational game, because he gestured with his briefcase for her to continue walking. Once she did, he fell into step next to her.

"Are you—are you accompanying me?"

"Apparently."

"But—why?"

He shrugged.

"Right," she said, slowing in confusion.

"It's not that I don't enjoy the cold," he said. "But I thought you had somewhere to go."

Apparently he was coming with her.

She sped up, glancing sidelong at him. He looked grim. To be fair, he usually looked grim. She wondered who had knitted the scarf for him—a sweetheart back home, perhaps?

"Your scarf is nice," she said. "Did someone knit it for you?"

"My mother," he said, the words short and to the point. After a pause, he continued: "She likes to knit."

Maria nodded. *His mother.* "So does my grandmother."

He lifted an eyebrow, but remained silent.

On the way to the tram stop, they passed a crew of workmen putting belated Fasching decorations up on one of the new department stores. Elijah nodded at it. "A local festival?"

She blinked at him. "I'm sorry?"

"The decorations. They're for a festival?"

"The . . . Fasching decorations?" She stopped. "Do you not have Fasching in America? Oh, I suppose you'd call it Carnival."

He shrugged again.

"But there are lots of Catholics there," she said. Evidently, he wasn't one of them.

"I'm an atheist."

"An—I don't think I've ever met an atheist before."

He simply looked at her.

"An atheist," she repeated, stunned. Should they be whispering? She wasn't even sure it was *legal* to be an atheist. "Is that why you were so flustered by the psychics?" she said, quietly. Just in case.

"I . . . wasn't aware psychics were part of a religion," he said, at his usual volume. "At least not Christianity. Your family is Catholic, isn't it?"

"Mmm, but we're not very devout," she said, wanting to be honest. It had been some time since any of the Wallners set foot in a church. "Still, though. You came to Vienna six days before Fasching and you didn't know? Didn't you have a spy training or something?"

"No. Because I'm not a spy."

Something annoyed in his tone, though, told her he agreed with her. Elijah Whittaker was not the kind of man who liked being unprepared.

A tram stopped, and they boarded it, sitting side by side on a wooden bench.

She decided to take pity on him. He was, after all, sacrificing his afternoon to escort her shopping. "Are you familiar with Lent?"

He nodded.

"All right," she said. "*Fasching*—Carnival—is the festival before Lent. It's like an enormous party before the austerity. Traditionally I think it was when people ate up the animal products that would go bad if they weren't eaten before the end of Lent. Now it's . . ." She struggled to find the words for what Fasching meant to Vienna. "It's the madness one needs to maintain sanity."

Elijah's frown deepened. "And when did it start?"

"The day after—" she paused. "The day before yesterday. The sixth."

"So all the . . . everything before the sixth . . . was Vienna's idea of sanity? The incessant waltzing? The balls? The parrot men?"

She laughed. "The waltzing and the parrot men are year-round," she said. "As for the balls . . . everything thrown between November and January sixth is really only a warm-up."

"A warm-up."

"The *real* balls are the Fasching balls. You haven't seen anything yet."

He paled.

"Ah," she said, as the tram slowed. "This is our stop."

They were slightly outside the Innere Stadt now, in the Viennese suburbs. As that was as close as the tram would take them, Maria hailed a cabdriver and engaged him for the afternoon.

A fifteen-minute drive took them to a large building, situated in a sparse area between the suburbs and the countryside. Maria knocked, and after a moment's wait, they were ushered inside.

Maria had expected the selection to be thin. She hadn't expected it to be nonexistent.

A few remnant pieces of furniture dotted the enormous space, like eddies of algae swirling on a vast pond. A lone fountain sat in an empty corner. A row of arches had fallen over upon each other across the room, like a line of dominoes that had simply given up.

"As you can see, it's—" The frazzled clerk gestured, as though he was too exhausted to speak.

"Yes," Maria said.

"Well," the clerk said, then nodded and left to return to a man Maria recognized as the manager of the Hotel Hoffmann. She frowned. The Hotel Hoffmann must be having a last-minute event in one of their smaller venues.

"How many guests are coming to this . . . er . . . Hotel-keepers' Ball?" Elijah asked.

"Five hundred," Maria said, dismissing the Hotel Hoffmann's manager and surveying the space. "There's another furniture warehouse, and we have furniture for a hundred and fifty at the hotel, but the other warehouse will be in a similar state." A plan was beginning to come to her. She nodded. "I can make it work."

She strode forward into the cavernous room, taking a notebook from her pocket. The theme was Fairyland, which was fortunate, because fairies could do whatever they wanted. Who said Fairyland would have matching tables and chairs? All they needed to be was shiny. Furnishings, perhaps, that the fey had stolen from kings and emperors over the centuries, like magpies.

That set of Louis XV chairs, for example. Well, not exactly a set—there were seven of them, obviously left over from a much larger order. She would take them, and the nineteen basic slat-back chairs in the gold lacquer, along with the six in silver. . . . She looked around for the clerk, only to find Elijah walking him toward her.

"I'm sorry, I have to—" But somehow the clerk didn't finish his sentence before he was maneuvered in front of her.

Elijah Whittaker really needed to stop being so . . . so useful.

"Hello again," she said brightly to the clerk. "I'm ready to start ordering."

The clerk glanced at the manager of the Hotel Hoffmann, and then at Elijah, standing completely still and expressionless.

"Yes, ma'am," he said, taking his order book out.

She talked as she walked. She needed around a hundred and fifty extra chairs, and an assortment of tables. It would be nice to have some decorative items as well, but she could manage without.

By the time she had walked around the room, she had spoken for every opulent, shiny, gold- or silver-colored piece of furniture in the warehouse. She could feel Elijah's distaste grow with every over-the-top decision.

"Fairies don't have taste," she said simply, when the clerk ran to the office to get a second order form.

He looked at her, and she thought—perhaps she imagined—that the corner of his mouth twitched.

"I see," he said.

She stopped in front of the fountain. Whoever had designed it made her tasteless fairies seem like Beau Brummel. It was three tiers, nearly as tall as she was and made to look like a series of open shells. Two women posed on either side, surrounded by several leering Cupids and . . . dogs? Possibly dogs. A goat danced near the top, probably to represent Pan.

A fairy bower, filled with the spoils of centuries of human folly and excess. She imagined the fountain covered with greenery and moss and strange looking flowers. Possibly overflowing with Hannah's almond cakes.

"Yes," she said. "It's perfect."

Next to her, Elijah sighed, but she was beginning to understand his sighs. This was fairly pro forma.

The clerk returned with the second order form.

"What price can you give me on the fountain?" Maria asked.

The man looked at her, looked at the fountain, and back. She shrugged, nonchalant.

"Err . . . three gulden?"

She snorted. The clerk glanced at Elijah.

"Two and a half gulden?"

"How about two gulden, and I'll take those two buffet tables as well."

The clerk glanced back at the manager of the Hotel Hoffmann, obviously eager to return to him, and nodded. "Fine," he said. "If you take it now. It's ugly. The other customers don't like it."

"Now?" Maria stared at him.

"It's plaster," he said. "Very light. Yes! I'm coming."

Maria stepped forward, tentatively lifting the edge of the fountain. "Well," she said. "It's not that light. But we have the carriage." She nodded to herself and picked it up.

Elijah frowned and tried to take it from her, but she ignored him. It really wasn't heavy. Just awkward.

A light snow had dusted everything when they stepped outside, some flakes still drifting idly down. The cabdriver was walking the horses nearby. He saw them and waved, bringing the horses back over. Maria set the fountain down while he hitched them.

Elijah stood next to her. She glanced up at him and found him looking back at her. He quickly looked away.

"I have to go to the next warehouse," she said.

He nodded.

"You really don't need to come with me," she said, suddenly very aware of the amount of time she'd spent inside.

"I'm coming," he said, mildly but absolutely implacably.

"But you must have things to do. Important spy things."

"I'm not a spy."

"Right. Important undercover things."

"I'm doing them."

"What?"

"Right now. I'm doing the important undercover things. I told you your attack might be related to the code thefts. So I'm following you."

"Oh," she said. "But I don't see how it could be related when I don't know anything about the thefts."

He shrugged. "Shall we go on to the next warehouse? It's cold."

She stared at him, then gave up and loaded her fountain into the waiting cab.

Chapter Sixteen

He explained everything. His family is making him marry her—he loves only me. How sad my doubt made him. He shed so many tears—my heart broke at his tragic fate, for this woman—Adelaide—oh, she's so cold. He swore he will never touch her; they will be husband and wife in law only, for I am the wife of his heart.

—Journal entry of Elisabeth Wallner, 2 June 1847

"This one is even farther out," Maria explained as she settled back against the bench, a few flakes of snow clinging to her coat. She took her notebook from her pocket and began to do sums in it.

"Sixty-seven more chairs," she muttered. "Eight more tables."

When Eli's mother had married his stepfather, she and Eli had been plunged into East Coast high society. Despite his best efforts, Eli had some idea what a major society event looked like. Chairs matched. Tables matched. China matched. Probably the damn candlesticks matched.

But he was beginning to understand that the woman next to him was more like a mountain climber than an East Coast society matron. She saw a problem, sized it up, and then . . . walked over it. Or around it. Or through it, like a tiny battering ram.

The light was fading quickly, and they were far enough from the city that no streetlights lined the road. Something prickled the back of Eli's neck, a whisper of wariness.

You've been watching all day, he reminded himself. *No one is following her.*

His instincts refused to listen. He looked out the window. The road was lined with thick trees, black in the low light. It was quiet.

Usually, Eli didn't mind quiet. But this was thick quiet, made dense by the heavy trees. It wasn't the kind of quiet you could hear people coming in. It was the kind of quiet that covered their steps.

The carriage slowed to a stop. Maria closed her book, her expression confused. "This isn't the warehouse."

Eli didn't say anything. Instead, he let his hand fall gently on the hilt of the knife he had concealed inside his coat.

The door opened, and the cabbie's friendly face was illuminated by the running lights. "Sorry," he said, with an apologetic smile. "Got something caught in the back wheel and now it's tangled in the undercarriage. If you'll get out for a minute so I can get underneath I'll have it sorted right away."

"Oh," Maria said, gathering her coat around her. "Yes, of course."

When Eli didn't move, she frowned. "Did you not understand him? He said there's something caught—"

"I understood him," Eli said, thinking quickly. In an attack, it was better to be outside, where they could run, than inside, where they'd be trapped. He slid out, extending his arm to help her descend.

"Thanks," the cabbie said. He looked at the fountain. "Better to remove this as well." He pulled it out and set it next to them, and then got on the ground to look underneath.

"Where are we?" Eli asked Maria, quietly. The road was narrow and empty, the snow-dusted trees pressing in on them.

"Somewhere in the woods," she said, apparently unconcerned. "I told you the warehouse was out of town."

"Hmm," he said.

"This is really stuck," the cabbie said. "Would you look
around for a branch or something?"

Eli frowned. "No."

Maria hissed at him. "Of course," she said, walking off
before Eli could stop her.

He strode after her, grabbing her wrist. "Don't leave the
ro—"

There was a sudden clatter of horse hooves. They turned
just in time to see the cab rolling at top speed away from them.

"Wait!" Maria called, dashing into the road while Eli swore.
"What—where—what—"

"Stay close," Eli said, pulling her next to him while he
scanned the trees. But no movement came from the tree line.

"I don't understand what's happening," Maria said. He
glanced down. Her nose was already red from the cold.

"We've been stranded," he said, slowly. "I'm just not sure
why." If they were going to be attacked—well, the best moment would have been while they were distracted by the carriage driving away.

Maria exhaled. "My luck," she said, with great gravity, "has
not been good lately."

Eli ignored this, still watching the trees. Nothing. Even
more confusing, his instincts, which had been on high alert
the entire carriage ride, were calming down.

Next to him, Maria shivered. Eli swore again and took his
coat off.

"Don't," Maria said. "I'm not that cold."

He draped the coat around her shoulders anyway.

She made a huffing sound. "You're very stubborn."

"So people have told me. Where does this road lead?"

"I have no idea," she said. "I assumed to the warehouse,

which is near the river harbor at Freudenau. But given what just happened—" She bit her bottom lip.

"There's no reason to believe he was even heading in that direction," he finished. "We passed a village a few miles back. We'll have to walk there."

She nodded, squaring her shoulders. And then, to Eli's disbelief, she picked up the fountain.

"No," he said.

"Yes," she said.

"It's at least a four-mile walk," Eli said.

"And I paid two gulden for this. It's going to be the centerpiece of the ball. It's coming."

"Fraulein Wallner," Eli said, with what he considered admirable restraint. "The fountain stays."

"It's not your decision. I'm the one carrying it." She started walking.

Eli clenched his jaw and stopped talking. She'd tire soon enough.

They walked in silence. Night was falling swiftly, and soon it started to snow again. Eli glanced at Maria. She wore the determined expression he was coming to associate with her.

Why had the cabdriver abandoned them? It was beginning to seem more like a malicious joke than part of a planned assault. No one was following them. This was not the work of the person who had attacked Maria in the greenhouse. That person had been a professional.

The snow started coming down harder. Maria stopped, put the fountain down, and took Eli's coat off.

"I'm hot," she said, handing it back to him. She picked the fountain back up and kept walking, leaving Eli frowning behind her.

He shrugged into the coat. It smelled like her, of the light floral perfume she wore.

After another fifteen minutes of silent walking, she began

to tire. Oh, she didn't say anything—in fact, her expression remained entirely the same. But she was slowing, her feet shuffling more.

When she stumbled, Eli had had enough. "You can't carry it the whole way," he said.

"I most certainly can."

"You almost fell over, just now."

"But, I think you'll notice, I *didn't*."

He narrowed his eyes. She smiled sweetly at him and continued walking.

"You're going to injure yourself. For a plaster fountain. An objectively ugly plaster fountain."

"It's objectively ugly *now*. When I'm done with it, it will be a portal into a beautiful, dangerous world of moonlight and stars and magic."

"The women don't even look human," he said. "I don't think they could stand up in real life. And that one only has four fingers."

"Well, it's not like the fairies would notice. I hardly think they go around counting humans' fingers—" She stumbled again.

Eli clenched his jaw and took a deep, calming breath.

"Give it to me," he said.

"I'm fine!"

"Give me the damn fountain, Maria."

Her name rang out in the forested night.

She stopped walking, putting the fountain down. Heat flooded his face. They were hardly on first-name terms. He needed to apologize, immediately.

"I—"

She cleared her throat. "All right," she said, sounding strangely out of breath. She didn't look at him as he picked it up, simply started walking.

He followed her.

The night grew colder. He estimated they'd walked about half the distance to the small village they'd passed, but it was dark, and he couldn't be sure. They needed to hurry.

He heard the trickle of water ahead with relief. He remembered the shallow creek. They had passed the village, and ten minutes later a lane to some hunting lodge or another, and not long after they had splashed through the water. They couldn't be more than a mile and a half from the village.

They came to the edge of the creek. It was hard to tell in the dark, but he thought the water looked pretty shallow. Still, it was dark, and he wasn't completely sure.

"Stay here," he said, taking off his shoes and socks. "I'll go first with the fountain, and then I'll come back across to help you."

It was fully night now, so it was hard to say how he knew Maria rolled her eyes, but he absolutely knew she did.

"I'm fully capable of walking across less than a meter of shallow water, *Elijah*."

His breath stopped. "Eli," he said, after a long, frozen pause.

"I'm sorry?"

"If you're going to call me by my first name," he said, his throat tight, "it's Eli."

"Oh," she said, sounding out of breath.

Eli nodded. Put the emotions away. Started breathing again. "Just . . . stay there."

She didn't reply, but he saw a motion he decided to interpret as a nod. Good.

He put one foot carefully in the freezing water, feeling the bottom. It was slippery, but he was sure-footed.

Eli was halfway across when he heard the rustling. He barely had time to shout a warning before an enormous *thing* charged them from the bushes. He had an impression of *big* and *hairy* and *teeth* headed straight for Maria and flung himself into the thing's path. It slammed into him, knocking him sideways as something sharp tore into his side, and then, just as quickly as it had appeared, it disappeared into the brush.

"What," Eli said, astonished to find himself still standing.

Maria was in the water next to him, touching his side gingerly. "Are you all right? No, he got you. All right. We need to—"

"What was that?"

"A wild boar," she said. "We must have surprised it. We're very, very lucky it didn't fancy a fight."

A wild boar. Of course.

"We need to get help," she said. "We need to leave this stream. Why are you still holding that damn fountain?"

Eli looked down at the fountain. He hadn't realized he was still holding it. "I'm fine," he said, just as his foot slipped on an algae-covered rock, and he landed flat on his back in the dark water.

Chapter Seventeen

She's expecting a child in November. I was at one of Anna's stupid parties—I only went because Heinrich said he might go—and it was all political talk, revolution this and uprising that. Right as I was about to nod off from sheer boredom, Mitzi slunk up to me and whispered it in my ear. She wanted to [writing is illegible and blurred] she's always been jealous . . . But how could he do this?

Maybe it's not his.

—Journal entry of Elisabeth Wallner,
13 August 1848, referring to the pregnancy of
Baroness Adelaide von Eder

He landed, absurdly, with his arms straight up, holding the fountain clear of the water.

Maria would be very happy if she never saw that damn fountain again in her entire life. She also felt that said life had been considerably shortened by the last two minutes.

She tried to take the fountain from him.

"I'm fine," he said.

She ignored him, yanking the fountain from his grasp. She set it on the muddy bank and went back to help him up, but the cursed man was already standing, streams of water pouring off him. She couldn't see his wound, but her hands had blood on them from where she had touched his side before he fell in.

Her breath was refusing to steady, her heart pounding in her chest. "We need to stop the bleeding," she said, her voice implausibly calm, given the tumult inside her body. She pulled the edge of her skirt up until she had access to a bit of dry petticoat and tore it with her teeth. "Can you walk?" she asked, handing him the bit of white muslin. He was a large man, but she would drag him if she had to.

Eli looked offended as he took the fabric and pressed it against his side. "Of course I can walk."

"We passed a hunting lodge near here. We can clean the wound and bandage it there."

He hesitated, but nodded. And then, the idiot, he tried to pick up the fountain.

"Eli Whittaker," she said, her voice perfectly even. "If you lay a single finger on that fountain, I will happily tell Frau Heilig *exactly* when and where you eat breakfast every morning. I know she's been *longing* to continue your conversation about the tarot."

He froze.

"Good decision," she said. "Let's go."

She set a slow pace. He didn't speak as they walked, but soon his mouth was tight with pain. They needed to get to the lodge. She needed to see the wound, and clean it, and get him dry—

There. She saw the opening in the trees that heralded the lodge's drive and almost shouted.

"There," she said instead, quite calmly.

By the time they reached the lodge's front door there was a perceptible hitch in his step. No light came from inside.

"No one's here," Eli said. "We'll have to go on to the village."

Maria ignored him and opened the door. "These lodges

are usually left open," she said, steering him inside. "For exactly this reason."

It was very slightly warmer inside, and very, very dark. "Stay here," she said, and fumbled around until she felt a lamp and—thank God—a box of matches. After two failed tries, she lit the lamp, and a low orange glow revealed their surroundings.

It was a simple structure—most hunting lodges were. This was a single large room, with a cast-iron stove in one corner and cabinets of supplies along the far wall.

She set the lamp atop a cabinet and pulled some blankets out. "Take your coat off and sit here," she said, kneeling before the stove. Fortunately, whoever had last been there had left the wood and kindling well stocked, and in a few minutes she had the fire going. Then she rummaged through the cabinets, finding the medical supplies in the second one. She took the kettle from atop the stove and hurried out to the well for some water, grateful it wasn't frozen.

When she returned, he had taken his coat off and was sitting on the blankets, leaning against the wall with his eyes half closed. He opened them when she put the kettle on to boil.

"Give me the supplies," he said. "I'll bandage it quickly and we can press on to the village. I'm sure your grandmother is worried."

"I doubt anyone has even noticed I'm gone," she said, placing the supplies in a neat line and lighting a second lamp before she reached for the buttons of his shirt. He made a motion to stop her, and she lifted an eyebrow at him.

"You were gored by a wild boar," she said. "Please trust that I'm not trying to seduce you right now."

He sighed and let his hand fall, his eyes half closing again. She pursed her lips and undid the buttons quickly.

When she peeled the shirt away, Maria had to bite her lip to keep from crying out. The skin of his side was torn badly, yellow bruising already starting down one side of his chest.

She gently prodded along his ribs, her suspicion confirmed when he winced halfway down.

"You've cracked a rib," she said. He nodded, the gesture telling her he'd already known.

The water boiled. She stood and carried the kettle over, pouring it into a bowl. "This is going to hurt," she said.

But Eli didn't cry out as she cleaned it, only the tightness of his mouth telling her how much it hurt. She worked as quickly as she could, making sure the wound was rinsed and clean. When she had done the best she could, she put a thick layer of ointment on and then wrapped the bandage around his torso.

"It's shallow," she said, sitting back on her heels. "But boar wounds are known to cause infection. You'll need to see a doctor, and be very careful about keeping it clean."

"Thank you for bandaging it," he said, and after a deep exhale, reached for his shirt. "It's getting late, but someone in the village will take us into town, for the right price."

Oh, this idiot.

He winced as he tried to put an arm in the sleeve. Maria made another quick decision.

"I couldn't possibly," she said.

He paused in his struggle with the shirt. "What? Why not?"

"I'm tired," she said, sitting next to him on the pile of blankets and making a show of yawning.

"You're tired," he repeated.

"Yes, surprisingly. Experiencing a boar attack and having to save you from bleeding to death rather drained me. I couldn't take another step."

"You stay then. I'll walk ahead to the village—"

She ended this extremely foolish line of thinking by putting her head on his shoulder and yawning again. "I'll just rest here for a few hours. We can press on in the morning."

"But—"

She closed her eyes, and after a moment he relaxed beneath her, his breathing steadying. It was strangely comforting, the rhythm of his breath, and the blankets were soft, and the fire was warming the room nicely, and it really had been an awfully long day—

When Maria next opened her eyes, the gray light of dawn was drifting through the windows.

She yawned and blinked against the light. She was snuggled against Eli's warm, naked chest. A chest that was very visible in the morning light. She sighed in appreciation. A weak, early ray of sunlight danced over his stomach, as though it too understood art when it came across it. The shoulder she was resting on was strong and hard, and the broad muscles of his chest—

She glanced up at his face to find him awake and looking firmly straight ahead. His jaw was clenched.

She wanted to climb into his lap, wrap her arms around his neck, and—

The wave of desire was so intense it robbed her of all intelligent thought for several seconds. When she could breathe again she pushed herself up and away from him. The man was wounded, for God's sake. She shouldn't be ogling him.

"How are you feeling?" she asked, when she had collected herself sufficiently.

Eli cleared his throat. "Fine," he said, his voice tight.

She looked at his bandages and reached for the medical kit. "We need to change those," she said.

"I'll do it," he said, still not looking at her.

"You'll hurt yourself—"

"I won't—"

"You have a cracked rib—"

"Mar—Fraulein Wallner, I very much need you to not touch me right now." His words were tense, almost desperate.

Maria drew back. Looked down. Comprehended the problem.

"I'll go wash up," she said brightly, after two seconds of fraught silence. She pushed the bandages toward him. "Just . . . be careful."

He jerked his head in acknowledgment, and she left the room.

Outside, she leaned against the rough wood cladding of the lodge. Her cheeks were aflame. Her whole body was aflame, actually, with no sign of cooling despite the icy air.

"Collect yourself," she hissed. "It's hardly the first time you've been attracted to someone."

But . . . Eli Whittaker was a man to be wary of. The kind of man you didn't want to walk away from. The kind of man whose touch stayed with you.

The kind of man you didn't move on from.

And that thought was like a bucket of cold well water emptied over her head. She'd lived through three decades of a woman refusing to move on from a man. She wasn't going to become that. No matter how tempting and gorgeous the man was, he wasn't worth . . . that.

The door opened and Eli came out, his coat already on. He looked tired, and embarrassed, two blotches of color on his cheekbones. He cleared his throat.

"It shouldn't be far to the village," she said, her voice light and free of tension. "Are you sure you can walk?"

He grunted in affirmation and handed her the reticule she'd left inside.

The silence between them as they made their way to the main road was thick and tight. Eli broke it first.

"Thank you," he said. "For . . . caring for me. Last night."

"Of course," Maria said. "After all, you've saved my life three times. This doesn't even even the score."

"I wasn't very gracious last night," he said. "I'm not used to . . . to accepting aid."

"You astonish me."

"I . . . I apologize."

"Accepted."

Twenty minutes later, they finally reached the village. It was hardly more than a cluster of houses, but there was a tavern, probably to serve vacationing hunters as well as the locals. As they entered the dark room, Maria was suddenly aware of their rumpled appearance. The blood on Eli's shirt was mostly concealed by his coat, but some had spattered onto his collar, and she could imagine her own state. Fortunately, the handful of locals inside didn't seem to care, and a few minutes of conversation with the tavern owner produced both a vehicle and a driver (the owner's son).

Half an hour later, Maria and Eli rolled away in the back of a simple farm cart, usually used for transporting vegetables, judging by the cabbage leaves left behind. It was only another thirty minutes until they stopped in the alley behind the Hotel Wallner.

"Thank you," Maria said, handing some coins to the youth who had driven them. The city seemed loud and foreign, even after only a few hours away. It had been so close this whole time, but there in the trees with Eli, it had seemed so distant.

She pushed through the back door into the kitchen, Eli behind her. "I'll call the doct—"

"Maria!" Elisabeth ran across the kitchen and collapsed in her daughter's arms. "Oh, thank God, thank all the spirits, you're safe, you're fine!"

Her face was streaked with tears; her silk skirts were crumpled.

"Mother—"

"I thought—I thought—oh!" She broke off in a cascade of sobs.

"I'm all right," Maria said, "I'm all right. I'm so sorry I worried you. We had an accident—"

"I thought it was *her*—I thought she'd *killed you*—"

The lobby door opened and Josephine came through, apparently only returning now as well, judging by the evening attire she still wore. She stared at the scene before her, and lifted a singular eyebrow at Maria. Maria shrugged, befuddled. It wasn't as though it was the first night she'd spent away from the hotel.

"Who is 'her'?" Eli said, behind her. "Who did you think killed Maria?"

Elisabeth said something that was lost entirely to the front of Maria's gown.

"I can't hear you," Maria said, engaged in a silent, confused conversation with her grandmother.

"*Adelaide von Eder,*" Elisabeth said, then, in entirely clear tones, and for a moment, there was nothing but silence.

Then Elisabeth burst, once again, into tears.

"It's far too early for this level of dramatics, Elisabeth," Josephine said sternly, crossing to the kitchen counter and looking around for something. "Did Hannah make coffee? Now why don't you sit down and tell us *calmly* what the hell is going on?"

Elisabeth sniffled, but obeyed. "I shouldn't have doubted him," she said. "Heinrich said he was *taking care of it.*"

Well, that was dire. As far as Maria knew, Heinrich had never successfully taken care of anything in his life. "What is Heinrich taking care of, Mother?" she asked.

"The curse," Elisabeth wailed. "Adelaide von Eder has placed a curse on our family."

Chapter Eighteen

I cried and threw things, like an absolute shrew. He explained everything, of course. He had no choice—his family required an heir. How could I have doubted him! He simply did his duty, my brave Heinrich, when touching her brought him no more pleasure than touching a snake.

—Journal entry of Elisabeth Wallner, 15 August 1848

"Oh, Lord," Maria said. "All right. I'm sure Heinrich has that in hand. Now, Eli was gored by a wild boar last night, so I'm going to send for a doctor, and then see him to his room—"

"It can wait," Eli said, sitting down next to her mother. "Forgive me. When you say a curse—"

"It cannot wait," Maria said, with what she considered admirable calm. "And if you tell me you can't see a doctor every time you're gored by a wild boar I will absolutely dump that pot of coffee—yes, Grandmother, it's over there—on your head. And then scream."

He continued speaking to her mother. "Adelaide von Eder is Heinrich von Eder's wife, yes?"

Maria threw her hands up and walked to her office for a piece of paper and a pen to write a note for the doctor.

Elisabeth sniffed hastily and dried her eyes. "Only the

wife of the law," she said. "*I* am the wife of his heart. And she's never forgiven us for that, *never,* and now she's trying to *threaten* me, but she's chosen the wrong victim, because I have *resources,* and my faith is *strong*—"

"When you say threaten," Eli said, "what do you mean?"

"She's placed a curse," Elisabeth said. "And she won't remove it unless I stop seeing Heinrich."

"She told you that?"

"She wrote me a letter."

"May I see it?" Eli asked.

Elisabeth sniffled, but pulled a crumpled envelope from her skirts. Maria, crossing toward the lobby door to summon a footman, stopped.

"That's the letter that came for you on New Year's Day," she said.

Elisabeth nodded and handed it to Eli, who apparently had no compunction about reading other people's correspondence, because he quickly removed the letter, his eyes scanning its contents.

Maria peeked into the lobby and flagged down Abe.

"Will you get Hans to run this to Doctor Svoboda as quickly as he can?" she asked, quietly. "Thank you. And ask Helga to send bandages and hot water to 306."

"I see," Eli said, closing the letter.

"Well, *I* don't," Josephine said, crossly, and Eli handed the paper to her. Maria went to stand next to her, and they read it together.

Dear Frau Wallner,

I am writing to inform you of the curse I placed on you and your family last night. As you may be aware, my daughter is to be married in a few months to a man of some consequence, and though I have suffered the embarrassment of your affair with my husband for several decades, I find myself unwilling to let it damage my daughter's future any more than it already has. Therefore, I present to you an ultimatum: end the public aspect of your relationship with Baron von Eder, and I will have the curse removed. If not, it will remain in effect. I am not personally a practitioner of the occult, but I consulted the priest of my hometown in Hungary, who is a well-respected master of the black arts and who is fortuitously visiting Vienna for the new year, and I am assured the curse is of the highest quality.

I thank you in advance for your attention to this matter.

Sincerely,
Adelaide von Eder

Maria stared at the message.

"You *have* been making a damn fool of yourself over that man recently," Josephine said. "Even more than usual."

"Mother!"

Josephine shrugged. "I don't believe in this stuff, you know that," she said. "But it seems to me that, since you *do* believe, the simplest thing is to simply acquiesce. After all, she's not asking you to stop seeing him. She's just asking you to stop doing it in public."

Elisabeth straightened, tilting her nose regally. "I will *never* give in to that woman. I have already taken my own precautions, and they are working *very well*." She glanced at the witch ball. "And Heinrich will make her remove it."

"Ten minutes ago, you thought your daughter had been killed by this so-called curse," Eli said, slowly.

"I should never have doubted Heinrich, *or* myself." She turned to Maria, her expression abruptly earnest. "Maria, I *promise* you this will be taken care of. Your father is going to make her undo it. You don't need to worry. That's why I didn't tell you—it's practically over already."

Maria didn't really believe in curses either. But—her mother did. And still, she'd chosen Heinrich.

It was unreasonable to feel hurt. Her mother was who she was; there was no point in wishing otherwise. Beautiful, and foolish, and selfish, and charming. She'd been that way for Maria's whole life, and presumably long before.

She sighed. "Eli, the doctor should be here shortly. I insist you rest in your room."

She felt his eyes on her, and finally, he stood. She turned and left the room, with him behind her.

They walked wordlessly through the lobby and up the two flights of stairs to the third-floor landing.

"Would you—" Eli shifted his weight. Cleared his throat. "Would you like a drink? Your brother left a bottle in my room."

Maria stared at the faded carpet. In her memories, it was a vibrant tangle of pink roses and lush, dark green leaves. Now the colors blended together in various shades of tan. "Yes," she said.

She trailed behind him to his room, waiting while he unlocked the door and then following him inside. She sat on the foot of his bed while he rummaged around the desk, finding a glass and pouring something gold inside. Whiskey, if she knew Mac.

"My brother was here?"

"He and your grandmother came to threaten me."

She nodded. "That's sweet."

There was a knock on the door, and Maria stood to answer it. Helga's eyebrows lifted when she saw Maria, but she didn't comment on it, simply wheeling the cart with the supplies inside. "Doctor Svoboda will be here shortly," she said as she left, closing the door behind her.

Eli handed Maria the glass. She took a sip—whiskey.

"You don't believe in the curse," he said, picking up a coil of bandage and looking at it.

"Not really," she said. She took another sip, feeling it glide warm and comforting down her throat.

"Your mother believes in it, though."

"Yes." Another sip.

"But you don't think she'll—"

"No."

Eli nodded slowly, as though organizing all the small facts of her life, and she found abruptly that she didn't want to talk about it anymore.

"The doctor will be here soon," she said. "You should clean up."

He glanced at her, and for one unnerving moment she had the sense that he saw right through her. Then he returned his gaze to the bandages, picked them up, along with the water and some clean clothes, and went behind the dressing screen in the corner.

Maria stared out the window, watching a group of street performers below. That's right, it was Fasching. She'd forgotten.

A few minutes later, Eli reappeared, clean and freshly changed, his hair neatly brushed. He sat across from her and leaned forward, his dark, deep eyes serious, and suddenly she was thinking about his damn mouth again. It was almost a relief. "I don't think it will shock you to learn I also don't believe in curses."

"It does not."

"What I do believe in, though, is motive. And Adelaide von Eder has just announced hers to the world."

"You think she's behind the greenhouse attack."

He leaned back in the chair. "I'm curious what you think."

He was interviewing her again, which she probably shouldn't find *quite* so attractive.

She cleared her throat. "I suppose it's possible," she said. "But . . . it doesn't seem her style. She's put up with my mother and father for—well, I was born the year they were married, so my whole life. Though . . ." She trailed off in thought.

"What?"

She shrugged. "I understand why she did it. They were more embarrassing than usual on New Year's Eve. Since then too, more public. But—she wants something very specific. If she was the one who attacked me, I don't think she would hide it."

He nodded slowly. "All right."

"You're going to investigate her anyway."

"Yes."

"Why? If she's behind it then my attack is completely un-related to your code thefts."

"Then I'll know that."

Her eyes met his, and for a few seconds they stayed per-fectly still, simply looking at each other. She couldn't believe she'd once thought his gaze cold. It wasn't cold at all—it was reserved, yes, but beneath that was warmth, and passion, and—

There was a knock at the door.

"That will be Doctor Svoboda," she said.

She stood to let the doctor in. He was a man in his early sixties, with frizzy gray hair and a grumpy expression that hid a soft heart. He had been the family doctor since before Ma-ria's birth.

"Hello, Maria," he said, and then frowned, taking in her rumpled attire. "Were you in an accident? The message said a guest was hurt—"

"I'm fine," she assured him. "This is Mr. Whittaker. He had an encounter with a wild boar last night, and I'd like you to examine him."

"Hmm," the doctor said, looking sternly at Eli.

"I'll leave you, then. He'll probably tell you he's fine," she said to the doctor. "But—"

"I'm accustomed to difficult patients," Doctor Svoboda said, lifting his bushy eyebrows. "I treat your grandmother, after all. Run along."

She mustered up a smile, and left the room. In the hall-way she glanced down at her skirts. They were caked in dried mud, streaks of Eli's blood mingled in. She imagined the parts of her she couldn't see looked much the same.

Pulling her watch out, she checked the time. Two hours before she needed to be at the front desk for her shift. She needed to hurry, then.

But her body refused to hurry. She pulled herself up the last few stairs to the family apartments, and let herself into hers with a sigh. Heaviness sagged through her muscles. She was suddenly terribly tired.

She made herself take off her filthy clothes before collapsing on her bed. Her mind flitted from problem to problem—the ball, Eli's wound, the greenhouse attack, Eli's mouth, whether their tablecloths were in good enough condition for the ball.

The curse her mother believed in, and hadn't told her about. Hadn't done anything about.

It was all too much. She didn't know if she felt cursed. What she felt was tired.

And none of that mattered, because she needed to be at the front desk in an hour and forty-five minutes, and her hair currently resembled a sparrow's nest—if the sparrow had just lost a particularly bloody battle. She sighed and pushed her-self off the bed. Curses and men and tablecloths were simply going to have to wait.

She had a hotel to run.

Doctor Svoboda left after dispensing a meticulous wound cleaning and a severe lecture encompassing at least three languages: Czech, which Eli thought was the doctor's native tongue; German, which he used to convey official medical in-structions; and English, for words he particularly wanted to stress. *Fool* was among the English words used, as were *death* and *bad*. Eli's two weeks of Czech study had not prepared him to receive a lecture in the language, but combining his small vocabulary with Doctor Svoboda's facial expressions made him reasonably confident that the doctor was expressing his extreme annoyance and displeasure with patients who were so bored they had nothing better to do than go out and get gored by wild animals, with no thought for the doctor they might be inconveniencing.

Fortunately, Doctor Svoboda didn't seem to need (or indeed welcome) his patient's participation in this discussion, and so Eli simply sat quietly, nodded at the instructions, and bit down on the provided thick stick of wood when it was time to clean his wound.

"You will need to limit your movement, you understand?" the doctor said in German, after packing his bag. He switched to English. "*Rest. Rest.*"

Eli nodded, and the doctor frowned at him before bowing slightly and departing.

The clock said that it was just past two in the afternoon. The events of the last twenty-four hours had left him unmoored, outside time. He needed to collect himself.

He walked slowly to the coat stand, searching through his coat pockets until he found his notebook, and then crossed to the desk, staring out at the white-and-gold city beyond. The decorations he'd seen the day before—or was it two?—were everywhere now. *Fasching,* Maria had called it. Carnival.

The madness one needs to maintain sanity.

The Viennese idea of madness seemed to be one of waltzing and laughing, of fun and glamour and illusion, of excess. Eli wondered what Maria would say if he told her the mirror image of that madness wasn't sanity, but another kind of derangement: a distorted image of sanity, a madness of dark rooms and silence, of purity and fanaticism. Of quiet, desperate tears instead of wild, desperate laughter.

His ribs gave a pain, jerking him back to the present.

Eli lived his life firmly, intentionally, in sanity. The Viennese madness might feel less . . . threatening . . . than the other kind, but it was every bit as destructive.

With a sigh, he opened his notebook, and wrote down the word *curse,* followed by a handful of names.

Did he see how Adelaide von Eder might be connected to the stolen codes? No. Under a strict understanding of his assignment, he had no reason to visit Baroness von Eder this afternoon.

He closed his notebook, and got up to finish dressing.

The bruising around his torso had fully set in; the adrenaline of the night before was entirely gone. He *hurt.* Getting into a fresh shirt had been a trial; his suit jacket was even more so. And then there was a struggle with his shaving gear, followed by an undignified debacle with his shoes, but at last he stood by the door, dressed and presentable, if not a particularly pleasing sight to look upon.

Maria's seen you look worse, he reminded himself, and then clenched his jaw as he grew warm. *Not that it matters what she thinks of your appearance,* he hastened to add.

Infatuations were really very foolish things. Briefly, he remembered the humiliating incident earlier, when he had woken with her body pressed against him and—

He clenched his jaw and thought firmly of other things.

The von Eders' city address was a mere five minutes' walk from the Hotel Wallner.

The Innere Stadt, the part of Vienna surrounding the grand, enormous court of the Hapsburgs, was densely packed, narrow medieval and Roman streets lined with grand, elaborate stone buildings. The Palais Eder was one of the more ostentatious on its short street, four stories high and seven large windows wide. Its front door sat beneath an entry of carved stone, supported by four imposing pillars, each one as wide as Eli.

He frowned at them and knocked on the door.

A butler in a crisp suit opened it, looked Eli up and down, said, "The trade entrance is in back," and would have closed the door in his face if Eli's foot hadn't gotten in the way.

"I'm here to see Baroness von Eder," Eli said, handing over his card. He was used to bullying his way into the homes of wealthy suspects.

The butler read the card slowly. "She's not at home to visitors. I'll tell her you called." He stared pointedly at Eli's foot. Eli stared back, and they might have stayed like that for some time if they hadn't been interrupted by a great clattering on the street.

Eli turned to see Mac driving a cabriolet at top speed toward the house. He drew the horse up at the last minute, tossed the reins to a scrambling footman, and jumped out before the carriage had even properly stopped.

"Good," he said to Eli, as he stomped up the walk. "You're here. Open the damn door, André."

The butler opened the damn door, and Mac stormed through, Eli following in his wake.

"I take it you heard," Mac said, pulling his driving gloves off and throwing them onto a side table. "I went to the hotel for coffee this morning. Hannah told me. André, where's my mother?"

"She said she wasn't to be disturbed," the butler said.

"I'm sure she did," Mac muttered. "I'll ask one more time. *Where* is my mother?"

"With Count von Kaufstein and his son," the butler said, glaring at Mac in disapproval. "They're having a meeting about the wedding."

"Hah!" Mac said. He nodded to Eli. "Come on."

Eli obeyed. He wasn't sure why Mac seemed to think of him as an ally, but if it got him access to Baroness von Eder, he wasn't going to fight it.

Mac strode down a wide marble hallway, with windows on one side framed by red velvet curtains and large oil paintings, presumably of past von Eders, hung on the other. An elaborate fresco occupied the ceiling, though Eli wasn't able to make out the subject while walking.

They turned at the end of the hallway and went through a series of large rooms, each dominated by crystal chandeliers and gilded walls, until they paused before a large set of doors.

"My mother's lair," Mac said briefly, before pushing the door open.

The room was pleasant and airy. Large, paned windows overlooked a hibernating rose garden, dusted prettily with snow. A grand piano sat in one corner, glossily reflecting the cold Viennese sky.

Four people sat around a low table near one of the windows: an elderly man, a younger man who resembled him, and two women who looked enough like Mac that Eli was sure they were his mother and sister.

All four were staring at them.

"Mac?" The older woman spoke first. She was probably in her early forties, blond and blue-eyed, with a kind of cool, contained beauty. She was dressed conservatively, her dress simply cut and almost without ornamentation.

"Mother," Mac said, bravado thick in his voice. His cheeks were flushed, half from anger and half from the embarrassment of accosting his mother, Eli imagined. "I need to speak to you."

She blinked at him. "As you can see, I am occupied," she said, turning back to the party gathered around the table. "After they leave the church, the procession will return here for the wedding breakfast—"

"I want a buffet," Mac's sister said. "They're all the fashion—sit-down breakfasts are so old-fashioned—"

"*Mother,*" Mac said. "I must request your attention."

Another man, one less curious and more polite, might feel awkward. Eli only wished he could pull out his notebook.

Baroness von Eder sighed. "I'm so sorry about this," she said, to her guests. The elderly man—presumably Count von Kaufstein—chuckled and waved a dismissive hand. "Annalise, we will be inviting the Emperor. I have no intention of entertaining His Imperial and Royal Majesty at a *buffet*. Mac, Secretary Berko is in his office. Please find him and make an appointment in the usual way. *Now.* At the wedding breakfast, the centerpieces will consist of white roses and orange blossoms—"

"Fine," Mac said, taking a deep breath. "I've just come from the Hotel Wallner—"

"*Enough.*"

The room fell silent at the Baroness's command.

She closed her eyes and took a breath. "I will speak to you briefly in the morning room," she said. "Wait there."

Mac nodded sharply, and left the room. Eli followed.

"My sister's wedding," Mac said, walking quickly down another hallway. "The groom's almost forty. Practically as old as my mother. But he's the son of the Imperial and Royal Chamberlain, and so I suppose that justifies . . . well, apparently it justifies anything at all."

"Imperial and Royal Chamberlain?"

"In charge of His Majesty's personal household," Mac explained briefly, opening the doors to a room that looked much like the last one, but without a piano. He flung himself down in a silk chair. Eli sat across from him. "Runs the place. In charge of the royal purse, too. Of course, the old man's a royal bastard, like Maria's grandmother. Half siblings."

The door opened before Eli had time to react, admitting Baroness von Eder.

In his time with the Secret Service, Eli had faced several of the more dangerous criminal bosses on the Eastern Seaboard. They were more diverse than one might expect. Some were merely small-time thugs who had, through luck and an appetite for brutality, risen in the ranks until they were on top. But then there were the *thinkers*. These were rarer; people who had wit and intellect and combined that with a perfect disregard for any ethical boundaries that inconvenienced them.

Eli's first impression of Adelaide von Eder was that she fit the latter category. Some people would disregard her, because she was a woman. But Eli had never been under the impression that women were weak—look at his mother and Maria.

They could also be dangerous.

He and Mac stood. Eli bowed.

"You placed a *curse* on the Wallners?" Mac exclaimed.

Baroness von Eder's expression, cold and composed, barely flickered. "I don't believe I'm acquainted with your guest."

"This is Eli Whittaker," Mac said, carelessly. "From the American Legation. Mother, how could you—"

"Forgive me, Mr. Whittaker, but I do not perfectly understand your involvement in this family matter."

"I—"

"He's involved because he's the one who keeps saving Maria's life," Mac snapped. "You need to remove the curse, and you need to do it *now*."

The Baroness lifted one eyebrow, a facsimile of amusement on her lips. "No," she said. "Mr. Whittaker, I really must ask you to leave. This is a private matter between me and my son."

"Forgive me," Eli said, before Mac could interrupt. "But it doesn't seem to be a private matter. At the very least, it seems to be a declaration of ill will against the entire Wallner family. Maria Wallner's recent troubles have intersected with a case

I'm investigating. I'd like to ask you a few questions about the letter you sent yesterday."

"Would you?" The Baroness smiled thinly. "I hardly think you have jurisdiction here, Mr. Whittaker from the American Legation. Besides, my letter was quite clear."

"Oh, it was clear all right," Mac said. "How *could* you? A curse against Elisabeth, fine, you've both done worse to each other over the last thirty years. But to include Maria and Josephine? What have they ever done? You cursed my *sister*, Mother."

"She is *not* your sister," Baroness von Eder said, her voice ringing coldly through the small room.

"She damn well is," Mac said. "And since you cursed her, she's almost died. *Twice.*"

Thrice, Eli thought, but didn't correct him.

"I'm surprised you believe in such things," the Baroness said, shrugging. "Anyway, if it *is* real, her mother has the power to save her at any time."

"*You* have the power—"

"She is not *my* daughter. I have my own daughters to worry about."

There was a tense pause.

"You don't believe in the curse?" Eli asked, mildly.

"To be honest, Mr. Whittaker, I don't care. Elisabeth Wallner believes, and that's all that matters."

"You—"

Eli waved a hand at Mac to quiet him. "I hope you'll forgive my ignorance," he said. "I'm unfamiliar with curses. What exactly is it you have done?"

"Apparently curses are a very advanced art," she said. "And the priest from my village, Father Ardelean, is the very best. It was a fortunate coincidence he was in Vienna this winter."

"And it's against the entire Wallner family?"

She nodded.

"This is black magic, Mother."

"Actually, I am confused about that," Eli said. "You're Catholic, yes? Do you mean you used a Catholic priest? I didn't know curses were part of that faith."

"They're not," Mac said, still staring at his mother. "But the part of Hungary my mother comes from—the priests there do it."

Eli nodded. Religions were odd like that. "Why all of the Wallners?" he asked. "Why not just Elisabeth?"

"I thought perhaps she loved them enough," the Baroness said, shrugging. "So far, of course, that seems like a silly bet. It was worth a try. And now I really must—"

"I won't be in this house while you do this," Mac said. His voice was firmer than Eli had ever heard it. "If this is the path you choose, I won't share a roof with you."

There was a short, empty silence.

"You must do as you think right," his mother said, and then she turned and left, leaving Mac staring after her.

"She—" Mac broke off, nodding slowly. "All right. All right."

He looked . . . heartbroken. Clearing his throat awkwardly, Eli stepped slightly closer. Just as he was debating patting the man's shoulder, Mac spoke.

"I knew she hated them. But I never thought—"

Eli cleared his throat again. "No child wants to believe the worst of their parent," he said, stiffly, after a pause.

"She chose this. I told her I would leave, and she still chose this."

"Yes."

Mac took a long breath, and another. "All right," he said, again. "That's that. I have to pack. André will see you out."

Chapter Nineteen

We served the last dinner in the restaurant tonight.
There were three guests. From tomorrow the restaurant
is breakfast only. Hannah and I cried in the kitchen,
afterward.

—Journal entry of Maria Wallner, 23 March 1875

The floors were done.

Eight years of damage, and three days of work had set them right. The workmen had departed that afternoon, and as soon as Maria had finished her shift she had sprinted up the stairs to see them, her earlier fatigue forgotten.

Now she stood in the middle of the Large Ballroom, heavy rain beating against the tall windows. It had begun a few hours earlier, and hadn't relented since. In the real, mundane world this meant soggy skirts and muddy shoes, and that tomorrow the roads would be impossible.

But here, in this marvelous room, Maria could feel the Hotel Wallner beginning to weave its old spell. The dark gray light turned softly gold when reflected off the newly shining floors, promising dancing, and ease, and warmth, and laughter. The rain beat against the window in three-quarter time.

Maria went to get the ladder. The hotelkeeper could only help weave the spell; she could not afford to be caught in it.

She'd been able to find a repairman who would fix the

workings of their damaged crystal chandelier for a reasonable price—practically a miracle on such short notice. She dragged the ladder beneath it and climbed up to begin removing the dozens of dusty crystal drops that hung there, to prepare it for removal to the repairman's workshop.

Would a woman who was cursed find a repairman to fix her broken chandelier in the middle of Fasching?

There were one hundred and fourteen crystal drops. She would begin polishing them while the body was being repaired. She considered herself quite a professional, after the chandelier in the Small Ballroom.

She hummed under her breath as she worked. It was a pleasant task. With plenty of time for daydreaming. She'd given up trying to banish linen closets from her mind; she would simply trust that she could keep the fantasy strictly where it belonged.

The door to the ballroom opened, and Hannah rushed in with a covered plate, her face pink and smiling. "The cake molds we ordered came."

"Ooh," Maria said, hurrying down from the ladder. "And?"

"And *voilà.*" Hannah whipped the cloth off the plate, revealing four palm-sized almond cakes, perfectly shaped like roses.

"Oh *Hannah*," Maria said, picking one of the cakes up and staring at it. "Oh. It's perfect. Look at the petals!"

"I know. You can see every one. I was afraid the ridges would dry out the cake, but they're delicious."

Maria took a bite, and moaned in pleasure. "My God. Are they better? Is that possible? I didn't think that was possible."

"It shouldn't have been possible, but *I think so too,*" Hannah said, her smile beaming.

"They're perfect. They're going to be the star of the ball. You'll have to make hundreds. People are going to devour them."

Hannah sighed, a sound of pure joy. She was never happier than when people were eating her food.

Maria finished the cake, popping the last bite in her mouth with relish.

"Here, keep the rest for later," Hannah said, walking across to the windows and setting the plate on a ledge.

"You know, I spoke to the owner when I placed the order," she continued after a moment, still facing the wall. "And I asked—just out of curiosity, and because maybe—maybe *someday*—anyway, I asked if they could do custom molds. Like this rose, but with the hotel's initials on it, in the middle. I thought—in the restaurant—" She broke off.

Maria lifted her eyebrows. "Yes?"

Hannah turned to face her. "That maybe—when we have the money—we could order some. And they could be our signature cake."

"It's a wonderful idea," Maria said, already weaving it into her vision for the future. The guests loved the almond cakes they served in the lobby at check-in. Now she imagined them not only in the lobby but the restaurant, advertising the hotel with every delicious bite. The idea sent a thrill down her spine.

"Really?"

"Yes, really. We can't afford it now, but you should get a quote from the owner. For . . . for when we're back," she said, the words sending an excited tingle through her chest.

Hannah nodded enthusiastically. "I will," she said. "I—" She broke off when the ballroom doors slammed open, blushing when Mac walked through them. "Oh," she said, abruptly sounding out of breath. "Mac. You must be here to see Maria. I'll just—"

She hurried from the room.

Maria hid a smile. Hannah had had a crush on Mac for years. Nothing would come of it; their class difference was too great for marriage, and unlike Maria, Hannah was not the type to engage in nonmarital relations. But . . . it was still sweet.

Mac strode forward, his expression thunderous.

"What on earth's the matter?" Maria asked, focusing back on her brother. "Are you all ri—"

He put his arms around her and squeezed tight.

"Oh," Maria said, wrapping her arms around her brother's waist. "Is everything—"

He pulled back. "Forget about me. Are *you* all right?"

"Of course," she said, confused.

"My damnable mother," he said. "I've moved out."

"You *what*?"

"I told her I wouldn't share a roof with her while she did this. You're my *sister*. You've almost died twice, and it's because of her!"

"What— Oh. The curse. Mac, I don't know that I believe—"

"How can you doubt it?" he asked. "She placed it on New Year's Eve, and the very next day a man shot at you in your own hotel!"

Not to mention the carriage that shouldn't have been there . . . She pushed the thought away. She had enough problems without adding a curse to the list.

"We've always lived an exciting life, Mac."

"I asked her to remove it," he said, and then swallowed. "She wouldn't. I *asked* her to."

"Oh, Mac," Maria said, softly. The expression on his face was heartbreaking: betrayal and love and horror all mixed up together.

Mac had lived a more protected life than Maria. Though he'd known about his father's other family—it was hard to avoid knowing—his mother had kept him away from the Wallners until he was old enough to seek Maria out himself. He hadn't grown up with the reality of his father's actions displayed before him. While Maria often felt there was nothing further her parents could do to disappoint her, Mac still nurtured a few fantasies.

One being that his mother was merely a victim, collateral damage of a love affair gone on too long.

This wasn't a terrible stretch. Adelaide probably *had* suffered the most of the three. Maria wasn't even sure she blamed her for the curse. Though she certainly should have left Josephine out of it.

"You need to take this seriously," Mac said.

"It's not exactly that I'm not taking it seriously," she said. "It's just—curse or no, I have a hotel to run. And a ball to throw."

Mac let out a long breath. "You're right. I'll deal with it."

"That's not what I meant."

"No. It's my mother. God knows you've cleaned up enough of Elisabeth's messes. I'll take care of it."

"Mac—"

"Is it all right if I move in here? To the hotel? I'll pay, obviously."

"Your mother will hate it."

"Good," he said, a look of anger she'd never seen before on his face. "Maybe she'll know how I feel, then."

Maria sighed in defeat. If she didn't let him move in, he would simply go elsewhere, and she'd rather have him where she could see him, if he was in this mood. "Fine," she said. "Let Abe know."

"Already did," he said, glibly, his mood abruptly restored. "Thanks, Maria. And don't worry. But also, stay away from duels. And dark, secluded greenhouses. Are those Hannah's almond cakes?"

"Yes."

He took one and turned to leave. "I'll see you at supper," he said. "This will be fun!"

She stared after him. Fun. It wasn't going to be fun when

Elisabeth and Adelaide found out. It was going to be an apocalypse.

She climbed the ladder and resumed detaching the crystal
drops. There was no more time for daydreaming, or stray rel-
atives, and especially no time for apocalypses.

It was then, of course, that a flood descended from the
heavens.

Chapter Twenty

This time I saw him—Beethoven, that is. I took Jose-
phine. There are no words for what we heard. His ninth
symphony. He has almost entirely lost his hearing, and
so the audience threw things in the air, determined to
show their love for him . . . Josephine and I threw our
hats, our handkerchiefs, our programs. . . .
—Journal entry of Theresa Wallner, 8 May 1824

Maria landed hard on the floor, the water knocking her off the ladder. She looked up through waterlogged hair to see the chandelier swinging wildly, three hundred pounds of crystal saved from shattering by only a thin rope—and *oh no* the floors—

She had to stop the water. Her floors. Her precious floors.

She pushed herself up, slipped and fell, and was about to try again when a very annoyed-looking man stomped through the pool of water.

"Are you hurt?" Eli shouted over the flood of water.

She shook her head. "But—"

He waved her off, righted the ladder, and peered around the torrent. His hair was already wet from it.

"Turn off the water," he shouted.

"How," she said, looking frantically at the rain outside. "I'm not God."

"What?" He turned, saw her gaze, and rolled his eyes impatiently. "It's a burst pipe. Your roof is three floors above us."

Maria said nothing, already running down the stairs to the basement, where the mechanical room sat next to the laundry. Quickly she turned the wheel that controlled the water to the bathrooms, until it was completely off. She tore into the laundry, grabbing an enormous armful of dirty sheets and towels waiting to be washed, and raced back up the stairs into the ballroom, where—*Thank God*—the torrent had stopped.

She threw the linens down and began frantically wiping the floors. Eli joined her, and when everything was soaked, she ran to the linen closet in the hall, threw every clean towel and sheet in it into the linen cart inside, and hurried back.

"Here," she said, hurriedly tossing the dry stuff out and loading the wet stuff in, before joining him in wiping.

"They're going to be fine," he said, pushing wet hair away from his forehead. "We got it before too much water accumulated. It didn't have a chance to sit."

Maria nodded, her throat tight. She didn't trust herself to speak until every last drop of water had been sopped up.

Finally, fifteen minutes later, she sat back on her heels. "All right," she said. "All right."

She looked down at her hands. They were shaking.

Eli walked in front of her and crouched down so they were eye-to-eye. "They're going to be fine," he said again. "Look. They didn't take damage."

Maria made herself glance around. The floors looked no different than they had before. Well, perhaps a little cleaner.

"The chandelier—"

"Is secure. I checked it."

She took a shaky breath. Released it. The floors were going to be fine. The chandelier was secure. Eli had checked. She took another breath. "Why are you so *competent*?"

He frowned, pushing wet hair off his forehead. "I believe I am of average competence."

Maria laughed. "Trust me, you're not. In the few days I've known you, you have disarmed a drunk aristocrat, bandaged your own gunshot wound, fought off a man trying to murder me, saved Jakob's orchids *and* my life some uncountable number of times, determined the cause of a flood, rescued my floors, examined my chandelier, and I'm *fairly sure* also learned to waltz. And that's only the things I know about."

Eli looked uncomfortable. "I just . . . do what is needed."

When she continued to stare, he shrugged. "When—when I was growing up, that was—there was—" He stopped talking. Frowned more deeply. Stood up. "I'll put these in the cart."

He gathered the last of the wet linens from the floor and dumped them in with the others.

There was what?

But the tense set of his shoulders told her there would be no more information forthcoming, and prying would only distress him. She went to look at the damaged ceiling instead.

It was bad. There was an actual hole in the plaster, about a foot across, and water damage a meter in every direction.

"It was intentional," Eli said from beside her, peering up into the hole.

"What?" Maria asked, beginning to add up estimates for a plumber and plasterers.

"The pipe," he said. "Someone cut it."

"*What?*"

"This plaster is all old, though, so they didn't go in from this side. What's above this?"

"Guest rooms," Maria said, faintly. "Not currently in use."

"Let's go look, then."

He didn't wait for her assent, simply striding from the ballroom. He'd taken off his suit jacket during the catastrophe, and she was briefly distracted by the line of his back muscles through his damp white shirt. She shook her head and followed him to the third floor.

It couldn't be sabotage. He naturally had a very suspicious mind, but surely no one had deliberately damaged her plumbing. Who would do that? And why?

Eli stopped on the third-floor landing. "Where?"

"This way," she said, leading him down the hallway opposite his own. From the hallway no one could tell these rooms were different. The carpet was clean and swept, the doors and moldings dusted and polished regularly.

Maria thought about the shape of the ballroom below her, and stopped before 316. "I think this is the one over the chandelier."

She unlocked the door and stepped inside, Eli behind her. It was dark inside, and she crossed the room to draw the curtains back. The weak, cloudy light illuminated the room, drifting over dust covers and torn wallpaper. Embarrassment heated her face.

"We're going to renovate this wing soon," she said, but Eli didn't seem to register the disrepair. He was looking at the floor.

"Someone's been in here."

She followed his gaze. Faintly visible on the dust-covered carpet were several clearly outlined footprints.

"One of the maids, maybe," she said, but she didn't believe the words even as she said them. There would be no reason for the staff to enter one of these rooms without her knowledge.

Eli followed the footprints to the bed, careful not to mar them. He looked beneath it, and when he straightened, his expression was grave. He pushed the bed away, and revealed a cut piece of carpet.

Maria swore.

Eli pulled the carpet up, revealing patched wood beneath.

A bit of effort brought that up, and soon they were looking through wood beams at the ballroom below.

"I don't understand," Maria said, blankly. "Why would someone do this?"

"Someone who doesn't want your ball to happen," Eli replied, putting the wood patch back in place.

"I don't— What has my poor ball ever done to anyone?" The sentence came out almost as a wail, embarrassing her. She prided herself on overcoming obstacles, but this— Were there not obstacles enough without someone intentionally damaging her plumbing?

"How difficult would it be for someone to access this room without you or your staff knowing?"

She shoved down the part of her wanting to burst into tears. "Not difficult at all. The easiest thing in the world on a night we have a ball, like New Year's, or if the person was a guest. Even if they weren't staying here, we aren't able to keep someone in the lobby every minute. If a guest needs us, we could easily be away from the front desk for several minutes or more."

The first thing to change, she thought. From now on, the person at the front desk stayed there.

"Even the other day, when we were in the ballroom—" She froze. "The man who interrupted us."

His gaze sharpened. "Middle aged. Slender. Gray hair. Mustache."

"There was no reason for him to be on the second floor," she said, slowly. "The restaurant is clearly marked."

Her body went cold as she thought about someone walking around her hotel, attempting to harm it right under her nose.

And then she thought about dark greenhouses, and strong hands around her throat.

"Do you think he was the man who attacked me?" She asked the question quietly.

Eli shook his head. "Your attacker was large. Perhaps just a little shorter than I am. The man in the ballroom was much smaller."

She didn't know whether that soothed her or frightened her even more. "I don't understand why all this is happening."

"Neither do I," Eli said. "But I'm going to find out." He stood, and held a hand out to her. She looked at it. His hand was broad and capable, like him.

"Why?"

He looked impatient. "Why what?"

"Why are you helping me? And don't say because of your investigation, because we both know someone sabotaging my ballroom has nothing to do with diplomatic codes."

"I know nothing of the kind," he said, his voice dismissive, the kind of formal tone government clerks tended to adopt when they were aware of a problem and had no intention of acknowledging it.

She kept looking up at him. The pale light from the window drifted over his harsh features, making his nose and jaw more severe. He frowned more deeply, his luscious mouth stern and set.

"Your side," she said.

"What?"

"Oh," she said, ignoring his hand and pushing herself up. "Your bandages must have gotten wet. You should change them."

He sighed. "You don't need to—you don't need to take care of me."

"Does anyone? Take care of you?"

Maria would have taken the question back the second it left her mouth if she could. He stared at her, a shadow from the curtains falling softly on his face.

"I do," he said, and there was utter finality in his voice. "*I take care of me.*"

"I don't think you're doing a very good job."

"I beg your pardon?"

There was a warning in his voice. She plunged on anyway. Recklessly. "I said you were competent, earlier, but that's not the whole truth. You're incredibly competent, for other people. But you also got shot and didn't see a doctor. I think, if I hadn't summoned one, you wouldn't have seen one for the wound in your side, either."

"I told you," he said. "I can hardly see a doctor every time I have a minor wound."

"Firstly, neither of those were minor," she said. "Being shot is not minor. Being gored is not minor. But secondly, *yes,* you can. You can absolutely go see a doctor every time you have a minor wound."

He was silent for a long time, his lips pressed tightly together. For a moment, she thought he would simply walk out.

"I don't think you're in a good position to lecture me," he said, instead. "You do the same thing."

Maria frowned. "No, I don't."

"Yes, you do. If the accusation is that I do a good job of caring for others and a bad job of caring for myself, yes, you do. You have all these friends and family, and they're all desperate to help you." He paused. "Well, maybe not your mother," he allowed. "But the rest. And you don't let them."

"I don't need their help," she said, not understanding.

"Of course you don't," he said, dryly. "Your life has been so smooth lately. Maria, you barely let me carry the damn fountain."

"It was my fountain," she said, confused. "And I *did* eventually."

An unwelcome memory pressed into her mind, of the rather delicious tone of his voice when he'd demanded she let him carry it. Frustration and command, wrapped up in one shiver-inducing package.

The truth was, she was letting him help her far more than she should. All her life, she'd seen her mother rely on others to solve her problems.

Maria never wanted to be that person. She would accept his help because the hotel was in jeopardy, but that was all. She couldn't get used to him.

She couldn't keep him.

"I suppose it's neither of our business," she said, suddenly tired. "Change your bandages, Eli."

She sent him a conciliatory smile, and left the room.

Chapter Twenty-one

*The Russians have declared against the Ottomans, and
what our own Empire is to do no one knows. . . . The
city is in a panic, Bosnia and Herzegovina on every
tongue, and yet no one, including our own ministers,
seems capable of locating the region on a map. . . .*

—Journal entry of Maria Wallner, 25 April 1877

January 10

Eli slept fitfully, his ribs hurting and the—argument? dis-
agreement? discussion?—with Maria looping through his
mind. He was awake before his small travel alarm clock rang,
sitting at the desk, staring out at the pale, icy dawn.

She'd asked why he was helping her, and he'd told her it
was because of the codes. That excuse was growing rather
thin, of course—even she saw through it. He should be focusing on Director Farrow and Secretary Collins rather than the
Wallners. But . . . something about the codes case was beginning to seem a bit thin as well.

Everything was off-balance, just like the ever-present waltz.
Vienna was chaos, the case was chaos, the Hotel Wallner was
chaos, but somehow, like the waltz, they all spun on. So, for
now, he would go where the chaos led him.

Chaos was a late riser though, so Eli spent an hour on

calisthenics, another hour on his Czech, and a third reading a chapter on Catholicism in one of his books. Yesterday's conversation with Baroness von Eder had made him realize how woefully underinformed he was on non-Protestant Christianity. By the time he had confirmed that indeed, curses were not standard practice, it was time to have breakfast in the restaurant and leave for the Legation.

The sun was bright above him as he walked to work. It had snowed again, a fine layer coating the magnificent buildings towering above him. Everything here was so fine—Vienna made Washington and New York look like farm towns. The city spoke of wealth, a kind of wealth unthinkable in America because it was the wealth of centuries, and of empire.

Eli hadn't truly understood what empire meant before Vienna. It sat beneath everything here—the soldiers on the street in their splashy uniforms; the ornamentation on the buildings; even the design of the city itself, the new, wide, beautiful Ringstraße and the old, magnificent, enormous Hapsburg court at the center of it all, the spider at the center of its web. Everything came together to proclaim the power of the Hapsburgs, the might of the Austro-Hungarian Empire, and to position Vienna as the pinnacle of it all. The grandest, richest city in the world.

He arrived at the Legation with the rest of the staff. They stared at him openly, some with simple curiosity, others with hostility. His questioning that week had been received with shock and suspicion, mingled with concern. Many of these men would have *something* to hide, even if it had nothing to do with stolen codes. The extramarital affair count was up to three, including one involving Director Farrow.

He settled at his desk and resumed work on his stacks of files. He *was,* after all, a financial investigator. This was what he was good at.

Around one, the office slowly emptying as people went

to lunch (lunch! they'd only been there for two hours), Eli reached the conclusion that there was *something* off in the account books. It was still mostly a . . . a feeling. The numbers weren't adding up, which could be a simple error, but the *way* they weren't adding up had an indescribably intentional feeling behind it.

He closed the book casually as he heard Secretary Collins approach, reaching just as casually for another file, as though he had simply scanned the accounts and moved on.

"Telegrams for you," Collins said, dropping two messages on his desk. Eli grunted in acknowledgment, waiting for the man to leave, but he lingered.

"How's the investigation going?" he asked.

"I'm not at liberty to discuss it," Eli said, picking up the first telegram. It was from Undersecretary Wallace. Apparently, he'd discovered that Eli was no longer undercover, and was displeased. Eli crumpled the message and put it in his pocket for later disposal.

"We're all so interested, you know," Collins continued. "It's the most exciting thing that's happened here in years."

Eli didn't bother answering. The second telegram was from his second-in-command, Robert Kasinsky.

Informing him that Senator Edward Markham had not been arrested.

Eli stared at the message, his fingers gripping it tightly, as Collins chattered on in the background.

Orders from higher-ups not to arrest Markham, the telegram read. *Charges dropped against everyone but Judge Roberts. Bantry investigation limited to "the criminal element." Team advised not to tell you but decided you should know.*

He read it again, then put it in the same pocket. He would burn them both later. He pulled the books back in front of him, and eventually Collins got tired of talking to himself and wandered away.

They hadn't arrested Markham.

The charges against the others had all been dropped, except against the least powerful and most obviously implicated person.

Further investigation had been blocked.

And suddenly, Eli understood very, very clearly why he'd been sent to Vienna.

Fury curled through him, tightening his muscles, shortening his breath. He wondered if Undersecretary Wallace had been bribed, or if it was as simple as a wealthy friend asking for a favor. That was how the world worked. They saw each other's crimes. They just didn't care about them.

Wealth covered even the most grotesque crimes.

For a minute he thought about marching straight to the ticket office and booking passage home, Vienna case be damned. He would go home, and *sort* things. Let them tell him to his face they weren't going to arrest those men because they were too wealthy and too powerful. Let them feel their complicity and their cowardice, let it sink into their bones.

But then he thought about Maria. And that too, was very, very clear. He would stay in Vienna. Not for the case, but for her. He would stay until she was safe.

Unfortunately, that only caused more frustration to course through his body. Every way he turned, there was a wall, until he felt angry enough to simply charge through one of them.

Instead, he went through the mountains of files and found the Legation's previous five years of financial records.

Send him on a wild-goose chase, would they? He'd just *see* about that.

Surprisingly, several hours spent investigating embezzlement didn't put him in a better mood, and as he made his way back to the hotel later, he felt as tense and tight as a wire on the verge of snapping. He'd spent *years* investigating the Bantry case, and those arrests had come close to breaking the entire gang. *Years* wasted, because . . . what, Senator Markham went to the same supper club as Wallace? And here—everywhere he turned, someone was doing something wrong, but what did they have to do with one another? Why couldn't he see the whole picture? He felt . . . impotent. Useless.

And then he walked through the lobby of the Hotel Wallner, and saw Maria laughing with Claude Girard, and something very dark and very petty roared to life in his chest.

Eli squashed the jealousy ruthlessly. He was not going to do that. He nodded to them and was going to go up to his room, when there was a sudden commotion in the kitchen, and Elisabeth burst into the lobby. There were tears streaming from her large, dark eyes, her hair romantically tousled. Hannah and Mac trailed sheepishly after her.

"Maria!" she cried. "How could you?"

Maria turned to Claude and excused herself. Eli stopped next to the staircase to eavesdrop.

"Let's do this somewhere else, Mother," Maria said, calmly and quietly. Elisabeth ignored her.

"The son of *that woman*! The woman who cursed me! The woman who took your father away from us! *Staying here! In my home!*"

She was truly distressed, Eli realized. It wasn't an act—perhaps none of it was. She was simply genuinely, ignorantly selfish.

"He's my brother," Maria said. "I told him he could."

"He is *not* your brother. He doesn't even *look* like Heinrich. Adelaide probably—"

"Do not finish that sentence," Maria said. Her voice was quiet still, but icy.

Apparently Elisabeth had some sense of self-preservation, because she immediately changed tactics. "I can't even *look at him,*" she said. "Do you know she had him seven months after you? *Do you understand what that means, Maria?*"

"That is your business, Mother, and Heinrich's, and Adelaide's. But not mine, and not Mac's."

"Elisabeth," Hannah said, her voice trembly but determined. "He left *because* he didn't approve of the cur—"

"I don't care why he left," Elisabeth snapped. "And you're on his side anyway, I saw you flirting with him when I—"

"*Enough,*" Maria said. "This isn't up for discussion. Mac stays."

Elisabeth inhaled sharply. "I absolutely forbid it."

"You can't," Maria replied. "I'm the manager. I decide."

Elisabeth's lips parted, and she stared, betrayal and surprise and anger in her eyes. "Maria! I'm your *mother!*"

Maria didn't reply. She simply waited. After several long, tense seconds, Elisabeth nodded.

"So be it, then. But I won't stay under the same roof as him. Do you hear me, Maria? I'll move out. I'll leave."

"That is entirely your decision," Maria said. "Now, if we're done here."

She nodded at the group, and returned to the front desk, leaving her mother standing in shock in the middle of the room. Finally, Elisabeth turned and flounced away, and the tension in the room broke.

Mac crossed the room to Maria, his expression deeply embarrassed. Hannah, her cheeks red, fled back to the kitchen. Eli continued to watch Maria, as Mac obviously unburdened himself to her. She was trying to listen, to be kind, but it was clear she needed time to recover. Her cheeks were flushed, her eyes bright.

Someone needed to think of her. Well, Eli was. But he couldn't think of a damn thing to do for her.

Unless . . . well. There was one thing she needed: for Mac

to be somewhere else. And one thing she wanted: that damn fountain.

And Eli could give her both those things.

He nodded to himself, pleased, and strode across the room.

"Mac," he said, interrupting them ruthlessly. Maria's eyes flew to his, and his hand twitched. He wanted to touch her, to comfort her. Her expression was glazed and brittle.

He couldn't touch her. But he could help her.

"I need your help," he said. Mac perked up immediately. "You do?"

"Yes," Eli said. "Now. An errand."

"Oh," Mac said, with clear interest. "All right." Sufficiently distracted, he hurried off to get his coat.

"Thank you," Maria said. Eli shrugged.

At that moment several guests came through the door, and Eli slipped away to wait at the foot of the stairs. Soon Mac came clattering down, one arm in his coat, the other holding his hat.

Eli nodded. "Let's go."

"Ooh, where are you going?" Claude asked, appearing next to them. "I want to come too."

Eli stared at him. "Why?"

Claude smiled. "Now, how can I possibly answer that politely? Perhaps I'm bored! Perhaps I've been stood up by my lover!"

"Perhaps you're snooping," Eli said.

"Perhaps," Claude said. "It is my job, after all. Oh, let me come. An outing! It is what my soul most desires."

"Let him come, Eli," Mac said, his good humor restored, only a slight trace of upset remaining on his face.

Eli shook his head, but in a half-hearted way that they apparently both interpreted as permission.

"Hurrah!" Mac said, and then tried to put the hand holding

the hat through the sleeve of his coat, resulting in a terrible tangle.

"Ah, allow me to assist you, *mon ami,*" Claude said, gracefully taking the hat. Eli rolled his eyes and went to hail a cab. By the time Claude had successfully sorted Mac's coat situation, Eli had given the driver directions. The three of them settled into the cab.

"Where are we going, Eli?"

"There's a fountain your sister wants, in the woods. We're going to get it."

"A fountain? What does Maria want with a fountain?"

Eli thought for a moment. "She wants to put almond cakes in it," he said.

Mac and Claude nodded, as though this made a great deal of sense.

"Ah," Claude said. "The woods. Exactly what my heart has been craving. A city provides everything one needs, but sometimes one must flee to nature."

Mac smiled at this gibberish. Eli stared out the window and regretted his choices.

Claude reached into his coat and produced a champagne bottle and two crystal coupes. Eli frowned at them. Where had they come from? There had been no sign of them under the spy's coat—

"I'm afraid I only have two glasses," Claude said, lowering the window and popping the cork out of it. "I'll drink out of the bottle."

"What a clever fellow you are," Mac exclaimed, taking his glass with glee. "It's like a picnic! I've always wanted to have a picnic."

"You've never had a picnic?" Eli asked, quietly. He hadn't either, until he was fifteen.

Mac shook his head. "It's not the sort of thing my family does."

Really he should leave it at that. "Because you're rich?" he asked.

"Oh no," Mac said. "Though I suppose rich-people picnics are quite different. More elaborate. But no, it's really because—I suppose we're not very fun."

Eli nodded, digesting this.

"Oh! I have some of Hannah's almond cakes!" Mac rummaged around, producing a paper bag, still warm from the kitchen. "Yes! Here."

He looked terribly proud of himself, and Eli felt the oddest impulse to praise him.

The almond cakes were passed around, and Eli found himself holding a champagne glass in one hand and an almond cake in the other. The two men looked at him expectantly.

He sighed. "I have some dried apricots. But I can't get at them holding these. Also, I don't drink alcohol."

Mac obligingly held his cake while Claude reclaimed the coupe and tossed back its contents. Eli found the apricots and distributed them.

The cab reached the edge of the Innere Stadt, and turned down the road Maria and Eli had taken back from the village.

"It's like a feast," Mac said, lining the apricots up neatly on his pant leg. He sighed. "I suppose you saw. Earlier."

Claude and Eli exchanged a glance. It wasn't as though anyone in that room could have avoided seeing it.

But Mac clearly needed to talk, and it was better he do so to someone other than Maria. So Eli grunted. "We saw."

That was enough for Mac. "I've put Maria in such a terrible position. And her mother—" He broke off. Swallowed. "Her mother shouldn't have to leave, because of me. I told Maria I'd go to another hotel, but she said not to. I don't—I don't know what I should do."

"Elisabeth Wallner is in charge of her own decisions," Eli said.

"But seeing me must be so painful—"

"You can't control how other people react to you. You can only control your own actions."

"For what it's worth," Claude said, "I think your sister likes having you there."

Eli thought so too, though he wasn't sure how he felt about Claude knowing that.

"I just—I feel like such a burden," Mac said. "I'm useless, you know? Utterly decorative. That's my whole purpose. Like my father. What has he ever contributed to the world, beyond children and drama? I'm shaping up to be exactly like him. Like father, like son."

"No." Eli said the word sharply. "That's an excuse. Don't do that."

"But—"

"*You* choose who you are going to be and what you are going to do. Not your parents. Not your position in society. *You.*"

Mac's expression was serious. "Do you really believe that?"

Eli nodded once, his jaw tight.

"I've always envied Maria," Mac said. "She's so . . . purposeful. I . . . I wish *I* had a purpose."

"So get one," Eli said, perhaps a little more harshly than was warranted, but the implication that Maria was better off than her half brother annoyed him.

"My American friend is right," Claude said gently. "Though he may say it too brusquely. And you may find you already *do* have a purpose. You simply need the confidence to pursue it."

Mac's brow was furrowed thoughtfully, and even as the conversation turned to lighter things Eli could see him turning the matter over in his head.

Shortly after, the cab passed the hunting lodge where

Eli and Maria had spent the night, and, a few minutes later, stopped.

"We're here? Where *is* here?"

Eli got out, picking his way through the brambles until he reached the creek. Sure enough, there was the fountain, a bit muddy and the worse for wear, but intact.

There was a rustling behind him, and then a burst of laughter.

"That is, without a doubt, the ugliest thing I have ever seen," Claude said. "It's marvelous."

"Maria wants *that*?" Mac asked, his voice laced with doubt.

"Yes," Eli said, lifting the damned thing and loading it into the carriage.

"*That?*"

"Yes," he said, oddly compelled to defend her. "It's for her *theme.*"

"Ahh," Claude said, as though this made everything make sense.

They got in the carriage and headed back toward the village.

"But is this all we're doing? We've barely been here at all!"

"I agree, we must stay longer," Claude said. "We must take time and fully appreciate the beauty of nature!"

"And the beauty of that wine garden," Mac said, rapping on the fiacre wall before Eli could stop him.

"Come now, my friend," Claude said, sotto voce, as the carriage swayed to a halt and Mac hurried out. "You wanted to rescue your maiden, and now you must pay. Ah! Speaking of maidens, I found the filthiest bookshop yesterday—"

He kept talking as he slipped out of the cab, heading toward a pleasant-looking outdoor tavern.

Maybe this would help Mac sort his feelings out, so he

wouldn't need to rely on Maria. Sighing, Eli grabbed his hat and followed.

A few hours after the disastrous scene with her mother, Maria stood in the Small Ballroom and auditioned musicians for the ball. Night had fallen outside the tall arched windows, and Vienna sparkled alluringly. The violinist currently in her ballroom played his music against a backdrop of revelers in the street below and the faint strains of a string quartet from the ball down the street.

"Thank you," she said, when he finished. "I'll be in touch."

He bowed, a tall man with neat black hair, and packed up his instrument. She didn't need to hire a full orchestra: she had a group of musicians she used regularly, but their numbers would need to be increased for such a large event.

Normally this was the sort of thing she enjoyed. Today . . . today she was tired, and her head hurt. All she really wanted to do was go to sleep.

She was about to call in an oboist when her mother came up the stairs from the lobby, a hatbox in her hand. Behind her, Franz the footman stood next to eight pieces of matching luggage. A gift from Heinrich some years before.

"Well, I suppose you've made your choice," Elisabeth said.

Had she? Perhaps. Still— "I'm not asking you to leave, Mother."

Elisabeth sniffed. She'd taken extra care with her hair and toilette; she looked more like Empress Sisi than ever. "Your actions have left me no choice."

Maria was too tired to continue this argument. "Where will you be staying?"

"Your father has arranged for rooms at the Hotel Hoffmann," Elisabeth said. Maria stopped her flinch. The choice of hotel was perfectly intentional—she wouldn't let it hurt her.

The plumber emerged from the Large Ballroom and hovered at the edge of Maria's vision.

"All right," she said. "Thank you for telling me."

There didn't seem to be anything else to say, and her head was pounding, and she needed to speak to the plumber. She knew she was supposed to plead with her mother; beg her to stay. Even if she wouldn't kick Mac out, she was supposed to demonstrate how much she loved Elisabeth.

But she was so . . . tired. So instead, she nodded politely and went to talk to the plumber. After a moment, she heard Elisabeth's "*Well!*," and the rustle of her skirts as she swept away.

Maria mustered a smile for the plumber. "How bad is it?"

"I'll need to replace the whole section of pipe," he said. "Someone did quite a job on it."

"Mmm," Maria said. She couldn't stop him from drawing his own conclusions, but she had no desire to confirm his suspicions.

"I'll need to go into the ceiling along the pipe," he continued, and Maria winced.

"Can you do it from the third floor?" she asked.

The plumber shook his head. "It stretches past three of your guest rooms. We'd have to go through walls."

It had really been a very, very long day. "All right," Maria said. "How much, and how fast can you do it?"

He named a price that made her stomach ache, and agreed to come the next morning.

So much for repairing the chandelier. The plumbing bill would wipe out her extra cash entirely.

She'd figure something out. She always did.

Straightening her shoulders, Maria walked down to the lobby and called the oboist up.

Two hours later, she'd seen the last musician, a French-horn player, and had a list of names to contact the next day. She saw the French-horn player back to the lobby, nodded at Abe behind the front desk, and passed through the empty kitchen into her office. She sagged down into her chair, pulling her journal from the shelf in front of her and recording the day's events, even the scenes with her mother.

When she was done writing, she pulled her to-do list over, making sure everything had been completed.

"The linens," she groaned, pushing herself up. She needed to make sure their linen supply was sufficient for them to skip a day of laundry, since the hotel's water was still off.

Maria dragged herself down the stairs to the basement, replaying the fights with her mother in her head despite her best judgment. The main linen storage was a large storeroom off the main laundry area. Neatly organized shelves reached toward the ceiling, and some of the larger laundry tools leaned in the corner, like the large, flat-ended wooden paddle the hotel had probably used for beating carpets since the days of Theresa Wallner.

She lit the lamp and started to count and sort her sheet sets. While she was here she might as well take what each floor would need the next day to their respective linen closets. It would save the maids unnecessary trips.

As she worked, she brooded.

She didn't know how to fix things with her mother. Even if she was inclined to, which at the moment was . . . also unknown. She had thought she'd finally learned to accept Elisabeth as she was, but—but Maria was hurt, too. Hurt her mother hadn't told her about Adelaide's curse. Hurt she would leave over Mac's presence. Hurt over the Hotel Hoffmann barb. Of all the things she'd done, that felt most like a betrayal. And to have Heinrich pay for it—

Yes, Elisabeth relied on others enough for them both.

She was stacking the sheets for the third floor when she heard a man's footsteps behind her, and the sound of the door shutting. "Abe?" she asked, turning.

The violinist from earlier stood between her and the closed door.

Maria froze, fear crawling up her spine. The man's expression was flat. Distant. *Professional.* And suddenly, she recognized his eyes.

"You," she said, her voice surprisingly calm and clear.

He didn't reply, simply took two long strides toward her.

Eli wasn't here. He was out with Mac and Claude. He wasn't going to save her.

Maria screamed, as loud as she could, even though the chances of someone hearing her down here were almost non-existent. The man closed the gap between them, one hand coming up to muffle her, the other pushing her against the wall, and she slammed her knee into his groin as hard as she could.

The practice with the skirts paid off. He wasn't prepared, and her knee made a perfect, damaging connection. He cried out, doubled over, his face closer to her level, and she didn't wait for him to recover. She slammed the base of her palm into his nose, feeling the soft cartilage crunch beneath her hand. He stumbled back, releasing her, but he was still between her and the door.

Eli had told her to run if she could, and to incapacitate him if she couldn't. So she grabbed the large wooden laundry paddle she'd used to beat carpets since she was strong enough to swing it, and brought it crashing around into his head.

He went down hard, hitting the laundry cart on the way.

And stayed down.

For a moment Maria simply stood there, the only sound in the room her own ragged breath and the rush of blood in her ears.

Her attacker was either unconscious or dead. She crept closer, saw his chest move up and down. Not dead.

What did one do after one knocked an attacker unconscious? Preferably not stand frozen within arm's reach of him, Maria decided.

Hands shaking, she pulled two clotheslines from the shelf behind her and set her jaw. "You can do this, Maria," she whispered, pushing the man onto his stomach and pulling his hands behind him. "You can do this."

Quickly, she bound his wrists, and then his ankles. He groaned once, scaring her, but didn't move.

"There," she said, straightening. "Now. What on earth am I supposed to do with you?"

She couldn't stop trembling. She didn't feel afraid anymore, but her body was shaking with the remnants of fear and anger and aggression, shuddering in long, uncontrollable waves.

"Maria? Are you down here?"

Eli. He would know what to do.

She opened the door. "Here," she said.

He came into view, holding—holding the damn fountain. Maria burst into tears.

Startled, he put the fountain down. "It's not damaged," he began. "It just needs a clean— Maria, what's wrong? What happened?"

Eli put his arms around her. He smelled like trees, and a bit like wine. She felt him stiffen when he saw the tied-up man in the room beyond.

Slowly, he released her. "What happened, Maria?"

"It's him," she said, wiping her tears away. Calm. She needed to be calm. "The attacker. He tried again. I'm not hurt. But, er, he is."

She didn't feel calm. The shakiness had turned into a kind of buzzing.

Eli walked to the man. Checked her ties. His pulse. Flipped him over and looked at his eyes. Surveyed the bloody mess she'd made of his face.

"You broke his nose," Eli said, his voice emotionless.

"Like we practiced," she said, sniffling. "I kneed him in the groin too. And then I hit him with that."

She nodded at the laundry paddle.

"You kneed him in the groin, broke his nose, and knocked him out with a laundry paddle," he said. There was a strange quality to his voice. It was slightly distant and choked.

"Yes?" she said, cautiously.

"He tried to attack you, so you kneed him in the groin, broke his nose, and knocked him out with a laundry paddle," he repeated, and then she realized.

He was laughing.

It was a wonderful sound. Oh, perhaps a little rusty, but it came out full-throated and surprisingly joyful. So she joined him. His laughter was utterly beautiful and utterly infectious.

He flipped the man back over and straightened, his laughter fading as he came toward her. "You're sure you're unharmed?"

"I'm sure. He barely touched me."

And then he smiled at her, and she lost her mind.

She went up on her tiptoes and kissed him.

Chapter Twenty-two

Two things happened yesterday: the great Ludwig van Beethoven died, and I gave birth to a daughter. I remember when Mother and I went to see him, just a few years ago. And now I'm a mother, and his tenth symphony will remain forever unfinished.

Mother still wants to know the name of the father. But him changing diapers was never in the arrangement. I suppose eventually she'll see that.

—Journal entry of Josephine Wallner, 27 March 1827

Her arms were around him, and her body was pressed against his, and her lips were caressing his mouth, and her smell, soft and wild, was all around him—

She was everywhere, and it was a tidal wave of sensation, and in the swirling, crashing waves of feeling he reached out and grabbed one lifesaving thought.

He could touch her too.

He lifted his hand to her cheek, stroking her delicate skin with his fingers. He thought they might be shaking—could she feel them shaking? Her skin was smooth and warm and soft and *hers;* he was stunned by the intimacy of this, the breathtaking feeling of touching another person, marveling at the sheer, incredible, advent of *her.*

Eli wrapped one hand around her head, wanting to draw

her closer, tangling his hand into her soft curls. He spread the other across her lower back and pressed her more firmly against him. She made a sound of approval that destroyed any hope of sanity, and her tongue touched his lips. He wasn't precisely sure how to do any of this, but Maria was a good teacher, and all he wanted in that moment was to learn. He responded, and she made more approving sounds, and then, somehow, they were against the back wall, with one of his arms still around her waist and the other bracing them against the wall.

Her lips were so foreign yet so familiar beneath his own, breathy little moans escaping between kisses. Another moment of experimentation informed him he could *produce* the little moans, by kissing her *like this* and holding her *like that.*

Vaguely, he was aware there was something else he should be doing, but he couldn't think what. His whole adult life had been spent repressing his desire, and now there was this woman in his arms, and *fuck* she was wrapping her legs around his waist, pushing her skirts impatiently out of the way, and his body felt like it might combust in a column of smoking desire, or perhaps it already had, and they were simply entwined in the middle of a conflagration—

His hand moved lower, and she pressed closer against him—

There was a groan behind him. "Oh," Maria said, breathlessly. "Him."

Whoever she was talking about was apparently not very important, because she leaned forward and caught his mouth again, and he was lost again, his senses tangled around her legs and her curls and the line of her jaw.

There was another sound from behind them. And finally, Eli's instincts, which had apparently been clamoring for some time, forced their way through the fog in his brain and made him turn to look behind him.

Where he saw the attacker Maria had taken out, slowly coming to his senses.

"Leave him," she said, breath warm against his ear. "I tied him up."

He almost did. And that moment, when he almost kissed her again, despite the threat a few feet behind them, shocked him back to himself.

He took a sharp intake of breath and pulled away, still bracing her so she wouldn't fall from the sudden change. For a few ragged breaths, he simply stared at her. He could barely think, confusion and lust and guilt and shock swirling in his head, and damn it, he *needed* to think, *she* needed him to—

She was so very, very beautiful. Her dark hair was mussed, her cheeks were flushed, her lips swollen. She was perfect. And she'd just been attacked, and he'd fallen on her like a—like an *animal*—and—

Maria's eyes met his own, soft and liquid and a little . . . doubtful. Like she was worried, or like hurt was considering creeping in, and that was just as intolerable as his actions had been, he couldn't hurt her, he *wouldn't*—

"I'm celibate," he said.

He saw the moment the word permeated. Her eyebrows scrunched briefly together; her lips parted then closed in confusion. "You're—"

"I just wanted you to know. I pulled away because . . . because . . . not because of you. You're perfect."

She sucked in a breath that made him want to kiss her *very much,* but he clenched his jaw and powered through it.

"Oh," she said. "Um. All right." She pursed her lips together.

"So." He didn't know what to do with his hands. At least she didn't look doubtful anymore.

"So," she said, and then—and then she *giggled.*

It was clearly a nervous response, utterly disconnected from any actual humor, but Eli found his lips suddenly twitching, a strange bubbly giddiness rising in his chest, cutting through the guilt that had been growing since he stepped away from her.

He didn't know what to do with that feeling, so he tucked it away for later analysis, along with all the other feelings racing through his body.

"We—we will talk more about this," he said. "But right now—"

"We need to deal with the man I knocked out?"

That damn lip twitch again. Why, of all times, had his body chosen *this moment* to remember how to laugh? It wasn't at all appropriate. "Yes," he said.

They turned together to the man lying on the floor, still flickering in and out of consciousness.

Maria pressed her lips together, considering. "I think I have to call the police, this time. I can't just let him go." She let out a long breath. "And I suppose I should do so now. Will you watch him?"

"Yes."

She cast one last worried look at the man on the floor, and hurried from the room.

Eli examined the man tied up before him. Maria's attacker was on the tall side, probably only an inch shorter than Eli's six feet one inch. He was in his mid-to-late thirties, with dark hair and a mustache. He was also bleeding from the back of the head, though the trickle of blood had slowed. Eli nudged him with a foot, but he only groaned.

It would take at least twenty minutes for the police to arrive. Plenty of time.

Eli began to search the man. A rummage through his pockets produced nothing except some banknotes and a handful of coins. His clothes were well made, his hands soft, save for

calluses on his fingertips. His fingernails were short and manicured.

Eli froze when he found a knife strapped against the man's
torso. *He didn't have time to draw it,* he reminded himself.
Maria stopped him. She stopped him.

He'd thought the man was a professional after the first
attack; now he was certain. There were two types of profes-
sionals, though: those who enjoyed the money, and those who
enjoyed the work.

Eli strongly suspected this man was the latter. He could
have snuck up behind her and slit her throat, cleanly and quietly. Instead, he chose his hands.

He liked the feeling of life fleeing beneath his fingers.

But dwelling on that made Eli want to use the knife himself, so he made himself go back, to the *professional* part.

Professional meant hired. Professional meant *paid.*

As if on cue, the man groaned again. Eli hauled him up,
propping him against the wall and squatting in front of him.

"Wake up," he said, clapping his hands sharply before the
man's face.

The attacker blinked his eyes open, and Eli found himself
making eye contact with the man who had tried to kill Maria.
Twice.

Eli shoved his rage down. Maria didn't need his emotions
right now. She needed him to do what he was good at.

He sat cross-legged in front of the man and waited calmly
while he tested his bindings. Eli had already checked them.
Maria knew how to tie a knot.

When the man had reached the same conclusion, he
looked at Eli. His eyes were flat, devoid of emotion.

"You seem to have the advantage," he said.

Eli didn't respond. You didn't begin an interrogation by
letting the suspect set the terms of the conversation. He held

the attacker's gaze until the man was forced to break eye contact. Only then did he speak.

"What is your name?"

The man laughed. "You can't believe I'd tell you my real name."

Eli simply waited.

If this man had been the kind of professional who didn't enjoy killing, Eli would have chosen a different tactic. That type could keep secrets. This type though—in Eli's experience, people who enjoyed killing also enjoyed talking about it. He would spill his secrets eventually.

"You can call me Mueller," the man said.

Yes. He wanted to talk.

"Who hired you?"

"How do you know anyone hired me?"

Eli let boredom steal into his gaze.

"Come now, you can't think I'll simply tell you all my secrets," Mueller said. He rested his head against the wall, wincing slightly. "Little slut surprised me. I'll be sure to pay her back."

Bait. Eli made himself ignore it.

"I assume she's fucking you," Mueller continued. "Fast work, but she's like that. You're not the only one, you know. She had another man in her bed a week before you arrived. I wouldn't be surprised if she's having the Frenchman on the side, too."

There, the first piece of information—he'd been watching her since before Eli's arrival.

The idea of this person following her, studying her, before Eli had even known her . . . it crept into Eli's chest and twined black vines around his lungs.

Focus.

"What was his name? Some count or another. They seemed

to have a *very* nice time—he didn't leave until four in the morning."

Eli added some amusement to the boredom in his expression, and continued to say nothing. A few minutes passed in silence. Mueller shifted.

"You're not her usual type, though," he said. "She likes the chatty ones."

"I've already told you what I want to chat about."

Mueller sighed. "Who hired me," he said. "You know, I have a terrible memory."

"Mmm," Eli said. "How about this. I'll tell you some names, and see if any of them ring a bell. Adelaide von Eder?"

The man laughed. "Ah, the Baroness. She'd be happy to erase the entire Wallner family tree, wouldn't she?"

"Frederic Farrow?"

"Who?"

"William Collins?"

"Are we playing a guessing game, then?"

"Elisabeth Wallner?"

"Surely she wouldn't hire an assassin to murder her own daughter," Mueller said, affecting shock. "Have you no respect for the maternal bond?"

"Heinrich von Eder?"

"You *are* a bastard, aren't you? That's the girl's father!"

"Mac von Eder?" Eli asked, guilt stabbing through him, because he was indeed a bastard.

"At least I understand this one," Mueller said, smiling. "Jealousy of his half sister being the motive, I assume. Perhaps!"

Eli supposed Mueller was not the least pleasant assassin he'd ever met, but he might be the most irritating.

The assassin laughed. "Is that all you have? But there are so many people who wish the Wallners ill."

"Really?" Eli said, blandly. "You should educate me, then.

You know I've only been here a short time. Who hates the Wallners enough to wish them dead?"

Mueller shrugged. "Oh, powerful people, I suppose."

"Are you a powerful person?"

"What?"

"The police are on their way. Are you a powerful enough person to avoid prison?"

"The person who hired me won't allow that to happen."

"But if they're so powerful, won't they simply arrange your death?" Eli said. "After all, you failed. Twice. Why would they have need of a failed assassin?"

There. A flicker of doubt.

"Are you trying to make a deal? What, I tell you their name and you cut these ties?"

"Tell me their name and they go to prison with you," Eli said. "Hard to kill you when they're in the same position you are."

"Prison doesn't feature in my future plans."

"Give me something, and I'll see what I can do," Eli said. "For example, if the stolen American codes have anything to do with this."

"The codes?" Mueller laughed again. "They're really the least—"

"Not another word," a low voice said from behind them. Eli jerked around.

The man from the ballroom stood in the doorway.

Maria stood in the alley doorway with the police officer she'd seized from the police station down the street, staring at four surprised expressions. Well, three surprised expressions (Hannah, Mac, and Josephine), and one vaguely interested one (Emilie).

208 ✦ Diana Biller

"There was an incident," Maria said, pulling the police officer toward the basement door. "I'll explain later."

"Maria Theresa Wallner," her grandmother said. "Stop right there. Explain."

Maria stopped, shifting her weight impatiently from one foot to another. "The man who attacked me tried again," she said. "But it's all right!" she continued in a rush, upon seeing Josephine's murderous expression. "I knocked him out."

Hannah made a distressed sound, her hand flying to her mouth. "Are you hurt? Did he hurt you?"

"I'm fine," Maria said. "I just need to—"

"I'll call a doctor," Mac said, standing. "You should sit down."

"I'm perfectly unharmed," she said, beginning to understand where Eli's impatience with doctors came from.

After all, if I saw a doctor every time someone attacked me I'd never have time for anything else.

I really *need to start getting attacked less.*

"But Eli is with him, and I need to get this police offi—"

"Where is he?"

"The basement," Maria told her grandmother, who was surveying the police officer with annoyance. He was young, barely in his twenties, but he'd been the first one she'd seen. He blanched under Josephine's scrutiny.

Maria's grandmother turned her eyes to her granddaughter. Maria resisted the urge to hide.

"You should have come to me first," Josephine said.

Yes, Maria thought, *but I didn't want to deal with disposing of a body on top of everything else.*

"Sorry," she said. Josephine narrowed her eyes like she'd heard the rest.

"Well, I suppose we'd better go see him," Josephine said, standing. Hannah and Mac hurried to join her. Emilie had left the conversation several moments prior, her attention returning to the composition in front of her.

"If this is a family matter—" the police officer started, taking a step back.

"It is," Josephine said.

"It is *not,*" Maria replied, taking a firm hold of the officer's sleeve and tugging. "Whoever is coming, let's go. Eli's been waiting long enough."

The five of them tromped down the basement stairs.

And found Eli engaged in a standoff with an unknown man standing in the doorway.

"Police," the young officer cried. Well, cried was overdoing it. Said, possibly. Certainly he at least squeaked it.

The man in the doorway turned, and Maria froze. "You," she gasped.

It was the same man who had interrupted her and Eli in the ballroom, right before the almost-kiss. She glanced at Eli, and saw the same recognition in his hard expression.

"Grandmother, that's the man I saw," she said, pointing at him. "In the ballroom. He shouldn't have been there, he had no reason—"

"Hello, Josephine," the man said, a small, almost wry smile flickering on his face.

Josephine took a quick, audible breath, and placed her hand on top of Maria's arm, pushing it down.

"What are you doing—"

"Send the police officer away, Maria," Josephine said, quietly.

"But—"

"Send him away." And the command in her eyes was underlined by something like . . . fear, so Maria obeyed.

"It appears there's been a misunderstanding," she said to the officer. "We don't need you after all. My apologies."

He was already backing away. "Not at all," he said. "Please don't regard it." And then he took the stairs at top speed, and disappeared.

"Hannah, take Mac to the Large Ballroom," Josephine said, never taking her eyes off the man in the doorway. "Get his opinion about the decorations. He's an aristocrat. He'll know what's fashionable."

Hannah must have seen the same thing Maria did, because she took Mac's hand and dragged him from the room before he could protest.

"I won't ask why you're here, Johann," Josephine said quietly. "Just take him and go."

"I'm trying to," the man—Johann—responded, that small smile still playing over his lips. "This American is being rather stubborn about it."

"Who are you?" Eli said. It was obviously a repeated question. "If you have the authority, simply tell me, and I'll move aside. If you don't—"

"He has the authority," Josephine said.

It was clearly not the answer Eli was looking for. "I was close to getting names—"

"I'll tell you everything," the attacker said, and just then, Maria caught sight of his face.

The man was terrified.

"I'll tell you everything," he repeated. "Just don't—don't let him take me."

"Who is he?" Eli asked Josephine.

"He has the authority," Josephine repeated. "Do as he says."

The two of them stared at each other. After a long moment, Eli nodded, his mouth creased in a tight frown. He walked across the room, to Maria's side.

"No!" the attacker cried. "I'll tell you, I'll tell you, it's the i—"

There was a loud explosion, and Eli grabbed Maria's wrist, yanking her into him, his hand pressing the back of her head into his chest, as a heavy thud sounded.

"No," Eli said, when she tried to pull away. "Don't look."

"—apologies for the mess," she heard the man say to her grandmother, his words faint against the ringing in her ears.

"—assume you'll send someone for the body," she thought Josephine replied.

"Of course," the man replied. "And I assume you'll ensure the secrecy of this event."

"I take personal responsibility for them both."

"Your word has always been good enough for me," he said. "A pleasure to run into you like this."

Her grandmother said something Maria couldn't hear, and then he must have left, because Eli's arms relaxed slightly.

"Close the door," he said. "She doesn't need to see that."

"I'm not a child," Maria said, yanking away from him and turning to look behind her.

Well. She wished she hadn't done that.

It had been a direct shot to the head. The attacker's body had slumped to the side, leaving a red smear along the wall behind him.

Nausea rose in her throat, threatening to overwhelm her. She made herself take a breath. Clamp down on the absurd impulse to cry.

Eli and Josephine were silent behind her.

"Who was he, Grandmother?" she asked finally. Her voice sounded thin in the silence. "The man from the ballroom. *Johann.*"

Josephine's expression was unreadable. After a pause, she stepped forward and shut the linen room door, blocking the body from view.

"You need to listen to me very carefully," she said. "I need you both to understand the extreme gravity of the situation we're in. But everything I say here *must* be kept secret. Do you understand?"

There it was again, that flicker of fear beneath Josephine's expression.

Maria wasn't sure she'd ever seen her grandmother frightened before. She nodded.

"That was Johann von Laziska," Josephine continued. "Head of His Imperial Majesty Franz Joseph's secret police."

Maria inhaled sharply. The secret police . . .

"He shot our only lead," Eli said, his expression severe. "Are you saying he did so on Franz Joseph's orders?"

"I don't know," Josephine said. "And I don't want to. This is done. Don't think about it, don't ask any more questions. Erase this incident, erase his name, from your minds. And above all, don't breathe a *word* of this."

"He murdered a man to stop him from talking," Eli continued. "To stop him from telling us who is behind the attempts on Maria's life. Because of him, she's still in danger."

Maria put a shaky hand on his arm. "Eli."

He shook her off. "And if, in fact, she has somehow come afoul of the government—"

"*Eli.*"

"Can he *do* that? The man hadn't even had a trial—yes, he was guilty, but von Laziska just *shot* him, on the Emperor's orders, presumably? But it seems like you're saying we're not even allowed to—"

"*Stop.*" Josephine's voice was sharp. "That, Mr. Whittaker, is exactly the kind of question you are never to ask again. If you'd like to keep yourself and everyone else in this room alive."

They stared at each other, her grandmother's expression steely, Eli's one of frustration.

"What my grandmother is not saying is that there's a hierarchy of danger," Maria said, quietly. "And the Emperor's secret police is at the very top of it. Von Laziska could murder every single person in this hotel and never stand trial for it. He could send us to some prison on the eastern border, to rot for the rest of our lives. He could *shut down the hotel.*"

"But—"

"The man who attacked me is dead."

"And whoever hired him can simply hire someone new," Eli said.

"Eli—"

Josephine blew out a breath and held up a hand. "He's right."

"What?" Eli and Maria said in unison.

"You're right," Josephine repeated, to Eli. "It seems that . . . *someone in the court,*" she said, careful even here, "has a misunderstanding about something involving Maria. We should clear up that misunderstanding."

Eli muttered something in English.

"But how?" Maria asked.

"I'll talk to Count von Kaufstein," Josephine said.

"Von Kaufstein? The man whose son is marrying the von Eder girl?"

"He owes me a favor," Josephine said, looking at Maria. "More than one, in fact. And . . ."

Maria filled in the unsaid part: *And he's family.* "Will he be able to help?"

"He'll help," Josephine said. "And if anyone will be able to take care of it discreetly, it's him."

Maria nodded, the tension suddenly draining from her body. "He'll help," she agreed.

Eli was unconvinced. "But how—"

"He's in charge of His Majesty's household," Maria explained. "There's no one better positioned. And he . . . he likes us."

"But you need to understand, Mr. Whittaker," Josephine

said. "There will be no justice here. I know you righteous types, you always want your consequences."

Eli looked about to protest, but Josephine kept going. "There will be no names. No trials. No accountability. This man"—she gestured to the closed door—"will simply disappear. As far as you are concerned, this is over. Do you understand?"

"I—"

"Because if you don't, if you choose to make a fuss, it won't be you who suffers. You're a foreigner, here on business for your government. Protected. The one who suffers will be Maria."

They went back to staring at each other, some complicated language passing between them. After some time, Eli nodded. "I understand."

"Good." She turned to Maria. "Get some rest," she said, and that was apparently her final word on the matter, because she nodded at Eli and went back up the stairs, leaving Maria and Eli alone.

Maria looked at the closed door. Behind it was a man with his head shot off. One minute he'd been alive, and then . . . not.

"Grieve if you need to," Eli said. "But don't forget he tried to do the same to you."

"I don't know what I'm supposed to feel," she said. "You're right. He tried to kill me. Twice. But . . . he was still . . . a person."

"Yes."

Maria stared at the door again. Doors were a funny thing. They created an illusion of distance. A closed door meant that whatever behind it was *there,* not *here.* But in truth the man's body lay only a meter or two away.

Eli rested his hand between her shoulder blades. His palm was warm through her dress. "I'll walk you to your apartment."

"Give me a moment." Quickly, she wiped her eyes. Smoothed her dress and hair. "There. Let's go."

He followed her up the stairs, his presence solid and re-assuring behind her. Fortunately, there was no one in the kitchen as they crossed to the servants' stair.

"I don't even know what time it is," she said, her steps slow and heavy.

"Late. Well after midnight."

"You found my fountain."

There was a long pause behind her. "I simply retrieved it," he said eventually.

"Thank you."

He made a soft grunting sound, and she smiled. Eli Whittaker did not like to be thanked.

They reached the top of the stairs. She opened the door to the Wallner family quarters, walking the handful of meters to her own door. "This is my apartment."

"I'll go in first," he said, opening the door.

It was strange, waiting for him in the hallway while he walked through her rooms alone. Not exactly how she'd imagined him seeing her apartment for the first time.

A few minutes later, a light flickered on in her sitting room and he reappeared. "It's empty. You can go in."

She nodded. Her head felt slow and heavy, as though someone had been slowly filling it with treacle.

"Your grandmother lives up here as well?"

"Two doors down."

"Good," he said. "Try to sleep. And if you can't, go see your grandmother. Don't try to—don't try to be strong. You experienced something hard tonight. It's all right to be affected by it."

He frowned, looking uncomfortable with this acknowl-edgment of emotion. "Go in. I'll leave after you do."

She let out a slow breath. "Eli, about earlier—"

"Sleep first," he said. "We'll talk tomorrow."

Tomorrow. Tomorrow sounded like a good idea. A fresh day, without bodies in it.

"Good night," he said.

"Good night."

Tomorrow. There would be time for everything tomorrow.

Chapter Twenty-three

*I met someone. Emilie Brodmaier, the pianist. She gave
a piano concert in the Small Ballroom last night. I was
running the event while Mother put Elisabeth to bed,
and after, when I was helping Emilie pack her music
up—I said something and she laughed. She laughed and
it was like—it was like the sun had decided to dawn
eight hours early.*

*Oh, I'm lost, I'm lost. It's merely an infatuation,
of course—she's married, and I'm a mother, and we're
both women—and yet I'm utterly lost to her.*

—Journal entry of Josephine Wallner, 25 August 1828

January 11

C*elibate.*

It was the first word in her brain when she awoke. Not
murder, or *attack,* or *corpse.* Not even *breakfast.*

He'd said he was celibate. But he had also kissed her back.
He had kissed her back like he was desperate for her, like she
was the last drink of water in the desert.

Did *celibate* mean he was a virgin?

She sat bolt upright, shoving the blankets to the floor.

Not necessarily, she told herself, heart suddenly racing
in panic. The celibacy could be new. Except, when they'd

kissed, he had been clumsy at first. Like perhaps he hadn't known what he was doing. She hadn't given a damn. When a man kissed you with the kind of intensity Eli Whittaker brought to the task, you didn't dwell overmuch on technique, but . . . it was *possible* he hadn't kissed anyone before. And if he hadn't kissed anyone, then it stood to reason he hadn't had sexual relations either.

Had she just . . . defiled a virgin?

No, no, kissing wasn't defiling.

Was it?

If you defiled a virgin, you had to marry them. Didn't you? She was sure she'd read that somewhere. Or heard it. Definitely there was an understanding—probably generally only true for women, and upper-class women of wealth specifically, but just because the rule wasn't *enforced* fairly or equally didn't mean she had an excuse—

But kissing wasn't defiling—

"Get yourself together, Maria," she snapped, taking several long breaths. Of course kissing wasn't the same as taking someone's virginity. Nor did she believe in such antiquated rules. She had once been a virgin, and she was certainly glad no one had made her marry the boy who had helped her depart that state, sweet though he had been.

Still . . .

She shouldn't have kissed him.

But he'd been so beautiful. When he had smiled it had felt like watching a rose bloom under the sun. She hadn't thought. She'd simply . . . gone to him, a bee drawn helplessly forward.

Her whole body warmed as she remembered the way he'd seized her in his arms. Her kiss had been light, playful, happy. His had been . . . possessive. Devouring. Claiming.

And that's why you can't do it again, she told herself. *Most definitely. No more kisses, playful or otherwise. And absolutely no linen closets,* she added, as her brain put forward another suggestion.

But *oh* . . . when he'd backed her against the wall and *caged* her . . .

Heat raced through her veins. She remembered pulling her skirts up to wrap her legs around his waist, and the feeling of his erection pressing through the fabric of his pants and her drawers, and the hardness of his chest under her hands, and the soft, crisp cotton of his shirt. . . .

She slid down in her bed, slipping a hand beneath the single sheet draped over her and pulling her nightdress up.

The man was not normal. Never had a man kissed her with that kind of *heat,* the kind of incredible intensity that made her feel as though she was burning from the inside out. Perhaps it was *because* he was celibate—

Probably a mistake to think about what several decades of denial might do to someone's sexual intensity, *certainly* a mistake to think about what it might be like to be the person they unleashed it on. There was some noise from the hallway, but she ignored it. This was a hotel after all. Instead, she thought of his face, his hands—

She was close, now, her eyes closed as thoughts of how he *had* touched her mingled with thoughts of how he *might* touch her.

There was another sound from outside her apartment, but she barely registered it, wondering if he touched himself like this, that luscious mouth parting on a silent cry of satisfaction—

"Maria."

Her eyes snapped open. Her hand froze. Surely—

Eli stood in the doorway of her bedroom, a strained expression on his face. "I knocked," he said, his voice hoarse. "There was no response. I thought— I was worried—" He stopped. Let out a long breath.

She didn't know what to say. Embarrassment had stolen all her words. She might never speak again. Or move. She was utterly frozen, one solid piece of humiliation.

Maria stared at him. He stared back. His body was tense, his fists clenched at his sides.

Then Eli spoke again. "Don't stop."

The words were quiet; raspy.

And hot. Impossibly hot. Hot like fire, like lava, like the sun itself. His eyes were locked on hers, intense and hungry.

She couldn't help it. She whimpered.

His jaw clenched. He gripped the doorjamb with one hand, as though tethering himself to it.

"Please," he said. "Don't stop."

It was a *terrible* idea. But when he spoke in that voice, there was probably nothing he could ask for that she would not grant him.

She didn't break eye contact as her fingers began to move again, and his hand tensed on the doorjamb until it looked as though he might splinter it. So serious, his eyes. So tight and intense. Standing over there, every muscle clenched, his suit perfectly neat and his hair perfectly brushed.

She wanted to see this man *undone.*

She didn't realize she'd said it aloud until he took a sharp, harsh breath and tensed even further, until he looked like an erotic statue.

Slowly, purposefully, she pushed the sheet away, never taking her eyes from his face. His nostrils flared as her hand went to the side of her nightdress. She hesitated.

"Tell me what you want," she said.

An expression resembling pain crossed his face, but he didn't hesitate. "Raise your dress, Maria."

She bit her lip and pulled the hem up, over her thighs, until her nightdress was bunched at her stomach and she was exposed to him.

His knuckles were white on the doorjamb.

"More," he said, his voice rough as sandpaper. "All the way. Please."

She had no choice. She complied. The nightdress went over her head and was tossed to the floor.

His face was pale, his eyes dark and burning as she resumed touching herself. All self-consciousness was gone. It was impossible to feel it when he looked at her like that. Like she was the most exquisite torture imaginable. Like he wanted to watch her forever.

She was embarrassingly close. Every stroke of her fingers sent the most delicious fire racing through her veins and over her skin; until her muscles trembled and her breath was ragged.

She moaned his name, and heard him swear. "I'm—so—close," she said, struggling to form the syllables.

He inhaled. "Then you should come, Maria."

Those words, uttered in his deep, serious voice, were all that were needed to send the orgasm crashing into her. She arched off the bed from the force of it, as wave after rolling wave of pleasure crashed over her. After, she collapsed onto the sheets, sweaty and limp.

That, Maria thought (once her brain was capable of thinking again), *was the most incredible sexual encounter I have ever had, and he didn't even touch me. The* potency *of this man.*

Even her thoughts sounded breathless.

Slowly, the muscles in her arms still trembling, she pushed herself up until she was leaning against the headboard. She didn't bother to pull a sheet around her—he'd certainly seen everything, and she didn't believe in late-onset modesty. She pushed sweaty curls out of her face and looked at him.

Eli remained in the doorway, every line of his body tense and coiled. Staring at him, she felt an unwelcome trickle of embarrassment. Had she really—

222 ✧ Diana Biller

"Your pleasure is beautiful," he said, and the absolute sincerity of his words banished any feelings of shame once and for all.

"Are you a virgin?" The question was out before she could stop it. Too late, she realized it probably deserved a more sensitive approach—

"Yes," he answered, without hesitation.

"Oh," she said, and then, confused, fell silent.

Eli's mouth did its half-smile thing, and Maria heard herself sigh—*actually* sigh—in appreciation.

"I came up here to talk about this," he said, releasing his hand from its grip on the doorjamb but staying exactly where he was. "I find you tend to disturb my plans."

"And what of my plans?" Maria said, laughing shakily.

"Have I disturbed your plans?" His smile lingered, but his gaze sharpened. "What were they?"

She had the sudden feeling she was being interrogated. Unfortunately, it did nothing to bring her back to her senses.

Rather the opposite, in fact.

"To think of you," she said, because a demon of mischief and bad ideas had apparently taken possession of her brain, "while I brought myself to climax." She shrugged. "I suppose you didn't disturb them very much after all."

Eli's hand went back to the doorjamb. His jaw clenched so tightly she saw a muscle twitch.

"Maria," he said, his voice sounding impossibly deep. He took a long breath. "I don't—I don't usually do things without thinking about them. And right now, I'm finding it very difficult to think at all."

The temptation to wipe every thought from this man's brain was overwhelming. But . . . she had so much more experience than he did, and perhaps, buried somewhere in his words, was a request to give him time for those thoughts.

So, she sighed, and pulled the sheet up to cover herself,

and then (because she was an absolute *saint*) she dragged the blankets she'd kicked away in the night up for good measure.

"I'll be good," she said, the words coming out breathier than intended. She cleared her throat and tried again. "I'll be good," she said, gruffly, waving a hand. "Let's discuss your virginity."

His lips twitched, though his expression was still strained. "I—have no idea how to have this conversation."

"I would think you have it all the time. Surely the women in America make absolute pests of themselves."

She found she didn't particularly like the idea of unknown American women flinging themselves at Eli. *Hypocrisy, thy name is Maria.*

"Not precisely," he said, dryly. He raked his free hand through his hair, rumpling it. "Do you think—could we talk— elsewhere?"

"Yes," she said, and catching sight of the clock, bit her lip. "But—"

"You have to work," he said, something between regret and relief crossing his face. She felt the emotion echo in her chest.

"I have to work," she agreed. "I have some work to do in the Large Ballroom tonight. You could . . . join me?"

"What time?"

"Nine," she said. "After dinner."

He nodded. "I'll meet you then."

He lingered in the doorway, and then, as though he'd made up his mind, bowed and left her room. A moment later she heard the apartment door close behind him.

Maria flopped back onto the bed. "Well," she said, staring wide-eyed at the ceiling, reliving the last twenty minutes in vivid color. The look in his eyes—how his hand had clenched— the way his voice had deepened, until it was as though it was rasping ever so slightly across her skin—

Eli wasn't the only one finding it difficult to think.

Another look at the clock brought her back to her senses. She had things to do. She had a meeting with Hannah to discuss the ball menu, and later she needed to finalize the event's entertainment schedule. She'd found a group of traveling dancers in town for an earlier event, who had agreed to stay on another week. They would be the entertainers of the fairy court, appearing suddenly throughout the evening to perform strange, sinuous dances and disappearing just as quickly. They would lend another touch of mystery and foreignness, a hint of the erotic—

And the erotic was the last thing she needed to think about right now. Grumpily, she threw the bedclothes off and got out of bed. Work. She was going to work, and focus on the ball, and absolutely not spend the next eight hours and thirty-six minutes daydreaming about Eli Whittaker.

Eli strode into his hotel room, shut the curtains tightly, and unbuckled his belt. He had work to do today. He couldn't afford to spend the day distracted by a damn erection.

Eli had no qualms about masturbation. Being celibate did not automatically rid one of sexual desire, and masturbation was a swift and simple way to deal with said desire. Furthermore, Eli found it usually left him with a clear mind and relaxed muscles.

He began in his usual straightforward and clinical manner. Tried to keep his mind empty.

Failed.

Maria hadn't touched herself efficiently. She'd played with them both, drawing her pleasure out until it was a tangible thing, until he felt as though he was living in it, breathing it in. What must that be like? What would it be like to help her find that pleasure, and to take his own with her?

He found his hand slowing. Found himself reaching for . . . for pleasure. Thinking of her.

She was magnificent. Standing in that doorway, watching her, he'd been overwhelmed. She was more beautiful than he could have possibly imagined, and the sight of her touching herself was . . . well, it was easily the most erotic thing he'd ever seen in his life, because he'd spent his life carefully not seeing erotic things, but it was *also* more erotic than he could have imagined, and Eli's imagination was actually quite good at . . . erotic.

He thought about her breasts, soft, with those hard, rosy peaks, and the incredible way they had moved when she arched her back. He wondered what they would feel like beneath his hands.

He thought about her pale thighs, slowly flushing as she approached her climax, and wondered what it would be like to kiss his way up them until he reached the dark curls between her legs.

He thought about her fingers, and the wet sheen of them as she'd touched herself, and wondered what it would be like to feel that same moisture on his own—

His orgasm hit him suddenly, a series of hard peaks slamming into him, robbing him of thought.

When he was done, he leaned his forehead against the cool wall. His breath was ragged, and his muscles were weak. His mind was not particularly clearer.

He sighed and walked to the washbasin.

She wouldn't have let you see that if she knew.

The voice was only a whisper in his mind, but it ran down his limbs like icy water.

You took advantage of her faith, it continued.

I'm going to tell her, he argued. *That's why I was there. To tell her. To find out if—*

The road to hell is paved with good intentions, Elijah.

Eli gripped the edge of the washbasin.

Once she knows, she'll never want to see you again.

Then she doesn't, he thought. He forced himself to release the basin. If she didn't want to see him again, then she wouldn't. He would respect her decision.

You should pull back now. Spare her.

It was a persuasive argument. For a moment, he considered it.

Then he thought about the woman who had knocked out an assailant with a laundry paddle. The woman who had doggedly carried a hideous fountain through the Vienna Woods. The woman who had bandaged his ribs when he'd been gored by a boar. The woman who had looked him right in the eyes as she brought herself to climax.

No. That woman made her own decisions. He didn't have the right to rob her of that.

The voice quieted. He combed his hair. Straightened his tie. Looked at his watch. Frowned when he saw it was well past eleven.

Chaos really was infectious.

By the time he arrived at the Legation, most of the staff were at their desks. Eli ignored Secretary Collins's smirk and dove back into the files.

The next seven hours passed slowly. There were years of records to read, but he had trouble focusing. Images of Maria that morning ran on a loop through his head, no matter how many times he tried to push them away, always accompanied by an uncomfortable mixture of anticipation and dread. Dread that when she knew everything, she'd never look at him with that same open expression again.

He punished himself for his wandering thoughts by staying late. Only when the street outside his window had transformed to its usual evening revel did he allow himself to leave.

To go to her.

He barely noticed his surroundings on his walk. The night was a series of sounds and images; horse hooves clomping on cobbled streets, gaslight reflecting off shiny black carriages, women laughing.

The Hotel Wallner welcomed him with light blazing in its windows, spilling onto the street below. It really was a lovely building, he thought. Distantly he remembered thinking the pink was frivolous; that the columns with their carved flowers and vines were strange, too much; that the Hotel Hoffmann, with its stern straight lines and pristine white stone, was more attractive.

How odd.

He was barely even surprised when he opened his door and found Josephine sitting at the desk.

"Good evening," he said, taking off his hat and coat and hanging them on the coatrack.

"You're late. I expected you half an hour ago."

His mouth—no, it wasn't a twitch. It was a smile.

He smiled. "My apologies."

Josephine sniffed. "I came to talk to you about the business last night," she said, her carefully chosen words signaling that even here, in the privacy of his room, they were to be cautious.

He nodded, sitting on the foot of the bed across from her.

"I spoke to my . . . my friend," she said.

"And?"

"He's agreed to look into it."

Eli nodded again. "All right," he said. That was all there was to say.

Josephine stood. "It's how things are here," she said. "I know it's not what you're used to."

"Maybe more than you think," Eli said, remembering the telegram from the day before. Maybe power worked the same way everywhere. Maybe this, for all its secrecy, was still more honest about its brutality. "Thank you for telling me."

"You're welcome," she said, standing. "I'd say I'm not sure how you came to be so tangled up in our business, but we'd both know that's a lie." She fixed him with a gaze that seemed to see right through him.

Yes, they both knew exactly how he'd become so entangled. He glanced at the clock. The reason was probably already in the ballroom.

Josephine followed his glance, and her expression softened. "Yes, all right, I won't keep you. I have appointments myself, after all. Good night."

He stood and bowed. "Good night."

"And Mr. Whittaker? Keep her safe when I can't."

Briefly, he fought the urge to throw her words from the previous evening in her face, but looking at her, there was no doubt she was doing everything she possibly could to protect her granddaughter. He had to trust her. So all he did was nod.

Chapter Twenty-four

She came back. I didn't know what to do. There she was, just sitting in the lobby, drinking a cup of tea and scribbling in a notebook. Composing, I later learned, because she's not merely a brilliant, world-famous pianist, she's also an actual genius who composes her own works.

And she's really, really pretty. Her eyes are so warm, like honey tea, and her hair is a cloud of the softest gold—

Anyway. She looked up at me, and smiled, and said "Oh there you are, I came to have lunch with you." I don't know if I said a word to her the entire time—I felt as though I couldn't speak. She must have thought me such a fool.

I'm sure I'll never see her again.

—Journal entry of Josephine Wallner,
28 August 1828, referring to Emilie Brodmaier

Eli paused in the wide doorway of the Large Ballroom. Two candelabras suffused the center of the room with a soft golden light, reflecting off Maria's dark hair as she bent over the fountain, cleaning it. The lights of Vienna sparkled softly through the freshly cleaned windows. The glass was old and warped, and it transformed the city from a busy, dirty, frantic place to something romantic and alluring. Fairyland, he supposed. A beautiful place one could never reach.

He cleared his throat, and Maria looked up, rag dripping into the large bowl of water on the floor.

She smiled, a little awkwardly, and nodded at the fountain. "You wanted someplace we wouldn't get . . . distracted," she said. "I thought there was nothing less erotic than this fountain."

There it was again. He was about to tell her something so serious, and yet a single wry comment from her had that champagne buzz, that *laughter,* rising in his chest. He wanted to play along, to remind her the fountain literally had naked women on it, that in fact every time they were around the fountain something erotic happened.

Instead, he cleared his throat, and nodded.

Maria watched him, and then, smile still clinging to her lips, handed him a rag.

He didn't know how to start. So he sat down across from her, dipped the cloth in the warm water, and started cleaning the fountain.

"Are you—are you all right? After last night?" he asked finally.

She sat back on her heels, apparently considering his question. "Yes," she said, looking around as if to make sure they were alone. "Probably less upset than I should be," she murmured, "considering a man had his head shot off."

"Was it your first time—"

"Seeing a man missing part of his head?"

"No!" Eli bit his lip, because *damn it* that was not funny. "Seeing death, I suppose."

"No," Maria said, her eyes drifting to his mouth. "I run a hotel. Things happen. But . . . violent death, yes." She paused, leaned forward to work on a spot of dried mud. "Not your first time, I think."

"No," Eli said, quietly, scrubbing some moss off a plaster seashell. "Not mine."

She nodded. For a few moments they worked together in silence. It was oddly comfortable, and Eli found himself clinging to the moment. Selfish.

He needed to do what was right.

He put his rag down and sat back. Maria seemed to sense his decision, because she mirrored his motions, tilting her head to the side with a slight smile. A stray curl fell across her face.

"There's something I need to tell you," he said. "It's going to shock you. I want you to be prepared."

She took a breath, settled more comfortably on the ball-room floor. "All right," she said. "Tell me."

He opened his mouth. Closed it. Firmed his shoulders.

"I killed my father," he said.

Four words.

Four words he'd never said before. Simple words, none of them more than two syllables. A sentence a toddler could say.

Maria stared at him, dark eyes wide.

Eli waited. He felt . . . flat.

"Oh, Eli," Maria breathed, and then, slowly, she was reaching out a hand—a hand?—and touching him, coming up on her knees so she could come closer—

Then her arms were around him, and she was *holding* him—

It was as though someone had stabbed a sword through his stomach.

The air rushed out of his lungs with something that sounded like a sob. He shook his head. She hadn't understood.

"I—" It was hard to get the words out, with her softness around him. He couldn't think, couldn't understand—

Gently, so as not to hurt her, he unwound her arms from his neck and moved back. She watched him; her lips pressed together.

"I'm sorry," he said, determined to get it all out. "I—I'm sorry I didn't tell you before we—before we became—before anything happened between us. I should have. To be honest, it's not something I allow myself to think about very often, and—and this—I didn't realize until we kissed. That I had misled you."

Her eyebrows were scrunched together. "Eli," she said, reaching out for him. He shook his head and evaded her. "Eli, what is this?"

"I know it must be very shocking," he said. "I'm not sure you've fully understood. I killed my father, Maria."

"I heard you."

"Then—do you not believe me—"

"I believe you," she continued, softly.

"It wasn't an accident." He needed to make her understand. "And I don't—I don't regret it."

"Oh Eli," she said. "I'm so sorry."

There was a long silence. The candelabras cast a circle of soft light around them, the shadows deep and dark in the corners. Through the window he could hear the faint strains of a string quartet.

"I don't understand," he said, finally. His words sounded unformed to his ears, almost childish.

"What don't you understand?"

"Why you're still here."

She frowned. "Was that the idea? You would confess to me, and what, I would see you for the monster you are? Run away screaming? Doesn't seem like me."

He . . . had nothing to say. His mind was perfectly empty. In no version of this conversation had he imagined . . . Well. He'd never imagined getting this far. He hadn't imagined having to say anything after those four stark, terrible words.

"I know you, Eli," she said, softly. "I know you wouldn't hurt me."

"How can you know that?" he snapped. "You *don't* know me. I've been in your life two weeks, Maria. Two weeks."

"You saved Jakob's orchids."

"What?"

She shrugged. "That's when I knew I could trust you, I suppose. I didn't realize it until a bit later. But . . . you saved a stranger's orchids, just to make me feel better. You picked them up so gently, and you covered their roots with soil, and you . . . you saved them. Not to mention my life." She smiled. "And let's not forget my ballroom floors."

He ignored this attempt at levity. "You can't base your estimations of a person's character on . . . on *horticulture.*"

She frowned, a hint of that regal Wallner expression in her eyes. "Of course I can."

Eli huffed out a breath, regarding her.

"Why are you trying so hard to convince me of your wrongdoing?" she asked.

"I . . ." He trailed off.

"Do you want to tell me what happened?"

"Do I—" He hadn't asked himself that. If he *wanted* to. His conscience had dictated that he tell her, but he hadn't thought she would still be around afterward to explain to.

"I never have," he said. "Before. People know. My mother. Others. Afterward my mother wanted to talk about it—but I—"

Hadn't wanted her to have to bear it, he thought. *The sin.*

"You don't have to," Maria said. "You don't have to—to hurt yourself. Not on my account. But if you want to talk about it, I'm here."

He didn't know what to do. So, after a long, still silence, he picked up a rag and started cleaning the fountain. A couple of breaths later, she followed suit.

He couldn't believe he was still allowed to be close to her, like this. Maybe . . . maybe she knew he was really no threat to her, maybe she would let him . . . stay. Help her. Nothing romantic—once she understood, properly, once it sank in, she wouldn't want that. But maybe—maybe she wouldn't look at him in fear.

"It was a long time ago," he said. "Seventeen years. Almost exactly. It happened in winter." He focused on a small patch of mold so he wouldn't have to look at her.

She made a soft, murmuring sound. "You were young."

"Fourteen."

It took a long time for the next words to come to him.

"I suppose I should tell you about him. He was . . . he was religious."

The word felt insufficient. A memory of the man came back to him, still making his stomach go cold and heavy after all these years.

"He was tall," Eli said. "Like me, I suppose. I don't have his face though. I think about that sometimes. What if I had to see him every time I looked in the mirror? He was thinner than me. That was part of . . . of his beliefs. He didn't believe in taking pleasure from food. So, we didn't eat much."

"I'm getting the feeling that when you say religious, you don't mean he went to church on Sundays."

"No." More quiet. Another bit of mold, vanishing beneath his rag. "There were years we didn't go to services at all. They usually weren't strict enough for his liking. He was the head of a congregation for a while, actually. But . . . it fell apart."

Strange, talking about these things as memories. They were simply facts, between him and his mother, never discussed. Remembering her back then—

"He was cruel," Eli said. He stared at his rag. Saw Maria in his peripheral vision. "He had rages. He . . . he hurt her. My mother."

He'd hurt them both. Sometimes he'd hurt her *because* of Eli. Those times had been, by far, the worst.

"I . . ." He cleared his throat. Made himself look across the fountain at Maria. "I don't say that as an excuse."

She lifted an eyebrow, and Eli almost smiled. It made her look so abruptly like her grandmother. He could read the expression. It hinted, very strongly, that Maria thought that a very fine excuse.

"I only say it so you understand the context. For what my mother did. But it . . . the whole thing was my fault."

He took another breath and dropped the rag.

Let himself go back, after all these years.

The cold of that winter night came to him first. His father had been a wealthy man, but he hadn't believed in the comforts of the body, so they'd only ever had enough coal to not freeze to death.

One winter, he'd fallen ill. His mother had defied his father's orders, using all the coal she wanted, just to keep him warm. When his father had come home, he'd dragged her to the hot stove and pressed her hand down on it. Her palm still bore the scars. That was before he was big enough to—

"It was my fault," he said. "I was fourteen. Suddenly I was almost as tall as he was. I'd started—I'd started fighting back. Not really. Just . . . defying him, I suppose. Two days before it happened, I came in the house and found him . . . hurting her."

He'd had her by the hair. She was on the floor, and he was standing over her, and she was crying . . .

"I lost my senses," Eli said, quietly. "I attacked him. Hit him. Bit him, even. It was so stupid. I might have grown a few inches, but he was so much stronger. I don't know what I thought I could do. He . . . he beat me. Badly."

Badly enough he'd thought, perhaps, that this was it. It wasn't the first time he'd thought his father might kill him, but it was the worst.

Maria made a small, wounded sound, her eyes glistening up at him.

"I don't really know what happened then. I was . . . I was in and out of consciousness, the next couple of days. I remember her whispering to me, telling me she was leaving but she'd be right back. The next time I woke up I heard him . . . I heard them in the next room."

He'd pulled himself off the thin little cot, clutching his side. He hadn't been sure he'd be able to walk—afterward, he'd learned that his leg and two ribs had been broken. He'd dragged himself to the door.

There, in the present, surrounded by Maria's glistening ballroom floor, with the ever-present waltz drifting in through the frosty windows, his throat closed up. For a moment, he couldn't even breathe.

"She'd tried to get help before," he said, looking down. He wasn't telling the story in the right order, but he wasn't sure there *was* a right way to tell a story like this. "Twice. She'd gone to the police twice. And twice they—they brought her back."

Maria made another noise. He didn't look up.

"I want you to understand that my mother—she's wonderful," he said. "She's the strongest, bravest person I've ever met. After the second time, she knew the authorities weren't going to help her. My father was rich, and he had a name, the kind that makes you immune to the law."

It was almost over now, the story. He couldn't bring himself to lift his eyes. The emotions of earlier had left him, and he only felt tired and empty.

"She'd gotten a gun somehow," he said. "I don't know how. He never let her have money, I don't know how she afforded it. But she'd gotten it, and I—I think her plan was to end it. Him. To save me. But it didn't work. I think she tried, but maybe she couldn't do it in the end, or maybe he saw her too early. He'd knocked it out of her hand. I saw it, lying there, a few feet away. He—he was going to kill her. I—I was sure. He was going to kill her, and no one was going to care. So, I picked up the gun."

The words were coming automatically, now. He felt so far away. Almost like he was floating. "He heard me," Eli said. "He turned and saw me. He looked into my eyes, and I shot him in the head. He was dead before he hit the floor. Afterward—she lit the house on fire. To cover it up."

He stopped talking. He felt . . . numb.

"Oh Eli," Maria said, and then she was next to him, her warmth and softness encompassing him.

"You saved her life," she said. "You saved your own."

"She only did it because of me. If I hadn't gone for him that day—"

"No, Eli," Maria said, softly. "You saved her life. And your own."

He was so, so tired.

"Your mother sounds like an incredible woman."

He traced a line along the floor. "She is." The words came out slurred.

"Where did you go? After?"

"She had a friend, from childhood. My aunt Mina. She lives in Boston with the woman she loves, my aunt Fred. We went there. We lived with them for a few years, until my mother met my stepfather, Ambassador Thomas. She's—she's happy now."

"Good," Maria said. "Good."

Her arms tightened around him, and he looked up. Her face was wet. He frowned, raising his hand to wipe the tears away. He didn't want her to cry, not for him, that was the whole point—

"No," she said, pushing his hand away. "This isn't one of the times you save me. Come here."

She stood, holding her hand down to him. He let her pull him up. His body felt stiff. So tired.

Empty.

She blew the candles in the candelabras out, and led him from the ballroom, up the stairs to his room.

"Unlock it," she said, stopping before the door.

She had keys—they were hanging from her side—but vaguely he remembered Maria had *rules* about the keys, so he pulled his out of his pocket and unlocked it. Gently, she steered him inside and closed the door. She sat on the bed, not bothering to push the sheets down, and tugged at his hand.

"Maria—"

"Just come here," she said.

And he really was very tired, so when she pulled again, he followed. He let her guide him onto the bed, let her tuck him into her side, let his head fall on her shoulder, and in the dim, warm, soft room, he let himself fall into a deep, deep sleep.

It was the second time she'd woken up pressed against Eli's warmth. They'd fallen asleep with him in her arms, but sometime in the night they had shifted. Now her head rested on the unwounded side of his chest, one of his arms around her. The hand playing gently in her hair told Maria he was awake.

"What time is it?" she asked groggily.

The hand froze. "Early," he answered. "Before dawn."

"Mmm," she said, closing her eyes. His chest shouldn't be so comfortable. "I have to go to the flower market this morning to place the order for the ball."

"I'll go with you," he said, his voice low against her ear.

She was about to tell him he didn't have to, that Hannah could accompany her, but then she remembered the look in his eyes the night before. The way he'd assumed she would push him away once she knew about his childhood, about his father.

"All right," she said. "Thank you."

She didn't move, and after a few moments, his fingers tentatively returned to her hair. The bloom of warmth in her chest was unnervingly strong.

"I suppose I need to change," she said.

"Yes," Eli said. "I do too."

"But I'm so comfortable."

There was a pause, and then a slight, hesitant rumble in his chest. Laughing. He was laughing again.

Maria hid her smile against his shirt before pushing herself up.

The remnants of humor were already fading from his face when she looked at him, his expression returning to its normal seriousness. She reached out, brushed a finger along one of his cheekbones.

"I used to think you looked severe," she said. "Judgmental."

"I am judgmental."

Her lips quirked up. "Eli Whittaker, you are one of the least judgmental people I've ever met."

One of his eyebrows lifted. "There are a number of people with contracts out on my life who would be surprised to hear you say that."

"So," she said, "first, we're going to set aside the words 'a number of people' and 'contracts out on my life' for a later discussion. And second, you are. Not many people can see past what society says is right to what is actually right. You can."

He grunted, a sort of doubtful acceptance. "Last night . . ." He trailed off. "Thank you. Again."

She shook her head. "Thank you for trusting me."

He looked up at her, examining her expression. "You aren't afraid of me."

The words hurt, sliced into her like little blades. That someone had done that to him, had given him that fear. "No," she said. "I don't think I could ever be afraid of you, Eli Whittaker."

He nodded, slowly. "You never asked me why I don't go by my real name."

"It wasn't my business," she said.

"He named me," he said. "It's from the Bible. I can't—I can't hear that name without hearing his voice."

She hummed in response. She didn't know what to say, so she simply touched him, tracing her fingers along the back of his hand. He turned his hand over, grasping her fingers with his own.

"I don't know what to do now," he said. "I hadn't planned this far ahead."

She snorted softly. "To be honest, it's the first virginity conversation I've had since my own, so I wasn't sure what to expect."

He chuckled, hesitantly. "I suppose I never quite got to that part."

"You don't have to," she said. "If it's too much."

"And if—" He broke off. Swallowed. "If I want to?"

It was her turn to examine him.

Hope. That's what was in his expression now. Fragile, delicate, nascent *hope.*

So, she looked at him again, in a different way. He was beautiful, leaning against the headboard: his hair mussed from sleep, his collar loosened, his shirt halfway untucked.

She hummed in appreciation. "You look rumpled," she said. "I like it when you're rumpled."

Predictably, he straightened, raising a hand to his hair. She laughed and batted it away. "No," she said. "I have an agenda."

"To see me undone," he said, and he looked quickly down at the sheets, a streak of color rising across his cheeks.

Maria bit her lip. There were things they still needed to say—indeed, more fairly serious conversations they needed to have—but she wanted to give him this. To let him have this.

She lifted her hand to his cheekbone again, delicately tracing the blush, before collecting herself and dropping it. "Really Eli," she said, sternly. "I'm trying to protect your virtue, but you have to *help* me. Stop being so—so *edible*."

He coughed. Laughed. Coughed again. Spluttered. "*Edible?*"

"Edible," she said, firmly, refusing to be distracted by his adorably wide eyes. "You're a flirt, Eli."

"I—a *flirt*—I most certainly—"

"You *are,*" she said. "A terrible one. You absolutely know the effect you have on me, because I've *told* you, and yet you persist!"

"I—"

"*Drop the damn fountain, Maria,*" she said, lowering her voice to a firm growl.

He was bright red, now, and laughing. "I don't—"

"I almost tore my clothes off in the middle of the Vienna Woods," she continued, struggling to keep her own laugh in check. "Though of course I would not be the first—"

"*Maria!*"

"No, you have to say it more sternly—"

A pillow hit her in the face. She gasped.

"You did not just throw a pillow at me, Eli Whittaker."

His lips twitched. "I am as surprised as you are."

"This is war," she declared, and proceeded to pick the pillow up and beat him around the head with it.

Predictably, the pillow fight did not last long, and in a few moments she found herself flat on her back, with Eli above her, holding her hands above her head.

She smirked, satisfied. "See?"

His lips opened as if to protest, and then closed. He released her hands and shifted so that he was on his side, next to her. He frowned, his eyes hesitant.

"You're still interested in me, then," he said, quietly. Doubtfully.

She rolled toward him, wishing she could simply kiss that doubt away. "Yes," she said, meeting his eyes so there would be no confusion on the matter.

He nodded, slowly.

"But," she continued, "flirting from both parties aside, it's a big decision for you." She paused, trying to choose her words carefully. "I want you to know it *is* your decision. Yes, I want to do all manner of sexual things with you, and no, your past doesn't affect that desire. If anything, it makes me admire you more. But I'm not going to stop—to stop liking you, if you decide you don't want to."

Eli's eyebrows came together. He looked at her in surprise.

To be honest, she was surprised too. Of course she wouldn't *stop* liking someone because they didn't want to sleep with her, but abruptly she realized how few people she really, emphatically *liked* to begin with. Oh, she was fond of the men she took into her bedroom, but it was a sort of surface fondness. Not true liking.

And somewhere in the back of her mind, a warning bell rang. This was the sort of feeling she reserved for a precious few. And never, never for romantic partners.

Never for anyone who could be *the man*.

But there was a flicker in his eyes that looked like hope, so she put her warnings away.

"I've spent a lot of time these last few days," he said, "thinking about why I decided to be celibate."

Maria hummed in encouragement, moving her hand closer to his on the sheets, so their pinky fingers rested side by side.

"Part of it was because I assumed—I assumed once I told

someone that story, which I still think I was morally obligated to do, they wouldn't be interested. So why put myself through that?"

She had thoughts, especially on the "moral obligation" part, but she kept silent. Perhaps she had been wrong about Eli's judgmental nature. Perhaps the more accurate statement was that he reserved his harshest judgment for himself.

"But the other part was more pragmatic," he continued. "There were women who indicated their interest. But— sexual relations are dangerous, and women are vulnerable. Socially. Legally. I didn't trust I wouldn't be—I wouldn't be taking advantage of them."

Like my father. He didn't say the words, but Maria heard them all the same.

"Sex doesn't have to be dangerous," she said. "There are many precautions one can take. Many precautions I *do* take, the most important one being the use of a French letter. I assume you know what they are?"

"A protective sheath," he said, nodding. "I know of them."

"I can't remember a time I didn't," Maria said, laughing. "Safety in sexual relations has always been emphasized in the Wallner household. It's actually a well-known benefit of our hotel—our long-term customers know there's a discreet box in the linen closet of every floor, with a stock of French letters inside. We don't print it on the brochures, but our footmen and maids are very good at getting the word out."

She paused, her eyes meeting his. "You wouldn't be taking advantage of me, Eli. We would be equal, in this. It's important to me that you know that."

After a moment his chin dipped, a small, hesitant acknowledgment.

"There's something I tell my prospective lovers," she said. "I don't know if it needs to be said here, since you live across an entire ocean and I think you know, but it's important to be clear. I don't have any intention to form a long-term romantic commitment. With anyone.

"Which means that, for me, sex is a thing I do for fun. It's separate—a thing that is enough on its own. You are returning to America when your case is over. If we engage in sexual relations, my hope would be that we would part as friends, and remember each other fondly."

She'd given some variation on the statement dozens of times, to dozens of different men. So why was this the first time it sounded sad?

He was watching her closely, some unreadable expression in his dark eyes. "I understand," he said. "And you're correct. It is what I already assumed."

Good. That was good. He understood her rules and accepted them.

So what was this feeling in her chest? The one that resembled disappointment?

He sat up. Adjusted his cuffs. "I want to."

And those three words swept away any confusing thoughts.

"Oh," she said. A little breathlessly. She wet her lips.

"I just wanted you to know," he said. "I don't really know what I'm doing. As you've undoubtedly already gathered. I suppose I wanted to be clear in my . . . intention."

"Intention," she said, her cheeks suddenly hot, as though *she* were the virgin in the room. She sat up as well. "All right."

"But I—I might be clumsy," he said. "And I might need a little time."

She almost laughed. He was so very dear. "How about this," she said. "Take all the time you want. You lead, and I'll follow."

Maria wasn't used to slow—wasn't used to following either. But for this man, for this dear, careful, bruised man, she found she wanted to do both.

"I lead," he said, frowning, like he was turning the idea over.

"You . . . set the pace," she said. "It's your first time. You should have that freedom."

He looked at her for a long time. "Freedom," he murmured. One side of his mouth lifted. "All right."

A half smile *should not* be able to rob her of breath like that.

"All right," she echoed, and then stood. "I'll go change. Meet you in the lobby in half an hour?"

Chapter Twenty-five

I'm in love with her.

I think we're friends? I want to be her friend. Except I also want to run my hands through her hair, to kiss her against a wall, to wake up next to her in the morning . . .

—Journal entry of Josephine Wallner,
12 October 1828, referring to Emilie Brodmaier

January 12

Freedom.

Maria had used a lot of words like that. She'd been so gentle with him, so careful. Made sure he understood it was his decision. His choice.

Said she'd like him either way (and that little sentence had already found his way into his heart and nestled there).

They were in a carriage, headed toward the flower market. It was barely dawn, the winter sky only beginning to lighten. Perhaps four in the morning had been a strange time to have a heartfelt conversation about sexual relations, but then, the past several weeks in Vienna had loosened his grasp on what exactly constituted "strange."

He'd known what her rules would be before she'd said them, though he appreciated her care in stating them. This

was not the beginning of a courtship, this was not . . . a romance. That was good. Eli had no intention of marrying.

*Yes, but you had no intention of breaking your celibacy,
either.*

He frowned at the thought, ignored it.

They should remember each other fondly, Maria had said.
Eli would always remember her . . . though *fondly* was a word
that sat clumsily on whatever emotion accompanied it. What
he hadn't said was that this was probably it for him. The one
time. That perhaps he wasn't so much stopping his celibacy
as making an exception.

They rolled over a stone bridge, the Danube icy and dark
below them. Maria was doing sums in her notebook.

If this was the one time, if this was it, then he should make
a good job of it.

Of course, the downside with all the talk of *freedom* and
choice and *leading* was that he hadn't the slightest idea what
to do.

A flirt, she'd called him. He only wished that were true.
He was certain it was what he ought to do now. Flirt.

"I can feel you thinking," Maria said, not looking up from
her numbers. "It seems very grave. What's one hundred and
twenty-four plus eighty-two?"

"Two hundred and six," Eli said absently.

"Thank you." She sighed and closed the notebook, peeking out the frosty window. "What are you ruminating on so
seriously?"

"Flirting." He waited for her to laugh, but when he looked
at her, she sat utterly still, a flush rising up her neck.

She cleared her throat. "Perhaps don't think *too* much
about it."

Eli let his gaze linger on her wide eyes, on the rise and fall
of her chest. *Interesting.*

248 ◆ Diana Biller

Once Maria had told him that he was abnormally competent. He didn't think that was particularly true, but he did try
to be good at whatever he put his hands to. One of the ways
he did so was to observe, carefully and faithfully.

And what he was observing was that she was having a
physical reaction.

To him.

A wave of pleasure rushed through him, and he casually
leaned back. "I want to be good at it."

"Mmm," she said, clearing her throat again. "You know, I
don't think you need to worry about it."

"I think I need to learn what you like," he said. "And then
do it."

She shook her head. Cleared her throat for a third time.
The flush had reached her cheeks.

It was like conducting a suspect interview. But . . . fun.

"I don't expect you to—"

"For example," he said. "You like my mouth."

She squeaked. *Squeaked.*

Oh yes. This was much more fun than a suspect interview.

"You mentioned it the first time we met, actually. And
sometimes, when we're talking, you watch it."

"You, ah—you noticed," she said, and he had to restrain
the smile threatening to take over his face. This new smiling
and laughing thing was going to be difficult to manage.

"I did."

She nodded, a little frantically.

"Mmm," she said. "Well. It's a—uh—it's a very nice mouth.
You're a very handsome man! You have many nice features!
Oh, look, we're here."

When the carriage rolled to a stop, Maria practically flung
herself from it, hurling some money at the driver and taking
off toward the flower market at a brisk walk.

Eli didn't bother stopping the laugh before he followed her.

The flower market was much larger than he expected. It was a series of long pavilions, underneath which sellers crowded. Buckets of cut flowers—obviously greenhouse-grown—filled the walkways, creating an explosion of color against the gray dawn. Vendors shouted at the top of their lungs as customers thronged around their tables. Eli caught up to Maria and refocused. There were a lot of people, and he needed to make sure none were assassins in disguise.

"Eli," she whispered, after the third time a man had gotten too close. "It's a public market. You can't just shove every person who gets within speaking distance of me."

"I'm not," he said.

"You are—you just did it again."

"He ran into me."

"He did not."

Eli shrugged. "Be thankful I'm not your grandmother," he said. "She would have put a gun to their head."

Maria made a strangled noise. "You're still holding on to that?"

"To the fact that your grandmother held a gun to my head?" He considered it as they wove through the crowd. "Yes. It's funny."

"Funny."

He turned the word over in his head. "I think that's right," he said. "I find things funny now."

"I regret everything," she muttered, and somehow that was funny too. He almost laughed, but then another man thought he could simply *jostle* Maria, and so he had to deal with that.

They went from booth to booth, as she examined the wares and talked to the vendors about what would be available, and when. It seemed to be a very complicated question, which he half paid attention to as he kept an eye on the crowd. She needed a lot of flowers for not a lot of money, so her solution appeared to be to take whatever she could get cheaply and make it work.

Finally, at the sixth booth she stopped at, the vendor conveniently had just had a large deal fall through. Eli listened in pleasure as Maria haggled, finally agreeing on numbers that left both parties satisfied. She gave the vendor the date of the event, took a variety of samples, and arranged for delivery the morning of the ball. He realized with a start that it was only two weeks away.

"And the day before I'll go to the Woods and cut some greenery," she said, speaking mostly to herself as they walked to the cabstand. "And we'll weave them together—I'll have to figure out the arrangements—all right. Yes. That will work."

"I'm impressed," he said.

Maria looked over at him, confused. "By what?"

"You. You're very good at that. The bargaining."

"Oh," she said, laughing. "I've had to be."

She flagged a driver down. "Do you want him to drop you off at the Legation?" she asked.

"No," he said. "I'll see you back to the hotel."

"But—"

He silenced her with a flat look, and she compromised by mumbling to herself as he helped her into the cab.

"No one is going to attack me in a cab," she said.

"A few days ago we were stranded in the Woods by a cabdriver, and I got gored by a boar," Eli said, resisting the urge to touch his bruises. "Which is still odd, by the way."

"Leave it, Eli."

"Your grandmother didn't say anything about the cab incident," he said. "Only that I shouldn't look any further into the assassin. Which I haven't."

Perhaps the end of that sentence turned a bit petulant, because Maria looked over at him with unimpressed eyebrows.

"I'm sure it was only a prank," Maria said.

He didn't answer, simply humming in a sort of neutral acknowledgment.

Still, the bit with the cab didn't make any sense. It didn't seem like Mueller's work. Maria hadn't been harmed; hadn't even been in danger except for the wild boar, and it wasn't like the assassin could have counted on the boar's appearance.

He was frustrated. He didn't like just . . . letting Josephine and von Kaufstein take care of whatever was going on at court. Perhaps this was something he could solve. Even if it *was* as simple as a prank.

He'd been warned off the assassin. No one had said *anything* about the cabdriver.

By the time they arrived at the hotel, the sun had fully risen. The smell of Hannah's fresh-baked bread greeted them in the lobby, and when Maria went into the kitchen, Eli trailed behind her.

He wasn't surprised to find Mac, eating a slice of bread with tea while Hannah shaped some buns on a baking sheet. What was more of a surprise was finding Claude Girard there too, slumped over the table like a dead man, the only sign of life a slight moaning coming from somewhere in his vicinity.

"Good morning," Mac said, turning to Eli and Maria with a bright smile. Claude whimpered, apparently in protest. "Where have you two been so early?"

"None of your business," Maria said, frowning at the men. "Hannah, what have I said about guests in the kitchen?"

Hannah shrugged, as if to say there was nothing she could do about it.

"Eli's a guest," Mac said. "He's in the kitchen."

Maria turned, looking up at Eli with a slightly puzzled expression. "Yes," she said. "Well. He's useful."

"That's a bit harsh," Mac said. "And anyway, I'm useful. Or at least I'm trying to be."

Maria lifted an eyebrow. "By eating Hannah's bread?"

He grinned. "She said she needed someone to make sure it was good."

"*Did* she," Maria said, staring at Hannah's back. Hannah pointedly did not turn around.

Eli felt his lips twitch. This smiling business was indeed getting out of hand.

"But that's not all," Mac said, and his tone suddenly serious, and his expression vulnerable. "Um. I'm making a list."

Maria took her coat and hung it up. She poured a cup of coffee and handed it to Eli, and then did the same for herself before sitting next to her brother. Eli took the chair next to her, beside the heap that was Claude. "What sort of list?"

"A list of ways I could be . . . useful."

Maria's eyebrows came together in confusion. "But—"

"Eli said I don't have to be like him," Mac blurted. "I mean. Our father."

"Mac," Maria said, her expression still confused. "You *aren't* like him."

"I could be," Mac said, quietly. "I haven't done anything, my whole life. I don't know how to. You can do everything, Maria. You can . . . you can place a food order, fix a broken toilet, manage your own accounts, make schedules. All of you are like that, actually. Hannah can bake anything in the world. Claude is a literal *spy*. Eli goes around randomly saving people's lives. What can I do? Spend money."

Hannah had turned around sometime during this speech, a soft frown on her pink face. She looked like she might be about to say something, but Maria spoke before she could.

"I— No, Mac," Maria said, covering his hand with her own. "I—I know I tease you. But you—you know the only reason you and I even have a relationship is because of you, right? You found me. I'll never forget it. You came up to me in the middle of a party, bowed, introduced yourself—like I didn't know who you were—and said, 'I'm your brother, and I'd like to be your friend.' You made that happen, and I'm grateful for it every single day. You *did* that."

Mac's face had a slight flush. "I'm grateful for us too," he said, quietly. Embarrassed. "But I want—I want more."

"Well," Maria said, a trace of confusion still in her eyes. "If that's what you want, I want that for you too. Show me this list, then."

Obligingly, he pushed the paper over. "It's not much," he said, hunching his shoulders. "A few ideas. Don't read it now. Just—maybe you could tell me what you think. Later."

Maria lifted her brows again. "All right," she said. "I'll look at it later."

The clock chimed, and Eli and Maria stood at the same time, facing each other, only a few inches between them. Eli stepped back, but not before noticing the flush starting at the base of Maria's neck.

She cleared her throat. "You're leaving for the Legation? I'll walk you out."

"I didn't know he felt like that," Maria said, after they'd left the kitchen. Her brow was still slightly furrowed. "He talked to you?"

Eli grunted in acknowledgment. "Don't worry about him. He'll be all right."

He meant it, too. There was more substance to Mac than at first met the eye.

"He's not like our father at all. I can't believe he thought he was."

And your children shall wander in the wilderness forty years, and bear your whoredoms, until your carcasses be wasted in the wilderness.

He heard the verse—Numbers 14:33—in his father's

voice, as he always did. This time, though, instead of simply ignoring and shoving it away, he stopped. Maria looked up, a question in her face.

"I told him we choose who we are going to be," he said, slowly. "I've spent my entire adult life trying to prove that to myself. But it's not entirely true, is it? It's right there in the sentence—my father has influenced my entire adult life. I've never escaped him."

Maria lifted a hand to his cheek. He should step away—he shouldn't need this comfort. Instead, he put his hand over hers, turning in to her touch.

"I like who you are," Maria said, softly, and he found himself smiling into her hand.

"I like who you are, too."

She rolled her eyes, and he frowned. He glanced around. The lobby was mostly empty, just Abe behind the front desk. With a sudden lightness in his chest, he took Maria's hand and pulled her into a shadowed alcove behind the grand staircase.

She giggled. "What are you—"

He kissed her.

He tried to put all the things he couldn't quite articulate into the kiss. That he liked *her*. The way she worried for her family. How doggedly she worked to keep them safe. Her determination. Her laugh. Her smile. *Her*.

When he slowly pulled away, she rested her hand against his chest, breathing hard. "So," she said, "that was the second time you've ever kissed anyone?"

"Mmm."

"I see," she said, clearing her throat. "Well. Competence has its virtues. So. Were you trying to distract me? Because it worked."

"I was—" Yes, what had he been doing? Trying to lighten her gaze, perhaps. Trying to lighten his own. "Seeking comfort," he decided.

"Comfort."

"Yes."

"Well," she said, her lips twitching. Laughter was never very far away from Maria Wallner. "You should probably practice more, then. I regret to tell you I'm not remotely comforted."

He felt the laughter echo in his chest as he put his arms on the wall she leaned against. "No?"

Maria shook her head. He could feel the rapid way her chest rose and fell. Her gaze fell to his lips. They curved under her scrutiny.

"What do you think about, when you look at my mouth like that?"

"Linen closets," she said, breathlessly, and then gasped. Her hands flew up to cover her mouth.

He . . . chuckled. Probably it was a chuckle. He would need to get better vocabulary around laughter.

"They must be very shocking linen closets," he murmured, and because he was so close, he pressed a kiss to her neck, right below her ear.

"Please forget I said that," she said, shivering under his touch.

"Can't," he said. Kissed her neck again. "Trained investigator."

She made a strangled sound. "Eli Whittaker, if you don't want to lose your virginity in the middle of my hotel lobby—"

He laughed again. "Then tell me. Tell me what you think, when you look at my mouth like that."

She hissed. "Eli—"

"Tell me, and I'll go to work." A third kiss. She let out a little moan and tipped her head back.

Yes, without a doubt the neck kissing was a success. He filed the information away.

"Fine," she said, after a few more breathless moments. "I

wasn't lying. I think about linen closets. You, on your knees in one. Pleasuring me. With your mouth."

Eli was aware of the sexual act, though he would need to acquaint himself with the specifics. "I believe I would enjoy that," he said, nipping at her bottom lip.

"Oh," she said, and then he kissed her again.

The clock in the lobby chimed half past eight. They pulled apart, hair and clothes askew. Maria giggled as she reached out to brush his hair back into place.

"You did say you wanted to see me undone," Eli said, deciding to try a joke.

She smiled. "Not quite there yet," she said, straightening his tie for him. He returned the favor, brushing her hair out of her eyes and running his hands over it.

"Have a good day at work," she said.

"You too," he said, giving one curl a fond tug.

She batted his hand away and hurried away toward the kitchen.

Eli felt the moment—sweet, warm, happy—sneak into his heart and curl up into a cozy little memory.

He was in love with her.

Apparently smiles could be mocking, too, because that's what the one on his face felt like. Of course he was in love with her. Of course.

Oh well. There was nothing to be done about it, and it didn't change anything. He would simply love her. There was nothing wrong in that.

He thought he would always love her.

And the best thing he could do for that love was to make sure she was safe when he was gone. With that in his mind, he turned and left the hotel.

Eli's day was full. Before going to the Legation, he stopped at the cabstand where he and Maria had found the driver who had stranded them. Casually, under the pretext that he'd left an important book in the cab, he described the man to the drivers who passed through. He offered a small reward for information, just enough to motivate memories. No one knew the man he described, but it was suggested the late-evening hours were much busier, and he'd likely have better luck then.

It felt good, *doing* something. Probably it would lead nowhere, but it was better than the frustration of being told to simply . . . look away.

To Eli, that was a kind of torture.

As he walked to the Legation, he reminded himself he still had his actual, official case, which no one could fault him for investigating. He ran up the Legation stairs eagerly, an almost savage anticipation in his chest, and spent the next six hours continuing to unravel the mess that was their financial records.

By afternoon, Eli understood the variety of crimes that had occurred. Both the Director and Secretary Collins were skimming from the events budget, in a way that was very difficult to track when done correctly. On the surface, no one would be the wiser. If they were careful and conservative, they could potentially keep the embezzlement going for years.

Perhaps unsurprisingly, neither the Director nor his secretary was careful and conservative. Rather, the Director wasn't careful, and Secretary Collins wasn't conservative, and they both had access to the books. Over the course of the day, Eli found three different instances where two different receipts had been entered for a given event, one for the real amount and one for the larger fake amount.

Secretary Collins was careful enough, but he apparently needed money more than the Director. There were several receipts for suspiciously large amounts, perhaps relying on auditors having no real idea what loaves of bread or sides of beef actually cost. Eli needed to check local prices before he could be completely certain, but he thought it unlikely that a dozen apples cost the equivalent of three United States dollars.

When he finally closed the last book, he smiled.

"I don't think I've ever seen you smile before," Secretary Collins said, stopping before his desk, an envelope in his hand. "It doesn't suit you."

"No?" Eli said, smiling wider and enjoying its effect. "I rather like it. Is that for me?"

Collins nodded, handed him the envelope, and cast one last repulsed look at him before walking away.

It was addressed to Eli Whittaker, American Legation, in a dark, angular hand. He opened it, and a short note fell out on Hotel Wallner stationery.

Spoke to my friend this morning, it said. *He took care of it. She's safe.*

It was signed Josephine Wallner.

Safe.

Just like that.

He frowned down at the message. It should delight him. And on one level, he *was* . . . if not delighted then absolutely, breathtakingly relieved.

But was it really this easy? Someone had cared enough to hire an assassin. Were they really dissuaded by a simple conversation?

If it was all a misunderstanding, he thought, *then yes.*

Still. It was as though a piece was still missing from the puzzle—

Because it is *missing,* he reminded himself. *At least, you'll never find it. That doesn't mean she's not safe.*

But—

You don't want to leave her.

He sat back in his chair, winded. That wasn't true, was it? He didn't want her to be in danger, just so he would have an excuse to be around her?

A thorough search of his conscience assured him that was not the case. Above all, he wanted Maria to be safe. If this was how that happened, then he would be happy.

He *was* happy.

And he didn't have to leave yet. There were still the codes, after all, no matter how much of a wild-goose chase that case was supposed to be.

He rubbed his eyes before glancing at the clock. Six fifteen. He had a few more hours before he planned to return to the cabstand. Plenty of time for the stop beforehand.

Half an hour later, he stood in the narrow passageway steps from the massive Stephansdom cathedral, looking at what appeared to be a highly respectable bookshop. It had a neatly painted wooden door, a stone front, and two small cabinet windows stuffed with attractive, popular titles, along with several luxuriously covered religious texts. Eli lifted an eyebrow. According to Claude, who had discussed the place at length over wine two nights before, this bookshop housed the largest cache of erotic books and ephemera in the empire, and quite possibly Europe.

He didn't bother double-checking the name. He was sure Claude was right.

And indeed, all Eli had to do was walk into the bookshop (conveniently empty of customers) and casually deliver the code sentence Claude had mentioned, before he was whisked politely away into a back room, and from there through a well-worn trapdoor into the dimly lit basement below.

Ah, Eli thought, taking in his surroundings. *Here are the customers.*

At least half a dozen men, careful not to make eye contact with one another, were browsing in what appeared to be a large network of cellars. The stone walls were rounded and thick, and the air was cool. Wooden shelves lined the walls, stuffed with books and piles of art and boxes of photographs.

It was a cornucopia of pornography.

Until now, Eli had stayed away from the stuff. Looking at pictures of naked women wasn't going to make remaining celibate any easier. He didn't need more images in his mind.

But now—well. When Andras Kovacs, the Hungarian scholar, had moved into the room next to his at the boardinghouse, Eli had learned Hungarian, to be polite. If Eli was going to end his celibacy, it similarly seemed only polite to the woman with which he was thinking of ending it to be properly prepared. Specifically, he needed details on the act Maria had mentioned that morning.

With this determination, he stepped forward into the stash.

It was fortunate that Eli had spent a great number of his days poring through stacks of financial records, because otherwise the scope of the rooms might have overwhelmed him. As it was, he spent at least half an hour wandering the aisles, simply trying to understand the organizational system. Finally, he located what appeared to be the educational section, and spent another half an hour locating the very few texts focusing on women's pleasure. When he was convinced he had identified all of them, he stacked them neatly and took them to the clerk sitting in a dark corner.

"These, please," he said.

The man looked at the titles as he wrapped them. "Oh," he said, with an approving smile. "This one has good illustrations."

Eli suspected illustrations would be helpful. He tucked the texts into his satchel, and, glancing at his watch, decided it was time to interview some more cabdrivers.

Chapter Twenty-six

She kissed me.
And I punched a man.
She kissed me.
—Journal entry of Josephine Wallner, 21 January 1829,
referring to Emilie Brodmaier and an unidentified man

Maria told herself she wasn't looking for Eli every time the hotel doors opened. She refused to let a man take up so much of her attention. She had things to do, after all: guests to check in; ballroom lighting to finalize; floral arrangements to decide on.

The doors opened, and her head jerked up.

Well, of course it did. She was working the front desk. It was her job to greet *anyone* who came into the hotel.

"Good evening, Maria," Count von Kaufstein said. The Count was dressed in eveningwear, here for a rare Saturday appointment with Mrs. Fischer.

"Good evening," Maria said, smiling at him. "Mrs. Fischer is already upstairs. Room 401, as usual."

"Thank you, dear," he said. "Are you all right? You look . . . tired."

"Do I?" Maria grimaced, before trying to inject a bit more sparkle into her voice. "Well, it's not easy," she said, smiling, "throwing the event of the season."

"Hmm," he said, apparently not fooled. "My offer still stands, you know. If it's money."

"No!" Maria said, flushing. "No. It's so . . . so kind of you. But we're fine. It's fine."

He nodded, watching her. "You know—I don't talk about it much. But you know who I am, yes? To you?"

Maria hummed noncommittally. Telling the Emperor's Chamberlain that you knew he was the illegitimate son of another emperor, and therefore your grandmother's half brother, was not the sort of thing you did if you wanted to stay alive in Imperial Vienna.

"Yes, I see you do," he said, his lips twitching slightly. "Well. Like I said, I don't acknowledge it publicly. But *privately,* it means—" He shrugged. "I suppose it means I wish you well."

"Thank you, sir," Maria said, taken aback.

He nodded, apparently as uncomfortable as she was. "Room 401, then?"

"Room 401." She handed him the key just as the doors opened again, and Heinrich walked through. The two men looked surprised to see each other.

"Count von Kaufstein," Heinrich said, bowing.

"Baron von Eder," the Count said, and then chuckled. "It feels strange to see you outside the wedding meetings. I feel as though someone is going to pop out brandishing a napkin arrangement at any moment."

Heinrich laughed, a little awkwardly. "Yes," he said. "We must remedy that. A drink, soon?"

"Soon," the Count said. "Well, if you'll excuse me."

He bowed again and departed, leaving Maria and her father alone in the lobby, staring awkwardly at each other.

"My mother isn't here," she said, before realizing Heinrich must know that. After all, he was paying for the rooms at the Hotel Hoffmann.

"I know," he said. "I'm here to see you."

Maria blinked at him. "Why?"

He let out a breath, shifting from foot to foot. "Can we sit?"

"Is she all right?" Maria asked, alarm spiking abruptly in her chest. "Is my mother all right?"

"Yes! Yes. I only want to talk."

There was a long pause as Maria digested this.

"I'm working," she said. She couldn't remember the last time she'd been alone with her father.

Heinrich was silent for a moment. "Please," he said.

He looked old, she realized. He was older than her mother, and he'd aged harder. His brown hair was mostly gray, now; his skin worn and . . . well, she wasn't the only one who looked tired.

"All right," she said. "Give me a minute."

Without waiting for his response, she turned and went into the kitchen, where Hannah was working on a test batch of taffy vines.

"Hannah."

"Mmm?" Hannah answered, focused on twining the vine around the makeshift trellis they had built that morning. When Maria didn't answer, she secured the vine and turned. Frowned. "What's wrong?"

"My father is outside. In the lobby."

"Why?"

"I don't know. He says he wants to . . . talk."

"Talk."

"Mmm."

"About what?"

"He didn't say."

"Your mother—"

"Is fine."

The two women stared at each other in puzzlement.

"What can I do?" Hannah asked.

"I guess—watch the front desk for me?"

Her friend was already slipping out of her apron.

"I'm sorry to ask—"

"It's fine," Hannah said. "I was getting frustrated anyway. I can't get the vines to hold their shape. A break will probably help."

"Thank you."

Maria pushed back into the lobby, Hannah behind her. Heinrich was standing by the fireplace, beneath Theresa's portrait. Maria gestured toward the restaurant.

Once, the restaurant had been open for every meal, stretching late into the evening for guests returning from balls, or aristocrats who simply fancied ending their evening with a cake and coffee, surrounded by the magic of the Hotel Wallner. It had been one of the first casualties of the Panic of 1873. Now it was empty, the tables made up for tomorrow's breakfast service.

Maria picked one at random and sat. Her father took the place across from her.

He sighed heavily. Picked up the neatly arranged napkin and began twisting it this way and that.

"This is hard," he said. "I don't know where to start."

There had been a time, perhaps, when Maria was very young, when she had craved her father's attention. Approval. She remembered a few outings with both her parents, her mother urging her to be charming and adorable. To perform.

She hadn't been very old when she realized she was simply another tool in her mother's arsenal, all of them directed toward a singular goal: to captivate Heinrich, to steal him away from his legal family. And Heinrich didn't see her as his daughter, not really. She was Elisabeth's daughter, and Elisabeth was the love of his life. That was all.

Once she realized this, life became simpler. No more worrying about whether she was funny enough, or pretty enough, or sweet enough to keep her father's attention. She simply dropped him from her consideration, and she'd never seen him care. In fact, she could probably count the number of times he'd spoken to her directly on one hand.

So why was he here now?

He really did look tired.

Perhaps a kinder woman would speak, find a way to ease his discomfort. Maria simply waited.

"I suppose I'm here to apologize," he said.

Maria lifted an eyebrow. "For what?"

"For—" He paused, frowned. "I haven't been much of a father to you, have I?"

A bubble of amusement rose in her chest. "No," she said, her lips curving slightly.

"I'm sorry."

Maria stared at him. He seemed to be waiting for something.

He grimaced. "More like your grandmother than your mother, aren't you? I suppose what I'm asking is if there's still a chance. For me to be your father."

The laugh that burst from her lips was harsh, sudden. Heinrich winced at the sound. "Oh," Maria said, pressing her lips together. A small giggle bubbled out anyway. "I'm sorry. But no, no there's not."

His mouth parted slightly, a confused expression on his face, as though he really had not considered the possibility of rejection.

"Err," Maria said, shifting in her seat. "Was that all? I do need to get back to work."

"I didn't know how to be a father to you," he said, speaking as though he hadn't heard her. "No one tells you, you know.

How to be a father to an illegitimate daughter. It's only now that my daughter is getting married that I see how badly I wronged you—how much I must have hurt you."

"I don't think of you," Maria said. "I don't mean that in a hurtful way. I have a family. I have friends. I have a home. It's been a long time since I felt your lack. Now I really must—"

"I understand. It must be hard for you to believe in my intentions."

"No, I—"

Heinrich stood, nodding with determination. "I will simply have to earn your trust."

"Really—"

"You can count on me, Maria," Heinrich said. "Things are going to be different from now on."

"But I—"

It was too late. He had already departed, with another firm nod.

"—don't want things to be different," Maria finished. The room was soft and silent around her. She rubbed her forehead, sighed, and dropped her head to the table.

She didn't know why this was the afternoon of biological relations remembering her existence, but she was ready for it to be over.

Her mother must have put Heinrich up to it. There was no other reason a man who had spent thirty years happily ignoring her would suddenly desire to be involved in her life.

With a groan, she lifted her head. Her shoulders hurt. She wanted a bath, a massage, and her bed.

But Hannah had her own work to attend to. And after Maria's shift in the lobby was over, she had flower arrangements to decide on. So, with another groan, she pushed herself upright and went back to the lobby.

It wasn't until an hour had passed that she realized Heinrich hadn't asked about Mac.

Abe took over the front desk at nine. By then Hannah had gone home, a successful test run of taffy vines buoying her energy as she left. There was another incident with the fourth-floor toilet, and then Maria wrote up the day's events in the hotel journal. She hesitated briefly before including her conversation with her father, but the Wallner policy was to write *everything* down, and so she did. Anyway, it was very unlikely anyone would read it. The journals were an insurance policy, but almost never used. Most of them were never opened again after they were tucked away in the hotel's hiding place.

It was almost midnight by the time she emerged into the empty kitchen. The room was lit by two lamps, and the alley outside the kitchen window was dark and quiet. The sample flowers from that morning—was it really only that morning that Eli had been flirting with her in a carriage?—sat in two water-filled buckets by the back door. She heaved them onto the kitchen table, took down several plain glass vases, and got to work.

The bulk of the order would be filler flowers—simple, cheap blooms no one really looked at. There would also be a small bundle of greenhouse roses, and three dozen precious white lilies. With this, and whatever she could forage from the Woods, she needed to create magic.

She hummed as she worked, trying to keep her energy up. When that didn't suffice, she made herself a cup of tea. And when that didn't suffice, and her shoulders had worked themselves into knots, and the fifteenth bouquet had failed to charm her, she put her hands flat on the kitchen table and swore.

"You're still awake."

Maria blinked tired eyes toward the lobby door. Eli stood, framed in the doorway, a familiar frown on his face.

Exhausted as she was, a smile tugged at her lips. God,

but he was handsome. She sighed in appreciation. "You're pretty."

His eyebrows rose. "Thank you," he said, stepping in and examining her failed floral attempts. He grunted.

"Yes," she said, feeling that the sound conveyed everything about the sad clumps sitting before her. "Believe it or not, I'm usually good at this."

"I believe you," he said mildly.

"But none of it's working," she said, the frustration bubbling up. "I can't find the . . . the right thing. It looks cheap, no matter which way I arrange it."

"Maybe you should rest," Eli said. "I find the solution rarely presents itself at one in the morning."

"I can't. One in the morning is the only time I have."

He casually slipped out of his jacket, hanging it over a kitchen chair before rolling up his shirtsleeves. Maria's mood was briefly improved by the appearance of his forearms.

"I'll help you," he said, his expression serious, and the sight of him glowering over the innocent stems on the table lightened her mood further.

"I didn't know you had experience with flower arrangement."

Eli's lips quirked slightly. "I'm competent, remember?"

"Oh, I remember," Maria said, and if her tone was slightly suggestive, well, it was very late and his sleeves were rolled up and suddenly her mood was brighter than it had been . . . since the last time she'd flirted with him.

"Don't distract me," he said mildly. "I'm focusing."

She snorted. His lips twitched, but he continued resolutely looking at the flowers, picking them up, rearranging them, frowning at her rejects.

"My father came to see me today," she said, not realizing she was speaking until the sentence was out.

"Mmm," Eli said, a hum of acknowledgment. Something

in her chest loosened at the sound. Maybe she could simply talk to him. He wasn't entwined with any of them. She could just . . . say things while he continued his newfound interest in flower arrangements.

"Suddenly he wants to be in my life. Well, he said—to be my father." She laughed. "I don't even know what that means—"

Abruptly, she stopped talking, the words suddenly reminding her why Eli might not want to listen to someone's father problems.

"Oh," she said. "I'm so sorry."

He lifted an eyebrow, confused. "Why?"

"Err—"

His expression cleared. "Maria, if I fell apart at the mention of *fathers* I wouldn't get through the day. Tell me what happened. It won't hurt me. And I'd like to know."

He returned to his bouquet, apparently unbothered, and tentatively, she resumed talking.

"We've never been close. Mac's not his only legitimate child; he has three daughters too, though I've never met them. My mother tried to push the two of us together when I was young. She wanted us to form a bond, probably thinking it would tie him closer to her. But—" She shrugged. "It didn't take. I don't know if he's even acknowledged the relation before today."

Eli's frown deepened. "Why today, then?"

"I assume because my mother somehow talked him into it," Maria said. She sighed in exasperation. "Why they've picked this exact moment to act even more foolishly than usual is a mystery. I don't blame Adelaide for snapping."

Eli grunted. She was beginning to become as familiar with his grunts as his sighs, and this one she thought was *disapproval*. Clearly, *he* blamed Adelaide.

That was rather nice, actually.

"It was uncomfortable," she said, lifting herself onto the kitchen counter. "Sitting across from him. I don't *know* him, really. I only know him and my mother, the couple. And that's ... fine. I'm blessed with more than the usual amount of people to love. What are you doing over there?"

"Mind your own business," Eli said, calmly, his body partially blocking her view. She snorted, and they fell into comfortable silence. It was nice, simply to sit.

"I have a lead on our runaway cabdriver," he said, a bit later. "Another driver identified him tonight. They said he was visiting his family, but would likely be back at the cabstand next Saturday evening."

"Oh." Maria frowned. "I didn't know you were investigating him."

"He doesn't fit," Eli said. "I know your grandmother said not to look into anything involving the assassin, and I'm not going to."

The clench of his jaw told her that was killing him.

"*But* I don't see how the cabdriver is connected. And I can't just—I can't simply sit still while you are in danger."

"All right," she said. "Thank you for telling me."

He nodded, a bit stiffly, and went back to work.

Two minutes later, as the clock chimed half past one, he stood back. "There," he said. "I think you should do it like this."

She slid off the counter to look at his attempt, her lips already curling in preparation. But when she saw the bouquet, she paused.

It was utterly simple. A plain arrangement of the filler flowers, no roses or lilies in sight. Just a few simple blooms, nestled lusciously in thick greenery. The plain flowers, that she was so used to dismissing, had been transformed into little jewels of color.

Magic.

"Fairies don't have the same attachment to wealth we do," he said, seriously, apparently having prepared a presentation while he worked. "We rank flowers based on how much they cost. A rose is more expensive than a carnation, so we think it must be the centerpiece. But a fairy would have no such association. They would simply pick something pretty."

Maria's lips formed a silent *oh*. She didn't know why tears were suddenly building in her throat.

"Do you—it's probably all wrong—"

"No," she said, crossing to him and kissing him softly on the lips. "It's perfect."

Chapter Twenty-seven

A guest was arrested today. Five of Metternich's hounds came right into the hotel dining room—my dining room!—and snatched him. A Czech journalist, can't be more than twenty-five, whose only crime appears to be the possession of a bright mind and a clever tongue.

I've written to Francis. It's been years since we parted, but he's always had a soft spot for me.

—Journal entry of Theresa Wallner, 13 November 1815

Well, I put on my prettiest dress and I smiled and flirted and laughed and cried a bit, and then I went back to his room with him, and at the end, the poor boy got to walk out of Metternich's prison with his heart still beating. I heard that Metternich is furious.

—Journal entry of Theresa Wallner, 14 November 1815

January 16

It had been another long day, and Maria was in the ballroom on the ladder again at the end of it. The plumbing had been fixed; the ceiling reassembled; the chandelier stabilized. There was no longer money to repair the chandelier, but Maria had a plan, and the plan still required the chandelier to sparkle. So as the clock chimed ten in the evening, and the streets beyond the lovely arched windows teemed with Fasching revelers, Maria unhooked its crystal drops.

It was an easy enough task. She let her mind wander while she worked, thoughts flitting from the edible bower Hannah was working on to Mac's List of Usefulness (yes, he'd titled it) to the troublesome plumbing of the fourth-floor bathroom. She was working the morning shift tomorrow, so she needed to be asleep by two, which hopefully would be enough time to take all these drops off and start cleaning them; and then tomorrow evening she needed to approve the final choreography of the dance troupe; and she still needed to find a violinist, since the last one had turned out to be an assassin and had been murdered, but fortunately Abe said he knew someone; and—

Before her to-do list could overwhelm her, she heard the ballroom doors open. She didn't turn; she recognized Eli's crisp footsteps.

"Good evening," she said, carefully unhooking another drop and placing it on the soft cloth on top of the ladder before she looked at him.

"Good evening," he said, coming to stand at the base of the ladder. He was dressed in one of his gray suits. She wondered how many he owned. His hair was neat as usual, despite a trace of fatigue on his face. He regarded the chandelier with interest. "What are you doing?"

"Cleaning the chandelier," she said, unhooking another drop.

He grunted in acknowledgment, wandering away to the table she'd set up nearby with the dirty crystals and a bucket of soapy water. The top of the ladder full, she bundled her drops and climbed down. By the time she reached the table he had his jacket off.

"What are you doing?" she asked, as he rolled up his sleeves and her brain momentarily stopped working. Really, the man needed to stop doing that. It was distracting. His forearms were strong and long; his hands large, with surprisingly elegant fingers. His skin was pale, with just a hint of gold.

"Maria?"

"Hmm?"

"Err, did you hear me?"

She blinked up at him. "No."

It really wasn't better, staring at his face, not when his mouth was sporting such a beautiful half smile. "I asked what you wanted me to do," he said, his voice slightly deeper than usual, the sound going straight to her stomach.

Her brain provided a number of answers to his question, complete with helpful visuals. *Not what he meant, Maria. Probably.*

"I don't—" Her voice was breathy, her train of thought obvious. She cleared her throat. "You look tired, and it's late. You should go rest."

He shook his head, rolling his shoulders. "Doing something physical will help me sleep. I've done nothing but sit at a desk and read account books all day."

Once more, her brain clambered in with helpful *physical* suggestions.

"You're washing the crystals?" he said, when it became clear she wasn't going to say anything. "I can do that."

"You don't have to—"

The half smile again. "Let me wash the damn crystals, Maria."

"I— All right."

Collect yourself, woman.

She took a breath. Attempted to compose herself. "Thank you."

He didn't respond, already turning to the table. She considered telling him how to wash them, but he was already reaching for the correct cloth, and really the best thing to do was put some distance between them. The less her restraint was tested, the better.

They settled into an easy rhythm. It was rare for her to work with someone else—she had colleagues and employees, but they rarely worked at the same time on the same task. It was surprisingly comfortable.

And she discovered, when she climbed down with the next batch of crystals and found two rows of brilliantly shining drops waiting for her, quite a bit faster.

They talked idly as they worked, about their days and the ball and even, briefly, about a letter Eli had received from his mother. It was all very easy, and it wasn't until Maria unhooked the last drop that she realized an hour and a half had passed.

She climbed down the ladder, setting the last crystals next to him and picking up a buffing cloth.

"What are you going to do about the lighting?" he asked.

"Decayed grandeur. The idea is that the fairies stole the chandelier, but they don't know how to work it. I'm going to decorate it with greenery, so it looks overgrown, and then stuff every candelabra the hotel possesses around the edges of the room. It's not ideal," she said, biting her lip. Of all her clever budget workarounds, this felt the weakest. "But at least if the chandelier is clean and polished it will reflect the light from the candles."

He handed her the last drop and reached for a cloth to dry his hands. "I like it. It sounds—" He thought for a moment, his face serious. "Pretty."

A smile tugged at her lips, helplessly fond.

"I assume you need to clean and polish the body of the thing," he said, squinting up at the chandelier, now stripped and barren. "I'll hold the basin for you," he said. "It'll go faster that way."

She probably should argue. She didn't.

And it did go faster. It took her only forty more minutes to wash and polish the body of the light, and then rehang the crystal drops, so that by the time she was off the ladder and staring up at their work, it was barely midnight.

"I don't know what to do with myself," she said, turning to clean up their worktable. "I thought I'd be working for at least two more hours."

"I—" Eli cut himself off, dropping into silence.

She looked over to him, noticing a pink flush traveling across his cheekbones. *Interesting. Very interesting.*

"Yes, Eli?" she said, trying to keep her voice from turning wolfish. "Did you have a suggestion?"

Judging by the way his flush deepened, she hadn't *quite* managed it.

"I—" He straightened and faced her. "I did some reading."

"Oh," she said. Not exactly what she'd expected. Not that reading wasn't good. She enjoyed it herself. Perhaps he was going to recommend a good book—

"On how to stimulate the clitoris with the tongue," he continued, and Maria choked.

"*Oh,*" she said, once she'd recovered.

"You mentioned an interest in the act," he said, words slow, his embarrassment apparently giving way to amusement and something . . . predatory. "And since you have an opening in your schedule . . ."

"In my schedule," she said, nodding stupidly. "Yes. Um. Well. Are you—Eli, are you sure?"

Another half smile. "Very sure," he said, stepping closer and brushing her face with his fingers. "I'll have to beg your indulgence, of course. I'm only familiar with the theory."

"Mmm," she said, as he pressed his lips against *that* spot on her neck, the one apparently connected to every nerve ending in her body. "I—err—practice is very important, of course, um—"

He kissed her, blessedly putting an end to her rambling.

"You mentioned a linen closet?"

"Yes," she said, breathlessly. "But I haven't fitted them out for sexual activities yet."

He chuckled against her neck. "Are you going to?"

"I—I think it's an amenity our guests would appreciate," she said. It was hard to talk with his mouth on her.

"I'm sure it would be," he said, his hand circling around the back of her head and sending jolts of pleasure down her body. "Take me to the linen closet, Maria."

She didn't argue—she wasn't a *fool*. She took his hand and led him from the ballroom.

The second floor was empty, the guests either in their rooms on the floors above or still out reveling. Still, Maria looked both ways before crossing to the linen closet and opening the door. It was the chivalrous thing to do—Eli had a reputation to protect, after all.

Quickly, she pulled Eli into the closet, shut the door behind them, and then stood perfectly still, listening to see if anyone had noticed. The closet was large enough for them to stand chest-to-chest, the light leaking through the wide crack beneath the door and casting a soft gray-gold light over them. The right-hand wall held shelves of neatly organized table linens and towels; the left-hand, shelves of cleaning products and assorted random objects the hotel required to run. The back wall was flat, lined with brooms and mops and buckets.

Once she was satisfied they had been unobserved, she released Eli's hand and looked up at him.

Only to find him . . . shaking with laughter.

"I beg your pardon!" she said, in an outraged whisper that apparently only made him laugh harder.

"I'm sorry," he said, though he did not look sorry *at all*. "It's just that I know multiple government agents who could take sneaking lessons from you."

"Well! Did you *want* to be discovered stealing into a linen closet to stimulate my clitoris with your tongue!"

Eli pulled her closer. "It's not something I'm seeking to hide, Maria," he said, still laughing as he kissed her. "Switch with me."

She did as he said and, head cloudy from his kisses, watched him efficiently clear a spot against the back wall. After a brief hesitation, he turned over a bucket, and left it against the wall, slightly to one side. Maria bit her lip, every breath suddenly feeling like champagne.

He regarded the wall, then turned to her, serious expression back on his face, and gestured. "Will this work for you?"

It was her turn to giggle. "I believe so," she said, attempting to mimic his serious tone. "You really *did* do reading, didn't you?"

"Of course," he said, taking her by the waist and switching their positions again, so she was facing the door. He kissed her jaw, and then the top of her collarbone where it peeked out of her neckline. "I like to be prepared."

"Mmm," Maria said, slowly running her hand through his hair, reveling in the way the thick, dark curls twined around her fingers. Eli breathed in sharply, closing his eyes for a moment.

"Your touch," he whispered. "Nothing has ever felt as good as your touch."

His words went straight to her core, flooding her with heat, and suddenly slow simply wouldn't do. Her hands went to his belt, and she yanked him forward, until his body was crushing her against the wall, and then her hands were touching him everywhere. Running down his back, marveling at the strength of his muscles beneath the smooth cotton of his shirt. Squeezing his arms as he wrapped them around her. Caressing his beautiful face with a whisper-soft touch, his skin smooth and warm beneath her fingers, his body going completely still as she stroked the delicate skin over his cheekbones, down the severe line of his jaw. Over his beautiful, luscious mouth.

His lips parted, his eyes intent on hers as he kissed her fingers.

It was as though the air itself was golden.

Eli reached up to catch her hand, turning it so her wrist was against his mouth, never taking his eyes off hers as he kissed his way down the sensitive skin. She was caught in the intensity of his gaze, the dark focus of it. No one had ever looked that way at her before. It was . . . intoxicating.

And dangerous, whispered a voice in the back of her head.

Eli nipped at the inside of her elbow, and the voice faded away into the buzzing, fizzy feeling of pleasure coasting over her skin and through her veins.

And then, he was kneeling.

Maria swore.

Even in the dusky light, he was indescribably beautiful, tilting his face up to look at her: dark eyes and pale skin; sharp angles and long limbs.

None of her fantasies about this exact moment had even come close.

He reached for the hem of her dress, moving hesitantly. "May I?"

"Yes," she said. Her throat was dry. "Yes."

Then he was raising her skirts, until they were at her waist, revealing her chemise.

"Hold these, please," he said. She complied with shaking hands.

Next was her chemise. And then she was standing before him, skirts about her waist, in nothing but her drawers.

"I can't believe I get to touch you," he said, voice so soft she could barely hear him. It sounded like a prayer.

Then he *was* touching her, his hands gentle as he reached around her waist to the drawstring tie of her drawers, loosening the garment until he was able to pull it slowly down to her ankles. He guided her feet out of her shoes and helped her step out of the drawers.

"Obviously you also researched women's underwear," Maria said, trying to smile, though she felt abruptly exposed and vulnerable. "Sometime you'll have to show me the text you relied on."

He didn't reply, simply sat back on his heels and looked up. His face was utterly serious, his eyes impossibly deep as he gazed at her.

"You honor me," he said. "I don't know if that's the right thing to say. But letting me—letting me do this. You honor me."

And then he put his mouth on her.

She wasn't prepared. If he hadn't been bracing her, she would have fallen right on top of him.

At first, he only kissed her. Between her legs, up her thighs, across the deliciously sensitive skin right above her curls. His hands were firm on her legs, their strength contrasting with the shattering gentleness of his kisses.

When she thought she might melt into the ground, he pulled back. She almost pouted, until she realized he was rearranging her, placing one of her legs on the overturned bucket. Suddenly she felt vulnerable again; nervous.

"Fuck," he said, in English, and the sound of the word uttered in that low, worshipful voice made her nerves depart. He swore again, and she almost preened.

That is, until he leaned forward, and dragged his tongue across her clitoris.

He sat back, swore a third time, and taking her thighs more firmly in his hands, leaned forward once more.

She should have known how it would be. Eli always learned things in the same way. There was a hesitant stage, a technical stage, an experimental stage, and then a competent stage. Perhaps all people learned this way. It was simply that Eli tended to compress all his learning into ten minutes or less.

At first he was gentle. Hesitant and perhaps, she thought, a little nervous. His strokes were slow, almost agonizingly so. He touched her like he was afraid to hurt her, and she let her hand rest softly in his hair, giving encouraging moans whenever something felt good.

Apparently he was encouraged, because suddenly he was sucking gently on her clitoris, and alternating that with long strokes of his tongue, and then there was some flicking, and suddenly her moans were not so much encouraging as pulled from her as he apparently worked through every technique in whatever *extraordinarily filthy* book he had gotten his hands on and—

"May I touch you?" he asked, pulling away. "With my hands. May I—may I put my fingers inside of you?"

"*Yes,*" she said, emphatically. She'd never had a man be quite so conscious of her consent during sex. Another thing she shouldn't have been surprised by. Eli was meticulous, and it was—it was extraordinarily attractive.

His face was between her legs again, and then he was touching her, and she heard him groan. She had to brace herself more firmly against the wall.

"So beautiful," he said, running his fingers over her cunny. Exploring. "Everything about you. You look beautiful. Taste beautiful. Smell beautiful. Feel beautiful." He slid one of his fingers into her, and she moaned.

"Sound beautiful," he said, following his finger with another one. "You sound really, really beautiful."

It was one thing to witness the Eli Whittaker learning

curve; another thing to *feel* it. He started playing with her, drawing moans and gasps from her, trying variations to see what would make her respond *more*. Learning if he licked her like that, if he moved his fingers like that, if he flicked his tongue like that—

He was learning *her,* she realized.

And it was overwhelming.

She didn't know when he stopped playing. All she knew was that suddenly her orgasm was building, and the only reason she was standing was that one large hand bracing her against the wall, and that she didn't know where she ended and he began.

"I'm going to come," she gasped, and he increased his pace, thrusting his fingers into her, until she was coming, moaning his name behind her hand in an attempt to muffle her cries.

He took his fingers from her and put them into his mouth, licking them clean.

Maria whimpered.

Slowly, Eli stood, tracing his hands along her thighs. She let her head fall back against the wall behind her. She was always wildly sensitive after an orgasm; it felt like he was painting her skin with fire.

She straightened when he reached her hip and helped pull her leg off the bucket. She'd forgotten it was there.

"Thank you," he said, leaning his forehead against hers. She felt his erection against her thigh, hard and long, but he seemed unconcerned about it.

Maria laughed softly, beginning to feel her strength return to her. "I'm fairly sure I should be thanking you," she said, letting her skirts fall and running her hand down the front of his chest.

He looked pleased, and she bit her lip. He was so—so sweet, and kind, and serious, and so very, very appealing, and he'd just given her the best orgasm of her life.

She reached his belt. "You know," she said, "you've given me two orgasms and I haven't given you any."

She saw him swallow. "One," he said. "I've given you one orgasm."

"Let's say one and a half. You certainly contributed to the one before this. Holding on to that doorway like if you let it go you might accidentally rip my clothes off."

Eli grunted. "Can't count that one. If we counted masturbatory orgasms involving the other person—"

He broke off. Flushed.

Maria grinned. "Thought of me, have you? That's only fair." She paused, her fingers still on his belt. "May I, Eli? May I give you one?"

He swore again in English, the harsh word soft on his tongue, and *oh* this man was delicious. She might never get enough of him.

Dangerous, that same part of her brain whispered.

It's not, she argued. *He's leaving. It's perfectly safe.*

"Yes," Eli said. "Yes."

Besides, it was hardly good manners to leave a sexual partner unsatisfied.

"What else is in that book of yours, I wonder," she said, slowly unbuckling his belt.

"Books," he said, his eyes fluttering almost shut, his eyelashes thick and dark against his skin.

Books. She smiled against his chest.

"I see," she said, schooling her expression into something more serious as she unbuttoned his trousers. "And were these *books* strictly about the art of stimulating a woman's clitoris? Or did they encompass other topics?"

He sucked in a quick breath as she pulled the opening of his pants far enough apart that she could reach in, stroking a finger down the firm line pressing against his underwear.

"Other topics," he breathed, after a moment.

"Mmm," she said, finding the place his drawers parted. "Did those topics include the ways I might give you an orgasm?"

Another pause. "Yes," he said, finally.

She smiled. It was rather delicious, slowly unraveling this man. "Ah," she said. "They were sort of general education books. So tell me, Eli Whittaker. How would you like me to bring you to climax?"

Closing his eyes, he drew in a ragged breath. "Touch me," he whispered. "Please. Touch me."

So she did, gently turning them around so he was against the wall. She pushed his trousers and drawers down, freeing his cock.

It was beautiful, just like him. Thick and curved and beautifully, outrageously hard. It was warm when she ghosted her fingers down it.

"Maria," he groaned. She closed her hand over his length, and slowly, enjoying every moment, stroked him.

He fell back heavily against the wall, and she leaned her weight against him so he wouldn't fall, enjoying this reversal. Enjoying being able to care for him.

No one had ever touched him like this, she thought, and suddenly she understood what he'd meant. "It's an honor to touch you too," she whispered.

It didn't take long—he'd been close, she realized, since before she touched him. Close, from bringing her pleasure. The thought was intoxicating, and she felt her own breath stuttering as she drew him closer and closer to climax.

She kissed him as he came, feeling some echo of his release ring through her body.

For a moment they simply stood there, tangled up in each other, her hand still on his cock, his on the back of her neck.

"Thank you," she said, repeating his words back to him as she stood on her toes to kiss him.

She meant it to be a peck, a sweet close to a sweet moment, but he held her close, kissing her firmly and deeply. It was a serious kiss, a serious kiss from a serious man, and it left her breathless and trembling.

Dangerous. The word slipped into her mind again.

"Here," he said, pulling a handkerchief from his pocket. "Let me—"

He pulled her hand toward him, where some of his come had spilled, and carefully cleaned her as best he could without water, and then himself.

"Are you—are you all right?" Maria found herself asking, a little awkwardly.

He looked up from carefully folding the handkerchief. His eyes softened when they met hers. "Yes," he said. "Will you—um—will you come back to my room? Not for any ulterior motive," he hurried to say. "To get cleaned up."

She could easily go to the second-floor washroom, a few meters away, or indeed to her own apartment, only a few floors up, but she didn't want to leave him just yet. She tried not to be an inconsiderate lover, and this had been his first time engaging in this kind of sexual activity. Only a cad would leave him so quickly afterward. Whether it brought her pleasure to stay around him was entirely irrelevant.

"Do you want to case the area again before we leave?" he asked.

She glared. "This newfound joking habit is going to get you in trouble one day," she said, but she peeked out the door carefully anyway before she opened it. "It's clear."

He snickered as he followed her out. *Snickered.* It was unbelievable.

"So," he said, as they walked up the stairs to his room.

"How are you going to equip the linen closets for sexual activities?"

And it was easy to fall into simply being with him, as she laughed and answered, and they brainstormed inexpensive ways to turn the linen closets into convenient locations for assignations. "*But what if the closet is already occupied?*" he asked, which prompted her to develop increasingly ridiculous things to hang on the doorknob but also was a very good point needing serious consideration. It was nice, and fun, and it continued being nice and fun when she washed up, and even as she said good night and returned to her own apartments with a smile on her face.

And it wasn't until she was lying down in bed that the warning came back. *He's dangerous,* it whispered, as she was on the brink of sleep, her thoughts filled with his touch and his smile and the adorable way he was learning to joke.

He's not dangerous, she told herself firmly. *It's not dangerous to like someone you're sleeping with.*

And with that, she turned over and went to sleep.

Chapter Twenty-eight

I heard there's a hotel in America with eight—eight!—indoor water closets. If we had even had half that number we'd be the toast of Vienna. . . .

—Journal entry of Josephine Wallner, 5 April 1831

January 19

"Eli!"

Mac and Claude caught him as he was descending the hotel stairs on Saturday night. He'd come back after work to change quickly—obviously a mistake. He should have gone directly to the cabstand.

"I'm busy," he said, attempting to weave through where they stood and somehow becoming tangled in Mac's arms instead.

"Eli!" Mac said, happily embracing him.

"You're drunk," Eli said, attempting to dislodge him.

"He's had two drinks," Claude said, having the nerve to laugh at Eli's discomfort. "He's just clingy. Where are you going?"

"None of your business," Eli said, trying and failing to prevent Mac from petting his hair. "Don't—you'll mess it up—"

"It's so stiff," Mac said, patting it happily. "You should use my product instead. I'll send it over. Oh—wait, no I won't.

I live here now. Eli! My extra pomade is at home! What will I do when it's empty?"

"Buy more? Let go, I have to—"

"Buy more! Of course! You're a genius."

Eli sighed. "Claude. Take him."

"No," Claude said, smiling. "But I might if you tell me where you're going."

"Why—*Mac, stop making my hair stand up*—why do you care?"

"I'm a spy? Remember? Honestly, why do I have to keep reminding all of you? Do I need to wear a sign? Obviously, I'm spying on you."

"But—*Mac, stop*—why?"

Claude shrugged. "You're fun when you're irritated! Come on," he whined. "Tell me!"

"Fine! Fine. I'm going to interrogate the cabdriver who stranded Maria and me."

"Ooh! What an excellent idea! I'll accompany you."

"No—"

"Come on, Mac, we have to help Eli."

Immediately Mac stopped climbing Eli and put his hat on. "I'm ready," he said, seemingly perfectly sober.

Eli stared at them. "No," he tried again.

"Afterward we can go to the bar that just opened on Kärntner Straße," Claude said, linking his arm through Eli's.

It was clear that if he wanted to leave he would be doing so with an audience. And he really did need to leave. So Eli allowed himself to be pulled from the lobby, and settled for occasionally grumbling under his breath as they walked to the cabstand.

"But when we get there, you have to let me do the questioning," he said, warningly.

"We will be absolutely silent," Claude said.

Mac mimed sealing his lips together. Eli frowned at them both. How did this keep happening?

He sighed. "Fine."

There were several carriages loitering at the stand, some drivers sitting on their boxes, others clustered together on the sidewalk. Eli surveyed the group talking and found what he was looking for.

"That's him," he said. "Stay here."

He didn't wait to see if they obeyed before walking toward the man. It was definitely him—Eli didn't forget faces. The man saw him approach, and for split second looked as though he was considering running away.

"Don't," Eli said. "I'll make it worth your while."

The driver hesitated. The men around him faded away, back to their carriages, obviously deciding there was no benefit in hanging around.

"I'm not here out of anger," Eli said, when he reached the man.

"Oh yes? Then why are you here?" the driver said, apparently deciding his best defense was belligerence.

"What's your name?"

"What's it to you?" the driver replied, but Eli saw a glint of guilt in his eyes. He was in his middle years, stout, with reddish-blond hair and a beard.

"There's money in it for you," Eli replied.

The man hesitated.

"Come now," Eli said. "Why not benefit twice? I can't imagine you owe anything to whoever hired you."

"Never seen him before," the man said. "How much?"

That had been a wild surmise, of course. Eli had simply been guessing, and it had paid off. He named an amount, pulling it from his wallet.

The man nodded. "What do you want to know?"

"Let's start with your name."

"Varga," he said. "Ján Varga."

"All right, Herr Varga. Tell me what happened two nights ago."

Varga licked his chapped lips. "Simple enough," he said. "Just a prank, I think, though for what it's worth I don't think it was on you."

"Why?"

"The man who hired me asked if I was *her* driver. The woman you were with."

Not surprising. "Why don't you tell me from the start?"

"I picked you both up. She—the woman—hired me for the afternoon. Said I was to take you to that warehouse, wait for you, take you to another one farther out, wait, then drive you back to the city."

Eli remained silent. The man licked his lips again.

"Um. There's not much else, really. I drove you to the first warehouse. It started to snow, so I was walking my horses to keep them warm. A man came out. Asked me if I was her driver."

Varga looked up, shifting on his feet. "I wasn't going to tell him, mind! But then—well, he offered me some money, and I thought it couldn't do any harm to tell him. And then once I had—he offered me more money. A lot."

"How much is a lot?"

"Enough to buy my services for a whole day," Varga said.

"And what were you to do for this sum?"

"Exactly what I did. Take you somewhere remote. Strand you. That was all."

"Was there an agreed-upon location? Somewhere specific you were to leave us?"

Varga shook his head, seeming confused by the question. "No, just somewhere it would be annoying. It wasn't supposed to be dangerous or anything. That's why I chose where I did, close to that village."

Eli decided not to mention he'd nearly been killed by a wild boar on the way to said village. "Can you describe him? The man who hired you?"

"Brown hair," Varga said, frowning as he tried to remember. "Slim. Probably in his mid or late thirties. He was wearing a brown coat; I don't know what he had on underneath, but he looked the type to be well-dressed. I—I can't remember anything else."

"That's enough. I know who you're talking about."

Varga's face cleared. "So it *was* just a prank then, between friends. Good, good. It's been on my mind."

Eli didn't answer; simply gave him the money. Varga nodded happily at him, pocketed the payment, and walked back to his carriage.

"Well?" Claude said, from right behind him. "Who is it then?"

"The manager of the Hotel Hoffmann," Eli said, frowning "He was at the furniture-rental warehouse too."

"The manager of the Hotel Hoffmann?" Claude said, looking offended at this apparent non sequitur. "What does he have to do with anything?"

"They were originally supposed to host the ball the Hotel Wallner is throwing," Eli murmured.

"It's not just the ball," Mac said, spreading his hands wide. "The Hotel Wallner and the Hotel Hoffmann have been rivals since—oh, before I was born, at least. They hate each other. It's been less serious since Elisabeth ran the Hotel Wallner into the ground. It seemed like the Hotel Hoffmann had won. But then they lost the ball, and now Maria's bringing the hotel back, and I'd bet the people at the Hotel Hoffmann hate that. Anyway, this is—what do you call it—*motive*! Don't you think that's a pretty good motive, Eli? Claude?"

"Yes," Eli said. "Yes, Mac, I believe it's a very good motive."

"Mac," Claude said, putting his hand on the other man's shoulder, his voice inflected with awe. "I've never been more impressed. I'm looking at you in an entirely different light. A master investigator. A genius. A—"

"All right, all right," Eli said, as Mac blushed bright red.

"So," Claude said. "To the Hotel Hoffmann?"

Eli grunted in assent. "But first I need to leave a note at the Hotel Wallner for Maria," he said. "She's at the vegetable market with Hannah, but she should know as soon as she returns."

"Oh, so you know her schedule now, do you," Claude said.

"Yes," Mac said, as they began walking back to the hotel. "I've been meaning to ask you about that. Exactly what are your intentions toward my sister?"

"Oh-ho," Claude cackled, an entirely unnecessary addition.

Eli's first instinct was to tell Mac that his intentions were entirely his own business, and none of Mac's. But—whatever his faults, it was obvious Mac cared deeply about his sister. And he looked serious. A serious question deserved a serious answer.

So Eli stopped. Turned to face him. "I like and respect her deeply," he said. "We have mutually agreed that whatever we are doing now will not develop into a long-term relationship. But you have my word I will care for her. Always."

Mac's lips parted, forming a surprised *oh*.

"Well," Claude said.

Mac swallowed. "I—uh, I didn't actually expect you to answer."

"It was a reasonable question," Eli said. "I will not ask if you approve. Maria's approval is the only one I require."

"Err, yes. Um, quite right."

"Then if we're done discussing this?"

"Yes! Yes. Done. Absolutely."

"Good."

He kept walking, and the other two quickly followed. He felt, rather than saw, them exchanging furtive, meaningful glances, but ignored them.

They reached the Hotel Wallner quickly, and Eli left a note with Abe, briefly outlining his findings. Perhaps it was strange to involve a victim so much in an investigation, but to do otherwise would feel like lying.

"All right," he said, sliding the envelope across to Abe. "Let's go."

The three men were quiet as they walked across the street to the Hotel Hoffmann, Mac and Claude's previous buoyancy replaced by something grimmer.

The Hotel Hoffmann was grand. It was much the same size as the Hotel Wallner, but it had an air of activity that the Hotel Wallner currently lacked. Its white stone façade was brightly illuminated; its lobby was busy despite the evening hour and its restaurant was open and full. Everything was freshly painted and lavishly outfitted with pink silk furnishings and gold-painted accents. A fountain tinkled in the center of the room. Obviously, the last decade had been good to the Hotel Hoffmann.

Eli didn't see the manager—there was another man behind the front desk.

"Is he here?" Mac asked, whispering. "Do you see him?"

"No," Eli said.

"So, what's the plan? Do we need to . . . break in? Search for him? Lure him out somehow?"

Claude hid a smile behind his elegantly gloved hand, and *damn it all* Eli refused to laugh in front of these idiots. He *refused*.

"We ask for him at the front desk," Eli said.

"Oh." Mac sounded disappointed.

"Cheer up," Claude said. "Maybe he'll make a run for it."

Eli ignored them, and walked to the desk, where a brief conversation resulted in the clerk leaving to summon the manager. Claude and Mac were whispering again; he ignored them.

A few minutes later, the man from the warehouse walked through the lobby doors.

And froze.

Ah. So he did recognize Eli. That, at least, simplified the matter of introductions.

For a few seconds he simply stood there, staring at Eli, obviously racking his brain for some smooth method of escape. Eli let him, content to wait. Either he would run, in which case Eli would catch him, or he would try to brazen it out.

Finally, he decided to walk toward Eli. "Hello," he said, bowing. "I'm Alfred Bucher, the manager of this hotel. May I help you?"

"Yes," Eli said, in the steady, professional voice he often used with suspects. It told people they could calm down, that maybe he *didn't* know whatever it was they had done. "Do you have a room where we can talk?"

"Well, I'm very busy—"

"I understand," Eli said, all polite firmness. "It won't take long. I'm happy to do it here, but I don't think it fits the tone of your establishment."

"Oh," Bucher said. "Well, all right." He frowned at them, and then at the busy lobby. "Yes, fine. Follow me."

He led them down a side hallway, to a room that appeared to be his office.

"Please, gentlemen," he said, gesturing to the two chairs across from the desk, and then staring at Mac, as though he had just realized he was a chair short and couldn't think what to do about it.

"I'll stand," Mac said smoothly, closing the door and leaning against it. The other three men sat.

Eli let the silence settle in the room. Claude was lounging next to him, a politely interested expression on his face. Bucher sat across the desk, growing steadily paler. He certainly was acting guilty.

"So," Bucher said, with a nervous laugh. "What can I help you with?"

"Well," Eli said, "I suppose you could tell us why you tried to murder Maria Wallner."

The effect was almost comical. Bucher jumped to his feet, the color drained from his face, and his eyes flew as wide as if he'd seen a ghost. "I didn't!" he cried. "It was a prank! And she didn't die, she only got stranded—"

Mac swore and pushed off the door. Claude stopped him with a touch to the wrist. "Let Eli handle it," he murmured.

"All he was supposed to do was inconvenience her," Bucher continued, so fast his words tripped over one another. "And you, I suppose. I certainly didn't try to kill her, it was a joke between hotels!"

"I see," Eli said. In terms of suspects, he'd had trickier customers. But then not every criminal was a mastermind, no matter what the papers wanted you to think.

"She's all right, isn't she? You know, we've always been like this, just a friendly rivalry, keeps us on our toes, you know."

"Mmm."

"Our grandparents were the same way, and it's all in good fun—"

Eli listened as Bucher went to great pains to paint the relationship between the two hotels as one of playful ribbing and mutually supportive competition. Unless the man was a master liar—and he wasn't—he wasn't connected to the attempts on Maria's life. But then, what about everything else that had happened? All Maria's so-called bad luck—

"Sabotaging the pipes in the ballroom wasn't in very good fun," he said. It was a guess. The only way he could make things fit.

And yes, there it was.

Guilt, written clearly on the man's face.

Bucher sat down heavily. "I didn't—"

"You did," Eli said.

"You don't have any proof," Bucher said.

Eli shrugged. "I haven't looked yet. Did you do it yourself, or did you hire someone?"

"I didn't—" Bucher gulped. "I didn't do anything."

Next to him, Claude sighed. "Eli, I'm bored. He's not a very good liar."

The manager winced.

"Suspect interviews don't exist to entertain you," Eli replied, keeping his eyes on Bucher.

"Sure they do," Claude said. "Let's hand him over to the police and go. I heard that new bar has a magic show at eleven—"

"No," Bucher said. "Not the police. I'll—"

A knock on the door interrupted them. Mac opened it, revealing Maria and Hannah on the other side.

Maria looked furious, but when she met Eli's eyes there was a slight softening. An acknowledgment, a reaffirmation of connection.

It was like being on a team, he thought. He and Claude stood, offering their seats to the two women.

"Maria," Bucher croaked.

"Alfred," Maria said. "Let's talk about sabotage."

Chapter Twenty-nine

I think men are watching the hotel.
　　—Journal entry of Theresa Wallner, 28 November 1815

Maria was indescribably pleased with herself.

Only a few seconds after she'd sat down, Alfred Bucher had confessed, to both the carriage incident and the sabotaged ballroom pipes. Oh, she'd been furious, of course—but Alfred had been very concerned about going to prison *and* about the three men standing angrily behind her (he probably hadn't been concerned about Hannah, but he should have been, because she had very distinctly seen her friend put a kitchen knife in her reticule), and he had quickly transitioned to the bargaining stage of guilt.

Which was how she currently had enough guldens in her pocket to pay *not only* for the repair of the chandelier, but for Hannah to make the floating gelatin lily cakes she'd dreamed up two nights ago.

The five of them left the hotel together, but soon Eli and Maria were left alone, Mac volunteering to see Hannah home and Claude vanishing after muttering about being de trop and sending her and Eli some very significant and slightly embarrassing looks. So now she and Eli were walking back to the hotel, the streets loud and bright around them.

A drunk man almost stumbled into her. Eli quickly whisked

her out of the way, and the man half fell past them, clinging onto a nearby lamppost and promptly vomiting.

Eli sighed, and she laughed.

"You look like you're about to be hauled away by the Spanish Inquisition," she said.

His lips pressed together as he steered her around a party of revelers, and he said something she only half heard, but that definitely included the word *torture*.

A man sat on the sidewalk playing an accordion, with two cats sitting on his shoulders. Maria fumbled for a coin and gave it to him, before pressing closer to Eli under the guise of being able to hear him better.

"And you look smug," he half shouted. She grinned.

"I am smug. I've one less problem, and a pocket full of money for the ball, *and* I'm very cleverly tucked into your side, and you're the best-looking man on the street, and I've received at least a dozen envious glances. Also," she said, pressing onto her toes to whisper into his ear, "someone brought me to a *truly* incredible climax a few days ago, and I'm still feeling the glow."

His arm tightened around her waist and his expression went momentarily blank.

Maria grinned wider and kept walking, even more pleased with herself than before.

Eli cleared his throat. "That—that brings me great pleasure to know," he said, his voice deeper than before.

She felt a shiver run through her, all the way to her toes. When he spoke in *that* tone, all she wanted to do was throw him on the nearest bed (and if a bed was unavailable, well, he'd already shown he was very innovative with a wall).

He leads, she reminded herself.

They came into a small square, where a fiddler was scratching out a tune for coins, and a few couples were twirling around

together, laughing as they danced. Eli frowned as she slowed
to watch.

She kept looking at Eli as she put some coins in the fiddler's case. She'd wanted to stop and dance but—he looked
uncomfortable, surrounded by so many people.

"Follow me," she said, tugging at his hand. She wasn't sure
if he heard her—it was very loud—but he followed as she led
them through a narrow passageway between buildings, to the
street on the other side. It was much emptier; less loud and
bright, but the music still floated in the air around them.

She looked up at him. "Will you dance with me?"

Suddenly, she was afraid he would say no. That he didn't
like dancing, that he didn't want to dance with her. But he
simply took her in his arms.

It was a clear, cold night, a few stars visible overhead. The
gas lamps twinkled, casting neat gold circles on the cobblestones. The fiddler was playing one of the Brahms waltzes that
had been all the rage when Maria was eighteen or nineteen.

"I've always liked this one," she said, as they waltzed on
the old stone street, Eli as serious as he had been in the Brodmaiers' ballroom.

"Why?"

"It's simple, I suppose. And a bit sad. And also I can play
it on the piano."

He gave a soft laugh, and for a moment she simply drank
him in: his smile, the golden lamplight on his skin, the expression in his eyes.

No one had ever looked at her like that before. With so
much . . . attention.

It was a heady feeling, to be looked at. *Really* looked at.

It was a short waltz, and the fiddler moved easily into the
next one.

"It's always waltzes, here," he said.

"That's not true," she said. "The Viennese love listening to all music. We're known for it, actually."

He grunted. "So why am I dreaming in three-quarter time?"

She hid a smile in his coat. "Well, perhaps we love *dancing* the waltz the most," she allowed. "And you are here during ball season."

"Ball season," he muttered, but without sting.

They danced for that song, and then another, and another after that. It was as though the night became still around them. Passersby ignored them—what was another waltzing couple in Vienna, after all—and not even a breeze ruffled the bushes along the side of the street.

Suddenly, Maria giggled.

"What?"

"I was remembering the first time we met," she said.

"When you were dancing in the street like a drunken idiot?"

"Yes, that time," she said, grinning up at him. "And now look at you, Eli Whittaker. You're not even drunk."

He looked down at his feet, as if to verify that he was indeed dancing in the middle of the street, and sighed deeply. "I was afraid of this," he said, in a tone of deep resignation. "The madness *is* contagious."

She snorted and batted at his chest. Was it flirtatious? Yes. She wasn't a *saint*.

Furthermore, the flirtation worked. He tightened his arms around her, brought her a little closer than what was strictly the proper waltzing distance.

Another satisfying result.

"Mac wasn't pleased that you didn't bring the police in for Bucher," Eli said.

"Do you think I should have?"

He shrugged. "You know the context better than I do."

She thought for a moment, simply enjoying the feeling of

his arms around her. "I suppose I'd rather have the money to set things right. I could sue him later, but it would be too late for the ball."

She waited to see if he would argue, but he nodded, accepting her reasoning.

"Mac also asked what my intentions were. Toward you."

Well, *that* was unexpected. And annoying. "That's not any of his business."

"And so I was tempted to tell him," Eli said. "But . . . he loves you."

Maria *hmph*ed. "That doesn't give him the right to meddle in my personal affairs. After all, I haven't asked him what his intentions are toward my best friend, though anyone can see they aren't precisely pure. And I love them both. What did you tell him?"

There was a brief silence before Eli spoke. "I told him I liked you. And that we would not be engaging in a long-term relationship."

Those words absolutely should not have hurt. They *didn't* hurt, she told herself. They didn't. They were her own words, for heaven's sake.

"I think he regretted asking."

Maria made herself laugh. "Good."

Dangerous, dangerous, dangerous.

It wasn't dangerous. It was fine. She liked him, all right. It was good to like the men you wanted to sleep with, even advised. The sex was often much better.

Dangerous—

She quieted the voice by kissing him.

He went still, surprised, and then his arms tightened, so she was molded to his body. When his tongue teased against her lips she moaned and opened for him. One of his hands came up to hold the back of her head, and slowly he walked them back until she was against a wall—the man really did do

302 ◆ Diana Biller

excellent work with walls—and the other hand was bracing them, and her brain was empty of everything except *I want him.*

"Maria," he said, pulling away slightly. His voice was soft. "May I stay with you? Tonight?"

It was probably embarrassing, how quickly she nodded, but—"Are you sure?" she asked.

His smile was a little rueful as he traced a finger across her lips. "More sure than I've ever been about anything."

"That's very sure," she said, aware of how stupid she sounded but somehow unable to stop. "You're a very sure person, in general, so that's really extremely sure—to be clear, when you say *stay with you* that's a euphemism, right?"

Eli was grinning. "It's a euphemism."

"And to be even clearer, that euphemism is referring to the sexual act in which—"

"I'd like to be inside of you, Maria."

"Excellent, excellent," she said. Why was she standing here in the middle of the street? She had a man's sexual education to get on with! "We should go."

She took his hand and tugged on it, and he followed her, laughing.

"You're in a hurry," he said. Absolutely teasing her. Who had taught him about teasing?

"*Yes,*" she said. "Unless you're interested in losing your virginity against an alley wall, *yes.* If you're still a virgin. Are you? After the linen closet?"

"Virginity is a strange concept," Eli said. "Perhaps I'm in a gray area? Or maybe one is a virgin for each permutation of sex one has not yet tried?"

"So what I'm hearing is, in order to really properly despoil you, we need to try *every* permutation of sex— Stop laughing! I take my responsibility to you very seriously!"

"I'm sorry, I'm sorry," Eli said, still laughing. Pulling her in to kiss her. "But do we really need to run?"

"*Yes!*"

So they ran, laughing, stealing kisses. She pulled him after her, her hand small and warm in his. Soon, they were pushing through the doors of the hotel. "My apartments," she said, leading the way to the servants' stairs.

He felt light. Was this what joy felt like? All fizzy and golden, like it was bubbling up through him and might lift him off the floor?

They reached the fifth floor, and he followed her to her apartment and waited for her to unlock it. She lit a lamp when they stepped inside, and then they were kissing.

Eli *really* liked kissing.

"Wait," she murmured, and he pulled back. "I have to tell my grandmother I'm back. Wait here for me, all right?"

He released her, and she darted in for one last kiss before hurrying from the room.

He looked around the apartment curiously. The two times he'd been in it previously he'd been focused on other things—a brief memory of Maria on her bed with her nightgown around her waist flashed into his mind.

It consisted of three rooms: a sitting room, a dining room, and a bedroom that lay beyond the doors behind him. The sitting room was the only one illuminated, so he walked idly around the small space, reading the titles of the books she had stacked on her shelves and looking at the art on her walls. There was a lot of art, of all sizes and styles and frames, clustered tightly together.

The furniture was old but well-kept, everything mismatched but melding together into a warm, happy whole.

One chair was identical to the one in his room, except for a replaced leg in a different color. There was a feeling of years passing, in the apartment. Eli wondered briefly what Maria had inherited, and what she had added—though he wasn't even sure it was the right question. Part of Maria's magic was legacy, the way she took what those before her had done, honored it, and made it even more beautiful. Even more . . . what it was supposed to be.

There was a small drawing leaning against the mirror over the mantel, and Eli walked over to get a closer look. He smiled. It was a caricature of Hannah and Maria. They were younger, maybe not even twenty, but the artist had captured their expressions well.

He heard the door open and felt one of Maria's arms steal around his waist as she came to stand beside him.

"When was this from?" he asked.

"The summer we turned sixteen," Maria said fondly. "We both have one. We went to a fair, and had this done, and ate our weight in funnel cakes and schnitzel, and Hannah got sick in the bushes on the way back, which she blamed on the cook, and not the fact that we'd eaten three servings apiece and then had an entire bottle of red wine. And I really don't know why I'm telling you a story about vomit when I'm trying to seduce you."

"I'm already seduced," he said. "It's unlikely a vomit story will change my mind."

"Yes, but should I risk it? Better to change the subject. Would you like a drink?"

Eli shook his head. She was talking fast—nervous. And perhaps it didn't say anything good about his character, but he liked it. He moved closer, and she looked up, her breath coming faster. She was flushed pink, and her lips were rosy from kissing.

"I don't really drink," Eli said. "But would you like one?"

She shook her head, then stopped. "Yes," she said, and marched determinedly to a side cabinet, where she poured some golden liquid into a glass and quickly tossed it back. He leaned against the mantel and watched her.

She glanced over and sucked in an audible breath. "You're so . . . big. I don't notice most of the time, except when I'm touching you. But standing here in my sitting room—you're just so . . ." She trailed off, gesturing in a way apparently intended to encompass his *bigness.*

"Maria," he said.

"Yes?"

"I need to ask you if you're sure about this, too."

"Oh," she said, laughing, a little breathlessly. "Thank you for asking, it's absolutely what you should do, and yes, I am. Sure, that is."

He nodded. "Then—may I touch you?"

She set the glass down. "Yes."

This was the moment, then. The moment he had never expected.

The person he had never expected.

Earlier, at the Hotel Hoffmann, as a tiny part of the mystery was solved, he'd remembered once again that this wouldn't last. Soon, he would solve his case, and go home. This was a beautiful moment in time, and it would never be replicated.

In this lovely, sweet bubble, he could live a different life. If only for a few weeks.

They met in the middle of the room. He pulled her against his chest, tilting her chin up so he could kiss her. His hands drifted down her body, gently at first, and then, as she moaned her encouragement, with more need.

"I want—"

"What?" she breathed. "You can have it. Whatever it is."

"I want to undress you. And then I want to touch you."

306 ◇ Diana Biller

She sucked in a breath. "*Yes,*" she said. "You should do that. Excellent idea. Here, let me—"

Her dress was complicated, with a bodice that had a bow to be untied and a row of buttons to be unfastened, and their fingers tangled together as they both attempted to free her from it.

"If I'd known this would happen, I would have worn something easier to get out of," she said, laughing.

Finally she was free of the bodice, revealing her corset and chemise and smooth, creamy shoulders, with little freckles he needed to kiss.

"So pretty," he murmured against her skin. "Can't believe I get to touch you."

"You've said—*oh*—you've said that before."

"Still true," he said, tracing a line across her warm, soft skin, down to her collarbone, up to her throat, everywhere the freckles tempted him.

Miracle.

That was the word in his mind. A miracle that he'd met her. A miracle that he could touch her. A miracle that she existed.

She was a miracle.

He couldn't say it. There were words he didn't say anymore. Instead, he turned his attention to her skirts, which had a different closure system, this one in the back. He'd gotten the hang of the buttons, though, so this one was easier to undo. When she was out of that there was a small bustle to deal with, and then Maria was standing there in only her chemise and corset and hose. Giggling.

"You look so serious," she said.

"I am serious," he said, concentrating on the next step, which he thought was undoing her corset. He realized that at some point in the undressing process she had stopped helping in favor of laughing.

"You missed a dirty joke in there. Something about being serious about getting me naked."

He looked up from examining her corset, giving her the dry look he knew made her laugh (when had her laughter become so precious to him?). "I *am* serious about getting you naked," he said. "It's not a joking matter."

She hit him then and laughed so hard she doubled over, which did not help his corset investigations, but did make something beat frantically and happily against his sternum.

"You need to unhook it there," she said, when she had sobered slightly. "And then—yes, exactly."

He figured it out from there, unlacing her quickly, and helping her out of it. Women wore a great many clothes, particularly women in "society." He'd known, but experiencing it firsthand was another matter.

But from there it was . . . simple. Her chemise went over her head, revealing her breasts, and the sight was so overwhelming, so intimate, that he stopped breathing for a moment, the cloth still crumpled in his hand.

"You've seen them before," she said, laughing again, slight embarrassment weaving through the sound.

Eli tried to think of some words that would convey *Yes, I've seen them before, but they're you, and you're perfect, and twice is not going to be enough times for me to become acclimated to any part of your naked form, and probably not twenty times, or two thousand either, because it's all you, you, you.*

He settled for "You're beautiful," and it was an impossible understatement, but she rolled her eyes in a way that suggested she was comfortable again.

"May I touch you?" he asked.

"You may assume you have permission to touch me anywhere you like, tonight."

He reached out, trailing his fingers down her form, from the delicate skin beneath her throat to the swell of her breasts.

It was still hard to breathe. The intimacy of this moment. Seeing another person unclothed; touching them so privately. He hadn't been prepared for this, not really. The reality of another person's body, beneath his fingers.

Eli stared at his hands, at the way her skin looked beneath them. Soft, soft, soft.

Miracle.

She let out a little sound, bringing his attention to her face. She was biting her lip, small white teeth sinking into the pretty pink of her bottom lip.

"Eli," she said, sighing his name in a way that immediately seared itself into his memory. "Feels good."

Another miracle—that he could touch her and make her feel good.

He let his fingers drift down to her nipples, brushing against them. She jolted hard, so hard he wrapped one arm around her to keep her from falling.

"I'm sorry—"

"No," she said, swallowing. "Good. That's good."

Interesting.

He recalled his reading. He'd been too overwhelmed to remember before, but her words brought it back. He could bring her pleasure. He'd studied.

Eli kept his arm around her, bracing her as he used the other one to trace around one breast, and then the other. She sighed his name again, closing her eyes and arching back. The light from the lamp flickered across her skin.

Tentatively, because he didn't want to hurt her, he took one of her nipples between his thumb and forefinger, pressing gently.

She moaned. All right, so that was good. What if he rolled it beneath his fingers, like one book had suggested—yes, she liked that. He did it again, then let his fingers travel to the other one—

"Harder," she said. "You can do that—harder."

He adjusted the pressure, and she let out a gasp and arched back farther, her body so beautiful across his arm, and finally—finally—he let his hand cover her, and she gasped again, and he stopped thinking for an unknown amount of time, marveling in the feel of her body, in the ways he could touch her and the ways she would respond.

His cock was hard, had been aching in his trousers since he'd kissed her earlier, and every luscious sound that fell from her mouth made its way directly there. He felt . . . tight. Hot. Coiled.

"May I—" His voice was raspy. He tried again. "The sofa?"

She nodded, her eyes wide and dark, and they moved to the sofa, his arms on either side of her body.

He swore.

She laughed, the sound airy and somehow needy. "Love when you look at me and swear. Makes me feel like a goddess or something."

Looking down at her, with her rumpled hair and huge eyes and soft, soft skin, he thought that if he ever were to worship someone, she would be it.

His fingers trailed down to the waist of her drawers, and slowly, relishing the moment, because if this was it, he wanted to remember everything, he untied the drawstring and pushed the fabric down. She lifted to help him, and then they were gone, and he pulled her hose away, and she was naked beneath him.

He swore again, and this time it sounded reverent even to his ears.

"The books said—" he started, breaking off when she giggled, throwing her arm over her face. He waited patiently.

"Sorry, sorry," she said, wiping her eyes. "It's just the first time a man who had me under him cited his sources. Please, do go on."

He bit his grin back.

"*The books said* an orgasm before penetrative sex might make the experience better for you. Is that something you like? To come beforehand?"

She stopped laughing.

"Was it wrong to ask? I just—I want to make you feel good."

"You want to make me feel good," she repeated, her voice high.

"Yes," he said, looking at her closely.

Her eyes were so, so dark.

"How good?" she asked after a pause.

Oh. She likes this.

Eli liked knowing things. He thought, perhaps, knowing things about Maria was what he'd been born for.

"I want to make you scream in pleasure," he said, idly smoothing one hand down her stomach, across the flat, front part of her hip.

"Then—um—yes, probably—if the goal is screaming— that's an ambitious goal for your first time—"

"I'm an ambitious man."

She swallowed. "Yes," she said. "You are. Um—then yes. Make me come first."

With that, he let his hand cover the curl-covered mound just above her legs, and *fuck,* there were no words for how she felt in his hand. So warm and *right.*

She was already wet as he pressed his palm against her. She moaned, long and low and needy this time, her head falling back against the arm of the sofa. And as he slipped a finger inside her slit, feeling the heat and wetness of her, he thought he might never recover from this. Maria Wallner beneath him, touching her, touching her, touching her.

Focus, Eli. Pleasure. Bring her pleasure.

"Tell me how you like it," he said, beginning to gently experiment. It was hard. *He* was hard, and it was . . . distracting. Important to make her scream in pleasure. Also important not to come in his pants first. He took a deep breath.

"That's—what you're doing is good—"

"Mmm, is it?" He varied the pressure, and her hips bucked up. It was different with his fingers than his mouth, though several principles were similar. "I bet it could be better."

"Um, a little harder," she breathed. "*Yes,* and higher, *yes, God, yes*—"

He filed it away, her expression, the need in her face, and then moved his fingers away slightly. She lifted her head, a pout forming on her lips, and he slipped two of his fingers inside her.

"*Oh,*" she cried, her head slamming back.

Perhaps efficiency was the important thing when Eli touched himself, but he found it was the enemy here. Pleasure should be stretched, prolonged, when it was Maria's pleasure. Her pleasure was a generous thing; it wrapped itself around him too.

So, he dragged it out. Thrusting his fingers inside of her, and then when she was pink and moaning and wriggling against his hand, moving up to that beautiful bundle of nerves that was her clitoris and starting over.

"*Eli,*" she said. "*Please.*"

"Mmm," he said, increasing the pressure against her nub. "But you look so lovely like this."

She tried to glare, broke off to swear and then made a sound halfway between a laugh and a moan. "Should have known . . . you'd be like this," she said. "I've created . . . a monster . . . *oh, Eli, yes, yes, yes*—"

When she came, there was still laughter in the air.

Eli pulled her toward him, kissing her face, her neck, the beautiful soft curve of her stomach.

"*God,*" she said, pushing sweat-dampened curls from her

face and staring up at him. She reached up and yanked on his tie. "Why, *why,* are you still dressed?"

He looked down. He'd forgotten about his clothes, in his focus on her.

"Off," she said. "Want to see you."

Compared to Maria's, Eli's clothes were easy enough to shuck. He did so efficiently, feeling somewhat self-conscious afterward, heat creeping up his face. He rubbed the back of his neck.

"Eli, look at me."

He obeyed.

She'd pushed herself up higher on the sofa, and *fuck* she was beautiful, naked against the worn red velvet upholstery, short dark hair messy and wild around her flushed face.

"Come here."

He went to kneel next to her. If he stood . . . parts of him would be very close to her face, and that seemed, well, extremely interesting, but rude.

She swung her legs around, so they were on either side of him, and leaned down to kiss him, long and messy until he was trembling with need. She pulled away, just an inch. "You're beautiful too," she said, kissing him again. "Beautiful"—kiss—"beautiful"—kiss—"beautiful."

She ran a hand through his hair, then pulled, so his face tilted back and she could kiss her way down the column of his throat. When she reached his collarbone, she *licked* her way back up his neck. Eli shivered.

"Remember I said I wanted to see you undone?" she whispered in his ear.

He nodded, light-headed.

"This is the undoing part."

And then she was slipping off the sofa onto his thighs, leaning deeper into their kisses, and *fuck fuck fuck* his cock was pressing directly against her slit, and she was rocking slowly, languidly along it, and Eli had never felt anything, *anything,* as gorgeous and all-encompassing and entirely overwhelming as that. He was barely aware that his arms were around her, bracing her, his hands mapping the straight line of her back and the soft, luscious curve of her ass.

There was nothing but Maria. Maybe there had never been anything but her.

She lifted slightly, pushing at his chest, and for a moment all his awkwardness came back as he tried to figure out the best way to lie back like she seemed to want, but she giggled and kept kissing his neck, so maybe it was all right.

Then he was on his back, and she was straddling him, leaning over to kiss him as she moved her hips, and he was so, *so* achingly hard it was hard to think. He needed to collect himself, get himself together, or this was going to be over before he was even inside her.

She slowed. "We should go to the bedroom," she said, beginning to rise off of him, and he definitely *did not* whimper in protest.

"Come on," she said. "I don't want your first time being inside someone to be on the floor."

Eli tightened his fingers on her hips. It seemed like a fine place to him.

She giggled. "*And* it's hell on my knees."

He released her immediately, and she rolled her eyes at him. He wasn't sure why.

They stood, Eli feeling abruptly cold. She was too far away, and she *had* said he could touch her wherever he wanted tonight, so he pulled her close, her back to his chest, and wrapped his arms around her.

"Of course you're a snuggler," she said, but there was a smile in her voice. "I have to get the French letters."

He buried his nose in her neck and didn't let her go. "In a minute. Don't want to let you go."

314 ◇ Diana Biller

"Eli," she said, wriggling, and finally he released her. Unhappily.

"Don't pout," she said, sneaking a look at him as she went to a cabinet in the corner, her eyes crinkled and merry.

Pout! "I don't pout." It was important for that to be made clear.

"Oh, I see," she said, laughing as she returned, a small envelope in her hands. "My mistake."

He pulled her back in. "Indeed."

"Bedroom," she said, weaving her fingers through one of his hands and tugging. Her bedroom lay through two closed French doors. She opened them, pulling him into the darkness.

"One moment," she said, letting go of his hand (he absolutely did not pout), and a few seconds later a lamp flared to life.

The light flickered over her skin, casting twisting, alluring shadows. "Come here, Eli," she said, taking his hand again, and he let himself be pulled down onto the softness of her bed.

They were lying next to each other, and the complete foreignness of the moment struck him. He, Eli Whittaker, was lying on a bed in Vienna, Austria, next to the most beautiful woman he'd ever seen. They were both naked, he'd already brought her to climax, and soon, he was going to be inside of her.

A few weeks ago, he'd still been in Washington.

"May I touch you?" Maria asked, the question immediately recalling his attention.

"Yes," he said.

She brought her hands to his chest. She moved slowly at first, almost lazily; letting her fingers play lightly with his nipples then drift slowly down to his hips.

Then she placed her hand on his cock.

The last time she'd touched him, he hadn't been able to see her do so—not properly, at least. Now he watched her, fascinated. Burning. He wanted desperately to buck up into her hand, but he willed himself to stay still.

"Maria—"

"Are you ready?"

"Yes," he said, staring at her face. Memorizing it. "If you are?"

She snorted, pushing up to get the envelope. "Let me show you how to use a French letter," she said, and then did so, and it shouldn't have been so alluring, the way she explained and demonstrated it so pragmatically, but it was.

"Did your books—" She stopped talking, breaking into laughter.

He leveled a glare at her. "Preparation is a crucial element of success."

"No, of course, of course—" She broke off in giggles again, and he sighed loudly. "Sorry, sorry, sorry, though where *on earth* did you find them?"

"In an erotic bookshop."

She stopped laughing. "An erotic— You went to an erotic bookshop?"

He shrugged. "Where else was I going to find the relevant texts?"

"That's so—" She put a hand to her cheek. Breathed out through her mouth. "Eli Whittaker, you are a very dangerous man. *Anyway,*" she said, apparently deciding she wasn't going to explain that, "what I wanted to know is if your books covered the basic sexual positions?"

"They did." He'd imagined her in all of them.

"And was there one you wanted to try first?"

He wanted to try all of them. It was an impossible question. "I just . . . I just want *you.*"

Her expression softened as she looked down at him. "All right," she said. "Tell me if you want me to stop. Any time you want to."

316 ◇ Diana Biller

"I will," he said, though there was no future in which he saw that possibility. "You too."

She smiled, and then she was straddling him, his hands coming to her waist, and then she was above him, and positioning him at her entrance, and—

And then she was sinking down on top of him, and he was inside her.

It felt like glory, and the home he'd never had, and heaven.

Maria's eyes were almost closed. She wasn't moving yet. Eli was grateful. If she moved, he wasn't sure he could control himself, and he desperately wanted this to last. He wanted to prolong the pleasure.

"Eli," she said, somewhere between a whisper and a moan. "You feel so good. You feel so good inside of me."

Fuck. That was not helping the whole control situation.

Slowly, painfully slowly, she started to move.

She was so beautiful, above him. Some part of him always associated her with a purple night sky, filled with stars, and with the light painting her skin, her head tossed back, it was as though she *was* the sky, and the night, and the stars, and all the colors in the world.

He loved her.

But he had just enough control left not to say it, which was impressive considering the feeling mounting inside him, this tight, furious, gorgeous feeling that made every other orgasm he'd ever experienced seem like a faint, penciled-in sketch compared to a Titian masterpiece.

Maria was moaning, and saying his name, and every movement of her hips was excruciating and perfect, and then his world was exploding, he was unraveling, he was coming undone.

Chapter Thirty

I'm going to add a stepladder to every linen closet.
And a lock.

— Journal entry of Maria Wallner, 15 January 1878

She collapsed heavily next to him. Eli was breathing hard, his eyes wide and stunned. It might be some time before he was back to his senses, she decided, dropping a kiss to his shoulder and pushing up to get a cloth.

But his hand reached out, pulling her against his chest. "Stay."

"I wasn't going anywhere," she said. "Just to get us something to clean up."

"Stay," he repeated, holding her tighter, and a warm feeling crept up in her chest, like the feeling of summer. She huffed, rolling her eyes for the principle of the thing, but she let him hold her.

After all, it had been his first time. She imagined it could be overwhelming.

It was overwhelming for you, too, that silky voice inside her whispered.

Yes, well. He's good at things, she replied.

And it had been good. Remarkably good, considering he'd never done it before. He hadn't *quite* achieved screaming in pleasure, but he'd come right up upon it.

Not to mention what he'd managed with his fingers before-hand. The man was a quick study. It would stand his future partners in good stead.

And that was a term that left a strange, sticky feeling be-hind it.

She was spared from dwelling, though, by Eli's grunt next to her.

"Are you coming back to the living?" she asked.

"Is it always like this?"

His question was quiet; serious. There were plenty of flip-pant answers she could give, but Eli—Eli deserved more.

"It can be," she said. "That was very good, though. At least for me."

"I thought about it. What it might be like." He ran a hand across his face. "I didn't come close."

She pushed herself up. "Are you— How are you feeling?"

Eli's lip quirked up. "Like I almost died."

Maria laughed. "Good. That's the effect I was going for."

He rolled over on his side. "And you? Are you . . . are you all right?"

"I'm wonderful," she said, softly, pushing some of his hair out of his face.

She'd achieved her goal. He looked undone. His hair was completely askew, his eyes glazed over. His mouth red and swollen. He looked like exactly what he was: a man who had just put his entire soul into fucking her.

And yet—the image struck her differently than she'd imag-ined. When she'd thought about this moment, it had always been in purely sexual terms, but now that she had him before her, in her bed, there was something else weaving through it. Something unbearably fond.

Beloved.

No, not that. Just—fondness. It wasn't surprising. She'd never liked any of the men she'd taken to her bedchamber as well as she liked Eli. Oh, she was fond of them too, but it was different with Eli. He felt more like—

More like home.

She stiffened.

No, home was a set group of people. Home was the hotel, and her grandmother, and Hannah and Mac, and Frau Heilig and Madame Le Blanc, and Abe, and even her mother. There had always been a clear boundary. There were the people she loved, and then there was everyone else, and those boundaries were solid and unchanging, they were forever.

The people you love—

"Maria? Are you all right?" Eli shifted, rolling onto his side so he could look down at her with a concerned expression.

"Yes!" she said, a little too forcefully. He gave her that uncomfortable piercing gaze he got when he was about to start digging at something, and she reminded herself that this was not the place to have an emotional collapse. "Yes," she said again, smiling more normally.

Because this still felt . . . normal. It was still easy, being next to him.

"But I *am* getting up to get us a towel," she said. "Your cuddling desires notwithstanding."

He sighed, but released her, and she pushed up to get a cloth, wetting it in her basin. When she returned, he'd already removed the French letter, tying it neatly.

As they cleaned up together, she could feel him growing increasingly self-conscious. She didn't want that. When he remembered this night later, she wanted it to contain only beauty. So she tugged at his hand, pulling them both back down onto the bed, where they lay facing each other.

"Hey," she said, softly.

"Hey," he said. He smiled back at her, and *oh* something in her chest hurt.

"Did you like it?"

He laughed, quietly at first and then louder, until the tension broke. "What do you want, woman, I already told you you almost killed me."

She shrugged. "I want you to tell me it was the most beautiful, perfect, exquisite moment of your life. Obviously."

"Obviously," he said, the smile still on his lips. "All right. It was the most beautiful, perfect, exquisite moment of my life."

She hit him with a pillow. He very graciously allowed it to land twice before catching it and taking it away, pulling her closer.

"Maria," he said, looking at her in that intense way she felt all the way down to her bones, "it was the most beautiful," he paused to kiss her, "most perfect," another kiss, "most exquisite moment of my life. Thank you."

"Oh," she said. Cleared her throat as she felt the blush begin.

"But—"

"But? What do you mean, but?"

"But I didn't achieve my objective," he said, and she expected him to smile, but he didn't. In fact, he looked utterly serious. "I didn't make you scream."

"Oh," she said. "Well. It was your first time. And you—you were far better than you really had any right to be, for a first time. I was very close—"

"You were not delirious," he said. "I can do better, now that I'm acquainted with the procedure."

She took the pillow back and covered her face with it.

"Who are you?" she muttered against the soft pillowcase, little spiky feathers poking her cheeks. "What are you? Where did you come from?"

"I'm serious," he said. "That is, unless you're too tired? Or sore? I definitely don't want to—"

"Do you mean *now*?"

"No," he said quickly. "I mean, we should have water first."

She hit him with the pillow again.

"People underestimate the importance of water!"

And again, and again after that, until he took it away, and *somehow,* she was on top of him and her skin was warm and tight and the air felt fizzy, and she was kissing him.

Kissing Eli Whittaker was beginning to feel a bit like breathing.

"Should I go get water?" she murmured, against his mouth.

"On second thought," he said, flipping her onto her back in one fluid motion, "water really isn't very important at all."

He achieved his objective the second time around. And when she thought he couldn't surprise her anymore, the third time, as well.

They fell asleep together, sometime in the early morning, and she didn't even question it, though she never let her partners spend the night. That wasn't part of the agreement.

But Eli was different, she argued with herself, as she let him pull her into his chest. He was new to this. She wasn't going to despoil the man and then force him out onto the streets. Or the perfectly nice guest room two floors below. She wasn't going to make him go down those servants' stairs at this hour! He could trip and break his neck.

So she let him cuddle her, because he really was quite clingy, even though she was sure she wouldn't be able to sleep, and then proceeded to fall very soundly asleep and not wake up until it was light out.

She woke the next morning still tucked into his side. Eli was playing gently with one of her curls. When he saw her looking at him, he paused briefly, and then continued.

"Good morning," he said.

He was pretty in the morning light, hair rumpled and eyes still sleepy. "Good morning," she said.

"I realize there must be some sort of etiquette for this situation," he said. "Waking up in a lover's bed. I'm sorry I don't know it."

One of his hands lay between them. She traced a line down one finger. "I don't, either, actually."

She felt, rather than saw, his frown. "What do you mean?"

"I don't usually let men stay the night," she said.

"Oh," he said, and then sat bolt upright. "Oh, I'm sorry. I didn't even think—I shouldn't have assumed—"

"No!" She scrambled up. "No, Eli, I didn't mean that. I wanted you to stay. Really."

"But—"

"I like you."

"That . . . sounded strangely combative, for a compliment."

His dry tone made her snort. She was being ridiculous. It was just Eli. Eli listened when she talked, and he never judged her. "I'm feeling defensive," she said. "I really do like you, you know. Maybe more than I'm used to, in this sort of relationship. I wanted you to stay."

"You like me," he said, a strange expression on his face.

"Yes?"

"Not many people do."

"Ah yes," she said. "The death threats. I'm glad we've circled back to that. Have you considered a less dangerous line of work?"

He flopped back on the bed. "I don't think it would help," he said. "I think it's me. And you changed the subject."

"Did I?"

"Yes. You were talking about how much you liked me."

Her snort turned into a laugh, which somehow turned into round four, because laughter seemed to do that for them. And that was different too. Oh, she'd laughed with the others, but not like this. That was half show, she realized. This was . . . being seen.

And that was too much, too close, too serious. So, after they finished, she stood up. "Now I really am evicting you, though. I have to be at the front desk in an hour."

He nodded and stood. "I have some telegrams to send, but I'll be back this evening. Is there anything you need help with?"

"I'm starting the ballroom decorations tonight," she said.

"I'll be there," he said. "Can I borrow a hairbrush?"

She pointed to one, watching as he put himself back together. "You don't have to—"

"I want to. What time?"

"After my shift is over," she said. "At six."

"All right." He leaned down, now perfectly neat and presentable, and before she really knew what she was doing she was tilting her head up for a sweet, light kiss. "I'll see you at six, then."

And then he left, Maria staring after him, before she remembered that brooding about men would contribute nothing to preparing for a ball.

Chapter Thirty-one

God in Heaven, they tried to kill us. My Josephine, they had their guns aimed at her—no. Can't think about that. I fixed it. They'll never come back. We'll be safe. Me, and her, and her children. I've made sure of it.
—Journal entry of Theresa Wallner, 25 December 1815

January 25

The next few days passed quickly, measured in items crossed off Maria's to-do list and kisses stolen in shadowy alcoves. And if there was a thrum of unease beneath the frantic preparations and flirting and laughter, well, there would be time to think about it later. Not that it didn't catch her, sometimes: in the warmth that bloomed at Eli's smile; or when she found Hannah teaching him how to knead bread, their expressions deadly serious (bread, they informed her, was not a joking matter). In these moments she remembered he *didn't* actually fit. That this was an illusion. She wasn't going to keep him. She didn't want to, something she was reminded of when her mother sent a stiff message requesting that Maria send more of her clothes to the Hotel Hoffmann.

And now, too, the day before the ball, standing in the lobby waiting for Hannah and Eli so they could collect some greenery from the Woods, staring once more at her father.

"Maria," Heinrich said, smiling at her. It was an odd feeling, her father actually looking at her. "I was in the neighborhood, and I thought I'd come see you. Perhaps take you to supper?"

She stared at him. "I'm busy."

His face fell. "Ah, well. Of course you are, you're young, you have friends—"

"I have a ball to host tomorrow."

"Ah! That's right, so you do. Well, you're sure I can't tempt you?"

"I'm sure," she said, slowly. She needed to put a stop to this, whatever "this" was. This misguided attempt at family.

There was motion on the stairs.

"Maria, Eli said you were—" Mac stopped, abruptly. "Papa."

"Son! I heard you were staying here." Heinrich moved forward, clapping Mac on the back. "Couldn't stand your mother anymore, eh? Well, young men need their freedom."

Mac looked at Maria, misery and embarrassment and love tangled up in his gaze. "You'll have to excuse us," he said, his tone formal. "Maria and I have an engagement."

"My children, together! Ah, it makes this old man proud," Heinrich said, ostentatiously wiping his eyes with his handkerchief. "Go, go, go. You were separated too long—not my doing, you know. Your mothers never really got on."

To her astonishment, Maria felt an abrupt need to defend Elisabeth rising in her chest. "My mother—" she began, but Mac was already speaking.

"Please don't speak of my mother so casually," Mac said. "Or of Maria's."

Heinrich blinked at them both, a strange blankness on his face before he composed it once more into genial lines. "Good children, both of you. Now off you go. I'll sit here in the warmth for a bit—maybe ask this young man to fetch me a brandy." He nodded at Abe, who immediately bowed and went to the kitchen to comply. Heinrich settled himself into one of the lobby's plush armchairs.

Maria frowned as he picked up a newspaper. Mac stood next to her, and when she glanced up she saw the same scowl on his face.

"I'm sorry," Mac said. "I know my mother—I don't know if I should have defended her, just then. After what she's done to you. Is doing to you."

"You don't need to apologize," Maria said, her attention still on her father. "I was about to do the same. I know—I know my mother has her faults. But—"

"He doesn't get to enumerate them," Mac said. His voice was firm.

"No. He doesn't. And thank you for defending my mother too."

Shrugging, Mac turned away from his father. "Eli said you needed help cutting greenery," he said, in a determinedly lighter tone.

"Oh," Maria said, an unexpected smile forming on her lips as she looked at her brother, dressed warmly with a thick wool scarf and a practical pair of heavy leather gloves. "Thank you."

He nodded. "But will that coat be warm enough? Should you—" He reached out to rearrange her scarf more tightly, and as she batted his hands away, Hannah and Eli emerged from the kitchen, deep in conversation about the logistics of the gelatin lily pond.

"Maria, there's been a—" Hannah said, wrapping her own bright red scarf around her as she crossed the lobby, and halting abruptly when she saw Heinrich.

Eli lifted his eyebrows and looked at Maria. A month ago, she would have said he looked cold and blank, but now she could see it; the little ways he was speaking to her. *Are you all right?* the crease on his forehead asked. *Do you need me to do something?* the tension in his shoulders inquired.

And underneath it all, the warm flicker in his eyes, that simply said, *Hello, you.*

She smiled up at him. "It's fine," she murmured, and, almost infinitesimally, he nodded. "Are you ready?" she asked the others.

"Well, there's been a slight change," Hannah said, as the kitchen door opened again and Josephine and Emilie stepped out, Josephine fussing with Emilie's coat.

"I still think it's too cold," she was saying, wrapping a length of patterned silk around Emilie's neck.

"Nonsense," Emilie said, reading a notebook as she walked. "The cold is exactly what I need. Perhaps it will freeze out some of these rotten ideas. Cleanse me. And if it doesn't, I shall simply lie down and die, and the snow will cover me, and then at least I will be freed from the indignities of this mortal coil."

"Well, if you must, you must," Josephine said, dryly. "I shall have Saint-Saëns played at your funeral."

Emilie gasped. "You shall *not*!"

"What do you care? You'll be dead."

"Sorry," Hannah whispered in Maria's ear. "Emilie said she wanted to come."

"And you would disrespect the dead with that . . . that *hack*?"

Josephine shrugged. "He seems fine to—What is *he* doing here?"

Ah. She'd found Heinrich.

"The carriage is ready!" Maria exclaimed, hurrying forward.

"Maria, what is that man doing in our hotel? Elisabeth isn't here."

"He came to see me," Maria said. "Don't worry about it."

"He came to see you? My granddaughter? He *dares* inconvenience *my granddaughter* in *my* hotel?"

The "my" did not escape Maria's notice, making her lips quirk as Josephine stared down her nose at Heinrich. Heinrich, for his part, appeared oblivious to them all, happily ensconced beneath the portrait of Theresa, reading his newspaper.

"It's taken care of," Maria said. "Come on, at this rate it will be dark by the time we even see a tree. Let's go."

She ushered them out of the lobby, not without difficulty. Mac appeared to be unburdening himself to Eli—that was an odd little friendship that had started up—and Eli had to remind him to put on his hat as he pushed Mac through the hotel doors, and Emilie forgot, at the last moment, where she had put her glasses, but eventually Maria had them all out on the sidewalk, walking to the fiacre stand.

When they arrived at the stand, Claude Girard was waiting.

"Ah, there you are," he said, bowing smoothly. "I thought perhaps I had the time wrong. I've already bespoken two cabs."

He busied himself helping Emilie and Josephine into one, and Maria tugged at Eli's sleeve. "Did you invite him?"

"No," Eli said.

"Then how did he— Mac, did you?"

Mac shrugged. "It's Claude," he said. "He knows things."

Eli frowned at this, but didn't argue, and it seemed rude to question Claude about it. Besides, she could hear Emilie laughing, and anything that took Emilie's mind off her composition problems could only be a good thing.

So she simply got in the closest carriage, Eli behind her. Mac and Hannah joined them, the other three in the second carriage, and they departed.

Maria pulled out her notebook as they drove, reviewing

her list and crossing off the items she'd already accomplished. The chandelier had been repaired that morning. When she'd seen it glowing brightly, for the first time in five years, she'd felt an odd pressure in her lungs, something that felt half like joy and half like sorrow.

"We're back," she had whispered, standing alone in the Large Ballroom after the repairman had gone. "We're back."

The rental furniture had been delivered in the early afternoon. Later that evening, when they came back with the greenery, it would be time to start setting everything up. Hannah had spent the last three days preparing—in fact, Maria was quite certain she would not be in the carriage now if it weren't for Mac—and would start in the kitchen at four the next morning.

Maria was measuring things in hours, now. Hannah in the kitchen at four, the flowers delivered at six, the orchestra there at three in the afternoon to set up, the dancers at five, the guests at seven. From there, the schedule was timed in minutes, and then—

And then what?

And then nothing, she told herself. *The Hotel Wallner will be back where it belongs. And I'll never let it fall behind again.*

That statement rang with the same love, the same intensity it always had, and Maria found herself relieved. She hadn't become her mother. She wasn't replacing the hotel with a man. The Hotel Wallner was, and always would be, her true love.

And until he left, Eli was . . . Eli.

Maria watched him listen seriously as Hannah discussed the lily pond, and the reinforcements necessary to hold that much champagne. He murmured something, and Hannah nodded vigorously, and took out *her* notebook—and Maria could already see it happening; *someone* was going to leave their notebook in the woods—and began sketching. Eli watched her, making a short comment in that deep voice of his, and Mac laughed and murmured something too.

They were so . . . impossibly dear. All of them. Yes, she would miss Eli when he was gone. She would miss him terribly. He wasn't *the man,* but . . . perhaps for a moment she let herself wish he were. That she could have this: the hotel and her family and him, all woven together. Laughing, just like they were now.

But she couldn't, and suddenly it felt as though she couldn't breathe.

"Maria?" Hannah was looking at her with raised eyebrows.

"Yes? Sorry, what?"

Her friend was looking at her, a flicker of concern in her warm brown eyes. "Where were you?"

Maria forced a smile. "Just thinking about everything we have left to do," she said. "What were you saying?"

Hannah narrowed her eyes, but allowed the redirection. "We were talking about the location. What if we extended the pond more along the window—"

She let herself fall back into the planning, debating table placement and the amount of space for dancing, and still her breath felt tight, as if she were having to remind her lungs to pull the air in and then expel it, over and over again.

It stayed like that, even when the carriages disgorged them in the Woods, even cutting the branches, even watching Hannah hesitantly flirting with Mac. Even when Eli touched her gently on the shoulder and asked what was wrong.

"Nothing," she said, laughing brittlely as she hacked at a branch. "Nothing. Really."

He took the knife and sliced the branch off easily, handing it to her with a look that said he didn't believe her.

Maria shook her head, sighing. "I think it's nerves," she

said, which must be the truth, after all. She'd never thrown a party this elaborate, or this important.

Eli watched her closely, his brow still furrowed. "All right," he said. "But, just so you know, it's going to be a triumph."

He turned back to the tree, choosing another branch to strip off, and Maria absently rubbed her chest.

A triumph.

She thought so, too. Didn't doubt it—had never doubted, she realized. This ball *was* going to be a triumph, and the Hotel Wallner *was* going to be returned to fashion. So why did the air itself feel sharp?

Nerves, she told herself.

Nodding to herself, she started to haul the cut branches back to the carriages.

Something was wrong with Maria. It had clung to her the whole time they were out, and by the time the carriages arrived back at the hotel, her smile was looking increasingly fragile.

They all stepped out, Emilie disappearing almost immediately, muttering about "that feeling of warmth from childhood; the innocence that must, inevitably, be shattered," followed by Hannah, muttering about gelatin molds. When they walked into the lobby, Eli didn't miss the way Maria's gaze went to the chair where her father had sat.

Perhaps he was even more than usually attuned to her today. Because something was wrong with Eli, too: that morning, he had received an answer from the State Department regarding the records of embezzlement he'd sent, and he had permission to use the information to pressure Director Farrow and Secretary Collins to reveal what they knew about the stolen codes. They knew something. On Monday he would find out exactly what.

And then what?

Codes, solved. Hotel sabotage, solved. Assassination attempts, solved. Apparently.

The Hotel Wallner had a kind of magic, he was realizing. A particularly dangerous kind: within its walls it was possible to feel safe. It even tricked him sometimes, luring him into laughter and flirting and easy, domestic tasks that made Maria smile. He didn't resent the magic—it had made it possible for him to love, too. But the Hotel Wallner was Fairyland, and he knew better than to forget the illusion.

It was all coming to an end. The bubble was about to . . . not pop, exactly. Dissipate into the air around it; be reabsorbed into real life. Life with corrupt senators, and his plain little room in his plain little boardinghouse, and his work.

You still have time, Eli reminded himself, when the wings of panic began to beat against his chest.

He ignored the voice that told him there would never be enough time.

He stopped in his hotel room to divest himself of his hat and coat, and then, without thinking about it, went to the Large Ballroom to see what Maria needed help with.

She was already there with Mac, her hands on the hips of the plain gown she'd worn to the Woods. He lingered in the doorway to watch her. He found himself doing that, lately: trying to capture the way she smiled; the way her skin crinkled around her eyes; even the way her curls twisted and sprang back from his hands. He would tell himself, *Ah, she has a freckle above her lip on the right side of her face,* or *Ah, see the way the light clings to her, as she stands by that window.* Mapping her. Mapping them.

"Eli!" Mac saw him standing there and waved enthusiastically, so he walked over. Maria smiled that same smile, warm, and lovely, and terribly, terribly brittle.

Perhaps it really was only nerves. In which case the best thing he could do was help her.

"What do you need me to do?" he asked.

Her eyes softened a bit. "I'd argue with you over that of-fer, but I have too much work. Can you take Mac and set up the tables?" She lowered her voice. "He won't stop fussing over me, after Heinrich's visit."

Eli simply nodded, taking the table map she handed him, and gestured for Mac to follow.

They got to work.

At some point in the evening Josephine joined them, sit-ting at one of the already-set-up tables and folding napkins with the ease of someone who had folded thousands of nap-kins in her life. Her expression was serious, but he detected a slight air of excitement in her motions.

After the tables and chairs were out, he turned to the lily pond he'd built that morning, giving it a final check to make sure it was champagne-tight. Hannah was running up and down, trying to decide a million different food-related things at once, and Eli, in a fit of romanticism, released Mac to go help her.

Probably nothing would come of them. He was an aris-tocrat, and Maria had told him Hannah was the daughter of a milliner, and even in America that was an impassable dif-ference in class, let alone in Imperial Vienna. But . . . maybe nothing *had* to come of them. Maybe it was enough that they both grew pink and happy whenever the other was near.

It was almost one in the morning when they finished. Maria had ordered Hannah home several hours earlier, and around midnight, Josephine had folded the last napkin, stood up decisively, and said the rest of the work was for younger people who had less interesting ways to spend their time.

"That's as much as we can do tonight, I think," Maria said, standing back from where she and Eli had maneuvered the arbor that Hannah would decorate with sweets the next morning. The lily pond was ready to be filled, the tables were ready to be set up, the chandelier shone brightly. Even the damn fountain was being used to good effect, standing at the top of the stairs, wrapped in greenery and fake moss, ready to welcome guests to another world.

Maria put her hands on her hips and surveyed the room, an expression caught between pride and longing on her face. "It's been so long since I've seen this."

Eli stood next to her, trying to see it through her eyes. "You never told me what happened," he said. "Why it came to this state in the first place."

She shrugged. "It's not a secret. My grandmother retired eight years ago and left the managership to my mother. Who . . . Well. This part you already know. The hotel is not the most important thing in her life. My father is."

Eli might have said that the most important thing to Elisabeth seemed to be herself. But it wasn't his mother, so he remained silent.

"Still, it was all right for a year or so. But then there was the Panic of '73. It . . . it decimated Vienna, or at least wealthy Vienna. Entire families, our patrons, were wiped out overnight. And to make things worse, the crisis with Bosnia started two years later, making financial recovery even slower. When I was trying to get a loan, I was told the banks are still only lending a tenth of what they did before the Panic. We flourish when the wealthy flourish, and the wealthy simply haven't been flourishing. My mother tried, in her way."

Maria didn't say anything more, and Eli filled in the rest. They stood together, gazing at the huge room, everything polished and sparkling.

"It's hard for me to believe it looks like this again. It looks like a memory."

"It's not. You did this, Maria."

She laughed then, a rueful sound, and looked down at the floors. She rubbed one foot along them. "I sold my great-grandmother's ring to pay for these floors, in the end."

"The woman in the portrait, right?"

Maria nodded. "She founded the hotel. It was something between a payment and a goodbye gift from my grandmother's father."

Eli raised an eyebrow. "Quite a goodbye gift."

"Little enough to him," she said. "And in the end, he turned out to be . . . Well. That's a family secret, and while I'm happy enough to give you mine—"

"It's all right. You don't need tell me."

She smiled at him. "Do you want to go on a walk?"

"It's late," he said, one hand gently touching her upper arm. He thought he'd never get used to this kind of casual touch. "Shouldn't you sleep?"

"I'm too nervous. Just a short one. Some fresh air."

"All right," he said. They took one last look at the ballroom, before they parted to get their coats. Everything was soft and quiet here.

It was busier outside, even though Maria told him there had been no major balls today. Crowds of people roamed the streets, laughing and dancing and stumbling from bars. She steered him surely through, guiding him until they arrived at the gates of a large park. It was still lit, gas lamps lining the winding paths, and couples drifting along arm in arm.

"This is a rose garden in the summer," Maria said. "But it's still nice now, and it's large enough to be quiet."

It was nice. It was nice to walk next to her, late at night, with the cold air nipping at his nose and her warm body pressed close to his.

He needed to tell her about the codes case. He'd put it off long enough.

"Maria."

"Hmm?"

"I can't give you the details," he said. "But I expect to have a break in my case on Monday."

She didn't say anything for a long time. He tried to look at her face as they walked, but all he could see was hair and shadow.

"That's good," she said, finally.

"Yes," he said, slowly. "Good."

"You think this will solve it." It wasn't a question.

"I don't know," Eli said. "But it's a possibility."

She nodded. "And your time in Vienna will be over."

The sentence—an entirely expected, entirely true sentence he'd said to himself at least thirty times in the last twenty-four hours—hit him directly in the chest. Winded him.

No, he wanted to cry. *It doesn't have to be. Let me, let me—*

But he didn't even know what to ask for.

"We should go back," she said. "I believe I *am* feeling tired, after all."

"Maria—"

She finally looked up, and the expression on her face— still open, still warm, with her mouth held so tightly, like she was determined not to cry—broke him. Froze his breath in his lungs. Laid his chest open and pulled his heart out. "I can't, Eli. Not tonight."

The ball was tomorrow. One of the most important days of her life. This was not the time. So he agreed. "Let's go back."

They walked quietly back the way they had come, their silence heavy, surrounded by the revelers.

"It's not as though we didn't know this day would arrive," Maria said, as they turned back onto Annagasse. "It was always—" She broke off, grabbing his arm. "Eli. What's that?"

He looked down the street, toward the hotel.

"Smoke," he said.

Chapter Thirty-two

Francis died yesterday. It's been so long since I saw him. I'll never know now if he knew about the assassination attempt—I'd like to think not. He gave me a daughter and a hotel, after all. The new Emperor will be his son Ferdinand. Josephine's half brother. I tried to speak to her today. After all, he was still her father. But she's an adult, with a child of her own, and harder for me to read. She asked if I was all right. In the end we simply ate our breakfast together and listened to the newsboys shout the news outside, over and over again.
—Journal entry of Theresa Wallner, 3 March 1835

She didn't think of anything as they ran down the narrow street. There was no room for thoughts; only pressing panic that felt like screaming.

By the time they reached the hotel a crowd had formed in front: hotel guests in their nightdress, passersby. Desperately, she scanned the crowd for her grandmother, for Hannah, for Mac.

"There," Eli shouted, next to her, his voice carrying over the din of the crowd. "There they are."

He turned her toward them, and yes, there they were, all three standing with Abe, counting the guests.

Maria pushed her way toward them. "Abe," she said. "What's the count?"

"All the guests are out," he said. "The Novotnýs went to a dinner party earlier and haven't returned. Everyone else is here."

She took the guest list from him anyway, scanned down it, matching names to faces.

"And you're all right?"

He jerked his head in confirmation. "I don't know what happened. I smelled smoke coming from the kitchen, and I panicked. I just got everyone out—I should have—"

"You did exactly what you should have," she said firmly, handing the list back to him.

Hannah's face was wan, tear-streaked. Mac stood next to her, her hand tucked firmly in his. "Maria," she said. "It must have been me. I must have left something on in the kitchen—"

"Stop," Maria said, taking her friend by the shoulder. "I don't care. All I care about is that you're safe."

The air smelled acrid.

"The fire brigade is coming," Abe said. "I sent a messenger."

She nodded. "I'm going to check on the guests. Stay here."

They were already turning to each other as she left, organizing a bucket brigade.

Her family was safe. The hotel could burn. But there was something in the hotel that kept her family safe, had kept them safe for decades, and that could not be allowed to burn.

The Wallner journals.

She pulled her scarf over her mouth as she neared the front doors. If the fire was in the kitchen, this was the only viable entrance. She glanced at the crowd, but in the chaos she didn't think anyone noticed her as she slipped into the lobby.

The air was hot, singeing the hair on her face and head. She coughed, sucking in more smoke, and steadied herself against a chair. It was dark, the only light coming from the streetlamp reflecting against the smoke, painting the room charcoal and orange. She couldn't see any fire, yet, but with this much smoke it must be growing.

She found her way across the room from memory. She made out vague shapes, the room a strange, apocalyptic version of the place she knew so well.

The journals were hidden behind the portrait of Theresa Wallner. It seemed fitting, since she'd been the first to deploy them, to keep her small family safe using information.

As far as secrets went, the one about the Wallner journals was fairly straightforward. A few years after Josephine's birth, Theresa had used the last of her influence with the old Emperor to meddle in something powerful people thought she shouldn't have. A few days later, an assassin had paid her and Josephine a visit in the same hotel her royal lover had given her. And Theresa had lied.

She'd made up the existence of journals. Said she'd written everything down—everything. All the petty court secrets, all the hidden affairs, all the clandestine meetings, all the way down to how the Emperor performed in bed. And then she said the journals were hidden somewhere far, far away, and that she had left careful instructions: if she died in a suspicious manner, they were to immediately become public.

The assassin left. He did not return.

There were attempts, of course, to find the journals over the years. But it seemed the powers that be had believed Theresa when she said they were far away, and so the searches usually focused on the town in Bohemia Theresa had come from, before she had been elevated to royal mistress. Eventually, two emperors later, the Wallners faded from focus.

But they never forgot that the journals had kept them safe.

Maria reached the portrait. She was light-headed from the smoke—it was an effort to pull a chair over to stand on.

Clumsily, she climbed on it and reached beneath the frame to the hidden latch. When she pulled on it, the portrait swung slowly open. She reached in to take the journals and—

Her hand met a bare shelf.

She felt along the opening, panic growing slowly and then all at once.

The journals were gone.

She half fell from the chair. Dimly, she knew she needed to leave. The hotel was on fire. She couldn't breathe. She was on the verge of passing out.

But the journals were gone.

The journals. Their protection. Sixty years of legacy.

Go, her brain was screaming at her. *You need to go. Now.*

She couldn't. She couldn't move.

The smoke grew thicker around her.

She heard the door slam open. "Maria!" Eli's voice called. "Maria, tell me you didn't—"

"Eli," she said, her muscles suddenly springing back to life. She coughed and stumbled toward him. "Eli, get out of here, you shouldn't have—"

"Don't," Eli growled. He seized her hand and was pulling her toward the door when he stumbled over a dark lump on the floor.

"What—" He squatted down. "It's a person," he said, his voice urgent.

"What? They said everyone was—"

He flipped the unconscious body over, and Maria saw her father, a large bag strapped to his torso.

"I'll carry him out," Eli said, hoisting him and pushing her toward the door in the same breath. "Come on, go."

Her foot connected with something as she took a step, making a very specific sound. As Eli pulled at her arm she hesitated.

"Maria! Now!"

She reached down quickly, scooping it up, and hurried after them.

The night air was cold and clear, hitting her lungs like frigid water. She coughed, and coughed some more, doubled over. In the corner of her vision she saw Eli hand her father to someone, and then a few seconds later his arms were around her. He led her across the street to the small park, gently pushing her onto one of the benches. The metal was cold beneath her skin.

"Here," he said, pushing a flask at her. "Water."

She nodded. Drank some. Choked a bit more.

"You too," she said, handing it to him.

"I wasn't in for as long—"

"Eli," she said, leaning back against the metal. Her throat was hoarse. "What if, this time, we *both* saw a doctor?"

He stared at her. "Are you making a joke?"

"Yes," she said. "But at the same time, no."

His lips quivered. "Give me the water," he said.

She looked up at the hotel. The bucket line was long, snaking from the alley into the street. When she could stand without fainting, she would go help.

"This is where we first met," she said.

"I remember," he said. "You were deeply concerned that we might have sexual relations in a public square."

"An entirely reasonable concern," she said. "Have you seen your mouth?"

He snorted, and just for a moment, it was like everything was going to be all right.

A mirage.

"There is something I've wondered, though," she said, looking down at the object in her hands.

He hummed in invitation.

"Did I vomit on you? That night?"

He burst out in surprised laughter. "No," he said, once he could breathe again.

"Oh, thank the Lord," she said, smiling at him before her gaze returned her hands.

"What is that?"

"This?" She turned it over in her hands. "This is a Wallner journal, which my father apparently had in his possession. Oh. I didn't ask. He is alive, isn't he?"

"He was waking up when I left him."

"Good," she said. "I was rather hoping to be the one to kill him. I think I can stand now. Let's go join the bucket line."

It was dawn by the time Maria was able to set foot in her hotel, a bright, silver-pink dawn that ought to have marked the end to some truly wonderful party.

It was a waste, this dawn.

The damage had been confined to the kitchen. A blessing. In fact, it had all been so much better than it could have been—the bucket line had been formed quickly, and the fire brigade had arrived quickly, and the entire back part of the kitchen was stone. There didn't appear to be any structural damage. Just a ruined kitchen.

Hannah let out a keening sound when she saw it. Like an animal with a mortal wound. Maria heard Mac whisper something comforting to her, and was grateful, because in this moment, she had no words.

Eli stood next to her. She didn't look at him.

In the night, in the panic, it had been enough that her family—her loved ones—were safe.

But as she stood amid the twisted wreckage of the fire, staring at the collapsed range, the half-charred kitchen table, the ruined ceiling—it was as though someone had reached into her chest and carved off a slice of her heart.

In the night, she'd thought, *It's only a building, we can rebuild.*

And it was only a building.

But—they couldn't rebuild. She'd made do, and made do, and made do, and finally she'd found something she couldn't make do around. She'd rested everything on the Hotelkeepers' Ball, and without a working kitchen there was no way they could hold it, and if they didn't hold it there was no way to restore the kitchen—

And that wasn't even including the money from the ticket sales, that she would have to refund when they had to cancel—

Josephine stepped into the room, picking her way to Maria's side. Maria let her hand fall to her side and take her grandmother's. Josephine's hand was delicate and warm. It was the sort of hand that should have felt fragile, but instead it was strong. A hand that had seen a lot, and done a lot, and survived a lot.

"Everyone's safe," Josephine said, quietly. "That's the important thing."

"Yes," Maria agreed.

They watched Eli poke around the room, lifting wreckage and staring at the walls.

"We'll find a way."

"Yes."

But she heard the fatigue in Josephine's voice. Felt it echoed in her chest.

"I did this," Hannah whispered, behind her. "I must have—I must have forgotten something—it's my fault."

Maria shook her head. "It isn't."

"But I—"

"You didn't start the fire."

Her friend stared at her, eyes wide and rimmed with red.

"I can't tell you everything right now," Maria said. "But I will. In the meantime, I need you to get some rest. Will you let Mac take you home?"

"No, I need to be here—"

"There's nothing you can do right now," Maria said. "But there will be later. There will be a lot of work, and I'm going to need you to be rested and strong enough to do it. So go home, rest, and come back."

Hannah sniffed hard, then took a determined breath. "All right," she murmured, and Mac quickly wrapped an arm around her shoulders and led her from the room.

"Tell me," Josephine said, once they were gone. The fatigue was gone, replaced by steel.

Maria sighed, pulling out the journal. "This fell from Heinrich's bag, when we found him. The others are gone."

She felt her grandmother stiffen. "Gone?"

"If it's any comfort," Maria said, "I don't think they went far."

Eli walked toward them, wiping his hands on his handkerchief. "Someone tossed something through that window." He nodded toward the window over the sink. "I can't say what, exactly. Maybe a lit rag in a bottle of alcohol."

Josephine looked at the journal, then at Eli.

"I'll leave," he said, apparently understanding the glance as a request for privacy. "But when you go to confront him, I want to be there." He turned to leave.

"Wait," Josephine said.

Eli stopped, and Maria looked at her grandmother in surprise.

"Grandmother?"

"He can know."

"But he's not, he's not—"

Josephine lifted her eyebrows. "If you can't even tell me whatever he's not, then I think we can assume he *is*. And he's useful. You have my permission to tell him."

But he's leaving, Maria wanted to say. In the next moment she realized how very safe that made him.

"It's one of our family journals," she said, slowly. This was not a secret she'd ever shared. "You've seen me write in them. We've kept them since the very beginning. They . . . ensure our family's protection."

"Blackmail?" Eli's expression didn't change, like he was refusing to assign blackmail a moral weight.

Maria shrugged. "Not recently," she said. "But a long time ago, yes."

Eli sighed as he stared down at the book in Josephine's hand. "And neither of you thought this was relevant to the whole assassination situation?"

"I mean a *long* time ago," Maria said. "Everyone involved is already dead."

"Excuse me," Josephine said.

"Sorry, everyone except my grandmother, who was very young at the time."

Eli frowned, apparently unconvinced. "And so, you were what, hiding them? And your father stole them? And set a fire to do so?"

They all sighed together, an enormous collective sigh.

"He really is a waste of flesh," Josephine said.

"Yes," Maria said.

Eli said nothing, but there was a flicker of something dark in his eyes. Maria reached out and touched his hand.

"I suppose we need to pay him a morning call, then," Josephine said. "Collect Mac as soon as he returns. This involves him too. I'm going to get my gun."

As the carriage came to a stop in front of Heinrich von Eder's home, Eli realized it hadn't been so long since he'd last been there. A little more than two weeks, really.

A lifetime.

There were four of them in the fiacre: Maria, Mac, Josephine, and himself. Mac's face was pale, his expression nauseated. Josephine looked firm, angry.

Maria looked . . . absent. When he helped her from the cab she stared up at the enormous building before them.

"I've never been here before," she said, her voice flat. Detached.

"I'm going to kill him," Mac said.

"We can argue about who's going to kill him after we recover the journals," Josephine replied. "And while we're here I have a few things to say to your mother as well, Mac."

She led the way to the front door. It opened just as they arrived before it.

"You're expected," the butler said, taking in their smoke-stained, filthy state and sniffing. He looked at Mac and bowed. "Young master."

"Where are they?" Mac asked.

"Your father's bedroom."

Mac turned to his companions. "This way," he said tersely. They followed.

Eli walked next to Maria down the corridor he had seen during his first visit, realizing that that meant he had been to her father's house one more time than she had. He supposed it wasn't unusual for illegitimate children to be kept separate like this, but seeing her eyes widen at the obvious wealth around her, he thought there was something deeply, deeply wrong with it.

He wondered if there had been a time when she loved her father.

There had been a time when Eli had loved his. It lingered at the edges of his memory, a flicker of a feeling before all the anger and beatings and hunger. Before the betrayal, he realized. No child comes into the world mistrusting their parents.

A child's love for a parent was supposed to be a constant—unkillable. Eli knew better. He didn't know when his love for his father had died, but it was long before the night he'd fired the gun.

He didn't know why he was thinking about that, either. But ever since he'd come to Vienna the memories had been pressing upon him, like they were desperately asking to be seen. Rearranged. So for once, as he followed Maria's family up the stairs, he let them.

Mac led them down another corridor, this one carpeted in lush burgundy, with burgundy silk wallpaper to match. He saw Maria lift her eyebrows at it, and then catch his eye in pale amusement. He snorted softly in return.

"Here," Mac said, stopping before a dark wooden door. "This is his room."

Josephine nodded. "All right," she said. "I'll do the talking, Mac—"

"Wait, Grandmother."

Josephine cocked her head, her hand already on the doorknob.

"I'll do the talking," Maria said softly. "I'm the manager of the hotel. And—and he's my father."

After a pause, her grandmother stepped aside. "I'll be right behind you."

Maria mustered a smile. "You always are," she said, and pushed the door open.

The room was dark, lit only by a single lamp on a table. Blinking, Eli made out Heinrich on the bed, apparently asleep. Adelaide sat next to the table in a reading chair, Heinrich's bag open and empty on the floor and a stack of books on the table. She looked up from what appeared to be a seating chart when they walked in.

She nodded at the pile of books. "Yours, I think," she said to Maria. "Hello, Frau Wallner. Macario. And Mr. Whittaker, from the American Legation."

Maria walked across the room to the books. They were

348 ◇ Diana Biller

dated, Eli realized, in small black writing on the spine. She ran her finger down the stack, and then looked at Adelaide.

"The rest are over there," Adelaide said, nodding toward the floor by the bed. "I didn't read them. None of my business. Would you like some tea?"

After a moment, Maria nodded. "Thank you."

"Please, sit."

She gestured to the sofa and armchairs across from her, and they sat. Adelaide rang for a maid, and asked for tea. The girl hurried away, leaving the five of them in silence.

"Do you know why?" Maria asked.

"Why?"

"Why he did it," Maria said. "Because he did, yes? He set a fire to steal our journals, and almost killed himself in the process."

"A pity he didn't succeed," Adelaide and Josephine said at the same time.

"Yes, well, he didn't," Maria said. She glanced toward the lump on the bed. "How is he?"

"He'll be fine," Adelaide said. "He was being unbearable about the pain, so I told the doctor to drug him. I don't know why he did it. But my guess would be—"

The door flew open. Eli twisted around in his chair and saw Elisabeth framed dramatically in the doorway, the butler hanging on to her arm.

"Let me go," she said, slapping him away and running across the room to the bed, which she promptly threw herself down on. "*Heinrich*," she sobbed. "*Heinrich, my love, my love, wake up, you must—*"

"He's not going to," Adelaide said, waving the butler away with a resigned sigh.

"What do you mean?" Elisabeth cried, pushing herself up and turning her tear-streaked face toward them. "*What have you done to him, you miserable bitch?*"

"Given him sleeping medicine," Adelaide said. "He'll be awake shortly, so you should probably save your histrionics for then."

"Sleeping medicine—oh Heinrich, the pain you must have been in—"

"Stop it, Elisabeth," Josephine snapped. "If you're not going to leave you may sit, but you *will not* embarrass me or your daughter any further."

Elisabeth opened her mouth as though to protest, but a whip-sharp *now* from Josephine had her shutting it.

"I will sit," she said, with great dignity. "And wait for my love to wake up."

Maria sighed, pinching the bridge of her nose, and turned to Adelaide. "I apologize for that interruption," she said. "Won't you continue?"

Adelaide's expression was flat as she looked at Elisabeth, but a few seconds later she nodded. "As I was saying. I suspect he stole the journals—"

"What?" The word was sudden and almost expressionless. For a moment Eli didn't realize it was Elisabeth.

"Yes," Josephine said. "Your precious love apparently set the fire at the hotel to steal our journals. Now please let Adelaide speak."

"No," Elisabeth said, still in that strange tone. "No. He wouldn't have."

"He was found with the journals in his possession," Josephine said.

"He must have been rescuing them," Elisabeth said, after a pause. "That's what happened. He ran into the building, knowing how important they are."

"And how did he know about them at all, Elisabeth?" Josephine said.

Elisabeth's face paled. "He's—he's a member of the family."

"Oh, Mother," Maria said, and suddenly her disinterested,

detached expression was gone, replaced by disappointment, and pity, and something that looked like love. "You didn't. You showed him where they were."

"It— He would never—"

"Oh, you foolish woman," Adelaide said. "Of course he did."

"You—what would you know, you've never loved him, you've only ever shown him coldness, you probably set this whole thing up to frame him!"

"I have found, to my regret, that it is almost never necessary to frame Heinrich for anything," Adelaide said. "Do you know, what I have never understood is how you haven't seen him for what he is, after all these years. He's nothing, Elisabeth. He's only a fairly stupid man, in his late middle years, who's made a fool out of two families for thirty years. He's a—a—"

"A curse?" Maria asked.

"Maria!" Elisabeth cried.

Adelaide stared at her for a long moment before she inclined her head, just slightly. Like a queen acknowledging a clever point made by a peasant. "Yes," she said.

"Maria, you take that back—"

"You're not what I expected," Adelaide said. "I'll tell Father Ardelean to remove it. Not that I believed in it, anyway."

Maria nodded. "You said you had a guess. About why he did it."

"Yes." Adelaide took a small black book from next to the journals and handed it to Maria. "His account book. The payments go back to '73."

Eli's fingers twitched. He wanted to see what was in that book.

Maria took the book and opened it. After a few pages she sighed. "Oh, he didn't."

Adelaide sipped her tea.

A few pages later, another groan.

"Who?" Maria asked.

Eli *really* wanted to see what was in that book.

"I have no idea," Adelaide said. "But the payments are regular. Every six months, for five years. It appears that, in addition to the sins I mentioned earlier, he also lost the entirety of his fortune in the Panic."

"Everything?" Maria asked.

"Fortunately, much of my money is inaccessible to him," she said. "Tied to Mac and myself. He would have needed my signature to access it. Which he asked for, last night. Obviously, I declined. That's when I searched his office."

Eli glanced at Mac, sitting next to him. He was pale.

"Mother—"

"Our money is perfectly safe," Adelaide said. "You don't need to worry about it."

"That's not what I'm worried about," Mac said. There was a tone in his voice Eli hadn't heard before. Maturity, he thought. "What did he do? Who did he borrow from? What about my sisters, how do we protect them? Their dowries—their reputations—"

"There's enough in my portion for their dowries. As for their reputations—" Adelaide paused, and suddenly she looked tired. "I suppose it depends on the answers to your first two questions."

Heinrich stirred and groaned, and everyone jerked their heads toward him.

"Heinrich," Elisabeth said. She stood, glaring at the others. "I've sat here and listened to this long enough. Heinrich would never do the things you've accused him of. He loves me. He wouldn't betray my trust."

She swept across the room and sat next to Heinrich on the bed, gently brushing hair from his forehead. "My love?" she whispered. "Can you hear me?"

"Ellie?" he mumbled.

"Yes," she said. "It's me. Oh darling, how do you feel?"

"What are you doing here? What happened?"

"You were injured," she said, and Eli saw tears rolling slowly down her face. Maria watched them, that flat, detached expression back on her face, before standing to go look at the stacks of journals by the door. "Oh, Heinrich, and I wasn't there— I heard there was a fire, and all I thought about was my mother and Maria, and I was so worried, and then I heard you'd been found— My love, you didn't have to try to save the journals, they weren't important, not compared to your life."

It didn't take a trained investigator to see the way Heinrich stiffened at the word *journals*.

"He did it," Mac said, softly, next to Eli. "He really did it."

Awkwardly, Eli lifted his hand and placed it on Mac's shoulder. He wasn't practiced at giving comfort, but somehow, this young man had become important to him, and he felt Mac's distress echoed in his own chest.

Mac took a deep breath, giving Eli's hand a single squeeze before he stood.

"Tell us why you did it," he said to Heinrich.

Elisabeth whirled around. "He *didn't*," she snapped.

Mac ignored her. "You set fire to—you *set fire to your daughter's hotel*. To steal her family journals. You're neck deep in something, and it affects everyone in this room, because you've *made* it affect everyone in this room. So, you need to tell us everything, and then we can figure out how to clean up this mess. If we can."

"I didn't do anything," Heinrich said, weakly. "It's as Elisabeth said, I was saving the journals, I—"

"There's one missing," Maria said, still crouched by the stacks.

Josephine frowned. "What do you mean, there's one missing?"

"I've counted them twice. Eighteen seventy-five is missing."

"It's probably at the hotel," Elisabeth said, tears still falling. "Or it fell out when he was being transported."

Mac, Eli, and Adelaide said nothing. They were all staring at Heinrich's face.

"Is this why you were trying to get to know me?" Maria said, straightening. "To get to the journals?"

"Maria, he wouldn't—"

"Let me explain," Heinrich said. His voice was raspy from the smoke. "I know it looks bad. But I did this for all of us."

Abruptly, Elisabeth stopped crying. "Heinrich?"

"Elisabeth, listen to me," he said. He took a deep breath. "You see, I'm a family man."

His family stared at him, and then, with the sole exception of Elisabeth, broke out into laughter.

"Oh Heinrich," Adelaide said, wiping her eyes with an embroidered handkerchief. "You really are the most useless man. It's extraordinary."

He ignored her, speaking solely to Elisabeth. "I didn't want to burden you with this. It's for the man to worry about, after all. But—'seventy-three was bad. I made—I was given bad advice, and made some bad investments. So did everyone, I don't hold myself responsible for that. We couldn't have foreseen the Panic. And that's the market for you, anyway. It goes through cycles. I only needed enough to get back on my feet. Let our fortune recover."

"Heinrich?" Elisabeth's lovely face was confused; her dark, carefully manicured eyebrows pulled together.

"But no one was lending," he said. "None of the banks, and my friends weren't in any position to do so; they all lost their shirts too. If anyone's to blame it's those damn bankers.

They're the ones who crippled the economy, you know—if they'd just been lending we'd all be back on our feet by now, but they got scared, and then they got scared again when all the damn fighting in Bosnia started—"

"We saw the payments to your account," Mac interrupted. "If they're not coming from a bank or a friend, where are they from?"

Heinrich fell silent. When he spoke again, his tone was aggressive, pugnacious. Daring the rest of them to find fault. "I had to go out of the country."

"What do you mean, out of the country?" Mac asked.

Elisabeth still looked confused. "But what does any of this have to do with the journals?"

"Father," Mac said. "*What do you mean, out of the country?*"

Heinrich pressed his lips together and fell silent.

But Eli was beginning to put the picture together.

"He means out of the empire," Eli said. "Probably not the Ottomans. Maybe the Prussians or the French. Or the Russians."

"Even he wouldn't be that stupid," Josephine said.

"Of course he would," Adelaide said, perfectly calmly. "Which is the worst option, of those three? Because whichever it is, that will be the one we currently owe money to."

"The Russians," Eli said, watching Heinrich's face. "The worst option would be the Russians."

"What do you know?" Heinrich snapped. "I'd like to know what you would have done, in my position. And I'll have you know that they were a damn sight more reasonable than anyone in this so-called empire—"

"I'm sure you did what was best," Elisabeth said. "But I still don't understand. What does this have to do with the journals? Whatever Heinrich does with his money is his business, and I, for one, trust him *completely.*"

"The Russians, Father? *The Russians?*" If Mac's face was pale before, now it looked as though he had lost every drop of blood in his body. "That's—that's—is it treason?" He looked desperately at Eli.

Eli knew the right question, now. He knew the question that would unravel almost everything. And looking at Mac's face, he wished he didn't have to ask it.

But the truth needed to come out. For all of them.

"What did they ask for," Eli said, "when you couldn't pay them back?"

There was a long, deep silence. Maria looked at her father, and then at Eli, and the detachment was gone. She knew it too.

"Nothing important," Heinrich said. "I had it all in hand. Have it in hand. They think they're the wily ones, but I have them exactly where I want them."

"What did they ask for?" Eli asked again, his voice soft and easy.

"They only wanted me to keep an eye out for anything interesting," Heinrich said. "Little pieces of information. Nothing that could hurt the empire, nothing *treasonous,* Mac—and how dare you accuse your father of such a thing! I've been feeding them bits of nothing for years. Just things I overhear. Favors I'm owed."

"Tell me about the American Legation," Eli said.

"Well, I will tell you, because in a way this is all your fault," Heinrich said, glaring at Eli. "I did give them your precious codes—Farrow owed me a favor. They were supposed to be the payment for the first part of the year."

"You sent a letter to them, from the hotel," Eli murmured.

"Well I could hardly send it from my house, could I? Anyway, do you know what they said? They didn't want them! They said no one cared what a backward ex-colony on the other side of the world was doing, and besides, they'd had your codes for years anyway. So they told me I had to find something better."

For a moment, the others merely blinked at him, rendered speechless.

And Eli—

Eli felt a terrible, almost overpowering urge to laugh.

"That must have been a hard position to be put in," he said, ruthlessly suppressing it. "What did you do?"

Heinrich sighed. "It *was* a hard position," he said, almost mournfully. "It didn't leave me with many options. I had to protect my family—*all* of it. I needed to give them something, and it occurred to me they might be interested in the journals. After all, Elisabeth said there was a lot of personal, embarrassing stuff in them about the patrons of the hotel, and the Russians like that sort of thing, you know."

"So that they can *blackmail people,*" Maria said, staring at her father as though he'd surpassed even her low expectations. "So that they can force people to commit treason. Which, by the way, is *exactly* what you've committed, under barely any pressure at all."

"Heinrich? You mean—you—you did take them? You were—you were stealing them?"

"Just one!" Heinrich said. "I only took one!"

Every head in the room swiveled toward the stacks of journals.

"At first," he said.

"You took 1875," Maria said.

"I just chose at random," Heinrich said. "I thought any of them would be good. I took it and I sent my contacts a message—"

A look of confusion crossed Elisabeth's beautiful face. "When?"

"What, my love?"

"When did you take the journal?"

"When I—when I asked you to show them to me," Heinrich said, and at last, he had the grace to look embarrassed. "My love! I didn't want to burden you, you must understand—"

"What was in 1875?" Josephine asked, looking toward Maria.

"Um, it's Mother and I," Maria said. "We both wrote in it. Probably about equally. Nothing I remember as particularly scandalous, but I'm sure there's plenty of blackmail material in there. Even if we only include our regulars, the number of extramarital affairs alone . . ." She trailed off, deep in horrified thought.

"You said you sent a message to your contact," Eli said. "What happened then?"

"Well, that's when things became complicated," Heinrich said, and Eli heard Mac give a bitter laugh.

"How so?" Eli asked.

"The journal disappeared," Heinrich said.

"It disappeared," Eli repeated.

"I don't know what happened to it," Heinrich said. "I've looked everywhere for it, but I can't find it. I'm worried one of the maids might have thrown it away—Adelaide, the way you manage the staff leaves *quite a bit* to be desired. Perhaps if you spent more time doing your job we wouldn't be in this situation!"

Adelaide stared at him. Eventually Heinrich lowered his gaze.

"That's why he was allowing Mother to be so flagrant," Eli heard Maria whisper to herself. "He wanted to be closer to her. To be closer to the journals."

"So the journal went missing," Eli said, determined to follow the string to its ugly end. "What then?"

"Then I knew I had to take drastic measures," Heinrich said, reaching for Elisabeth's hand. "My contacts were already here. They didn't—they didn't like it when I told them what had happened. So I—I—I created a ruse. And I took the rest of the journals. I thought I could parcel them out—which is still a very good idea! Perhaps it's better that you all know, now. I didn't want to burden you, but now that you've insisted, maybe it's better everything is out in the open!"

"I'm going to gut you open like a pig," Josephine growled. "You useless, sniveling—"

"You set the fire?" Elisabeth asked, slowly pulling her hand away from him.

"My love, I had to! I knew it wouldn't do much damage; actually I think it was rather clever of me."

"My mother and daughter live in that hotel," Elisabeth said. She stood up, and it was as though the whole room held its breath. "Heinrich. My *mother* and *daughter* live in that hotel."

"And they're fine! They're right—"

"*My mother and daughter,* Heinrich. *My mother* and *my daughter. Your* daughter. Yours. *And* your son! He was staying there too! You set *fire* to the hotel your son and daughter live in?"

"Ellie—"

"No," Elisabeth said, backing away. "No, you wouldn't. You wouldn't. Your daughter, Heinrich."

Maria was staring at her mother, blank shock on her face.

"My family," Elisabeth whispered. "And the hotel. The Hotel Wallner, Heinrich. *My* family. *My* last name. And you— you *set fire to it*?"

"Mother," Maria said, cautiously reaching a hand out. "Are you, er, all right? You don't need to—"

"Yes, Maria, I absolutely do," Elisabeth said, and she

whipped around to her mother. "Mama, may I borrow your gun?"

Josephine stared at her with interest, then shrugged. "Yes," she said, reaching for her reticule and pulling it out. "Here."

For some reason no one moved until after Elisabeth raised her hand. Heinrich dodged just in time, rolling off the bed in his haste, and the bullet went into his pillow, sending goose feathers flying into the air.

That released them. Maria grabbed her mother's arm, and Mac and Eli dashed between Elisabeth and the cowering Heinrich. Adelaide and Josephine stayed where they were, watching with impartial expressions.

"Elisabeth! My love! You've misunderstood—you're not in your right mind!"

"*My mother and my daughter,* you pile of horse manure! You rotting piece of roadkill! You absolute bag of whale blubber!" She wrenched her arm out of Maria's grasp and tried to climb across the bed.

Maria grabbed her ankle. "Mother! We're all right! Look, Grandmother and I are all right! And you shouldn't kill him. You'll regret it."

"I won't," Elisabeth said. "Let go of me, I'm going to put him out of our lives forever—"

"No—Mother—*Grandmother, say something!*"

Josephine sighed. "Your mother has a point, Maria."

"*Grandmother!*"

"If I might contribute something," Eli said, holding his hands up, "bodies are very difficult to hide, and a murder charge would be highly inconvenient."

"That's a valid concern," Josephine said. "I'll have to send a message to Johann. I'm sure when we tell him what went on he'll dispose of the body."

"*Grandmother!*"

Josephine sighed again. "Oh, all right, Maria, but you really must do something about this sentimental streak. Elisabeth, *stop.*"

Elisabeth stopped. "But *Mother*—"

"I know," Josephine said. "And I've never been prouder of you, my girl. But it would upset Maria."

Elisabeth looked at Maria, and then, abruptly, collapsed in a pile of silk and tears. Eli could vaguely make out the words "my fault" and "whale blubber" and "sorry" in between the sobs.

Gingerly, Maria picked up the gun. Josephine held out her hand, and Maria frowned at her. "I'll just . . . keep this, for now," she said.

"Elisabeth." Heinrich took a breath. "*Please,* my love."

"Father, if you don't want to have a bullet in your chest, please stop. Just stop." Mac's voice was impossibly tired. "You've already ruined so much. Our family. The Hotel Wallner. Maria's ball."

They all fell silent and still. Heinrich with Eli and Mac on the floor, Maria patting her mother awkwardly on the bed, and Josephine and Adelaide looking for all the world like they were at a slightly tense tea.

And then Eli had a very brilliant, very strange idea.

For a moment he simply looked at it. It didn't seem like an Eli Whittaker idea, so he was suspicious of it. He turned it this way and that. No, it was not an idea the old Eli Whittaker would have had.

But it was a damn good idea anyway.

"Not the ball," he said.

Maria jerked her head up. "We can't have a ball without a kitchen, Eli."

"No," he said. "But the kitchen doesn't necessarily have to be on-site, does it? It would be more work, but really it only needs to be nearby."

"Theoretically," she said, watching him closely. "But there aren't any we could use. It has to be a huge kitchen, and we can't afford to rent one, even if there was one available—"

"There's been a lot of talk about blackmail today," Eli said, slowly. "It gave me an idea."

Chapter Thirty-three

The Austrian Empire is officially no more. Now we are the Dual Monarchy of Austria and Hungary, and the Hungarians have won back some, if not all, of their rights. His Imperial Majesty Franz Joseph still sits over it all, of course—we're still an Empire, though for how much longer . . . Well, I say well done them—and now, I imagine, the Czechs and the Bohemians will try as well. It seems to me that it was easier to be an Empire when I was a child.

— Journal entry of Josephine Wallner, 28 July 1867

Eli's idea was devious, simple, and satisfying: blackmail the Hotel Hoffmann into letting the Hotel Wallner use its kitchen. The only problem was that it was already nine in the morning, and if the ball was going forward, they had to get to work. Immediately.

The Wallners and Eli left quickly, Elisabeth hanging half conscious on Eli's arm. Mac stayed behind, murmuring a quick apology to Maria as they left.

"Don't apologize, Mac," she said, softly. He looked so tired; like he'd aged five years in a single night. "I know it's a mess. I'm—I'm so sorry this happened."

He winced. "Don't. My family has greatly wronged yours. I don't know how to make it right."

"It's not your responsibility to make it right," Maria said. "Stay with your mother. We'll figure everything out."

"My mother and I will have to pay the Russians off," he said. "If we have even the slightest chance of keeping this secret. After that and making sure my sisters are provided for—well. I was looking for a purpose, wasn't I?"

Maria smiled ruefully. "I know avoiding ruination wasn't exactly what you had in mind."

"Not exactly," he said, with a tired smile of her own. "But it's what has presented itself."

"Make sure you get some rest, in between reading account books." Maria lifted her hand, rubbing away some soot still clinging to his cheek.

"I'm sorry I won't be there tonight. I—I wanted to see it. Your triumph. I love you, Maria."

She squeezed his shoulder. "I love you too."

When she reached the carriage, her mother and grand-mother were already inside, along with the journals. Eli was waiting for her outside.

"Well," she said, smiling up at him. "Let's go blackmail a hotel."

He nodded gravely and helped her into the carriage.

The staff of the Hotel Hoffmann was slightly disconcerted by the appearance of three smoke-stained, grubby people—and one heavily weeping woman—demanding to see the man-ager, but once they gained admittance to Alfred Bucher's office the blackmail took hardly any time at all. Especially once Elis-abeth heard about the sabotaged pipes and grabbed the letter opener off Bucher's desk.

Maria was going to need some time to adjust to this new Elisabeth, who was so much like the old Elisabeth, and yet so very different in such a very important way. On the way to the Hotel Hoffmann, and again on the return home, Maria found herself sneaking looks at her mother.

She'd really chosen them. When it had come down to it, she'd chosen Maria, and Josephine, and even the Hotel Wallner, over Heinrich. Yes, she'd done so in a dramatic, over-the-top, ridiculous, scene-stealing way. But that was just her.

She'd chosen them.

And it really shouldn't make Maria want to cry. Shouldn't shake her off her footing like this. But ever since her mother had aimed that gun, Maria felt like she was living in unmapped time, after a life spent living in Fate.

She didn't know what would happen next. And there were so many questions still. But for now—

For now, they needed to throw a ball.

The first thing was to find Abe. In her absence he'd thrown open all the doors and windows, but the acrid smoke smell still clung to everything. She imagined the entire hotel would need a fresh coat of paint. But for tonight, the hotel would simply smell like smoke.

Maria could work with that.

She found Abe wiping down the staircase. "We need to get the word out that the ball is still on," she said, without preamble.

He stared at her.

She stared back. "Abe. Abe. Hello."

"Maria, we don't have a kitchen."

"We blackmailed the Hotel Hoffmann into lending us theirs. But we need to—" She exhaled in a sharp burst. "We have *a lot* to do."

"We have a kitchen?"

"We have a kitchen. But we need to tell everyone it's still happening, fire and all. That's the angle—the ball must go on. Vienna does *not* stop dancing because of one, single, tiny fire."

Abe was looking at her like she'd lost her mind, but he was

nodding slowly. "Yes. Yes, all right. I'll round up the news-boys."

"Good. Is Hannah back?"

"Cleaning up the kitchen," he said. "Well. Crying in the kitchen."

"Thank you," Maria called, already heading to the kitchen, where Josephine had apparently just told Hannah the news.

"Maria," Hannah said, looking over with red eyes. "It's real? It's happening?"

"Yes," she said, grabbing Hannah's coat and wrapping her in it. "You need to get started. I know it won't be as good as you'd planned. Focus on the almond cakes, pick one of the fancy desserts, and then work on the buffet food. We already planned for it to be plain. The Hotel Hoffmann has agreed to lend you two assistants."

Hannah was nodding frantically. "Yes. Yes! It's going to happen." She was halfway out the door when she stopped, her face falling abruptly. "Oh. But the flowers, Maria. They sent a message saying they'd heard about the fire, so they sold them to someone else."

"They sold the flowers?" Maria felt a pang of loss. She'd loved Eli's flower arrangements. "All right, we'll figure something out. Go, go." She ushered Hannah out.

"I'll take care of the flowers," Josephine said. "Leave it to me."

Maria nodded. "Thank you," she said, and hurried away to the ballroom.

Eli was already there, cleaning the windows where smoke had reached them. He'd disappeared after they'd reached the hotel, saying something about telegrams, but here he was, hands dripping with soapy water.

Maria stood in the doorway, feeling like someone had just kicked her in the chest.

Oh. Oh, oh, oh.

He must have heard her, because he turned a smile her way before resuming his task. He looked tired and rumpled, still wearing the shirt he'd been in the night before.

For her.

The tears threatened once more. She shoved them down, pinned a smile on, and got to work.

They worked for three hours, the two of them. Around noon, her mother entered, carrying a platter of sandwiches. Maria put the tray of silverware down and cautiously approached her.

"Mother? Shouldn't you be resting?"

"No," Elisabeth said. "I've rested plenty. You haven't eaten, and Hannah's not here. I made sandwiches for you."

Made them? Maria looked at the sandwiches. They were clumsily built, and she didn't actually recognize one of the vegetables, but her mother had made them, so Maria would be eating them.

"Thank you," she said, taking one. Eli took another, nodding his thanks before returning to his task (dismantling the lily pond—the jellies meant to float in it had been ruined in the fire and there was no time for a new batch).

"What else can I do?" Elisabeth asked.

"Mother, you don't need to—"

"Maria, *what else* can I *do*?" Elisabeth's expression was pure Wallner—determined, arrogant, and a little angry.

"Um, you can finish the place settings," Maria said, handing over the silverware.

Elisabeth nodded graciously, and began to do exactly that.

"Huh," Maria said, watching her for a few seconds she didn't really have to spare.

Around three she started to worry about the flowers. Josephine had said she would take care of it, but was it even possible to get such a large number of flowers on such short notice? In February? Perhaps she could wind the greenery from the Woods with colored ribbon—

A clamor on the stairs interrupted her.

"Maria," Abe said, breathing heavily. "Come see."

She glanced at Eli, who looked just as confused, and they followed Abe down the stairs, through the ruined kitchen out to the alley.

Where they found three wagons, their loads covered with cloths, and Jakob and Emilie Brodmaier fussing over the contents.

"Emilie?" Maria asked, wrapping her arms around herself to ward off the cold. "What are you—"

"Josephine said you needed flowers," Emilie said. "Jakob brought his orchids."

"We need to move them quickly," Jakob said, looking up from one of the wagons. "They're sensitive."

"You—you—" The tears finally pushed their way to the surface. Jakob's orchids were his most beloved possession. That he would lend them—go to all this trouble—

"Your mother has done enough crying for us all today," Josephine said, from behind her. "Let's get these inside."

Maria wiped her eyes, laughing, and started unloading the wagons. Josephine was right, she *was* getting overly sentimental.

But she found herself watching them all as she worked. Eli, busy helping Abe with the buffet tables, even though he had absolutely no reason to do so. No reason to help, other than—

Other than that he cared for her.

And Elisabeth, busy arranging the orchids and draping the greenery around them with a genuinely artistic eye. Emilie, who had tried very hard to stay interested in ball preparations, until the orchestra had arrived and was now "overseeing them," which apparently meant terrifying them while she watched them warm up with narrowed, intense eyes. Josephine, watching Emilie and smiling fondly when she thought no one was looking. Jakob, monitoring his orchids with passion, his beautiful orchids that he'd had no reason to share, except that an old friend had asked.

Maria had been born long after Emilie and Josephine had fallen in love; she'd never had much reason to think about their arrangement. Jakob knew, had apparently always known. He and Emilie had been childhood friends, and though Maria didn't know the details, it was very obvious they were *still* friends, and that he and Josephine were friends too.

Josephine's love was all-encompassing, but it wasn't destructive. She'd loved Emilie and loved the hotel and loved Elisabeth and Maria and even loved Jakob. It hadn't ruined any lives—it had only broadened them.

And even her mother, whose love was absolutely destructive, even her—when it had mattered, she had chosen her family. Not *the man.*

It wasn't quite that easy, of course. Elisabeth had chosen Heinrich many times before, and those times had mattered. Those wounds wouldn't simply disappear because of one moment. But that one moment mattered too.

The man. For so long she'd let his specter haunt her. All through her twenties, when Vienna had laughed and speculated and she'd had to pretend she didn't mind. All the times her mother had talked about him. But in the end, there was no *the man.* He didn't exist. He was a prophecy built solely from gossip, and she'd been so scared of him. She had been so scared to love, and it had happened anyway.

She was in love with Eli Whittaker, who was not *the man,* but himself. Stern on the surface, and impossibly soft and kind beneath, with a smile that opened like the first summer rose. She loved him. She didn't know when it had happened: maybe love didn't work that way. But now that she recognized it, she found it everywhere; it had climbed inside her like a flowering vine on an arbor. Everywhere she looked, love bloomed back.

And he was leaving. In those terrible moments in her father's room, she hadn't missed that Eli had solved his case. The knowledge had thrummed beneath the revelations of her father's betrayal, present like an open cut. Leaving, she'd thought as her mother had lunged across the bed. Leaving, she'd thought, as Eli had walked away to send telegrams to America, certainly related to his case.

And then—there he'd been. In the ballroom. Washing the windows.

And ∴ . . maybe he was leaving. But before he did, she was going to tell him how she felt. And maybe—maybe—

Maybe he loved her too.

When the clock said six, after everyone but Eli had left to change, Maria stepped back and looked at what they had created. She stretched and yawned.

"We didn't sleep," she said.

He hummed in acknowledgment.

"It's perfect," she said, gazing at the ballroom.

It wasn't Fairyland. They'd had to change too much. There was no champagne lily pond, and no edible arbor (though the fountain had survived, and was overflowing with almond cakes, waiting to greet the guests). It was simply a lovely room, filled with well-decorated tables, good food, and beautiful flowers.

It was so much better than Fairyland.

"You did it," Eli said.

She shook her head. "We did it," she said, and, feeling rather brave, she snuck her palm into his. He looked down at their joined hands, a slight furrow in his brow, but didn't let go.

"You should change," he said.

"Mmm," she said. "We both should."

He went still next to her. She glanced up and found his face oddly . . . blank. "Eli."

"Yes?"

"You . . . you are coming to the ball." She didn't phrase it as a question. It wasn't one.

"I—"

"Eli!" She dropped his hand as giggles threatened to overcome her. And, oh, it was lovely to laugh.

"I didn't— You never invited me!"

Her mouth dropped open. "I assumed you knew you were invited!"

"Why would I assume that?"

"So you've just been helping me this whole time and thinking you weren't invited?"

"It didn't bother me," he said, making a sort of befuddled gesture. "I helped you because I wanted to."

Oh. Oh, oh, oh.

She pushed away the heady need to swoon, instead putting her hands on her hips. "You are coming to this ball."

"But—"

"You *are* coming to this ball, because it *is* going to be the most triumphant night of my life. And on that night, Eli Whittaker, you *are* going to dance with me."

There was a flicker in his expression when she said it. She felt her smile falter.

Quickly she pinned it back into place. "Come on," she said, tugging on his hand. "I'll help you pick out what you're going to wear."

Eli let her pull him to his room, Maria stepping politely aside when they reached his door so he could unlock it. Watched her as she flitted past, heading for the armoire. It wasn't as though there were options—he possessed only one formal suit, the one he'd worn to the party at the Brodmaiers'—but he didn't say anything, simply sitting on the edge of the bed.

He would go to the ball. He would dance with her. It was what she wanted.

It was also goodbye.

He hadn't realized it, in the excitement over saving the ball. He'd been pleased to solve the case, but it wasn't until he excused himself to write the telegram to the State Department, naming Farrow as the leak, that he realized this was the end.

He didn't have *time* anymore.

And he didn't know what he was going to do about that.

She was safe. Supposedly.

So why did it feel like leaving her would be like severing his own arm?

He didn't have time, and he needed it, at least a little more. Just until he could convince himself she was safe. Maybe he could stretch Farrow's investigation out, he thought frantically. Or perhaps he could take that rest Wallace had suggested. Sure, he'd offered it only to get Eli out of his hair, but that didn't *matter* now.

And what if you never convince yourself?

He refused to answer the question. He would, and then he would go home.

Home. The word didn't feel the same as it used to.

"Eli?"

"Hmm?"

"Pay attention," she said, laughing. "This is very important."

She put his suit on the bed next to him, and came to stand in front of him. Unconsciously he spread his legs to make room for her to stand between them—when had he become so comfortable with her body?—and she clasped her hands behind his neck, bending down to kiss him softly on the lips.

It was selfish, but he pulled her closer. He didn't deepen

the kiss, let it be soft and sweet and easy, but he held her close. Memorizing her.

When she pulled away, he let his hands fall. "Get changed," she said, her face still close to his. She kissed him lightly on the brow.

He stood, taking the suit and walking behind the screen.

His chest hurt.

For weeks, he'd let himself sink into this . . . this moment. The spell of the Hotel Wallner. Oh, he'd told himself that he saw the risks, that he knew the ending. But that had been a lie.

It was only now, at the end of the moment, that he understood exactly what he had done. He had fallen in love with a woman he could not keep. Their arrangement was temporary, but the love was permanent, irrevocable. And he'd *known* she wasn't for him. How could she be? She was sweet, and laughing, and soft like the night sky, and he was . . . none of those things. He was broken and cold and harsh, and a few weeks of laughter didn't change that. He would take her joy and ruin it.

She probably knew that. She'd been clear about their arrangement from the beginning—it had been one of the things that reassured him. Made her safe.

Eli looked down and discovered he had somehow dressed himself. He touched his tie, patted his suit, and stepped out from behind the screen.

Maria stood by his desk, her back to him, the lights of Vienna sparkling brightly through the window next to her. When she heard him behind her she startled.

Her expression was serious, but she offered him a rueful smile. "You caught me," she said, her voice tight. "This time I was snooping." She held up the copy of the telegram he'd sent, which he certainly should have destroyed. It was a sign of how very far from home he felt that he didn't care at all.

He didn't say anything, simply watched her put the paper back on the desk.

"It must feel good," she said, shifting. "You solved it."

"Not particularly," he said, the words working just as well for either statement. It didn't feel good, and he hadn't done much to solve it. Just been in the right place to ask the right question.

He wished the right question hadn't chosen *that* moment to reappear.

She twisted her hands together. "You look nice."

There were things they needed to say, but not tonight. Not before her ball. "Thank you," he said. "You should go get changed."

"Yes," she said, but she didn't go. Instead, she bit her lip.

"Are you nervous?" he asked.

"Yes."

"You've been so confident until now," he said. "You've worked hard. Everything will go just as you want it to."

"I'm not nervous about the ball."

He frowned. "Then what?"

"You," she said, laughing breathily. She ran a hand through her hair. "I need to say something to you. I thought it could wait, but—" She nodded toward the telegram. "I realized I have to say it now."

Eli took a long breath. She wanted to end things. He understood, but—"It's been a long day, Maria, and it'll be a longer night. Whatever you need to say can wait. I'll be here tomorrow."

"Yes, but will you be here the day after?"

The question burst from her lips, startling him with its intensity. She was already waving her hand.

"I'm sorry, I'm sorry," she said. "That's not—I'm not good at this. I've never done it before. What did you say? *I have no idea how to have this conversation.*"

It seemed important to her that they talk about this now, so Eli sat, calmly. There was no reason to feel like his chest was splitting open. They had agreed beforehand, after all.

"It's all right," he said. "You don't have to . . . treat me gently. You can just talk to me like you talked to the others."

"That's the problem," she said, with a choking laugh. "There haven't been any others. Eli Whittaker, I—I love you. I know this is probably a surprise. And I know it's inconvenient. I don't expect anything. But you're leaving, and if you—if you didn't want to, if you felt the same—you could stay." She broke off, bit her lip. Looked quietly at her hands as though she was listening to everything she just said, and nodded. "You could stay."

The room was completely silent. Perhaps there were sounds beyond the window, or from the orchestra warming up, but he heard none of them.

"No," he said.

Her eyes flew up to his. Her lips parted slightly. "Oh."

Another long, long silence.

She stood. "I'm sorry," she said. "I—I didn't mean to make you uncomfortable. I'll, um, I'll just—"

"You don't."

She huffed out a breath, looked at him in confusion. "What?"

"Love me," he said. It sounded like his voice was coming from very far away.

"I think that's my business," she said. "Um, you don't have to accept it, or reciprocate it, but—look, I haven't done this before but I'm quite sure it's the person who's in love who gets to say, um, whether they are or not—" She pursed her mouth. "That got confused, but the point is, yes, I do."

"But you said we couldn't have a relationship."

"I did say that," she said. "But—things changed. For me. I

thought maybe they had for you too. But it's all right that they haven't. I understand."

If she loved him, he could hurt her.

The thought made his stomach twist. "You've developed a crush. It can happen."

Maria lifted her eyebrows. "Like I said. You have the right to reject me. You don't have the right to tell me what I'm feeling."

"But it makes sense," he said, feeling relieved now that he understood. "It will pass. It might be uncomfortable right now, but you'll see—"

"Eli Whittaker," she snapped, and there was a disturbing amount of her grandmother in her tone. "Don't you dare talk down to me like that. Do you think I'm a child? An idiot who can't hear her own feelings? Do you think I came to this conclusion on a whim? It's fine if you don't feel the same way. Well, it doesn't *feel* fine, but it . . . it will be. But this is *hard* for me, and I haven't done it before, and you *will not dismiss me* like that. I love you, you absolute ass, though *just in this moment* I am struggling to understand why. All I know is you do not get to take that away from me."

"But—"

"*Don't,*" she said, and in the silence that fell, they simply stared at each other across the room. She looked furious. He felt numb, and distant, like someone had just knocked him on the head.

In the distance the clock chimed half past six.

"I should go," she said.

He didn't say anything. There was nothing for him to say; all the words had left him.

After a moment she nodded, and left.

Chapter Thirty-four

What made them stop in the end? I told them I'd drawn
a picture of the Imperial Member. I hadn't.
   Now I have.
   —Journal entry of Theresa Wallner, 26 December 1816.
         Text is followed by an explicit illustration.

The Hotel Wallner was, indisputably, back.

They'd given Vienna the story of the season—the hotel that had risen, literally, from the ashes. And everyone who was present would have the distinction of telling the story: that they were *there,* at the Hotel Wallner's Hotelkeepers' Ball, flirting and waltzing and laughing while the smell of smoke still clung to the walls.

It was a triumph.

And it didn't matter that the triumph felt like ash in Maria's mouth. No one would know, as she spun around the room. Flirting and waltzing and laughing.

The room was packed. Abe's newsboys had done their job well. Maria could barely see her beautiful floors beneath so many well-shod feet.

The chandelier shone bright and beautiful. The ceiling was white and smooth, no sign of the plaster patch job.

The grand arched windows let in the lights of Vienna, so much brighter than the night sky. The orchids had been much

admired, Hannah had sent over her third batch of replacement almond cakes, and the orchestra played exquisite waltz
after exquisite waltz.

Vienna and the Hotel Wallner were dancing together again,
and Maria vowed that this time, the waltz would never end.

She'd already lost Eli. She wouldn't lose the Hotel Wallner.

Maybe she shouldn't have told him. Then, at least, he
would be here, with her, and they could dance together. He
would have done that for her, even if he didn't feel the same.
He would have danced with her.

But she didn't really regret it. All waiting would have done
was delay the pain.

She smiled even more brightly, as her chest threatened to
close. Every moment she wore that smile it felt like a piece
of her heart was being peeled away, but the Hotel Wallner
needed her to smile, and so she would.

"Maria?" She turned to see Count von Kaufstein, his face
unusually anxious. "I'm sorry to bother you—"

"Is everything all right?"

"Well, not exactly," he said. "I can't find anyone else, and
it's, well, it's a bit embarrassing—"

"No, please," she said, touching him lightly on the arm.
Making him feel comfortable.

"There was a line for the washroom," he said, his face
flushing. "So I went to the one on the fourth floor, and—"
He made a face.

"Oh," she said. Probably she should feel something other
than relief at being able to escape this room for a few minutes,
but she didn't. "Thank you. I'll take care of it."

He nodded apologetically, and she shook her head, reas-
suring him, before hurrying away. She needed to take care of
the problem immediately, lest there be a flood. *When we're
back I can have the plumbing fixed,* she thought, out of habit.
Then she realized that they *were* back, and she probably *could*

have the pipes fixed, after the kitchen repairs were completed, but instead of bringing pride and pleasure, the thought felt empty.

She hastened up the stairs to the empty fourth floor, stopping at the linen closet to get supplies before crossing to the bathroom.

When she entered, though, everything looked normal.

"Huh," she said, frowning down at the toilet.

And then someone pressed a cloth over her nose and mouth. She breathed in, surprised, and the smell of something sweet hit her nostrils. She thrashed, but her muscles were already too weak, and darkness closed over her.

Eli hadn't moved since Maria had left his room.

He'd heard the guests begin to arrive; heard the first waltz begin.

Once, he thought he heard her laugh.

She didn't love him. She was mistaken. That, at least, was clear.

How could the night sky love him? He was nothing. Broken. Cold like a rock, but without the rock's integrity.

He'd killed his own father. Shot him in the head, and driven away while his body burned.

Had his mother loved his father? If she had, it only brought her pain. So much pain.

There was a great emptiness inside his chest. He had the ridiculous idea that that was where the laughter had lived.

But what if she is? In love with you?

She's not.

But what if she is?

Then that was the worst thing that could possibly happen, he told himself angrily, not realizing he'd stood until he was already striding across the room. He stopped when he came to the door. There was nowhere for him to go.

But she told you to dance with her.

If he could still laugh, he would. *That was before—*

Before she confessed her love to you and you didn't believe her?

Well. When he put it like that, it sounded—it sounded bad.

I was protecting her, he said. A little hesitantly.

Silence.

Eli sat back down on the bed and put his head in his hands. He loved her. He didn't want to hurt her; he'd rather throw himself out the window than hurt her, but—he had.

What if she's in love with you?

And that thought should feel like the apocalypse. But the truth was—the truth he'd hated so much that he'd denied her words even when he could see the veracity in her eyes—the truth was, it felt like a miracle.

Maria Wallner loved him.

Maria Wallner *loved* him.

Maria Wallner loved *him*.

It was impossible, of course.

That's why it's called a miracle.

And that word was so full in his chest, so all-encompassing, that it became the air in his lungs, and the bones of his ribs, and his heart itself, until there was no place left in his body for it, and so he started to weep.

Eli Whittaker didn't smile. Eli Whittaker didn't laugh.

And Eli Whittaker didn't cry.

He hadn't since long before that fateful night, so long he couldn't remember when the last time had been. There hadn't been any point. He could have cried, or he could have survived.

And afterward, when they were safe—

That was the thing, though, he realized, as he slid down the edge of the mattress to the floor.

He hadn't felt safe.

It wasn't until now, this moment, sitting in a hotel room an ocean away from his room in Washington and his mother and his job and what was left of that cold, spartan house in Boston, that he finally felt safe enough to cry.

The tears felt as though they would last forever. He wept for his mother. He wept for Maria, and even for Mac.

And when it felt as though he was the ocean itself, he wept for himself.

He didn't know how much later it was when, finally, there were no more tears. For some time longer he simply sat, numb and empty, staring at the wall opposite him.

And then he remembered.

He needed to dance with Maria.

Chapter Thirty-five

There's an uprising somewhere I've never heard of before, a province of the Ottomans called Bosnia. Apparently, they resent the loss of their lands and demand autonomy.

—Journal entry of Theresa Wallner, 2 February 1831,
referring to the failed Bosnian uprising of 1831–32

Maria woke in the dark light of a swaying carriage. Her mouth tasted funny, and her arms hurt. She blinked and tried to shift to release the pressure in her wrists.

Which was when she realized they were tied together.

It was a sign of how many times she'd been in danger in the last several weeks that she didn't waste time saying anything silly like *what's happening.* Her brain, fuzzy as it was, immediately produced the obvious conclusion: she'd been drugged, had her wrists and—yes, also legs—bound together, and then been kidnapped. Or had the kidnapping technically begun with the drugging? Eli would probably know; he seemed like the sort of person who would be familiar with the technical elements of crimes, even in foreign countries.

And thinking about Eli made the thing even worse, because on top of being kidnapped, she'd been rejected.

Later, she told herself. There'd be time to wallow later.

After she dealt with whatever this was. Beginning with who-ever her kidnapper was.

She looked up from cataloguing her restraints and squinted across the carriage. Two men sat on the other side.

"Father," the one on the right murmured. "She's awake."

The man on the left made a sound of disapproval, and leaned forward, out of the shadows.

"Count von Kaufstein," Maria said, even more confused.

"Maria," the Emperor's Chamberlain said, his wrinkled face filled with distress. "My dear, I'm so sorry. I didn't want it to come to this."

Her head was pounding. And she felt sick to her stomach, between the swaying of the carriage and the—"Did you *chloroform* me?"

His blue eyes showed nothing but regret. "Yes. I had hoped to avoid direct involvement, thinking it less painful for us both. But in the end, I had to step in, and—well."

She waited, hoping for his sentence to continue and *make everything make sense,* but he was already leaning back. Like explaining, wasn't, in the end, very important. Like he didn't need to, because he didn't plan on having to face her ever again.

"You're planning to kill me," she realized. "Which means—you were the one who hired Mueller? But—but if the Emperor wanted me dead he simply could have told von Laziska, and von Laziska was the one who *killed* Mueller—"

There was a break in the trees—*we're in the Woods,* she thought—and the moonlight briefly illuminated von Kauf-stein's face.

"Oh," she said, reading the line of his mouth. "Not the Emperor. You."

He didn't deny it.

"*You* hired Mueller. *You* chloroformed me. And now *you* are taking me to the Woods to kill me, which makes sense, because you could hardly do it in the middle of the hotel."

Maria was taking this very calmly, and after a moment, she realized why.

She was going to be fine.

She felt this with the same surety she'd known the Hotel-keepers' Ball would be a triumph. She *knew* she was going to be fine, because Eli was going to come and get her, and if he didn't (he would, even though they'd fought, but *if he didn't*) then she was going to save herself. The details weren't particularly important. They would work themselves out.

"If it helps," von Kaufstein said, "your death *is* for the empire."

Oh yes, it helps enormously, who wouldn't *want to be chloroformed and murdered for the empire,* Maria wanted to say. She resisted, just barely, an idea forming.

She sniffled. Schooled her face in helpless lines. "For the empire?" she said, sniffling a little more. "But Count von Kaufstein, I don't *understand*."

"I know," he said, sighing heavily. "I know."

"Father," said the man next to him. "Don't talk to her. We should drug her again."

Ah, he was von Kaufstein's son, the man engaged to Maria's half sister. Well. She couldn't say she approved of the match.

Think about that later, she told herself. *Avoid being drugged* now.

"I won't talk if you don't want me to," she said, in a pleasingly helpless-sounding whisper. "But—if you told me *why,* I think it would help me make my peace. With God."

Von Kaufstein sighed again, reaching out and patting her cheek. "You've always been a good girl, Maria."

"I try to be," she said, with a touch of a whimper.

"And it's not your fault. God will know that. You're going to die for a worthy cause—for the safety of the empire. Not only the empire—the safety of Europe."

This revelation left her momentarily speechless, so she simply sniffled again, assessing the men across from her.

The son. She couldn't remember his name—he'd never been particularly important to her, despite being her illegitimate . . . cousin? Second cousin? She tried to remember what she *did* know. He was engaged to her half sister. Heinrich's daughter. And Heinrich had tried to burn the hotel down, because he was in bed with the Russians and owed them secrets, and he'd stolen the 1875 journal to give to them, but the journal had gone missing, after he'd sent a message—

And von Kaufstein was trying to kill her, and he'd hired Mueller—and his son was engaged to Heinrich's daughter, and when had that engagement happened exactly? Not long ago, right before the New Year's Ball, which was when Heinrich had started acting so oddly—

What if von Kaufstein had somehow intercepted the message?

If you were engaged, you could go in and out of your fiancée's house, without much question. There were all kinds of events and dinners and meetings. Plenty of time to search a house for something, then steal it—

"The journal," she said, making sure to keep her voice soft and unthreatening. "The 1875 journal."

"Stop talking," the son snapped, and she made a show of pressing back against the carriage seat and whimpering fearfully.

"There's no need for that," von Kaufstein said, glowering at his son, and really it was extraordinarily funny, the way this old man was going to extend chivalry to her right up to the moment he put a bullet in her brain.

All right. Maybe she wasn't completely calm.

What happened in 1875?

Something that involved von Kaufstein, or his son. . . .

It wouldn't be an affair. Von Kaufstein's relationship with

Mrs. Fischer was well-known and so long-standing it was respected almost as much as his actual marriage had been.

Perhaps something about his paternity? But his status as an Imperial bastard wasn't precisely a secret. Certainly all the people who would care, like Emperor Franz Joseph, would already know.

1875 . . .

Two years after the Panic. The year the revolt in Herzegovina and Bosnia had begun. The feeling in the city had been tense. Afraid. The Ottoman Empire was collapsing, and the Russian Empire was growing, and the Hapsburg Empire was caught in the middle, desperately clinging to a status quo that seemed, with every dire headline, a thing of the past—and what *exactly* happened when an empire collapsed?

What had happened, when Rome fell?

At the hotel, the feeling that what had been a slump was becoming increasingly irreversible. The Large Ballroom was already unusable. That was the year they stopped serving supper in the restaurant. No one was coming except a handful of regulars, and it had been too expensive to keep the ingredients on hand, and the waitstaff. Near the end, Maria had served as the sole waitress, a job more time-consuming than difficult, as some nights there were only one or two patrons.

Von Kaufstein had been there, though. Oh, at the time, she'd been so grateful for him. He liked to bring people there. Sometimes he had business meetings there, and then he would use the small dining area they could close off, for privacy—

Had she overheard something?

"You were simply in the wrong place at the wrong time," von Kaufstein said. "Though, Maria, you shouldn't have written it down. That's a nasty habit you Wallners have. Had I known, I never would have used the hotel for Imperial business."

"But I don't know what I wrote down," Maria said, and this time she didn't have to feign the slight whine in her voice.

"You probably don't," he said, not unkindly. "You probably wrote it down without even knowing what it meant. But someone else, some enemy of the empire, would know. And if they knew you remembered, then they could use you. Turn you against the Emperor. Hurt him."

But it wasn't the Emperor who was trying to kill her. She racked her brain, trying to remember.

1875, 1875, 1875. The mood in Vienna had been dark—the mood in Europe, generally. What else? She'd been preoccupied by the hotel—all she remembered was that things had been tense. That people who, three months earlier, had never heard of Herzegovina or Bosnia or the Balkans were suddenly opining that the revolt was the spark that could ignite the continent.

The spark . . .

And like that, she remembered.

It had been a day in the early part of the year; January, probably. Months before the revolt had started. It had been cold outside. Von Kaufstein had brought three men for supper and asked for the private room. That wasn't unusual, but she hadn't seen the other three men before, and that was. She had the impression they were other officials, but perhaps ones from outside the city. She'd thought von Kaufstein was trying to impress them with the magnificence of Vienna.

She'd taken their orders and left them alone, knocking before coming in. But she *had* overheard a sliver of their conversation, when the door hadn't closed properly and she'd had to push it closed a second time. And yes, she'd written it down that night. She could even remember what she'd written: *von Kaufstein was in tonight with some men; something about Dalmatia, and needing only a spark.*

Was that what all this had been about? A single line in a

three-year-old journal? A line she hadn't even remembered and that, perhaps most insultingly, she still didn't understand?

Well. Now she was annoyed. She had a ball to run. A triumph to bask in. And, she thought, as the annoyance blossomed into anger, a man to dance with.

She kept her expression sweet and afraid, and thought quickly.

Dalmatia was a region along the Adriatic coast, controlled by the Austro-Hungarian Empire, bordering Bosnia and Herzegovina. There were rumors, of course, about Bosnia and Herzegovina. That while the Emperor pretended he only wanted to keep the peace between the Russians and the Ottomans, he'd be quite happy to gain control over the territory himself. That was something many observers said would be on the table during the summer treaty negotiations, though Russia seemed intent on claiming it, and the Emperor's foreign secretary had as recently as a month ago proclaimed that the empire had no interest in it.

Needing only a spark. The region had revolted before, a rebellion the Ottomans had put down brutally. The most recent revolution had likely only been a matter of time—but *what* time, and on whose schedule, Maria had never questioned.

And probably she should keep her mouth shut, but if von Kaufstein was really going to kill her over one line in a journal, then at the very least she should understand why.

"The revolution in the Balkans," she said, and the men stiffened.

"I told you," the son said.

Von Kaufstein was looking at her like she had just betrayed him. "So you knew, all along."

"I know that whatever you did," she said, slowly, "you did on your own."

"What I *did,*" von Kaufstein said, and suddenly there was no pretense of chivalry, "I did for the empire. Franz Joseph is a scared old man; scared of change, of power. Not like his ancestors. Barely a Hapsburg. I'm closer to the true Hapsburg line than he is. I understand the nature of strength. We can't save ourselves by cowering, by helping our enemies just so everything will stay the same."

"So you—what? Went off on your own and—created a spark?"

He shrugged. "There were enough of our people in Dalmatia that it was easy enough. We simply funneled aid to the rebels. Of course Franz Joseph knew nothing about it—and I was proved right, when the rebellion started and he immediately wanted to help both sides, just to keep the peace. When Bosnia was *right there* for the taking. Oh well, we'll take it in the end anyway, and the right people will know whose hand was really behind it. Ah, here we are."

The carriage came to a halt. No light came through the windows except that of the carriage lantern.

"Now don't make this harder than it needs to be," von Kaufstein said. "Out you go."

Eli stood in the doorway of the Large Ballroom, searching for a familiar dark head. He felt light, wrung-out. He didn't know what he would do once he found her.

Dance, he supposed. Even if he had missed his only chance with her, he still had a promise he needed to keep.

The ball was a smashing success. Even his unpracticed eye could tell that. The orchestra played a romantic, sweeping waltz, and elegantly dressed couples spun wildly, as though under a spell. Guests stood around the dance floor laughing, the light bouncing off jewels and luscious satins and champagne coupes—even, in quick flashes beneath decadently shod feet, off Maria's beautiful, precious floors. The smell of smoke mingled with perfumes and the faint smell of sweat.

The air itself was still hazy with it, lending the ballroom an air of the fantastic after all.

And nowhere, in this triumph, was the woman who had made it all happen.

He plunged into the crowd, dodging roving platters and men who'd had too much champagne. She would be somewhere here, making sure everything ran smoothly. Maybe by the buffet—

Or on the balcony—

Or talking to the orchestra leader—

But she wasn't in any of those places. He found her mother, who hadn't seen her, and her grandmother, who hadn't seen her. By the time he got to Claude, panic was starting to rise.

"When was the last time you saw her?" he shouted, and then, frustrated, pulled the man out of the room, so he could hear him.

"Not in at least half an hour," Claude said, his brow furrowing. "You're worried."

"Yes," Eli said.

"Can you think of anywhere else she would have gone?"

He began to shake his head, then stopped. "The bathroom," he said. "One of the bathrooms has plumbing problems. I can't remember which one, but—"

"Go check," Claude said. "I'll find Josephine and Elisabeth—"

Eli was already running. It wasn't the one on the second floor, judging by the quickly moving line. And there wasn't one on the first floor, which meant it was on the third or the fourth.

There was a small line at the third floor as well. Rather than wait to see if it was moving, he pushed his way to the front, ignoring the outraged squawks of those waiting, and banged on the door. When it was opened by a red-faced, gray-haired man, Eli paused only long enough to look inside before running up the stairs again.

No one had ventured to the fourth floor in search of the toilet. The door was slightly ajar; the room empty when Eli pushed into it. Panic was high in his throat, and when he saw she wasn't there, he turned to leave, already running through other possibilities.

Something caught his eye as he spun around. A glimmer, a reflection—he turned back, frowning as he searched the floor for the small glint. He shuffled awkwardly along the cold, white-tiled floor.

And then he saw it, tucked slightly out of sight behind the bottom of the toilet. A hairpin with a crystal star on the end, glittering prettily and incongruously from its position on the bathroom floor. A hairpin he'd last seen tucked into dark, glossy, wavy hair.

"Damn it," he said, and before the curse had finished leaving his lips he had the pin in his hand and was running down the stairs.

He pushed his way through the crowds in the ballroom, shoving rudely and wordlessly until he saw Josephine's steel-gray hair in a corner.

"Where is she," she said, when he was in earshot—a demand rather than a question.

"Someone took her," he said. "I found her hairpin in the fourth-floor bathroom."

It was hard to breathe. He needed to stay calm, to think clearly, but all his muscles screamed at him to *move*. Maria was in danger—had been in danger—

She could be—she could be—

No. She will be fine. You will find her, and she will be safe.

Claude pushed his way to their sides. "Have you—"

"Someone took her," Eli repeated. "Who? Damn it, *damn it,* if either of you know anything, you need to tell me *right now*. Josephine, you've known more than you've let on this whole time—"

Josephine shook her head. "Nothing Maria herself didn't know," she said. "That there are things one isn't *allowed* to know—"

"That man," Eli said. "The one from the laundry room, the Emperor's secret police—"

Josephine closed her eyes. "I don't think he'd hurt her," she said, shaking her head firmly. "Not unprovoked. But yes, he might know something. I know where to find him, I'll send a message—"

Eli wanted to shout that they didn't have *time* to send a message—

"If you mean von Laziska, he's upstairs," Claude said.

Josephine and Eli turned in unison.

Claude shrugged. "I'll go get him."

Elisabeth pushed in as Claude left. "What's going on?" she asked. "Have you found Maria?"

"No," Josephine said, and then briefly—almost ruthlessly— explained.

"I don't understand," Elisabeth said. "Is this—is this about Heinrich again? Do you think he could have done something to her?"

Eli had already asked himself that question. But no matter how many ways he looked at it, there was only one puzzle piece he couldn't make fit—the piece tentatively marked *His Imperial and Royal Majesty.*

"Josephine." Von Laziska's voice came from over Eli's shoulder. "The French spy tells me your granddaughter is missing."

"Johann," Josephine said, and there was something different in her voice. Fear, yes, and tension, but also . . . something familiar? Had it been there the first time as well? "Please. For old times' sake. Help us, if you can."

They stared at each other a long time.

"All right," he said. "The usual warnings apply."

"We won't breathe a word of anything," Josephine said, and then stopped. "Actually, Elisabeth, you need to leave."

"Mother!"

"When more than twenty-four hours has passed since the revelation that you revealed the hiding place of our family journals to your lover, I might reconsider. Until then, I am unlikely to think you can keep a secret."

"Mother!"

"*And* someone needs to keep that damn Hotelkeepers' Ball running," Josephine continued. "Go on. Do a good job. Maria needs you to."

After a tense moment, Elisabeth nodded sharply and left.

"The French spy needs to leave too," von Laziska said, and Claude winked.

"I'll get a carriage ready," he said.

That left the three of them, just Eli, Josephine, and von Laziska.

"I don't know everything," von Laziska said. "All I know is that there's a rumor. About a Wallner journal, from 1875. And that it contains damaging information."

"About Franz Joseph," Eli said.

Von Laziska shrugged. "I doubt it, actually. That's why I've been around more than usual. But the more I've learned, the more I believe His Imperial Majesty isn't involved at all. That doesn't mean it couldn't hurt him, though."

"That's why you shot Mueller," Eli said, slowly. "You thought he was about to name the Emperor. He was about to say 'Imperial.'"

Von Laziska did not look repentant. "Better safe than sorry."

"Imperial," Josephine said, frowning. "Yes, he could have been about to. But there are a lot of people with that in their title—any number of them. Imperial and Royal comes before—"

"Like the Imperial and Royal Chamberlain?" Eli said, suddenly, and two pairs of eyes flew to meet his. "Maria introduced him to me. Von—von Kaufstein, right? He's getting married to Heinrich's daughter. And Heinrich—"

"Had the journals," Josephine finished. She looked pale. "He— No. He's my half brother. He wouldn't."

"He's what?" Eli shook his head. "Sorry, he's Maria's uncle? She didn't tell me—"

"It's supposed to be a secret," von Laziska said, a little condescending, like it wasn't trying very hard to be a *good* secret. "Both Josephine and von Kaufstein are royal bastards. Von Kaufstein's mother wasn't quite as difficult, though."

He said this last part fondly, as though he rather approved of difficult.

"We need to find out if he came tonight," Eli said.

"He did," Josephine said, her voice hard.

"Then we need to find out if he's still here."

They didn't waste time searching the ballroom, going straight to the boys out front managing the carriages. And sure enough, thirty minutes before, the von Kaufstein carriage had been called for.

"Where would he take her?" Eli asked, almost growling the words. *Now,* he needed to find her *now.*

"He has a hunting lodge," Josephine said. "In the Woods. Probably there, or near there."

"Good," Eli said. He looked around for Claude, saw him standing next to a carriage. "Let's go."

The three of them ran to the carriage and piled in.

Chapter Thirty-six

*I suppose there were times, when Josephine was very
young, when it was lonely. Oh, I didn't want a
husband—despite my origins as an Imperial mistress,
I've never much craved romance or sexual affection. But
friendship—that was lacking in those first few years. It
was the hotel that finally gave that to me. Friends that
became family.*

—Journal entry of Theresa Wallner, 20 July 1849

Maria couldn't exactly step out of the carriage, so in the
end she was hauled out of the carriage and dumped on
the ground like a sack of potatoes.

This wasn't ideal.

They were in the Woods, seemingly far from anything.
They'd been driving for a while even after she'd woken, which
meant they were quite a way out of the city. There were only
dark trees around her, for as far as she could see.

She still wasn't worried.

As she saw it, her main objective was to buy time. Even if
she could manage *somehow* to get out of her restraints, the
likelihood she could defeat two men *and* their carriage driver
was low. Especially when the son had a gun.

So she needed to stall until Eli got there, an eventuality she
still had complete faith in. After all, she really had only two

choices: either she believed he was going to save her, in which case the worst that could happen was that he didn't, and she died but she didn't die afraid; or she could believe no one was coming, and still die, but all the parts before the dying would be a lot more unpleasant.

The son stepped forward with the gun. That wouldn't do. She sniffled. "I don't want him to do it."

He rolled his eyes. "No one cares."

"Count von Kaufstein cares," she said, blinking back fake tears. "He's always been"—sniff—"kind to me. I don't even know your name."

"That doesn't matter!"

"It matters," she said, sniffling again, directing her gaze toward the Count. "I understand why you have to do this, sir. It's for the empire. All these political things are so beyond me, but everyone says you're brilliant, so I know"—sniff—"I know you must be doing the right thing, but I *am* scared, and it's so dark—"

She'd just been saying things at random, but that was actually quite a good idea.

"—and I'm so *scared* of the dark," she said, bursting into tears and hoping no one came close enough to notice there was no actual moisture. "Maybe, before you do it, could you bring that lantern over? I just—I want to see the light, before I go."

Von Kaufstein rubbed a hand over his face, and were those *actual* tears she saw? "All right," he said, sounding defeated, and nodding at the coachman. "Bring the lamp over." He looked at Maria. "You should prepare yourself, my dear."

Another excellent idea. She wasn't the best, most observant Catholic in the world, but she thought she could find *quite a few* things to say to God on this occasion. Preparing herself for death would take some time, if she had her way.

She pushed herself into a kneeling position, bringing her

hands together and pretending to close her eyes while she watched the men. They were arguing. The son wanted to kill her now. The coachman seemed to be on his side. Von Kaufstein was on her side, though—well, at least as much as someone who absolutely intended to murder her and had, indeed, instigated the entire murder thing could be said to be *on her side.*

And then von Kaufstein stepped into the carriage and shut the door.

"He'll do better if he doesn't have to see it," the son said to the coachman.

All right, that wasn't good. A bolt of fear speared through her. She kept watching them, kept pretending to pray, trying desperately to think of something, anything to buy a little more time—

The son had the gun. He walked toward her with it.

She realized she *was* praying, in a way. *Eli,* she thought. *Let him find me. Or let him—if he's too late, let him know nothing about this. And, if it's not too much, let him know I love him. I love him. I love him.*

Von Kaufstein's son raised the gun and pointed it at her.

She closed her eyes in earnest and heard the gunshot.

And waited.

And waited some more.

Had he . . . missed? How embarrassing. These von Kaufstein men really weren't very competent.

There was a second gunshot, startling her. This was probably the one. She waited to feel it.

"Maria. Maria!"

Someone was shouting at her. She cracked an eye open, and then another one.

"Oh good," she said. "You came."

"Are you hurt? Did he hurt you? You're tied up, hang on, let me—"

The ropes around her wrists gave way, followed by the ones around her knees and ankles.

She saw von Kaufstein's son and the coachman lying on the ground.

"Von Kaufstein is in the carriage," she said.

"I know," Eli said. "Your grandmother and von Laziska have him."

"Good. Oh, hello, Claude," she said faintly, as the man bent over von Kaufstein's son, checking his pulse.

"Hello, Maria," Claude said, bowing neatly. "May I say, for someone who has just been kidnapped and almost murdered, you look lovely."

"Thank you," she said, easily, and then, just as easily, she slid into tears.

Eli's arms came around her, and she leaned into him, feeling their strength and their warmth. "You came," she said.

"Of course I came."

"I knew you would."

"Good," he said, squeezing her more tightly. "Good."

"But you did cut it a bit close."

"I did," he said.

"And *also,* before the kidnapping and murder situation, you were a *complete* ass."

"I was."

"Good, so long as you know," she said. "Wait. You know?"

"I know," he said. "I knew before you left my hotel room. I knew—I was coming to tell you—Maria, I almost lost you. I can't do it again, I can't—"

There was a commotion by the carriage, as von Laziska pulled von Kaufstein out of it. Josephine followed him.

"You don't know what you're doing," von Kaufstein said. "You're making a terrible mistake. This is all on the Emperor's behalf. This is his private business!"

"And all this should probably wait," Eli said, sighing.

He helped Maria to her feet, and they walked toward the others.

"I'll take him in for questioning," von Laziska said. He was looking at Josephine, some complicated unspoken code passing between them.

"And when I am questioning him," he continued, "there will probably be others in the room. Who might hear what he has to say and feel obliged to act upon it. As they should. For the good of the empire."

Josephine held his gaze a moment longer, and then, perfectly smoothly, shot Count von Kaufstein in the head.

They watched as his body crumpled in a heap on the cold ground of the forest.

There was a long silence.

"Ah, Josephine," von Laziska said. "Now I'll have to get rid of three bodies."

"We both know that once you have two a third makes no difference at all," she said, wiping her hands with a handkerchief.

"Well," von Laziska said, staring at the body. "For old times' sake, I suppose."

"Indeed," Josephine said, dryly. "It's all right if we leave you with the von Kaufstein carriage?"

He waved his hand at them, which her grandmother apparently took as consent, because she steered the other three back through the forest, to a very confused cabdriver who absolutely didn't understand why they had decided to go hunting so very late at night.

"Grandmother," Maria said quietly, tugging on Josephine's sleeve before the older woman stepped into the carriage. "Exactly how do you know von Laziska?"

"Oh," Josephine said. "He's your grandfather. I do hope Emilie hasn't gotten worried about my absence, I told one of the footmen to tell her."

She climbed in. Maria looked at Eli.

"My grandfather," she said.

"I heard," he said, staring at her grandmother as she settled herself in the carriage. "You know, your family tree is somewhat complicated."

"Yes," she said, tucking this revelation neatly away for later examination. "Well. We have a ball to get back to."

The ball was still whirling when they returned. No one had noticed their absence, too wrapped up in the music and the food and the flowers and the bright, sparkling city lights beyond the windows to care. Elisabeth had nurtured this spirit, apparently handling every disaster that had erupted with unexpected grace. Eli saw the look of hope Maria gave her mother when Elisabeth embraced her. That would never be a perfect relationship, Eli thought, but perhaps, with time, it could be a better one.

Hannah was there too, falling on Maria's neck in relief. "You're all right," she said. "I was so worried. Now I have to go. Two of the buffet dishes are empty."

Maria laughed, patting her friend on the shoulder and sending her off with a smile.

Then it was just her and Eli, standing at the foot of the grand staircase. Claude had excused himself, citing a need for fresh clothes, and Josephine had gone in search of Emilie.

"I suppose I should change, too," Maria said.

His hand reached down, closing around hers. "Wait."

She looked up at him.

"I didn't say it, earlier. I did a lot of things wrong, earlier, but that was the worst one." His grip on her hand tightened. "I love you too, Maria. I'm in love with you, and I think I have been since you wandered into the street drunk and were almost flattened by a carriage."

400 ♦ Diana Biller

"Oh," she said, and then her hand wrapped around his neck, and she pulled him down to kiss him.

He'd thought he would never be able to kiss her again.

"You know, that carriage wasn't supposed to be there," she murmured, between kisses. "The street was closed."

"So you said at the time." With a bit of regret, he pulled away. "There's more I need to say."

"All right," she said, and he saw caution creep into her expression.

"I'm sorry I said you didn't love me. It was so—it was terrifying. The idea that you could. Because it's vulnerable, loving someone."

"It is," she said, softly.

"I didn't want you to be vulnerable."

"Personally, I'm more concerned with surviving all the assassination attempts than surviving love," she said. "But—I believe I understand. A little."

"It was an excuse, though," he said. "I think I didn't want to admit that I *could* be loved. It's easy, to be a stone. Loving alone, for me, was easy. Being loved—"

"Being loved is being vulnerable too," Maria said.

"Yes."

"You told me I could stay," he said, taking her hand. "Is that still true?"

"Yes," she said. "Oh, Eli. Yes."

"Oh," he said, and for a moment both his throat and his brain closed up and all he could do was stand there and stare at her. "Oh. Good then."

"Yes," she said, smiling. There were tears on her face. "Good."

"It'll probably be complicated," he said. "My mother is still in the States, we'll have to visit often, which will be difficult with your schedule."

"We'll figure it out."

"There's a case I need to properly wrap up in Washington."

"I believe in you."

"I'll have to find a new job."

"You're abnormally competent."

"And I'll probably want to get married."

"Wallner women usually don't," Maria said, laughing. "But we can discuss it."

"All right," he said. "All right."

"Is that everything?"

"Yes. I think so."

"Then I'm going to kiss you again."

She made good on this threat, kissing him thoroughly, her hand still in his, and he felt—he felt. Just then, it was as though he felt everything. All their moments and memories, all the laughter and tears and fights and kisses.

There would be so many more of all of those, he realized. A miracle.

"Wait," he said. "There's one more thing."

She pulled away, lifting her eyebrows. "What now? Do you somehow have a secret love child you need to bring over? Because really, Eli, that hardly warrants stopping a perfectly good kiss."

"Will you dance with me?" he asked.

"Oh," she said. "Of course."

"Not here," he said, gesturing up the stairs. "Up there. In the moment you made."

She smiled, then bit her lip. "I should change . . ."

He shook his head. "You look perfect."

"I have blood on my dress."

"These things happen."

And she laughed, and it turned out that the empty space

in his chest where laughter had lived was full again, because he joined her, and then he tugged on her hand and pulled her into her beautiful, triumphant ball, and put his arms around her.

And they danced.

Acknowledgments

I t's easy to fall into the habit of dismissing one's art, of minimizing it, or rendering it frivolous. I've been guilty of this my whole life. It's only in the last two years—over the course of writing this book—that I've begun to challenge the belief that I need to.

What if our art is not small? What if it is not silly? What if we took up space? What if we took ourselves seriously?

What could we do then?

It is the people in these acknowledgments who showed me that I *could* ask those questions.

Rachel Paxton has been my writing partner since before I ever finished a book. She is one of those people who have creativity coming out of their ears—she's a talented writer (as well as being my personal plotting consultant), *and* a painter, baker, embroiderer, and jewelry maker. I am blessed beyond words to have her in my life.

Patty and Tim Billings were among the first people in my life to take my writing seriously, when I was sixteen and lost. Brianna Billings inspires me every day, with her strength, grace, and artistry. Rose, Sean, and Calyssa Savard have supported me unquestioningly every day since they entered my life.

My friends Isaac Skibinski, Rachel Kellis, Kaitlyn Sullivan, Hilary Richardson, Morgan Smalley, and Anna McGregor are all people who make my life richer simply by being in it. Through their eyes, their talent, and their art, the world becomes a much bigger place. I also want to thank Martha Reynolds, who is a constant lesson in grace, and Michael Vu, who made a beautiful playlist just for me when I was writing this book.

My agent, Amy Elizabeth Bishop, is an invaluable partner. She possesses one of the keenest story senses in the industry. There is also no idea too bonkers for her.

I am so fortunate to have met my editor, Vicki Lame. Her genius for editing and story is combined with kindness, grace, and a true passion for books. I think that is a rare combination.

One of the wonderful things about publishing a book is the wildly talented people one encounters along the way. This is particularly true of the team at St. Martin's Publishing Group: Hannah Jones, Lisa Davis, Diane Dilluvio, Terry McGarry, Marissa Sangiacomo, Brant Janeway, and Sophia Lauriello. I particularly want to thank Vanessa Aguirre, for her contributions and support, and Kerri Resnick, who created the breathtaking cover.

My husband, Timothy Savard, keeps a copy of all my books on his desk. Not just the final version, either—*every* version. The uncorrected manuscripts. The advanced reading copies. When my first novel debuted, he sent an email about it to his coworkers. He supports me in so many enormous ways, but in so many small, everyday ways as well. Thank you, Tim. I love you.

Finally, I want to thank my readers. You, every one of you, are important to me. And if I can say one more thing to you, it's this: please treasure and protect the things *you* do that make the world a richer place. Please take yourself, your creativity, and your art *seriously*.

About the Author

DIANA BILLER is the author of *The Widow of Rose House* and *The Brightest Star in Paris*. When she isn't writing, she enjoys snuggling her animals, taking "research" trips abroad, and attending ballet class. She lives with her husband in Los Angeles.